Praise for Martha Waters' delightful Regency rom-coms!

'Superbly entertaining' *Booklist*

'Irresistibly irreverent' *Publishers Weekly*

'A laugh-out-loud Regency romp – if you loved the Bridgertons, you'll adore *To Have and to Hoax*!'
Lauren Willig, *New York Times* bestselling author

'A worthy addition to the trend for historical romantic comedies and highly recommended for fans of Evie Dunmore' *Library Journal*

'Sweet, sexy, and utterly fun. A love story with depth to match its humor, and refreshingly frank communication between its two headstrong leads – I adored it'
Emily Henry, *New York Times* bestselling author

'Packed with saucy banter and delightful period details, this Regency rom-com is completely charming'
Hannah Orenstein, author of *Head Over Heels*

'Pure fun on every page'
Sarah Hogle, author of *You Deserve Each Other*

'Endlessly charming … absorbing and clever and at times laugh-out-loud funny'
Kate Clayborn, author of *Love Lettering*

'A delightful battle of wits that's funny and touching all at once' Jen DeLuca, author of *Well Met*

'A perfect little whipped-cream confection of a historical romance' *BookPage*

By Martha Waters

To Have and to Hoax
To Love and to Loathe

To Love and to Loathe

MARTHA WATERS

HEADLINE
ETERNAL

Published by arrangement with Atria,
An Imprint of Simon & Schuster, Inc.

First published in Great Britain in 2021
by HEADLINE ETERNAL
An imprint of HEADLINE PUBLISHING GROUP

1

Cataloguing in Publication Data is available from the British Library

ISBN 978 1 4722 8387 0

Offset in 10.08/15.82 pt Adobe Jenson Pro by Jouve (UK), Milton Keynes

Printed and bound in Great Britain by Clays Ltd, Elcograf S.p.A.

Headline's policy is to use papers that are natural, renewable and recyclable
products and made from wood grown in well-managed forests and other
controlled sources. The logging and manufacturing processes are expected
to conform to the environmental regulations of the country of origin.

HEADLINE PUBLISHING GROUP
An Hachette UK Company
Carmelite House
50 Victoria Embankment
London EC4Y 0DZ

www.headlineeternal.com
www.headline.co.uk
www.hachette.co.uk

For my grandmothers,
Rosa Elizabeth Holland Best
and Alice Kirkland Waters

Prologue

Diana Bourne was only eighteen, but she knew one thing already: men were fools. Adorable fools sometimes, enticing fools occasionally, but fools one and all.

This was not a complaint—for Diana's purposes, the fact that most men of her acquaintance seemed to have little more than a few bits of cotton wool floating around between their ears was really rather ideal. Because Diana's purposes, quite simply, were to be wed to a man of means—one did not need to possess intellect to boast a hefty purse, and furthermore, in her experience thus far, the two qualities seemed to be mutually exclusive.

Take her brother, Viscount Penvale. Penvale was a touch addle-pated, of course, by virtue of the male anatomy he possessed, but he was well-read, a deft hand at cards, and, at times, unsettlingly observant—a shining beacon of intellect compared to other gentlemen of his set. And yet, he had pockets to let. The poor boy didn't have two pennies to rub together—which, unfortunately, meant that she was in similarly dire straits.

"And what are you hunting for tonight, dear sister?" His voice came from behind her, startling her out of her thoughts as she stood, glass of ratafia in hand, at the edge of a crowded ballroom.

She turned, schooling her features into the expression of bland innocence that she knew men found so appealing—which would not fool her brother for a moment.

Sure enough, he arched an eyebrow at her in amusement. He refrained from comment only because next to him stood Jeremy Overington, the Marquess of Willingham, one of his best friends. And, *oh*. If only a handful of men could be said to be enticing fools, Willingham was one of them. Tall, golden-haired, and possessing shoulders that were just the right width to be attractive without making him appear unfashionably brawny, Willingham made female heads turn in every room he entered. Aside from his objective aesthetic appeal, there was something about him—a certain knowing gleam in his eye, a heaviness to his gaze—that set Diana's heart beating just a touch more rapidly than it should have done whenever she was in his presence.

This was inconvenient, because despite his aforementioned positive attributes, he was also overly fond of drink and women and, most disqualifying of all, deeply in debt. Useless in regard to her current objective, in other words. It was therefore maddening that her traitorous heart sped up each time he came within fifty feet of her.

"Lord Willingham," she said coolly, pleased to hear that her voice sounded bored rather than breathless. "Would you be so kind as to remove my irritating brother . . . elsewhere?"

"Angry I've caught you out?" Penvale asked genially, never one to be put off by a barb from her. "You needn't pretend for Jeremy's sake; I've told him you've been calculating marriage the way some men consider an investment scheme."

"And aren't they more or less the same thing at heart?" Diana asked sweetly.

Lord Willingham let out a surprised laugh, which relieved her—he had been watching her in a way that made her feel quite unsettled, and she was pleased to have broken his calm.

"Too true, Miss Bourne," Willingham said. "Why don't you tell me all about your hunt whilst dancing this waltz with me?"

Diana consulted the dance card attached to her wrist. "I've promised this waltz to Lord Snidewhistle."

Willingham leaned in close. "Snidewhistle is up to his ears in gambling debts; it's not widely known yet, but it will be soon."

This was, in fact, rather disappointing—despite his unfortunate name, Snidewhistle had been one of the younger gentlemen on her list of potential husbands, and one of the few with whom the idea of sharing a bed had not been entirely repellent.

"In fact," Willingham continued, "I saw him at the hazard tables not five minutes ago, and he was so deeply immersed in his game that I doubt he remembers what day it is, much less that he is engaged to waltz with so charming a lady as yourself." These words were laced with the slightest trace of sarcasm.

Diana scowled at him. "I will dance with you," she said, lifting her nose into the air, "but only because I cannot stand to be a wallflower."

Her brother snorted.

"I don't think you've much to worry about there," he said.

And he was, in some sense, correct. Diana had attracted her fair share of male attention in the weeks since her debut—unsurprisingly, given her honey-colored hair, hazel eyes, and a bosom that one Almack's patroness deemed "rather vulgar." However, she also had a decided lack of fortune—indeed, her pin money amounted to a sum

3

that would have made a lesser lady weep—and, as a result, she found herself with a decided lack of decent proposals.

And with a fair number of indecent ones.

"Come, Miss Bourne," Willingham said, taking her arm without so much as a by-your-leave and leading her onto the dance floor as the opening notes of a waltz drifted through the room.

"I suppose you expect me to thank you for the tip about Snide-whistle," Diana said as they took their positions, her hand on his shoulder, his hand at her waist.

Willingham flashed her a grin. *Thump, thump*, went her heart. "I would never be so foolish as to expect the Honorable Diana Bourne to thank me for anything," he said, pivoting her slowly about the room as the waltz began. "Though, of course, if you wanted to consider yourself in my debt, I shouldn't object. . . ."

"I promise you, sir, that I shall ensure to never do anything that would find me in your debt. I cannot think of a less trustworthy gentleman to hold such power over me."

"Come now, I'm not so bad," Willingham said lightly—but something about his voice made her glance up sharply into his eyes. Had she wounded him? Surely not. In her entire acquaintance with Lord Willingham—dating back to the years that her brother had brought him home with him from Eton to their aunt and uncle's house during school holidays—she had not once seen him so much as wince from one of her hits. Surely this one hadn't landed?

"Aren't you?" she asked, watching him closely. His hand was firm on her waist, his motions smooth and effortless. The man was an exemplary dancer—no doubt because he had honed his skill in his pursuit of every ineligible woman in London, but impressive nonetheless.

He seemed to realize that she was baiting him—the slight tightness around his mouth that she had noticed a few moments prior had vanished, to be replaced by one of his more usual facial expressions: the alluring, slightly cheeky smile of a devil-may-care rogue, intent on charming the skirts off of every lady with the misfortune to cross his path.

"I'm not," he said easily. "In fact, I think you should set your sights on me as your next target."

Diana stumbled, missing a step; Lord Willingham steered her back into the rhythm of the waltz, hiding her error, while she continued to stare at him, mouth agape.

"You cannot be serious," she managed after a few moments' silence.

"Why shouldn't I be?" His tone was casual, unconcerned; if he hadn't been waltzing, she was certain he would have shrugged. "You seem to be quite eager for a husband. I am, in fact, excellent husband material."

"By what qualifications, precisely, are you excellent husband material?" Diana didn't allow him a chance to respond before continuing. "You drink too much, and you seem intent on weaseling your way into the bed of every widow you encounter."

"I do say," Willingham sputtered, and Diana awarded herself a mental point for managing to embarrass him before she'd even completed her thought.

"You don't take anything seriously, and, worst of all, you've no fortune." She pronounced the latter as though it were a death sentence—which, as far as marriage prospects went, it was. She had spent a childhood acutely aware that she was a burden on her aunt and uncle, understanding the expense her presence incurred. She was determined that once she married, she would never have to obsess over something so vulgar, so endlessly tiresome as *money* ever again.

Willingham watched her with a steady gaze as she spoke, his face never changing expression on the surface, and yet she could somehow sense the feeling building beneath his calm demeanor. "I see," he said, and there was a clipped tone to his voice that was somehow gratifying—if she was going to verbally wound a man, she'd like evidence of the effort. "And I suppose that you have received so many offers this Season that you are in a position to be so choosy?"

Diana didn't flinch, but it was a near thing. "I have indeed received quite a few offers," she hedged, which wasn't untrue.

Willingham's gaze sharpened, and a furrow appeared between his eyebrows. "Have men been propositioning you?" His grip on her waist tightened, and some primitive part of her thrilled at the touch. "If they have, I will call them out."

Diana rolled her eyes. "I think, given the number of married ladies' beds you frequent, you're in enough danger of winding up in a duel without deciding you need to challenge any man who is a threat to my virtue," she informed him. "I can take care of myself, and I certainly don't need you barging in like a knight in shining armor, no doubt mucking it all up."

"So you *have* been propositioned," he said darkly.

"What do I have to tell you that will convince you that your concern is entirely unwanted?" she asked through gritted teeth, managing with great effort to keep a ballroom-appropriate smile upon her face. Judging by the skeptical look Willingham gave her, it likely made her appear slightly deranged.

"Let me be sure I have this correctly," he said, ignoring her question entirely, as most men tended to do. It was astonishing that nearly all of them considered themselves to be the more intelligent sex, considering that they seemed to lack rudimentary listening skills, but one had to manage with the poor fools as best one could.

Willingham continued. "You are possibly being subjected to indecent proposals on the part of lecherous gentlemen, you've no marriage prospects in sight, but you still refuse to consider me a candidate for the position of your husband?"

Up until this moment, Diana had been certain that he'd been jesting. She could not think of a single gentleman of her acquaintance less likely to wish to settle into matrimony than the Marquess of Willingham. Had he not been rumored, just last week, to have been discovered in the Countess of Covendale's bedchamber? Discovered by the earl himself, no less? This hardly seemed like the behavior of a man desperate to settle down to a life of quiet domesticity.

And, furthermore, he wasn't the sort of man she wanted to marry. She wanted someone dull, someone safe. Someone wealthy.

Lord Willingham was not at all dull, nor did he feel particularly safe—especially not when he was gazing at her as though he could see right through her, as he was at this precise moment. When he looked at her this way, neither of those qualities—dullness or safety—seemed terribly desirable, while *everything* about Lord Willingham did.

But the third quality, wealth, was the one she refused to negotiate on, and the fact remained that the marquess was a second son who had unexpectedly inherited his title upon the death of his brother—and who was currently scrambling to pay the death duties from the depleted Willingham coffers. He would never suit.

And for that reason, she had to make him stop—stop gazing at her with his peculiar intensity, as though he saw right through her carefully built shell, right to the heart of her. To *her* heart.

That was, quite simply, unacceptable. She had decided long ago that she wouldn't let anything so foolish as her heart have any part in deciding whom she married.

And so, to make him stop, to remove herself from that unsettling gaze at all costs, she said the first thing that sprang to mind, razor sharp, guaranteed to wound.

"Even if you *weren't* in debt . . ." She trailed off, letting his focus sharpen on her even more, granting the moment its full weight. "I certainly wouldn't consider *you* for a husband. I can't think of a man who would be less devoted to his wife."

Because this was the Marquess of Willingham—rakehell, charmer, and seducer—he didn't allow his flirtatious smile to slip for even an instant. But something in his gaze dulled and shuttered, and internally, Diana cheered.

Even as a small part of her, buried deep inside, cracked.

This, Jeremy supposed, was what you should expect when you attended a ball sober.

He couldn't recall the last time he'd been at one of these affairs without the comforting warmth and distance provided by a blanket of brandy, fogging his senses, making him genial and fond of everyone he encountered. A glass of brandy or three made him more appealing to the ladies—smoothed any possible rough edge, any trace of bitterness, leaving behind only the Willingham they wanted to see: handsome, charming, and without an iota of depth. He had learned in his Oxford days not to fool himself—the ladies he lured to his bed were not interested in conversation, or feelings, or anything other than his face and physique. This was a state of affairs that was, naturally, entirely satisfactory to him—he was certainly not looking for any sort of emotional entanglement. He liked his life the way it was: simple and full of pleasure. At least, that was how it *had* been, prior to his brother's death. These days, chasing that pleasure took a rather more concerted effort on his part.

So why, then, had he skipped his brandy, knowing that a certain Miss Bourne would be in attendance tonight, a lady on whom his charms seemed wasted? And what had further propelled him not just to ask her to dance, but also to half-seriously suggest matrimony while doing so? He could not think of anyone less suited to marriage than himself, no matter how appealing Miss Bourne was, with her hair gleaming by candlelight and her rather spectacular bosom evident even in the modest gown she wore. There was something about her that always had this effect on him, from the moment he had first met her, when he was a young buck at Eton and she still a skinny little hell-raiser galloping about her aunt and uncle's estate. Even then, she had never lacked a biting retort to anything he threw at her, and it had done nothing but make him want to rile her even further. It had been maddening, then.

Now, it was still maddening, but there was an undercurrent of tension to it that he was not enough of a fool to mistake for anything other than attraction. The fact was, Diana Bourne was beautiful and intelligent, and that was a dangerous combination. And something about her still made him want to best her at any endeavor, including simple waltzing conversation. And so, listening to her coolly explain marriage as a financial transaction, he had wanted nothing more than to shock her, set her off-balance. And he had done so in the most obvious way he knew how.

He had not expected her to say yes. Had not *wanted* her to say yes. Marriage to Diana Bourne was something for a stronger man than himself—or so he reminded himself now, as they continued to turn about the room, sharing a silence that was growing tight as it stretched between them.

"I expect you have a list of acceptable mates inside that scheming head of yours," he said, adopting the bored tone that was his lifeline and his shield in moments when he felt anything other than suave, confident, and entirely in command.

"Of course," Miss Bourne said, without a trace of embarrassment, and this was yet another thing he liked about her. She was no worse, really, than the majority of the debutantes on the marriage mart this year, and yet they hid their scheming behind giggles and insipid smiles and, truly, a disturbing number of feathers. Miss Bourne stated her intentions plainly—and, mercifully, without a feather in sight.

"Might I hear the list?" He gave her a roguish wink. "I'm certain I could help you narrow it down to an acceptable choice."

"I don't think so." Her voice was cool and distant—this was the voice that never failed to make him want to provoke her. He dampened the impulse with great difficulty. Where had that instinct gotten him not five minutes before? Offering marriage to a woman who would no doubt use this as a weapon in every argument they engaged in for the rest of their lives. It had been an amateur mistake, and one he certainly wouldn't make again.

"You see," she continued, "this isn't a game to me, like it is to you. I have my looks and my family's name and the bloom of novelty, and not much else. Not much to attract any man looking for an intelligent match. I need to marry this Season, and I don't need *you* making a joke out of it."

"I wouldn't make a joke of it," he protested, even as he realized that that was, in fact, precisely what he had been doing. Miss Bourne did not even bother to dignify this obvious falsehood with a response.

"So no, Lord Willingham," she concluded—and never had his title been pronounced more scathingly than it was in that moment—"I will not share anything about my matrimonial hopes with you, and I think it best that we end this line of discussion entirely."

Jeremy was a bold man, but not recklessly so. And it would have been a reckless man indeed who forced Diana Bourne to continue a conversation she clearly wished to avoid. And, deep down, Jeremy thought it might be rather unsporting to do so—she had, of course, just rejected him, and many men in his shoes might have considered themselves to be the wounded party. But Jeremy knew better. He was, at the end of the day, a man, and she was a woman. He could end the evening with a woman of his choosing, engaging in behavior that would have ruined an unmarried woman had she attempted to follow his lead. And he might have pockets to let at the moment, but he was still a marquess, and with that came power and freedom the likes of which no woman—not even a princess—could ever hope to achieve. Miss Bourne was charting her own course in search of a mere scrap of the freedom he enjoyed every day, and he could not fault her for it.

But a small part of him wondered what he would have done if she had said yes.

And it was that thought that, at the conclusion of their waltz, sent him in search of something stronger than lemonade to dull the senses, to cast that warm, golden light upon the evening's proceedings.

He did not see Miss Bourne again that night. One month later, her betrothal to Viscount Templeton was announced.

One

There was no place like a ball for a good, old-fashioned wager,
Diana always said.

Or, rather, she was going to *begin* saying now, effective this evening,
in the wake of having made just such a wager.

It was July, and they were inching toward the end of the London
Season, Diana's sixth in total and her third since the death of her
husband, Viscount Templeton. She was in a crowded ballroom at the
home of Lord and Lady Rocheford, whose end-of-Season soiree was
one of the most coveted invitations among the *ton*, for reasons that
frankly escaped Diana at the moment, as she was sweltering in the
heat of tightly pressed bodies and an incalculable number of candles
burning above and around her.

Diana was, in truth, finding the entire evening rather tedious. She'd
been experiencing this sensation more and more often of late, which
was a bit unsettling in its novelty. She had been so eager to escape her
aunt and uncle's home when she had debuted, flinging herself into the
social whirl of London the instant she had made her curtsey before the
queen, not letting up in the slightest upon her marriage to Templeton.

13

His death two and a half years later had slowed her considerably, of course, but she had been eager enough to rejoin society when her mourning period was over, once again immersing herself in the relentless cycle of balls and dinner parties, Venetian breakfasts and nights at the theater, musicales and outings to Vauxhall Gardens.

Lately, however, she had felt something . . . missing. She had, seemingly, everything she had once dreamed of acquiring: a wealthy, titled husband who had seen fit to conveniently expire, leaving her a wealthy, titled widow; a London town house filled with servants to attend to her every whim, and as many painting supplies as she could possibly dream of; dear friends to liven up her days; any number of handsome gentlemen to flirt with of an evening.

And yet, this evening, as she chatted idly with her friends, watching her friend Emily twirl about the dance floor in the arms of the slightly scandalous Lord Julian Belfry, she found herself feeling vaguely . . . dissatisfied.

Which was why it was so convenient that the Marquess of Willingham chose that moment to open his mouth—a decision that was for him, as it was for so many men, often a mistake—to offer her the following warning:

"You're making a mistake if you think to match Belfry with Lady Emily. A less likely man to marry I've never seen. Have you heard nothing of his reputation?"

Diana turned slowly to face him, arching an eyebrow. "Mmm, yes," she agreed, giving Willingham a sweet smile. "But I didn't think it was any worse than yours, my lord."

Willingham's mouth quirked in that infuriating half smirk he favored; his was an exceptionally handsome face, all blue eyes and cheekbones and strong jaw, and that smirk somehow, unfairly, made it more attractive rather than less so. "Touché. And yet I've no intention of marrying either, so my point remains."

"So you say," Diana said with great skepticism. "But need I remind you that you are a marquess? At some point, you'll have to produce an heir."

Willingham shrugged. "I've a cousin who I've no doubt would be quite pleased to inherit. He has a very fertile wife, if I recall."

Diana tossed her head impatiently. "Don't be absurd. Of course you'll marry." She was dimly aware that their friends were beginning to take notice of this conversation; she could sense their attention focusing on her and Willingham, even as she did not look away from Willingham's face. The friends in question were their closest ones—Diana's friend Violet, along with her husband, Lord James Audley; Diana's brother, Penvale; and Lady Fitzwilliam Bridewell, a new friend of Violet's and, until very recently, Willingham's lover.

Willingham shrugged again, the gesture so irritating that Diana promptly forgot about their audience once more. "If you say so," he said. "I've yet to meet a debutante I didn't find insufferable, so you'll forgive me for remaining unconvinced."

"You knew me when I was a debutante," Diana said through gritted teeth.

"Did I?" Willingham asked, his surprise so patently false that, had he been anyone else, she would have been tempted to laugh. "Oh, I do believe you're right."

She could hardly miss his rather marked failure to apologize.

Diana took a breath, attempting to calm herself. Willingham possessed the infuriating ability to rile her without even trying to, and so it was perhaps not entirely surprising that the next words out of her mouth were spoken before she had time to even properly consider them. "I'll wager you'll be married within the year. I could find you a bride in three snaps."

Willingham laughed out loud at that. "That would be money in my pocket, Lady Templeton."

"Then you'll take the wager?" Diana pressed. "And you'll allow me to send a parade of marriageable misses in your direction?"

"Why not?" Willingham asked with the misplaced confidence so typical of his sex. "I somehow think I'll be able to resist the temptation. What shall we make the bet?"

Diana paused, considering; if she was going to do the thing, she might as well go all in, so to speak. "One hundred pounds." She stared directly into Willingham's eyes as she spoke, daring him to balk at such an exorbitant sum; he paused for the merest fraction of a second.

"Done," he said briskly, then extended his hand. "Shall we shake on it?"

Considering that she had just bet the man a sum that would pay a good number of her servants' annual salaries, it was slightly absurd that *now* was the moment she hesitated, but she was not used to shaking a man's hand like an equal; she was more accustomed to men hovering over her hand in excessive displays of gallantry, attempting to catch a glimpse of her bosom. Nevertheless, she extended her hand and shook his firmly. His grip was strong and surprisingly reassuring; the latter was not generally an adjective she would have applied to anything about Willingham.

And so it was settled: Willingham would be married within a year, or Diana would pay him one hundred pounds. Diana would freely admit that agreeing to this wager had not, perhaps, been her most well-considered decision. Now that she'd challenged him before their friends, she could hardly admit that she thought the idea of Willingham marrying in the next twelve months to be unlikely in the extreme. Nevertheless, it might be good for a laugh, introducing Willingham to every unmarried lady of her acquaintance at every social event for the next year. That alone would be worth the loss of one hundred pounds.

Still, nothing terribly serious might have come of it had she not, less than an hour later, encountered Willingham's grandmother.

The Dowager Marchioness of Willingham was something of a legend among the *ton*. Widowed for decades, she lived in London year-round and was admired and feared in almost equal measure. Her sharp tongue had skewered more than one reputation, and she had somehow performed the magic trick of saying whatever she liked to whomever she chose, without losing an ounce of her social power.

Naturally, Diana adored her—though she could not say she was entirely pleased to see her at the moment. Diana had just returned from a trip to the retiring room with Violet and Emily; Violet had vanished in search of her husband, and Emily had promised a dance to a blushing, stammering young buck just down from Oxford and clearly terrified to be dancing with one of the most beautiful ladies of the *ton*. Diana consulted her own dance card, realizing that she had promised this dance to Audley. Given the determined expression on Violet's face when she had gone off in search of him, Diana hardly thought it likely that he would be appearing to claim this dance.

Instead, she made her way around the room, stopping to chat with several ladies of her acquaintance and to gaze flirtatiously at several gentlemen. Henry Cavendish, who was the second son of an earl and a thoroughly disreputable rake, had caught her eye and just begun to make his way through the crowd toward her, a promising smile playing at the corners of his mouth, when she felt her elbow seized in a strong grip.

"Lady Templeton, I'd advise you to reconsider that one."

Diana turned, recognizing the voice even before she caught sight of its owner. "Lady Willingham," she said, giving a curtsey. "I cannot imagine what you possibly mean."

Jeremy's grandmother was dressed in a demure evening gown of lilac silk, her diminutive figure held in rigidly proper posture. Her white hair was swept smoothly back in an elegant coiffure, a few curls framing her face, and she was in possession of a fan that Diana personally felt to be doing more work to allow its owner to gossip freely than as a cooling instrument.

"Don't play coy with me, my dear girl," the dowager marchioness said severely. "Young Cavendish is trouble, mark my words—his father must have counted his blessings many a time that that idiot was born the younger twin by a few minutes. Always felt twins a bit unnatural," she added, shaking her head in disapproval at the very notion. "Too many babies at once, if you ask me."

"It is a pity our heavenly father did not think to consult you before coming up with such an arrangement," Diana agreed.

"That's quite enough of that, now," the dowager marchioness said, frowning. "You're as bad as my grandson."

"Did mine ears detect the sound of my name?" came Willingham's voice from somewhere to Diana's left. Stifling an internal groan, she turned, watching as he sauntered toward them, placing a kiss on his grandmother's cheek that one could only accurately describe as smug. "About to describe my many charms?" he asked sunnily, a brief nod of his head his only acknowledgment of Diana's presence.

"It would make for a rather short conversation," Diana said sweetly.

"Lady Templeton likes to flatter me," Willingham confided to his grandmother in conspiratorial tones.

"Over before it even had a chance to begin," Diana continued, tapping her chin thoughtfully.

"If you're finding it so difficult to describe my many charming qualities, I wonder that you were so confident that I'd be married this time next year."

Like a hunting dog detecting a scent, the dowager marchioness's attention—which had wandered slightly toward a number of couples in close proximity to them—snapped onto her grandson, razor-sharp.

"I beg your pardon?" she asked in tones of barely concealed glee.

"Er," Willingham said, clearly intelligent enough—just—to sense danger.

"I wagered Lord Willingham that he'd be married within a year," Diana explained cheerfully. It was worth every penny she stood to lose, just to see Willingham squirming under his grandmother's piercing gaze.

"Did you, now?" the dowager marchioness asked slowly, a speculative gleam coming to her eye. "What a positively delightful notion."

"I should note," Willingham said, seeming to feel the need to exert some sort of control over the direction the conversation had taken, "that I was quite happy to take that bet. Not considering myself in any great danger, you understand."

"Yes, dear," his grandmother said absently, patting his shoulder as one might pat a dog begging for attention. "That is what men always say."

"Yes, Willingham," Diana agreed innocently. "Surely you wouldn't presume to contradict your grandmother, who of course is so much wiser in the ways of the heart than you are yourself."

"You are laying it on a touch thick, Lady Templeton, but I do applaud the general sentiment." The dowager marchioness's fan increased its rate of flapping, seemingly in time with the pace at which the cogs in its owner's brain were turning. "Jeremy," she said suddenly, turning to her grandson, "did you receive a reply from my secretary to your invitation to your house party?"

"I did indeed, Grandmama," Willingham said mournfully, his blue eyes impossibly wide. "It naturally struck at the soft parts of my heart to read yet another crushing refusal from you, but I trust I will eventually be able to recover from the disappointment."

"Enough, Jeremy, you're not half so charming as Lady Templeton is." Diana quirked a single, self-satisfied brow at Willingham in response to this in a show of restraint that she frankly felt worthy of a saint.

"I think I have changed my mind, however," the dowager marchioness continued. "I really ought to thank you, Lady Templeton," she added, turning her attention—and the breeze generated by her fan's vigorous flapping—in Diana's direction. "You have made me see that I've allowed matters to go on quite long enough. It's time to take charge of things myself."

"Yes," Diana said uncertainly, not entirely understanding to what she was agreeing.

"Excellent," the dowager marchioness said briskly, her gaze flicking between Diana and Willingham. "I shall look forward to this house party immensely. I anticipate it will be most productive."

Diana was too busy cackling internally at the look of alarm on Willingham's face to take much notice of the scrutinizing look the dowager marchioness cast her way. She would soon have cause to reflect on, and regret, her mistake.

Two

For the next couple of weeks, Diana's life continued on much as it ever did. She spent her afternoons painting in her solarium, and her evenings at a dwindling series of dinner parties and balls as the *ton* began to scatter to their various country estates in early August.

Since that evening at the Rocheford ball, Violet and Audley, whose marriage had been strained in recent years, had reconciled in predictably nauseating fashion. This reconciliation had been the culmination of nearly a fortnight of Violet feigning a case of consumption in order to get her husband's attention—an endeavor that had severely tried Diana's patience—but husband and wife were in the throes of matrimonial bliss once more. While this was overall a satisfactory outcome, it did mean that one could not spend too much time in the company of the recently reunited couple without feeling moderately ill. As a result, Diana had not spent quite as many hours at Violet's Curzon Street house as she was accustomed to—which did have the advantage of meaning that she'd not been forced into Willingham's company much of late. She'd heard from her brother that he'd wasted no time in taking up with a new mistress, now that his love affair with Lady Fitzwilliam, the former Sophie Wexham, had ended, but this was such quintessentially Willingham-like behavior that it scarcely warranted notice.

This was the state of affairs when, one morning in August, as she was lying abed, her butler arrived to announce an entirely unwelcome visitor.

"Lord Willingham," she repeated, clutching her wrapper tightly to her throat to ensure that poor Wright did not accidentally see even an inch of inappropriate flesh—she wasn't sure his heart could handle it, poor dear. "Lord Willingham, to whose country estate I will be retiring in a matter of days? Shouldn't he already be there? Doesn't it take *time* to prepare for a country house party?"

"I could not say, my lady," Wright replied stiffly, his gaze focused somewhere over her left shoulder. Despite Diana's modest attire, clearly the fact that she was in her bed was too much for his nerves to bear. "Would you like me to tell him that you are not at home?"

"No, no," Diana said, her curiosity piqued. "Tell him I shall be with him shortly." *Shortly* was, of course, a relative word, and Willingham would understand as much. She was a lady of style, after all. She did not simply roll out of bed and instantly become the delectable creature who graced ballrooms in the evening. This transformation took time.

She instructed Toogood, her lady's maid, to dress her hair as simply as possible once she had shimmied into her favorite pink muslin morning gown. Not fifteen minutes later, she was smoothing her skirts as she entered her drawing room, where the Marquess of Willingham was waiting for her.

Her first thought, as she entered the room, was that he was ill at ease. This was laughable—she was not sure she had *ever* seen Willingham anything other than confident and secure of himself, with the notable exception of his elder brother's funeral six years prior. He crossed the room to bow over her hand, entirely correctly, but there was something ever so slightly *off* in his manner that made her gaze sharpen as she took a seat on the most comfortable settee.

"I must confess, I am surprised to find you here, my lord," she said politely, lacing his title with the slightest layer of sarcasm, as was her wont. The tone she used when she referred to him as *my lord* always implied that he was anything but, and an amused glint in his eye acknowledged the slight and congratulated her for it. She never addressed him as Jeremy, only ever as Willingham or *my lord*. He hated his title, and none of his friends used it; their refusal to do so made her all the more determined to be scrupulously correct in her address, just to needle him. "Do you not have guests arriving at your country house in less than a week? And . . ." Here she paused, as though the thought had only just occurred to her. ". . . you don't have a wife to assist you! Who is helping the cook set the menu? Who is ensuring that all the rooms have been aired out? Who is setting an agenda of activities? I know you have a large staff, Willingham, but they do need *some* guidance."

Willingham waved a lazy hand. "I assure you, they do their best work when I am well out of their way. Were I to show up at any time other than at the last possible moment, it would set them all aflutter, the poor creatures."

Diana narrowed her eyes. "Spoken just like a man."

Willingham gestured to himself, the motion somehow encompassing his perfectly knotted cravat, the riding boots polished to shining perfection, and every artfully mussed golden hair upon his head. The gesture asked, *Am I not a perfect specimen of well-bred masculinity?* Diana had too much self-respect to allow herself to reply with even an internal sigh.

With a firm mental shake, she refocused her attention on the matter at hand. "What can I do for you, Willingham?" she asked briskly. "And won't you please sit? You're making me nervous. I do hate to watch anyone expend more energy than is strictly necessary. Except, of course"—and here she allowed her voice to take on a flirtatious note—"in certain situations when it is entirely desirable."

Willingham allowed his gaze to slowly rake her from head to toe as he sauntered toward her, and Diana's pulse quickened, much as she willed it not to.

"It is interesting that you mention that, Lady Templeton," he murmured as he drew near her and proceeded to sink elegantly upon the settee next to her, despite the availability of a pair of armchairs nearby.

"Exercise?" Diana asked innocently, ignoring with some effort the proximity of his thigh to her skirts.

"Of a sort." He reached out without warning and seized her hand. He had removed his gloves at some point before she had joined him in the room, and the feel of his bare skin against her own sent an embarrassing tingle racing through her.

"I find myself thinking," he continued, maintaining his firm grip upon her hand, "that as we are both unattached, young, attractive individuals . . ." He trailed off as he lifted her wrist to place a kiss upon her pulse there. "We might find our way to some sort of arrangement."

"An arrangement?" Diana asked, and was distressed to hear that her voice was not quite as steady as she would have liked. His lips were warm upon her wrist, and he withdrew only enough to allow himself to speak, his breath heating her skin with each word.

"I'm sure a lady of your experience doesn't require me to elaborate further upon the sort of arrangement I have in mind." His eyes met hers, bright with amusement, and it took a moment for his words to filter through Diana's sluggish mind. After a moment, however, they did, and a particular phrase—*your experience*—was as invigorating as a blast of freezing wind.

She stiffened and withdrew her hand from his grip. "My *experience?*" she asked coldly, inching herself away from him as much as was possible on the tiny settee.

Willingham seemed not to realize that he was treading on dangerous ground. "Well, yes," he said blithely, shooting a flattering smile at her. It was an attractive smile, there was no doubt, but at the moment it left Diana entirely cold. "You're a widow, with a certain reputation . . ." He trailed off, clearly intelligent enough to realize that he would gain no favor by further elaborating upon that point.

Ah, yes. Her *reputation.* Diana was no fool, and was, of course, aware of the whispers about her among the *ton.* She had, in truth, done much to cultivate such rumors—she had flirted and batted her eyelashes and worn revealing gowns because she liked the feeling of power it gave her. She was a woman in a society that thought women were helpless and weak, and she had spent her entire life subject to the whims of men. Now, at last, she was subject to no one's whims but her own—she was a widow with a title and a healthy bank account, and she was young and beautiful and she knew it. Why shouldn't she flirt—and more?

But it was the "and more" that was the sticking point. Because, in truth, her reputation was entirely founded on rumors rather than action. She had married, at eighteen, a man old enough to be her father, who had consummated their marriage for legality's sake and then taken little interest in matters of the bedchamber from that point on. He had also, rather expediently, made her a widow.

And so here Diana was, young, full of certain . . . urges, with a reputation that preceded her and, in truth, no idea how to seduce a man.

Or, rather, she thought she could seduce him quite easily, but she'd not much of an idea of precisely what to do with him once she'd lured him to her bedchamber. She had experience with the act in its most basic iteration, of course, and had a fair understanding of what brought her pleasure, but she lacked . . . finesse. And, as she was not a person who liked to admit to weakness, this bothered her.

With Willingham, at the moment, it seemed that little effort would have to be expended in the seduction. He was directing his charm at her so forcefully that she was surprised her legs hadn't fallen open of their own accord. However, her momentary return to sanity had been enough to allow her to reclaim her naturally suspicious nature, and it was a wary glance she now leveled at the man beside her on the settee. Willingham was charming and flirtatious, it was true, but he was laying it on too thick.

She smelled a rat.

"Do remove yourself from my settee, Willingham," she said briskly, proceeding to rearrange her skirts with such gusto that the man had no choice but to retreat to an armchair to avoid the risk of suffocation by muslin. "And tell me what your true plan is here. I've been out of mourning for positively ages and you've never so much as quirked a brow in my direction until now."

Willingham sank into the armchair and crossed one leg elegantly over the opposite knee, his fingers drumming against the arms. All traces of flirtation had vanished as quickly as they had arrived, though Diana was distressed to note that she found him all the more appealing for their absence. He sighed heavily. "I should have known better than to try my usual tricks with you."

"Yes, you should have," Diana said severely. "Now explain."

"I recently had a somewhat traumatizing experience." Willingham's eyes turned round and soulful. Diana, unmoved, waved her hand for him to continue. "I was in a . . . shall we say, *private* situation with a lady of my acquaintance, and at the end of the proceedings, I felt obliged to tell her that I thought it time our liaison came to an end."

Diana raised a hand to stop him. "Just to be clear, do you mean to tell me that you rejected your lover *after* you bedded her?"

Willingham blinked. "Well . . . yes," he said, as though this should be obvious. "It would have rather spoiled the mood if I'd done so beforehand."

"But you could have just told her and then left!"

"But I wanted to have one last time with her to remember," Willingham said, his eyes misting nostalgically.

"But the time *prior* to that would have been the last time for you to remember."

"But I didn't *know* then that it would be the last time. I hadn't quite made my mind up, you see," Willingham said, as though attempting to force a toddler to see reason. "But by the evening in question, I had decided, and so I wanted one last memory before it was all spoiled."

Diana stared at him in disbelief. "But don't you think it would all have been a bit *less* spoiled if you'd ended things in a gentlemanly fashion?"

Willingham sighed. "Well, as it turns out, you may be correct in this case. She was . . . somewhat perturbed, let us say, when I told her. I had to dress in rather a hurry to make it out of there before she woke the whole house with the insults she was flinging at me."

"You told her whilst you were *still in bed?*" Diana had never considered herself to be someone with an overly strong moral compass—anyone who, at eighteen, forms a mental list of eligible mates and sets about seducing one with cold-blooded calculation cannot reasonably claim such an honor—but even she, it seemed, had her limits. "Willingham, I daresay you deserved every insult she threw at you, and quite a few she didn't."

"I admit it might not have been my best decision-making," Willingham said, leaning forward to brace his elbows upon his knees. "I'd had a few drinks too many that evening, I should add—liquid courage and all that, eh?"

"So let me be certain I understand this," Diana said, provoked to the unthinkable—standing!—as she spoke. "You appeared at the home of your paramour, foxed. You took the lady to bed. Then, whilst lying in her warm embrace, you ended your liaison." She had begun to pace as she listed his offenses. "And then you fled whilst she gave you the set-down you so richly deserved?"

Willingham considered. "That is about the shape of it, yes." His eyes tracked her movements back and forth across the drawing room. "Are you quite well?" he asked, genuine concern evident in his voice. "I don't think I've ever seen you pace before."

"It's been a very trying month," Diana snapped, her footsteps continuing unabated. "First Violet spends weeks wheezing into a handkerchief, all to lure back a man who was already in love with her, and now you appear in my drawing room, panting all over my hand and describing your bad behavior in such detail that I feel compelled to slap you just on principle."

"Please don't," Willingham said, raising his hands defensively. "Last night's brandy is still sloshing about in there and I don't think my poor head can take much more abuse."

"Well, I cannot take much more of this!" Diana waved a hand expansively about the room. "Why must all my friends insist on behaving like utter fools? Next thing will be Emily eloping with that odious Mr. Cartham of hers, and I don't know what I shall do then!" Her friend Lady Emily Turner had been persistently courted by the owner of a gaming hell to whom her father owed a rather large debt. Thus far, Emily had succeeded in keeping a proposal at bay—and had, with Diana's encouragement, been escorted by Lord Julian Belfry to a handful of recent *ton* events. Belfry was handsome, wealthy, and had enough seedy connections that Diana suspected he would be more than a match for Cartham, should Belfry decide to court Emily in earnest. But with the way things were going lately, Diana had no doubt that disaster among their set lurked just around the corner.

"If we can return to the matter at hand," Willingham said, rising and placing himself directly in her path, forcing her to halt abruptly. "I've not told you the worst bit."

Diana threw her hands up. "What *else* could you possibly have done to make this worse? Shot the poor lady's husband in a duel?"

"*That* I am innocent of," Willingham said, sounding rather proud of himself. "I managed to escape the home before that admirable gentleman returned, sparing the lady in question that bother, at least."

Diana, who knew well the way that servants gossiped, wasn't certain that Willingham should breathe a sigh of relief just yet, but she held her tongue, curious to hear what his true complaint was.

"The lady . . . well . . ." Willingham looked, Diana thought, truly uncomfortable, for possibly the first time in her lengthy acquaintance with him. She leaned forward eagerly, curious in spite of herself. "She critiqued my performance in the bedroom," Willingham said all at once, the words emerging in such a rush that it took Diana's brain several long moments to piece together the meaning of what he had said. While she was puzzling this out, Willingham himself began to pace, and after a moment he continued to speak, her lack of a reply clearly making him all the more uncomfortable.

"I mean to say, it is of course nonsense, just spoken in anger, but it . . . well, it's lodged itself in my mind and I can't stop thinking about it. I shall never bed a woman again at this rate if I can't get myself into an amorous situation without the blasted woman's words echoing around in my head the second things get interesting."

"Has that happened to you, then?" Diana asked, finding her tongue, torn between glee and an unexpected rush of indignation. She had always rather prided herself on having cornered the market when it came to crushing set-downs delivered to Willingham, but this unnamed lady had clearly usurped the crown.

"Well, no," Willingham admitted, still pacing, "but it's only a matter of time. I need to just, er, get back in the saddle, as it were, but I'm finding the task a bit daunting." Diana, watching him closely, thought she detected a telltale flush rising in his cheeks. Was Willingham *blushing*? She had not thought such a thing possible—when roughly a third of the widows in London had seen one in the nude, she would have thought that one would be above (or below?) blushing.

"Why are you sharing this with me, of all people?" Diana asked belatedly. This should, truly, have been her very first question, but she had been somewhat taken aback by the unexpected nature of his revelation, and her mind was not moving at its usual rapid pace. "Wouldn't Audley or Penvale be a more likely confidant?"

"Good God, woman!" Willingham stopped in his tracks and turned to face her, looking truly appalled. "This isn't the sort of thing I can tell another man. I'd be a laughingstock! I'd never be able to look your brother in the eye again." He paused, a shrewd look coming into his own eyes. "Which means that you aren't to tell him, either. I should have gotten your agreement on that count before I began. I've gone about this all the wrong way." He shook his head. "See? I'm addled! Not thinking clearly! Lack of bedsport isn't good for any man—look at Audley's behavior recently, if you need proof of that. It dilutes the power of the brain. Makes us soft."

Diana's mouth quirked up. "I'd rather think *soft* is quite the opposite of what it would make you."

He shot her a quelling look. "This is not the time for bawdy jokes, Diana."

It had been many years since he had addressed her by her Christian name—when they were young, tumbling about her aunt and uncle's estate on his visits with Penvale, she had been Diana and he had been Jeremy. Or, more often, names had been forgone entirely in favor of more insulting monikers. But once she had made her debut in London, emerging onto the scene as the sophisticated debutante she'd worked so hard to craft herself into, she had been Miss Bourne, later Lady Templeton, and it had been more than five years since she'd heard him call her anything else.

None of this explained, though, why hearing her name on his tongue did such odd and uncomfortable things to her insides. She had long since resigned herself to the fact of her own body's unwanted, traitorous responses when in the presence of this man, but with firm mental control and self-discipline, these reactions could be ignored. And so she proceeded to do just that.

"If it will ease your mind, I am happy to inform you that the thought of discussing your difficulties in the boudoir with my brother is one of the more horrifying prospects I have ever considered," she said. "But you have still failed to answer my question: why on earth are you telling me this? We're hardly in the habit of trading confidences."

He heaved a sigh and stiffened his shoulders, as though steeling himself for a daunting task. Diana scarcely had time to contemplate what said task could possibly be when he took a few steps forward, seized her hand, and dropped to his knee in front of her.

"Lady Templeton," he said solemnly, his handsome face gazing earnestly up into her own. "I have a proposal for you."

Three

It was entirely worth it just to see the look on her face, Jeremy thought.

Diana, he knew, prided herself on her control, every move she made calculated to have maximum impact, each word honed to sharpness before launched. The sight of her standing above him, jaw slack, a look of abject horror on her face, was one of the most satisfying Jeremy had ever witnessed.

It took only a moment for Diana to come to her senses and wrench her arm from his grip. "Get up off that floor at once," she said, waving her now-liberated hand at him imperiously. "Have you lost your mind?"

"I don't believe so, no," he said, leisurely climbing to his feet. "But I am hurt, truly, that you were not willing to hear me out."

"Hear you out?" she repeated incredulously. "What could possibly have possessed you to think that I'd wish to hear a *proposal* from you? Have I not made it abundantly clear in the past that a marriage proposal from you would be entirely unwelcome? How better can I explain it so that you finally get it through your thick skull that I wouldn't marry you if you were the last man in London?" She paused. "Unless you are indicating your desire to concede our wager?" She batted her eyelashes at him. "I suppose I could nobly suffer matrimony

33

if it meant I'd win one hundred pounds, and the lifelong satisfaction of knowing I'd bested you."

"My dear Lady Templeton," he said, smiling his most winsome smile at her, "as charming as it has been to hear you yet again elucidate your disgust at the prospect of sharing a life with me, I fear you may have gotten a bit ahead of yourself."

"How so, precisely?" Diana asked icily. Her words were so clipped that she scarcely needed to move her jaw to speak. She was magnificent when she was angry—hazel eyes blazing, cheeks flushed, and that rather spectacular chest of hers doing all sorts of interesting things with every slight movement. This was, of course, no small part of the appeal of riling her.

His smile widened. "My proposal," he said slowly, drawing the words out, enjoying himself immensely even as her eyes flashed dangerously once again, "was not one of marriage."

He paused for one beat, then another. Her brow furrowed slightly in confusion, and then smoothed just as quickly as realization sank in. She arched a brow at him and took a step back, crossing her arms over her chest as she gave him a slow once-over.

"Just to be certain I understand this," she said, her gaze seemingly fixed—surely he was mistaken?—somewhere just south of his navel. "You want me to be your mistress?" He could not help noting that she sounded less insulted by the prospect of being his mistress than by that of being his wife, but decided not to take offense. When he had been mentally reviewing the list of women of his acquaintance, he had discovered that the number he had not dallied with in the past was almost embarrassingly small—and that the number of those who remained who would not be appalled by his proposition had shrunk even further. All the way down to one, in fact.

"I think *lover* would be more accurate," he said by way of reply. "*Mistress* implies a certain financial arrangement that I don't think would be necessary between us." He cast a wry glance at the priceless works of art upon the walls of the drawing room, and at the emerald ring upon her hand. "And, indeed, it also implies a power imbalance, which would not be my intention at all. I'd expect us to enter this arrangement as equals, each receiving benefits."

Diana's other eyebrow joined its twin in a race toward her hairline. "And what benefits, precisely, would there be for me? You've just informed me that your performance in this context has been receiving somewhat tepid reviews of late, have you not?"

"I am certain those are naught but the angry words of a bereft woman," Jeremy said, with a touch more confidence than he actually felt. Could women feign pleasure? He supposed they could do so far more easily than a man, and the idea raised a number of unpleasant possibilities in his mind. How was a man ever to know if a woman was truly enjoying herself, if her response could be feigned? What if every woman he'd ever dallied with had been internally critiquing his performance? It seemed unlikely—he did, after all, have something of a reputation. But, of course, it wasn't impossible. Improbable, yes. But not impossible. And he needed to know, just to be sure.

"If you're so certain," Diana said, echoing his thoughts, "then why are you propositioning me in my drawing room? I assume that's what this is about, is it not? Take me to bed, get a complimentary review of your efforts, head back out into the world reassured of your manly prowess?"

This was, in fact, precisely what Jeremy had in mind, but when she stated it so baldly, it sounded a bit . . . well, pathetic.

"Something along those lines," he hedged. "But you would benefit as well, of course." Seeing the skepticism writ plain on her face, he rushed on. "I've heard your discussions with Violet, all this talk of taking a lover. And yet no rumor of a love affair has reached my ears, so unless you are being remarkably discreet, you must continue to sleep alone. Which begs the question: *why?* You're young, you're beautiful, and, er . . ." He floundered, unsure of how to put into words the quality she exuded, the one that made every man halt and turn as she passed, the one that made it impossible to look at her for more than five seconds without imagining her a great deal less clothed and more vocal. Or, rather, he *did* know how to put it into words—but not words that were appropriate for a lady's ears.

"You . . . attract men," he finished, which was true, but an enormous understatement. She was like a magnet. She could have bedded every eligible man of the *ton*—and a good many of the ineligible ones, too. He was surprised the suitors hadn't been beating down her door before her husband was cold in the ground. He knew—had known for years—that he had this damned weakness where she was concerned, but he also knew he was far from alone in these sentiments.

"And that should make me *more* likely to share my bed with a man who, apparently, has no idea what to do once he's gotten there?" Her face was calm, her voice neutral, but he could see the spark of laughter in her eyes and knew that she was baiting him. For once, he refused to rise to her efforts.

"My point is, you seem not to know how to make men understand that you are, er . . ." The first phrase that sprang to mind was *open for business*, but he was fairly certain that even he, with his legendary charm, wouldn't be able to recover from that one. "Open to a liaison," he settled upon instead. "But a brief, discreet affair with me would send all the right signals."

Diana looked skeptical. "I'm not certain that the signal I'm looking to send is that I've joined the legion of women who've lifted their skirts for the Marquess of Willingham. I'm surprised they haven't formed a society. With matching hats."

Jeremy did laugh at that, unable to help himself, and he saw suspicious twitchings about her mouth.

"You don't have to give me an answer today," he said, wrestling himself back under control. "You can let me know once you've arrived at Elderwild," he added, naming his family seat in the country.

"Shall I do so by waiting for you in your bedchamber one evening?" Diana asked, clearly amused.

"I rather thought a discreet note might do the trick just as well, but don't let me stand in the way of your desire for theatrics."

"I don't need to wait, Willingham, I can tell you right now what my answer will be."

She meant that it would be no—he could see it written on her face, could hear it in the tone of her voice. And who could blame her? He'd bungled this, there was no doubt about it.

He raised a hand before she could give voice to her refusal. "Just consider it," he said simply, then dropped his voice. "If nothing else, it would finally dispel whatever this is between us," he added, waving his hand at the space between them, which always seemed to take on a charged quality as soon as they were in the same room. "And don't tell me you don't know what I mean," he said as she opened her mouth. "Because I know you do."

Before she could speak a word, he took a couple of steps forward and reached for her hand, pressing a kiss to it and allowing his lips to linger there for two heartbeats longer than was proper. And then, with a murmured word of farewell, he took his leave.

His intention had been to remind her of the strange, potent connection between them, to leave her wanting more. He had no idea, he reflected ruefully as he strode through Mayfair toward his club, if he'd accomplished that aim—but he'd undoubtedly succeeded at reminding himself.

Four

Both the advantage and the disadvantage of an unmarried friend was the fact that she was entirely too easy to shock.

Diana, being a naturally devious person by nature, occasionally took advantage of this fact in her conversations with Emily—there was, after all, a fair amount of amusement to be had from casually discussing indiscretions among the *ton* and watching Emily's fair cheeks turn rosier and rosier with each word. At other times, however, when she wanted a piece of good advice, she had less patience when Emily came over missish.

Emily, however, was the next person Diana saw after her discussion with Willingham in her drawing room, and therefore had no choice but to be the recipient of her conflicted ramblings.

"But . . . you and Willingham can barely spend ten seconds together without arguing," Emily said, once Diana's somewhat incoherent explanation of Willingham's proposal had finally come to an end. It was the afternoon of the same day, and they were walking in Hyde Park, a footman and Emily's abigail trailing a discreet distance behind them. It was not entirely private, of course, but about as close as she was likely to get.

It had been tricky to explain Willingham's proposition without revealing his reasons for doing so—fortunately, however, given the man's general behavior, Emily hadn't seemed to have much difficulty believing that he'd just taken it into his head that Diana would be a likely enough candidate for a roll or two between the sheets.

"I do find him more irritating than any other man of my acquaintance," Diana agreed.

"What promising groundwork for romance," Emily said, straight-faced.

Diana shot her a reproving look. She had known Emily for close to ten years; Emily's parents were good friends with Violet's, meaning the Marquess of Rowanbridge and his family were frequently paying visits to Violet's parents, the Earl and Countess of Worthington, and Diana's aunt and uncle had lived on the adjoining estate. The three girls had been thick as thieves since well before their debut Season.

And yet, even after all that time, there were still moments when Diana found Emily exasperatingly difficult to read. She had the best mask of the three of them—she possessed an almost eerie ability to project the image of the serene, innocent, uncurious lady that society so desperately wished her to be, with no sign of the quick mind that lurked beneath. Diana admired this skill, except when she was on its receiving end.

"So, what do you intend to do?" Emily asked, breaking into Diana's thoughts. They were approached by a cluster of ladies they knew, walking in the opposite direction, and for several minutes their conversation was interrupted by an exchange of pleasantries and a perhaps excessive amount of cooing over Lady Julia Hornby's new dog, which was being paraded about by a footman. Diana did not care for dogs—too noisy, too energetic, and too smelly. She rather liked the idea of acquiring a cat at some point, though—she admired their lazy grace, as well as their ability to force everyone around them to do their bidding. It was a skill she was constantly trying to hone in herself.

At last they were alone again, continuing their walk down the public footpath that ran alongside Rotten Row, a soft breeze now rustling the leaves on the trees around them. "I've not decided yet," Diana said, without preamble; Emily did not so much as blink, apparently having no difficulty in picking their conversation up where they had left it. "It occurs to me that there might be some . . . advantages to the arrangement."

Emily's smooth brow furrowed, the only imperfection to her appearance; she was dressed in a gown of blush pink, her golden curls pulled neatly into a knot at the nape of her neck, her blue eyes wide and guileless. She appeared so perfect a specimen of English womanhood that the sheer absurdity of her unmarried status hit Diana with greater force than usual—and, not for the first time, Diana wished she could shove the Marquess of Rowanbridge, whose gambling debts were the cause, into the nearest body of water.

"What sort of advantage?" Emily asked, but the words had scarcely left her mouth before her confused expression cleared, replaced by an alarmingly rapturous one instead. "Oh, Diana!" She stopped in her tracks, turning to face Diana full-on, clasping her hands together in barely contained glee. "Do you mean to say . . ." She trailed off, momentarily overcome by emotion.

Diana, who had stopped walking when Emily had, eyed her friend with some degree of trepidation. "No," she said quickly. "I don't know what you're thinking, but whatever it is, the answer is no."

"*Do you mean to say*," Emily repeated, ignoring Diana's words entirely, "that you have a *tendre* for Willingham?"

"No!" Diana said; the words came out as nearly a screech, and she darted a quick glance around to ensure that she had not drawn any undue attention. Behind them, her footman and Emily's abigail dawdled, clearly waiting for their employers to begin walking again, but no one else appeared to be paying them any mind.

"No," she repeated at a more normal volume. "I mean nothing of the sort. What I meant . . ." She trailed off—much as she loved shocking Emily, she hesitated at the thought of explaining why it was that she was considering Willingham's offer.

Really, it should have been easy to say no—Willingham certainly hadn't done a very convincing job of selling the proposition. But the fact remained that there were years of history here—years of her spine tingling whenever he walked into a room, of a prickling awareness of his gaze on her when he thought she wouldn't notice. It was so tempting to just work this—whatever *this* was—out of her system once and for all and be done with it.

There was also another, more logical reason for accepting his—highly indecent—proposal, one that Willingham could not possibly have known when he appealed to her sense of reason, but which existed nonetheless: her need for a bit of practice in the bedchamber.

While the thought of Willingham possibly noticing her inexperience was mortifying, she thought she could bear it better from him than from any other gentleman of her acquaintance. Despite their constant barbs, she somehow knew that he wouldn't use this particular weakness as ammunition in their future battles, if for no other reason than that he prided himself on besting her fair and square, and would no doubt consider sinking to underhanded tactics to be beneath his dignity, or some similar nonsense.

The thought of explaining this to Emily, however—innocent, virginal Emily—was mildly daunting.

Instead, she decided to fall back upon the excuse that Willingham himself had provided for her—which itself was not entirely without merit.

"If I have a brief affair with Willingham and word gets around, it makes it that much easier for me to take my next lover," she explained in businesslike fashion. Emily, predictably, looked somewhat scandalized by this explanation, though she did not interrupt.

"It's so much easier to allow the men to come to me than to have to hunt for them myself," Diana continued. "Once it becomes clear that Willingham and I had a liaison—but are no longer doing so—I shan't even have to crook a finger to find another willing partner."

"The men already come to you," Emily pointed out. "Your dance card is always full. Afternoon calls at your house are practically a parade of eligible gentlemen."

"Yes, yes," Diana said. "But some of them seem to have distressingly proper intentions. I only want the ones with decidedly *improper* intentions, you see. Bedding Willingham should make that abundantly clear." The more she spoke, the more obvious it became that to accept his offer would, in fact, make perfect sense.

Her mind thus settled, she decided to turn the conversation to Emily's own romantic prospects. They were nearing the end of Emily's sixth Season. Her first Season—when both Violet and Diana had themselves married—she had received several offers, but the Rowanbridges had insisted their daughter reject them, deeming none of Emily's suitors sufficiently high in the instep for a marquess's daughter. Her second and third Seasons had been missed entirely—the second because of a scandal involving her imbecile of an elder brother, who had fought a duel and killed his opponent, forcing him to flee to the Continent; the third, due to her mourning period for said brother's death abroad. And for the past two years, Emily had been escorted about by a certain Mr. Cartham, owner of a gambling hell whose disinclination to call in the marquess's debts was entirely dependent on his daughter's presence on his arm at society events.

Cartham himself was hardly what her parents would consider appropriate marriage material; his ability to weasel invitations for himself to a surprising number of *ton* events was surely testament to the fact that the Marquess of Rowanbridge was not the only aristocrat in his debt. And everywhere he appeared, Emily was at his side; he had thus far displayed no intention of actually marrying her, seeming to find the presence of one of the most beautiful unmarried ladies of the *ton* on his arm satisfactory enough, but Diana was not about to risk the possibility that his plans could change.

"We've spoken enough of me," she said cunningly, reaching out to link her arm with Emily's as they walked. "I'm positively desperate to hear how Lady Tarlington's musicale was." She herself had missed the event, having already accepted an invitation to the theater that evening instead. Emily, however, had been present—and in company of which Diana highly approved.

"It was lovely," Emily said calmly. "Mozart is so soothing, don't you think?"

"Did you find the company . . . invigorating?" Diana asked slyly.

"Lady Fitzwilliam was there," Emily said slowly. "I had a nice opportunity to speak to her—I do like her quite a bit, I'm so glad Violet introduced us. We weren't able to speak for long, but West was there, too, and I saw them in conversation for quite a while."

This was, indeed, quite an interesting piece of gossip, as Emily well knew—West, as the Marquess of Weston was known to his friends, was Audley's elder brother and had been Lady Fitzwilliam's beau when she was still Sophie Wexham. Diana, however, did not allow herself to be distracted.

"Anyone other than West and Sophie of particular interest?" she asked casually. "A certain gentleman who owns an oh-so-scandalous theater, perhaps?"

Emily sighed. "Lord Julian escorted me, as you are perfectly well aware, so you can stop beating around the bush and just ask me whatever it is you wish to know."

Lord Julian Belfry was an acquaintance of Penvale, Audley, and Willingham from their Oxford years; Diana had never gotten the impression that they were terribly close, Belfry being a couple of years ahead of the others, but they had recently renewed the friendship—and he had shown more than a passing interest in Emily.

Belfry was the second son of a marquess but was considered rather scandalous; his father had disinherited him, and he'd used his inheritance from a relative to start a theater that catered to gentlemen of the aristocracy in search of a night out without their wives. Belfry was still invited almost everywhere by the *ton*—he was, after all, handsome, wealthy, and second in line to a marquessate—but he caused whispers and gossip wherever he went.

Diana could scarcely think of a less likely suitor for prim, proper Emily—which was of course why she was so entirely delighted by the whole thing.

"Did you two discuss anything of interest?" she asked. "Music? Art?" She paused, looking idly around. "Matrimony?"

Emily stumbled a bit, but Diana's grip upon her arm was firm and she quickly regained her footing. "Should I take that as a yes?" Diana asked gleefully.

"No," Emily said, very firmly. "And even if he were to offer such a thing—which he has given no indication he intends to do—I don't see how my parents would possibly permit it."

"Belfry is, by all reports, exceedingly wealthy," Diana pointed out. "Perhaps he'd be willing to pay your father's gambling debts and free you from Cartham."

"I'm beginning to wonder if there's more to it than simple debt," Emily said slowly, worrying her lower lip. She paused for a moment, clearly considering her words. "Do you recall last Season, when Viscount Trevelyan showed an interest in me?"

"Of course." Trevelyan was in his mid-thirties and owner of a famously lovely country seat in Cumbria. "He never actually proposed, though."

"No," Emily agreed. "My mother told me he had known I had no dowry, but hadn't realized he'd need to pay Father's debts, too." She paused. "But Lord Julian said that he had it on good authority that Trevelyan *had* offered to pay my father's debts, and he was still rebuffed." She looked up at Diana. "Which doesn't make any sense at all!"

No, it didn't—unless, as Diana was all at once coming to suspect, the Marquess of Rowanbridge's debt to Cartham went beyond money.

"Did Belfry add anything?" Diana asked curiously; she still couldn't figure out what, precisely, the man's game was. That he would find Emily lovely was entirely unsurprising; that he should take such an interest in an unmarried lady with no fortune was somewhat more so—as Willingham had noted, Belfry did have something of a reputation as a rake.

"He said . . ." Emily trailed off, blushing a bit. "He said that he intends to be at Lord Willingham's country house party next week, and he wished to know if I would be attending."

"Oh *did* he?" Diana said, resisting with great difficulty the urge to cackle. "And what did you tell him?"

"That Lord Willingham always invited me, but my mother never wants to chaperone me—she and my father would normally already be back in the countryside by now, and she has little interest in delaying our return home further. He seemed somewhat disappointed."

"Of course he did," Diana said cheerfully. A thought struck her. "Do you think your mother would find a different chaperone acceptable?"

Emily frowned. "You know she won't let you act as my chaperone for a trip to Wiltshire, Diana. It's miraculous enough she allows me to accompany you to the park or the theater without her."

"I didn't mean myself," Diana said, waving a hand dismissively. "I was thinking, though, that Willingham's grandmother said she planned to attend—and isn't she friends with your mother?"

"*Friends* might be stretching it," Emily hedged. "She stops by for an afternoon call periodically and terrifies Mother into buying me a new pair of gloves or something along those lines. She was friends with my grandmother, you know, and seems to think it her duty to see that we're all behaving appropriately."

"Perfect," Diana said, making a mental note to call on the dowager marchioness the very next afternoon. "I think I know just the chaperone for you."

"I don't know," Emily said doubtfully. "And besides, I'm not at all certain I wish to attend Lord Willingham's party—I don't understand what Lord Julian's aim is, precisely, but he hardly seems like the sort of man to just suddenly take an interest in an eligible lady for no reason," she added suspiciously, echoing Diana's own thoughts on the matter. Diana was forced to admit that this did not precisely sound like the beginnings of a legendary romance, but perhaps Emily and Belfry simply needed more time together.

Time in a romantic pastoral setting, even.

"I'm sure Lady Willingham won't object once she learns that a matter of the heart is at stake," Diana said dramatically.

"Stop that," Emily said repressively.

Diana pouted. "I don't want to." She tugged Emily even tighter to her side. "This is all going perfectly, if I do say so myself. Tricking your mother into allowing me to take you to Belfry's theater is the best thing I've ever done."

"I don't think—"

"Your babies will be so adorably blue-eyed."

"I hardly—"

"You're right, you're right," Diana conceded. "Mustn't get ahead of ourselves. Let's focus on the wedding first."

Emily sighed, clearly recognizing a battle she was not going to win, and evidently decided to change tack. "I'd much rather speak of *your* wedding," she said, casting a sly glance at Diana.

"An event that has happened once and is never to be repeated," Diana said firmly.

"Don't you ever wish to marry again?" asked Emily a bit tentatively.

"Why should I?" Diana asked blithely. "I've done it once, and now that I have the advantage of a widow's portion and the accompanying freedom, I don't see why I should ever wish to tie myself to another man again."

"But . . ." Emily trailed off, hesitating. "If you intend to take a lover—Willingham, or anyone else—does it not seem possible that your emotions might become involved? What if you fell in *love*?"

Diana laughed. "Emily, don't be absurd," she said. "The last thing I ever intend to do is something as unutterably foolish as to fall in love."

Five

It did not escape Diana that a somewhat unpleasant task lay ahead of her: telling Willingham that she accepted his offer. That she was dreading the conversation so much was alarming—she, who prided herself on a level head, on never losing her composure. But the prospect of presenting herself at his bedchamber door, armed with a seductive smile and an enticingly low neckline, made her balk, even in her mental imaginings. She enjoyed being bold—she *wanted* to do just that—but she thought she would have to send a note. She had never done this before, after all; perhaps one had to build up to this sort of thing. Begin with a note, but eventually work up to the point of appearing in a gentleman's bed, naked and inviting.

Yes, she decided firmly. Best to start slow.

She was still mulling it over the following Monday when her carriage at last halted in front of Elderwild, the sudden stop jostling Toogood—who had spent the entire journey dozing across from Diana in the carriage—awake with an amount of grumbled profanity that Diana personally felt was out of proportion to the offense.

"Careful, Toogood, or my innocent ears shall never recover," she offered as a parting shot as she accepted a footman's hand down from the carriage. Toogood's reply was muttered in an undertone, thus sparing

Diana what would have undoubtedly been another string of colorful epithets. Whenever she heard aristocratic ladies of her acquaintance lamenting some imagined slight on the part of their ladies' maids, Diana had to stifle a laugh: she undoubtedly had the most openly hostile maid in the *ton*.

The house before her was, as ever, striking; Willingham's ancestral pile was an imposing manor of weathered stone, featuring an impressive number of turrets, pinnacles, and mullioned windows. It was surrounded by immaculately maintained lawns that sloped gently into a scenic lake to the front of the house, and which devolved into woodland in the hills that rose behind the manor. It was these surroundings that made Willingham's invitations so coveted; his shooting parties each August were said to be among the best of the *ton*, since the woods that surrounded Elderwild were full of deer and pheasants, and the nearby hills boasted even the occasional grouse, unusual so far south. The hunting, of course, had nothing to do with Diana's annual attendance at these events; Willingham also had well-stocked cellars and a talented cook—and, furthermore, by August she was usually desperate to be out of the oppressive heat of London.

She now allowed herself to be ushered into the house, divested of her outer garments and baggage, and steered into the red drawing room for tea before she was able to get so much as a word in edgewise—the master of the house was nowhere in sight, but his staff, accustomed to the firm guiding hand necessary to manage a degenerate, unmarried marquess, had little trouble bending her to their will. She blew an errant lock of hair away from her face as the drawing room door clicked shut behind her, feeling rather as though she had just survived a small, efficient tempest.

"Diana!"

Violet rose from her spot on a settee, where she had been re-clining next to her husband until Diana's entrance, and crossed the room quickly to seize her friend's hands in her own. Diana realized that both Violet and Audley were looking a bit flushed in the face and, noting that they had been the only occupants of the room prior to her arrival, had little doubt as to the cause. People worried about debutantes requiring strict chaperoning, but Diana thought the ones who should really be watched were married couples recently reunited after a lengthy estrangement, if one wanted to leave at least some of the furniture in the house with its virtue intact.

"Where's Willingham?" Diana asked, extricating herself from Violet's grip and dropping into an armchair next to the settee. Audley, who had stood upon Diana's entry to the room, sank back down into his seat, drawing his wife down beside him with a tender look that was equal parts endearing and nauseating.

"Greeting the Rothsmeres still, I believe," Audley replied, examin-ing the contents of the tea tray on the cart before him.

"Rothsmeres, plural?" Diana asked, a feeling of dread stealing over her.

"I'm afraid so," Audley replied, finally settling upon a fat tea bun that he proceeded to consume in a methodical fashion.

"Jeremy merely invited the earl," Violet added, picking up the story where her husband had left off in his baked-good-induced distraction. "But I gather the countess hounded Rothsmere until he secured an invitation for his sister as well." She heaved a mournful sigh.

"The good news is," Audley added, swallowing his last mouthful of tea cake, "it's a large house. If you're clever—and, knowing you, Diana, I am certain you will be—you might avoid her entirely, except at mealtimes."

"I shall certainly endeavor to," Diana muttered. The Earl of Roths-mere was one of Willingham's friends dating back to his days at Oxford. And he was decent enough, as far as men with titles went; however, his sister, Lady Helen, was an entirely different sort. She was in her third Season now, still unwed, and in Diana's limited interactions with her she had received an overwhelming impression of grasping ambition. Diana wondered idly if Lady Helen's presence at this house party indi-cated that she'd set her sights on a certain unmarried marquess.

"What have you been occupied with in the past few days, Diana?" asked Violet, handing her a teacup and then proceeding to somewhat clumsily refill her own. "I've not seen you in nearly a week."

"Mmm," Diana said, her mouth curling up as she surveyed her friend over the rim of her teacup. "And whose fault is that? I didn't dare call on you, lest I inadvertently stumble upon an amorous scene that might have damaged me permanently." She was delighted to see that, instead of denying this charge, both Violet and Audley flushed. She gave them a moment to stew in their own discomfort, then took pity on them and continued. "But to answer your question, I've been exceedingly busy fending off every gossip in the *ton* eager to hear about your reconciliation, of course. And painting."

This was a bit of a lie by omission—Diana was certain that Violet would be very interested indeed to learn of Willingham presenting himself at her home, confessing his bedroom woes, and propositioning her, but she didn't care to enlighten Violet and Audley at the moment. Or perhaps ever—she was already somewhat regretting having let even Emily into her confidence.

"What have you been working on?" Violet asked curiously.

Were she speaking to anyone else, Diana would likely have down-played her work, dismissing it as merely dabbling in watercolors or something similarly inane. (In fact, Diana loathed watercolors.) She didn't like to speak of her painting overmuch—even with Violet, her oldest friend, who had seen and admired plenty of her art. It was impossible to put into words the sense of stillness and calm she achieved when seated before a canvas, and any attempt on her part to articulate this made her feel frustrated and fraudulent. Because who was she, other than the daughter of a viscount who had had a drawing master as a child? She was hardly Botticelli.

She was aware, of course, that she had some talent, but she also knew that society wouldn't value her art beyond a cursory compliment now and then. She was proficient at painting, and this earned her a tick mark next to that item on the list of desired qualities in a lady of good breeding. It didn't really matter to anyone that she was better at it than any other lady—or man—she knew, and so she tried not to let it matter to herself, either.

She did not say any of this to Violet, of course. Instead, she merely said, "I've been attempting a still life, with mixed results." She'd been working on it in her sunroom for the better part of the past two weeks. She had been distracted by her thoughts of late, and found the unceasing attention to detail that a still life required to be the only thing that could make her mind go blissfully blank. She wasn't entirely pleased with the painting yet, and she'd left it behind in London; perhaps a change of scenery and some practice with landscapes here in the countryside would give her renewed energy for the project upon her return.

Before Violet could prod her further on this score, the drawing room door opened behind them, and the lord of the manor himself joined the party. Willingham looked vaguely harried, which Diana uncharitably but fervently hoped was on account of having spent a quarter hour in the company of Lady Helen but which, knowing him, could just as easily be on account of his cravat not having been elaborately knotted enough that morning.

A moment later, though, he proved the cause to be the former. He produced a flask from somewhere within his jacket and took a hearty swallow before muttering, "Women."

Diana smiled sweetly. "I have been given to understand you are rather fond of the sex, Willingham."

He narrowed his eyes at her as he took another sizable gulp. "In certain contexts, undoubtedly. But in my own home, in the form of an eligible miss, I have the gravest qualms."

"You invited her, old chap," Audley said unsympathetically, with all the smugness of a man who is safely married.

"I was backed into a corner by Rothsmere," Willingham said, replacing the flask in his coat and crossing to sit in the armchair next to Diana's. "Hard to say no to an old friend, you understand."

Violet arched a brow and Audley looked skeptical in the extreme, but it was Diana who gave voice to the thought: "He has some sordid story about you he's holding over your head, doesn't he?"

"If he did, I'd hardly admit to it, now, would I?" Willingham said, grumpily enough that Diana knew she was correct.

"Was it the time you cast up your accounts in the lap of that French actress you were attempting to seduce?" Audley asked.

"No," Willingham said, giving him a withering look. "But thank you so much for bringing up *that* particular cherished memory."

"Or the time you accidentally kissed your mistress's sister on a balcony at Lady Montlake's ball because it was dark and you couldn't tell the difference?" Violet asked.

"They were *twins*," Willingham said, a pained expression upon his face. "And I'd had a bit to drink," he added grudgingly.

"You might as well tell us," Diana informed him. "We could go on like this all day."

Willingham took a deep, fortifying breath. "Let us just say I was once . . . *friendly* with a lady whose husband publishes broadsides. He was somewhat irate when he got word of our liaison and printed a rather unflattering one about me detailing some, er, unconventional bedroom activities he claimed to have learned about from one of my former mistresses." He shuddered a bit at the thought. "Rothsmere knows the man and bought them all up and had them destroyed once he got wind of what was afoot, but he saved one for blackmail purposes," he finished darkly.

"I see you made it safely, then," he added quickly, giving a curt nod in Diana's direction before she could ask any of the numerous follow-up questions she had about this tale.

"Is that what passes for welcoming a guest to your home these days?" Diana asked, taking a sip of tea. "I remain more convinced than ever that a wife would do wonders for you, Willingham."

"And Rothsmere's been kind enough to deliver an eligible candidate directly to your doorstep," Audley added, with considerably more than his usual degree of cheer. "Couldn't be easier."

"I am not looking for a wife," Willingham said darkly; clearly the past quarter hour had been somewhat harrowing. "I can't let Lady Templeton win our bet, now can I?" he added, more jovially. "I've still eleven months of evading the parson's mousetrap ahead of me before I can claim my prize."

"*My* prize, you mean," Diana said serenely. "I have glorious plans for all the feathers I plan to spend my winnings on."

"Feathers?" Willingham asked blankly.

"For elaborate headdresses for your future wife," Diana clarified.

"You won't be able to get within five feet of her without a feather prodding you in the eye. It will be glorious."

"I find the glee with which you contemplate my future misery chilling," Willingham said, not sounding remotely concerned—indeed, there was a knowing look in his eye as he met her gaze that thrilled her to her core.

That reminded her of her other aim this evening. She gave an enormous, entirely feigned yawn. "I fear my journey was rather tiring, and I'd like to rest before dinner." She batted her eyelashes at him. "Would you be so good as to show me to my room?"

Willingham rose with alacrity, cottoning. "It would be my pleasure." He offered Diana his arm, which she took.

Violet and Audley watched this display with interest.

"What . . . is this about?" Violet asked slowly, her gaze flicking from Diana to Willingham and then back again.

"Can't a gentleman chivalrously escort a guest to her bedchamber without garnering raised eyebrows?" Willingham asked.

"Not if it's you and Diana," Violet said bluntly.

"It's like watching Napoleon offer Wellington his arm," Audley murmured.

"Why do I have to be Napoleon?" Willingham objected. "She's shorter!"

"Audley clearly realizes, deep down, that I would make the better general," Diana said smugly.

"I hardly think—"

"We were just leaving, were we not?" she said, tightening her grip on his arm and giving him what she hoped was a significant, meaningful sort of look.

He heaved a great sigh, conceding the point. "If you'll excuse us," he said to Violet and Audley, then steered Diana out of the room before either of them could make a reply.

Once they were in the hallway, Diana dropped his arm immediately and took off in the direction of the main staircase.

"I don't believe I'm contagious," Willingham drawled, following her at a leisurely pace.

"Given your romantic history, I don't know that I'd be so sure," she said darkly, and was gratified to hear a sound behind her that could only be described as a sputter. "I'm only joking," she relented, slowing her pace slightly and, in what she considered an admirable show of goodwill, reaching out to take his arm once more. "That's what I wished to speak to you about, in fact."

"The pox?" he asked acidly.

"No, your romantic history," she said, lowering her voice. They had reached the staircase, and she suspected that every word they spoke could be overheard by nearby servants. As such, they remained silent until they reached the second floor and were walking down another empty corridor.

"I take it you've come to a conclusion about my offer?" Willingham asked in a low voice. He kept his gaze fixed firmly in front of him, but Diana could feel his arm tense slightly under her hand. Her answer mattered to him, she realized with some surprise.

"I've decided to accept your proposal," she said, and his head turned, his eyes catching hers with unexpected intensity for a moment before he jerked his head forward once more.

"But," she added, as he opened his mouth to speak, "I have conditions."

"Of course you do," he agreed. She narrowed her eyes at him, but he refused to meet her gaze. They drew to a halt before a door midway down the corridor, which he proceeded to open.

"This is your room," he said. "Mine is just down the hall."

"Mighty certain of my response, weren't you?" she asked, arching an eyebrow.

"Not at all," he said with that irritating, irresistible cheeky grin of his. "But if you did say yes, I wanted to be prepared. Shall I pay you a visit this evening once everyone has gone to bed and we can discuss your conditions?"

"I suppose," she agreed. "For now, you should probably rejoin Violet and Audley in the drawing room."

"Ah," Willingham said, nodding sagely. "So they don't become suspicious of my overlong absence in your company?"

"No," Diana said over her shoulder as she turned to enter the room. "So that they don't debauch any more of your furniture."

It was extremely satisfying to shut the door on Willingham's horrified face.

Six

It was with some relief that Diana reentered the drawing room before dinner that evening to find Violet and Audley fully clothed and deep in conversation on opposite sides of the room. Giving the settee a sympathetic pat on her way across the room, in light of the activities the piece of furniture must have borne witness to that afternoon, she made her way toward Violet, who was chatting animatedly with a familiar-looking golden head.

"Emily! You've arrived!" The head turned, revealing the almost impossibly lovely face of her friend. "My brilliant scheme worked, I see?" Diana added, crossing the drawing room in great eager steps.

She seized Emily's hands, looking her friend up and down. Emily looked . . . tired. She was as beautiful as ever, her hair neatly dressed, her trim figure garbed entirely appropriately in a simple white evening gown. But there were dark smudges beneath her eyes that Diana had never seen there before, and a faint crease in her brow that implied repeated furrowing of it. Diana wondered how many events she had recently attended with Mr. Cartham—and how many quarrels she'd had with her parents on the subject.

"Even my mother is powerless in the face of the Dowager Marchioness of Willingham," Emily said with a smile.

"As are we all," Diana agreed. She turned as she spoke, scanning the room for the lady's white hair. This was more difficult than it sounded, because the dowager marchioness was barely five feet tall, and did have a tendency to get rather lost in a crowd. So, instead of looking, she stopped and *listened*.

And, sure enough, a moment later she heard the sound of the dowager marchioness's voice, far louder than was proper for a lady of good breeding—but then, such considerations had never stopped the woman from behaving exactly as she wished. Which was precisely why Diana adored her.

She, Violet, and Emily approached the group of people clustered nearby and found the dowager marchioness holding court before half a dozen amused gentlemen, including James's brother West and several friends of Willingham's from his Oxford days, regaling them with the tale of her husband's rather infamous demise.

". . . and then the fool tossed the empty wine bottle to me as if I were his groom," she said, every word infused with just the right degree of disdain, "flung himself into the saddle, and took off at full speed toward the gate in question. I could see from fifty yards away that he didn't stand a chance of making it, and sure enough, the horse—sensible creature—shied just enough to fling him off into the shrubbery." She sighed, accepting a glass of sherry from one of her many admirers. "Broke his neck instantly, of course," she said matter-of-factly, as though she were describing the death of a particularly unbeloved family dog, rather than that of her own husband. "And the worst bit was that because he landed in the bushes, the brambles scratched his face something awful, so he looked positively dreadful in his coffin. His good looks were really all he had in his favor, and even those abandoned him in death."

"A lesson for us all, really," came Willingham's voice from just behind Diana, and she started—so absorbed had she been in the story, she hadn't heard him approach. His eyes were dancing as he surveyed his grandmother. "And how lucky my dear grandfather is to be survived by a wife who describes him in such devoted tones."

The dowager marchioness snorted, taking a sip of sherry. "Don't be absurd, Jeremy. The man was a nuisance who nearly bankrupted this estate—though your own dear father did plenty of work in that regard, too, so there's enough blame to go around, I daresay—and who no doubt has a litter of bastards running around the nearby countryside like so many unwanted puppies."

At this, West choked on his claret; behind Diana, Emily seemed to be choking on air.

Willingham moved past Diana to press a kiss to his grandmother's cheek that somehow managed to be both affectionate and sarcastic. Diana wished she could learn the trick of that, as those were the exact set of contrasting sentiments that she wished her own kisses to convey to him.

"You made it safely, I see, and even managed to extract Lady Emily from her mother's clutches without injury," he added.

"Yes, well, it was a very near thing, I don't mind telling you." The group surrounding them had begun to break up at the conclusion of her tale; Diana watched as West crossed the room to join Audley, who was deep in conversation with Sophie, who had arrived an hour or two before. Given Sophie's romantic history—both her affair with Willingham this summer, and her near-engagement to West years ago—Diana found her presence at Elderwild highly intriguing, and it was with no small degree of interest that she watched West bow over her hand, saying something to her as he straightened that made Sophie's mouth quirk in a sort of half smile that seemed inexplicably intimate.

Belatedly realizing that she was neglecting the conversation at hand, however, Diana rededicated her attention to her companions, who now had been reduced to just the dowager marchioness, Willingham, Violet, and Emily. The dowager marchioness gave Emily an approving look. "That young lady is not half so tiresome as most ladies her age. And what's more, she knows how to shut her mouth and allow a feeble elderly woman some much-needed rest."

Emily smiled her prim, proper smile. "That's very kind of you, my lady, though not entirely how I remember it." She paused, then added, "I do think I was above-average reticent, but only because you spent most of our journey explaining to me all the qualities necessary in a future husband."

"And what qualities would these be?" Willingham asked. "All ones that I, your beloved grandson, already possess, I assume?"

"There you would be wrong, my boy," his grandmother said sternly. "You are as much a fool as most of the other young bucks I see running wild these days, although I will grant you that you've the face of an angel, which softens the blow."

Diana rolled her eyes, which Willingham of course noticed. He grinned at her, then widened his eyes in an approximation of angelic innocence. She stared back at him, stony-faced.

"But the more angelic the face, the more devilish the man, that's what I always say," his grandmother added, giving her grandson a suspicious look. "I'm certain I only hear a quarter of the appalling gossip about you, and that is entirely too much already, I assure you. I wish I could say your father would be ashamed, but he was a scoundrel through and through."

"But," Emily began hesitantly, "wasn't he your son?"

"That he was," the dowager marchioness agreed without a trace of sheepishness. "He would no doubt be delighted to see his own son following in his footsteps." She paused dramatically. "*I*, however, have higher hopes for this family. It's about time the name Willingham came to mean something more than drunken womanizing." She gave her grandson a hard stare. "I applaud your efforts and your stamina, my boy, but you've made your point."

Violet let out a cough that Diana was certain was a hastily concealed laugh, then said, "Well, I, for one, am glad that you were able to see Lady Emily here safely, at least."

"Yes," Emily agreed, and smiled at Willingham. "Thank you for the invitation, my lord. I know that eligible misses are not traditionally counted among the numbers at your house parties."

"We seem to be bucking that tradition this year," Willingham said darkly.

"Yes," the dowager marchioness said, "I have been given the charge of chaperoning Lady Helen Courtenay—her mother can be fiendishly determined, when she wants something." She cast a quick glance around the room. "Sparing us her presence this evening, though, is she?" It did not seem to give her even a moment's pause that she had only now noted the absence of the lady whose virtue she was supposed to be so carefully guarding.

"Lady Helen professed to be fatigued by the journey and has requested a tray in her room," Willingham said in tones of thinly veiled relief.

"Hmph," snorted the dowager marchioness, in a way that suggested that was all that needed to be said about such deviant behavior. "She's an odd one, that Lady Helen."

"What do you mean?" Diana asked, turning back to her.

"She's developed rather a reputation as the most desperate, marriage-minded girl of the *ton*—men are terrified to dance more than once with her, as I understand it."

"Yes," Diana said. "But what about that is odd?"

"I knew the girl when she was growing up, and she was nothing like that at all," the dowager marchioness finished thoughtfully. "She seems so different a creature these days as to be entirely unrecognizable."

"It just goes to show how dreadful the marriage mart is," Violet said sternly, her gaze softening as her eyes fixed momentarily on her husband across the room.

"Which is why marriage is an institution I've no intention of entering into," Willingham said smugly.

"That's what *you* think, my boy," his grandmother said, swatting him on the arm. "That's what you think."

Diana grinned at this—it seemed the dowager marchioness had well and truly taken Diana's casual mention of her wager with Willingham to heart. She was rather looking forward to the next couple of weeks—if it was going to involve the dowager marchioness flinging Willingham at every unmarried lady of quality who crossed his path, she thought this might make for the most entertaining country house party she'd attended in years.

Watching Willingham suffer was always an experience to savor, after all.

Dinner quickly taught Diana that she had been overly hasty in her glee. It began as soon as they were seated, whereupon the dowager marchioness made rather a production out of her concern for Emily's bare arms, claiming that her seat—directly to Willingham's right— was in the line of a mysterious draft that would naturally cause one with such a delicate, fragile constitution (Emily, in fact, was rarely ill) to take a chill.

"Lady Templeton, why don't you trade places with her?" the dowager marchioness asked, in a tone of voice that made it perfectly clear that this wasn't really a question at all. "You're much sturdier and heartier than Lady Emily, I'm certain you won't be at risk."

"Thank you, Lady Willingham," Diana said sweetly, rising to follow orders. "I've never heard myself described quite so similarly to a horse."

A few seats down, Penvale made a sort of aborted neighing sound—aborted, Diana was fairly certain, because Violet had elbowed him in the stomach. On her other side, Audley looked as though he was trying hard not to laugh. Under different circumstances, Diana would have been pleased to see him looking so cheerful—the past few weeks of marital bliss had turned him nearly unrecognizable from the overly serious man she had known for so long—but at the moment she was not feeling terribly charitable.

With this promising start, Diana took Emily's abandoned seat next to Willingham and the meal commenced.

Things naturally only got worse. Over the soup course, the dowager marchioness—ignoring all dinner table etiquette as to her conversation partner—subjected Diana to a lengthy inquiry about her childhood, marriage, and whether she preferred cats or dogs. Over fish, she regaled the table with anecdotes from Willingham's misspent youth, casting a rosy, sentimental sheen upon the conclusion of each story that Diana was certain was wildly out of step with the reality of the events.

Over dessert, she mercifully subsided, allowing herself to be drawn into conversation by West, who had been sitting to her left and tolerantly observing this show over the course of the past hour, exchanging an occasional raised eyebrow across the table with Sophie, who was seated directly opposite him. This respite was not as relaxing as Diana might have hoped, however, given that she could still feel the dowager marchioness watching her out of the corner of her eye even as she gave the appearance of being entirely distracted by whatever West was saying.

Were she a religious sort of person, Diana might have thought that a divine power was punishing her for years of misbehavior; not being terribly pious, however, she merely decided that this was a cautionary tale about grandmothers.

She had been perfectly delighted at the prospect of Willingham's grandmother devoting all of her considerable energy toward seeing him married to some insipid virgin; it was quite another thing entirely to realize that the prospective wife the dowager marchioness had set her sights on for her grandson was Diana herself.

"I would have thought your grandmother more subtle," Diana said under her breath to Willingham, raising a bite of blackberry tart to her mouth.

"Indeed," Willingham agreed, gazing down the table at his grandmother with narrowed eyes. "Perhaps she is growing desperate in her dotage."

Diana suppressed a snort with great difficulty. While the dowager marchioness was certainly getting on in years, she was as sharp and wily as ever. "Or," she suggested, "perhaps she thought that we would require only the merest push to fall into each other's arms." She batted her eyelashes at him, adopting a look of lovesick adoration.

Willingham leaned closer. "She's not entirely wrong on that front."

Diana fought the impulse to shut her eyes at his proximity—this close, she could feel the heat of his body, see the faint traces of evening stubble shadowing his jaw. "I'm looking forward to my visit this evening. To discussing ... conditions."

He leaned back then, leaving Diana embarrassingly breathless. The word *conditions* had never sounded lewd to her before. The house party was only hours old, and it was already proving highly educational.

$\mathcal{S}$even

Jeremy was nervous. It was late; his guests had retired to their rooms more than an hour before, and the hallway outside his bedroom door had grown quiet, no longer full of the footsteps of servants rushing back and forth. He himself had dismissed his valet, Snuffgrove, and now stood barefoot in breeches and a loose shirt beneath his favorite blue banyan, a glass of wine in hand. He had imbibed less than usual this evening, not having joined the other gentlemen in their after-dinner port or in their brandies in the drawing room once they rejoined the ladies. Now, however, the weight of the glass in his hand was a comfort as he contemplated the evening ahead.

He had no intention of throwing himself at Diana like a green boy this evening, much as the cut of her bodice at dinner had made him want to do just that. If Jeremy wanted reassurances that he was the consummate lover he'd always believed himself to be, he'd hardly serve his cause well by rushing into this without taking the time to lay the groundwork.

The problem was, of course, that he felt as though the groundwork between himself and Diana had been lying there, ready to be used, for years. Every encounter he'd had with her since she was eighteen years old had somehow involved flirtation. Of course, Diana flirted with everyone—and so did he. But it felt different between them, as though it had some purpose beyond making the other smile or—dream of dreams!—blush.

He, of course, had never made her blush. He wondered if she were even capable of it.

He would very much like to find out.

It was that fortifying thought that had him draining the rest of his glass and striding to the door. He opened it carefully and poked his head into the corridor, ensuring that it was indeed deserted before continuing. When, prior to his guests' arrival, he'd asked his housekeeper, Mrs. Foxglove, to give Diana a bedchamber on the same hallway as his own, she'd given him a long, suspicious look.

He crept down the hall and scratched at her door. The door opened a second later—had she been standing there, awaiting his knock?—and he quickly slunk inside before she closed it behind him.

It was only once they were safely ensconced in her room together that he took a good look at her. She had changed from the evening gown she'd worn to dinner and was dressed as simply as he had ever seen her, in a plain red muslin dress with nary a jewel in sight. Her glorious hair was no longer in an elaborate coiffure but instead spilling over her shoulders in waves that shone in the candlelight, and she held a small glass of wine in her hand, just as he had minutes before.

"Diana," he said, unable to use anything other than her Christian name in a setting as intimate as this. He strove to inject his voice with its usual sarcastic drawl. "You look . . . informal."

She rolled her eyes before casting a skeptical look at his own clothing. "At least I'm wearing attire that could be decently worn in a drawing room," she said, stepping back to allow him entrée to the room.

Deciding that perhaps a bit of flattery was in order, given his aims for the evening, he attempted: "You look beautiful."

This was similarly unsuccessful. "Please don't start mooning, Willingham, or I shall never have the slightest temptation to allow you to remove my clothing." With that, she turned and walked deeper into the room, leaving Jeremy standing there, slightly nonplussed, watching her go. One had to admire her way with words, he supposed. He shook his head once to clear it, then followed her.

The guest room Diana had been given was one of the larger ones in the house. The walls were papered in a blue and white floral pattern that was feminine, but not overwhelmingly so. A fire burned in the grate—though it was August, the evening had turned chilly—and Diana sank down onto the settee before it, beckoning him to her side with a single, imperious wave of her hand.

Jeremy was tempted to follow without hesitation—she presented such an enticing picture, her lovely face bathed in firelight, her smooth skin glowing white where it rose above the modest neckline of her gown—but he resisted, feeling that to allow her to summon him now would set a tone for the entire endeavor that he would find difficult to change.

Instead, just to irk her, he took a slow turn about the room, examining one of the sketches by his late mother on the wall and testing the plushness of the cushion atop the window seat. Behind him, he could sense Diana's attention, but he would not turn and acknowledge it. Not yet, at least.

At last she broke the stalemate: "Are you quite finished?"

Mentally, Jeremy grinned in satisfaction, awarding himself a point in their never-ending war. Externally, however, he was all innocence as he turned to face her. "I beg your pardon?"

"Willingham," she said through gritted teeth, "*you* are the one who suggested this meeting. I propose you sit down and speak to me before I eject you from this room and never open a bedchamber door to you ever again."

This prospect was more alarming than Jeremy cared to admit, and he conceded this battle and strode toward her. Ignoring entirely the armchairs situated to either side of the settee on which she reclined, he sat down next to her, so close that her skirts brushed his breeches and that had he wished to take her hand, only a matter of inches of movement would have been required to do so.

"Now," she said, her tone all business, entirely incongruous with the languid, seductive picture she presented at the moment, "we need to discuss the conditions of our arrangement." Hearing her discuss said arrangement in such businesslike terms should have had a rather dampening effect on his lust for her; instead, somehow, it provoked the opposite reaction. There was something to be said for a woman with a face and a bosom like Diana's, sitting there coolly discussing an affair as though it were a business matter rather than a carnal one. It should not have been remotely enticing; instead, it was absurdly so. In that moment, he wished for nothing more than to reduce this calm, collected woman to a state in which she could not muster any words at all.

"The first term," she said, holding up an index finger, "is that we should be discreet."

"Of course," Jeremy said, wounded. He did not pride himself on many things, but his discretion was one of them. He had something of a reputation, it was true, but he was fully aware that as a wealthy, titled man he had little to lose from these liaisons, while the ladies often risked a fair amount more. He therefore did his best to keep his associations a secret. Was he to blame if some ladies, smug over having caught, even temporarily, the infamous Marquess of Willingham, allowed their tongues to loosen more than was wise?

"I don't mind if word gets out to a select few gentlemen," she added. "After all, I do want it known in some circles that I am open to similar liaisons. You might even be of some help to me here, mentioning it to a few well-placed people who might be of interest to me."

"You make me sound like a brothel owner," Jeremy said, nettled.

She rolled her eyes. "Don't come over missish on me now, Willingham."

He nearly howled. *"Missish?"*

"The second term," she said, ignoring him entirely and raising another finger, "is that this liaison will last only the duration of this house party."

"Done," he agreed readily. He really, of course, only needed to bed her once, just to receive reassurance that his skills were all that they should be, but he had a sneaking suspicion that one time in bed with Diana wasn't going to be enough. In fact, he suspected that a fortnight wouldn't be enough, either, but he'd worry about that when the time came.

"The third and final term is that you are not to ask me any questions regarding matters of the bedchamber."

Jeremy frowned. "I beg your pardon?"

"No questions," Diana repeated, quite firmly.

"Don't you think that might present some difficulties?"

She frowned, too, her own expression matching his own. "I can't see why it should." He thought he detected the faintest hint of uncertainty in her voice.

"How am I to be assured of your consent?" He might be a rake, but he'd never bedded an unwilling woman, nor done anything within the confines of the bedchamber that had not been entirely consensual, and he did not intend to start now. Particularly not with her.

"Willingham, will my presence in your bed not be indication enough?"

"Yes, but what if I want to try something and you don't like it? I need to be able to ask if you are enjoying yourself, at the very least."

"Very well," she said impatiently. "I revise the term. No questions about anything other than whatever sordid act it is that you are trying to convince me to engage in."

"Well, now you've made me sound like a deviant," he objected.

She threw her hands into the air. "What else am I to assume? A man of your reputation suddenly expressing some great concern that I shan't enjoy whatever it is that you want to do . . . It does rather raise questions, Willingham."

"As does your insistence that I not ask you any. What the devil is this all about?"

"It is none of your concern." She made rather a production out of smoothing her skirts around her. "I just don't wish you to ask me about my . . . past experiences, shall we say."

He frowned. This conversation was growing more puzzling by the moment. "Did your husband do something . . ." He trailed off, not certain how to phrase the question; delicacy had never been his strong suit. "Was your marriage bed an unpleasant one?"

"No," Diana said quickly, and her expression softened as she looked at him. Somehow, he felt certain she wasn't lying, and something within him loosened. "I just don't wish to speak of the past. So you may ask any questions necessary to ensure my consent, and to receive the critique you're so desperate for."

"'Desperate' might be an overstatement," he objected with what dignity he could muster.

She ignored him. "Do we have an agreement?"

"Would you like me to have it drawn up by my solicitor and signed before witnesses?"

"I do not think that will be necessary," she said, refusing to rise to his bait. "A mere handshake will suffice, I think." She held out her ungloved hand to him and, after arching an eyebrow at her, he reached out and shook it firmly. Then, as his hand was still clasped within her own, she pulled him forward and kissed him.

Eight

Diana had always felt that when there was a daunting task at hand,
there was nothing gained by delaying it. While she would not precisely
classify bedding the Marquess of Willingham as *daunting*, she was
feeling a decided pang of nerves over the entire thing, and did not see
any point in postponing the inevitable.

Which was how she found herself on her settee, his hand still
clutching her own, being kissed by said marquess quite urgently.

She wasn't even certain when the kiss had changed hands—when
it had ceased to be her kissing him, but rather the reverse—but she
could not complain about this outcome. The only coherent thought
she could manage at the moment was that whatever complaints his
ex-paramour could have had with him, they could not possibly have
been with his kisses.

After a moment's hesitation, during which, as usual, she was forced
to do all of the work herself, he took control, freeing his hand from her
grip so that he might slide it around her waist, pulling her closer, elim-
inating the slight space between them on the settee. His other hand
reached up to cradle her cheek, the gesture unexpectedly tender. His
mouth, however, was anything but, moving over hers with an expertise
that she knew came from years of practice with scores of women.

But she didn't want to think about them—and she didn't want him to, either. She wanted him to only think of her, and of the fire that was slowly building between them.

She felt his kiss . . . everywhere.

In her heart, which was pounding so hard that it felt as though she were at risk of it beating out of her chest entirely. In her head, which suddenly felt fuzzy, all of her senses overpowered by the smell of him surrounding her and the taste of him on her tongue. And in the pit of her stomach, where heat seemed to grow and spread throughout her body, turning her limbs heavy and her movements languid.

She slid her hand into the short hair at the nape of his neck, keeping him close, while her other hand rested on his chest, underneath his banyan, gratified to feel his heart pounding in rhythm with her own.

She felt his tongue at her lips and parted them with a sigh as his hand at her waist began a steady journey north, stopping just below her breasts as though silently asking permission. Without breaking the kiss, she reached down and picked up the hand in question, placing it on her breast. He needed no further encouragement—somehow, despite no time seeming to elapse at all, his hand had slipped beneath the fabric of her gown, the warmth of his palm on her sensitive skin causing her to gasp aloud.

He broke the kiss with a shudder, resting his forehead against her own, his eyes shut, as his breath fell unevenly on her neck.

"Why—" she gasped, then paused to catch her breath. "Why," she tried again, "did you stop?"

He opened his eyes without moving his head; he was so close to her that all she could see was the brilliant blue of his gaze, consuming her entire field of vision. His eyes were the blue of the sky on the first perfectly crisp autumn day.

It was likely for the best that he had broken the kiss. If this was what happened to her mind after a few minutes spent kissing, she was beginning to have grave concerns about the effect of this experiment upon her mental faculties.

"Believe it or not," he said after a moment, his voice a trifle uneven, "I didn't actually come here for this."

She leaned back slightly, breaking the contact between their skin, and arched a skeptical brow at him. "You came to my room at night after everyone was abed for innocent purposes?"

"Well," he hedged, "not entirely innocent, perhaps. But I didn't think we'd dive right into the main course this evening."

She untangled herself from him, creating some much-needed space between them on the settee. She couldn't speak rationally— couldn't *think* rationally—when he was so close to her, invading all of her senses. The settee, however, was only so big, so the foot of space she managed to create between them was hardly insurmountable. Still, it was better than nothing.

"What was this, then?" she asked, trying to inject her usual imperious note into her voice. "An appetizer?"

His mouth quirked up in amusement, his eyes crinkling a bit at the corners. "Something like that."

She preferred this version of Willingham so much that it scared her. While the public version—the flirt, the rake, the seducer— possessed charm in abundance, as well as the most well-tied cravats of any gentleman of the *ton* (and, as any lady knows, a well-tied cravat is nothing to take lightly), there was something brittle about him. He was all flash and no substance.

This version, however—the private Willingham—was far more dangerous. His golden hair was mussed from her hands, and his cheeks were appealingly flushed. His loose shirt had shifted enough for her to see the faintest hint of hair on his chest, and she was determinedly *not* looking any lower than that, lest she see something that would distract her completely.

She realized that she was . . . enjoying herself. The man was insufferable 95 percent of the time, of course, but there was something to be said for getting to see him like this, unguarded and relaxed. It was perhaps for the best that he had called a halt to the proceedings—she had responded to his kiss more passionately than she'd expected, and she needed to settle herself a bit before taking things further.

It was only for the next fortnight, she reminded herself somewhat sternly. She could enjoy it while it lasted, but then it would be done. She felt a slight pang of uncertainty at this thought, but surely two weeks would be sufficient time for them to indulge in and then dispel the strange attraction that coursed between them.

Given the uneasiness of her thoughts, she thought it best to be rid of Willingham as quickly as possible for the evening. "Well," she said lazily, stretching, falling back on her old tricks. And, sure enough, Willingham's gaze dropped to her bosom, just as she had intended. She arched her back for a moment longer than was strictly necessary. "If that's the best you can manage for this evening, I suppose I'd better send you on your way. Disappointing, but hardly surprising."

Disappointing, of course, was the last word she could honestly use to describe that kiss—but nowhere in her agreement with Willingham had she promised him honesty.

Much to her chagrin, however, Willingham glanced up, met her eyes once more, and appeared anything but chastened. Instead, he looked even more amused than he had a moment before—appreciative, to be sure, but definitely amused, as though he knew precisely what she was doing, and bowed to a worthy opponent.

"Perhaps the critiques I recently received were entirely fair after all," he agreed mournfully.

"Well," she said briskly, refusing to reward him with a smile, much as her mouth had a mind of its own and seemed desperate to curve upward, "I shall have to wait until another evening to pass judgment on that. Your efforts were reasonably satisfactory."

"O, fair maiden," he proclaimed, clutching at his chest dramatically even as he rose. "Have ever such flattering words fallen on mine ears?"

"Do go away, Willingham," she said crossly, sorely tempted to give him a satisfying kick in the shin—or somewhere rather more sensitive. "If you're not going to make yourself useful to me, please leave me in peace."

He dropped his hand to his side and, reaching down, pulled her to her feet. The movement was unexpected, and she stumbled slightly as she tried to gain her footing, finding herself suddenly leaning against him rather intimately. All traces of laughter had vanished from his face, and he was looking at her in a way that made her feel hot and flustered and entirely too self-conscious. "Diana," he said in a low voice that did unspeakable things to certain unspeakable parts of her person.

"Yes?" she asked breathlessly.

He paused. Leaned closer. Diana's eyelids fluttered downward.

"Your efforts were reasonably satisfactory as well," he said in a low voice, his breath warm against her cheek.

And, with that, Diana lost all reason entirely and, seizing the closest weapon at hand—her half-drunk glass of wine—proceeded to fling its contents into his face.

It had, she later reflected, been a very trying evening, but the sight of the Marquess of Willingham blinking at her incredulously with claret dripping down his face made it all entirely worthwhile.

Nine

Breakfast the next morning was a lively affair.

The remainder of Jeremy's houseguests were due to arrive that afternoon, but the party had already grown to a respectable size of a dozen in the past twenty-four hours. One late arrival the night before had been Lord Julian Belfry, whom Jeremy had invited on a whim and hadn't entirely expected to come.

Belfry was unable to stay for the entire duration of the house party, but had accepted the invitation to visit for a few days nonetheless. Diana and Violet had noted his arrival the night before with expressions of speculative interest that had made Jeremy decidedly uneasy, but he'd learned long ago that the best thing to do when a woman looked like that was to stay as far removed as possible, so he'd not inquired about whatever scheme they were hatching.

The truth was, he had very little excess mental energy to dedicate to anything other than his ... *situation* with Diana.

He was, all in all, feeling rather pleased with himself; matters with Diana were proceeding nicely, and a few weeks in the country were certain to pass more pleasantly with female companionship than they would have done otherwise. He'd left her the night before with wine dripping down his face and an almost uncontrollable desire to laugh at the look on hers—part irritation, part smugness, and entirely, utterly *her*. He was beginning to realize that their liaison was going to be . . . fun. He'd get past his difficulties in the bedroom—as well as his tendency to start mentally undressing Diana whenever they were in the same room—and be able to move on to his next affair with complete ease of mind.

True, it was a trifle unexpected just how much he'd enjoyed the kiss they had shared the night before, but surely the allure would fade fairly quickly.

In truth, he had assumed a somewhat limited experience on Diana's part; her husband had been considerably older than she, and had shuffled off this mortal coil fairly early in their marriage. Despite her reputation as a flirt, he'd never heard a single piece of reliable gossip linking her to any man in particular. However, that kiss had not seemed like the innocent kiss of a repressed widow. It was the kiss of a woman who knew exactly what she wanted—and how to take it.

It was . . .

. . . not something that made for appropriate breakfast table contemplation, if one wanted to avoid shocking one's guests.

With some difficulty, Jeremy steered his thoughts away from this pleasurable detour and back to the present matter, which was the unfortunate appearance of Lady Helen Courtenay at the breakfast table. Jeremy heaved a heavy internal sigh; he supposed he could not have expected her to remain in her bedchamber indefinitely, though a man could dream.

Lady Helen was tall and willowy, and moved with a certain elegant grace that Jeremy reluctantly had to admire. Her hair was a pale blond, her eyes very light blue, her complexion fair and unblemished. She was an entirely pleasing creature to look upon.

Until she opened her mouth.

"Ahahaha! My lord, you are *too* droll!" she said to Penvale as she entered the room, his arm grasped tightly in her clutches. Jeremy guessed his friend had had the misfortune to encounter the lady in the corridor on his way into the breakfast room, and—judging by the barely concealed grimace upon his face—was heartily wishing he'd lingered in bed a few minutes longer.

"Jeremy," Penvale said loudly as soon as he spotted his host. "I was fortunate enough to encounter Lady Helen on her way down to breakfast and offer her my escort."

"Yes," Jeremy agreed. "Most fortunate." He blinked, and peered closer at Penvale's arm—were Lady Helen's fingernails actually digging into his flesh?

"Oh, my Lord Willingham!" the lady trilled, dropping Penvale's arm—to the visible relief of its owner—and coming toward him, arms outstretched. "How positively *delightful* to see you this morning."

"Likewise, Lady Helen," Jeremy said, rising to his feet and offering a rather listless excuse for a bow. For perhaps the first time in his life, he experienced a moment's longing for a wife—if there were a lady of the house, he could pass Lady Helen over to her to entertain with whatever it was ladies liked to chat about. Gloves, perhaps. Watercolors. Handkerchiefs. Et cetera.

However, as the sole host for the house party, Jeremy had no one upon whom he could foist Lady Helen without appearing abominably rude, and so he resigned himself to a never-ending breakfast with the eagerly chattering lady at his side. He did his best to tune out her prattle—at one point, he distinctly noted that she was discussing the relative merits of fichus versus exposed necklines, and he promptly rededicated himself to the stack of generously buttered toast before him.

At some point during the proceedings, Diana entered the room; he glanced up and caught her eye, watching as she registered his captive state, her mouth twitching as she clearly fought to suppress a grin. He gave her a look that he hoped implied his promise that she would shortly suffer from mocking his misfortune, but the effect did not seem to be as threatening as he might have wished, for her mouth twitchings widened into a proper smile in response.

Meanwhile, farther down the table, Penvale and West were deep in conversation, no doubt regarding something exceptionally dull, like irrigation. Or sheep. Penvale's family estate had been unentailed and sold to cover his parents' debts upon their death, and he was obsessed with reclaiming Trethwick Abbey, his ancestral lands. West, who as Audley's elder brother was heir to a dukedom, no doubt had all sorts of frightfully dull insights about estate management.

It never occurred to Penvale to ask Jeremy any of these questions, despite the fact that Jeremy was, in fact, a marquess—and one who had rescued his family estate from the brink of ruin, no less. Penvale knew this, in theory. In practice, however, it seemed that no one could imagine asking the merry, freewheeling Marquess of Willingham for advice on land management.

Which was exactly how he had liked it. He had spent many years creating the reputation he now had—he couldn't reasonably complain that the results of these efforts were exactly as he had intended. Even if, sometimes, he wondered if there was anyone who saw beneath it.

Next to Penvale, Violet and Audley were sitting perhaps closer together than was strictly necessary at the breakfast table. Violet was speaking rapidly, as usual, about something Jeremy couldn't hear, and Audley was watching her as though she'd hung the moon. Jeremy was pleased that these two had reconciled their marital differences, but he did feel they took things a bit far, at times. Last night at dinner, Jeremy had observed Audley miss his mouth with his fork. Twice.

Belfry was in deep discussion with Henry Langely, another of Jeremy's Oxford friends. Langely was a decent sort—second son of an earl, rather bookish. He and Jeremy didn't run in precisely the same circles these days—Langely had never been known as a womanizer, having had the same mistress for years now. As such, Jeremy couldn't imagine what on earth he and Belfry had to talk about. Belfry's reputation was even less savory than his own—thumbing one's nose at one's aristocratic father and being disinherited before going on to found a semirespectable theater did tend to have a damaging effect on one's reputation.

It was all the more intriguing, then, that Belfry was here, trailing around after Lady Emily, of all people. Jeremy was hardly a matchmaker—indeed, he shuddered at the very thought—but he could not help wondering what precisely Belfry's aim was where Emily was concerned. There was the obvious fact that Emily was almost ludicrously beautiful, but he'd never gotten the impression that Belfry struggled to find female companionship. Whatever Belfry's interest was, he had little doubt that Diana would sniff it out before too long; she and Violet were taking quite an interest in the proceedings between Emily and Belfry, and he could hardly blame them, given that the alternative was Emily's continued courtship by Oswald Cartham.

Cartham was a seedy sort, born in America to a younger son of an aristocratic family; he'd returned to England in his teens and had remained ever since, operating a legendary gaming hell and, from all Jeremy had heard, keeping more than a few aristocrats in his pocket by virtue of a combination of gambling debts and blackmail. Belfry was a bit scandalous, but by comparison with Cartham, he represented the height of respectability.

Jeremy had little time to contemplate this, however, because his attention was drawn to his grandmother, who had just entered the room.

"Ah, Lady Templeton," she said, sounding as pleased to see Diana as if she'd last seen her twelve months ago, rather than twelve hours. "I do hope that seat next to you is being saved for me, because I have been so wishing to have a cozy little chat with you."

Diana's face, Jeremy was amused to note, bore a look of barely concealed alarm; she was as aware as he was that "cozy little chats" with the dowager marchioness frequently led to ladies shutting themselves up in their rooms in tears. He was certain Diana could bear his grandmother's sharp tongue with equanimity; the two ladies were not dissimilar. He wondered if Diana would be something like his grandmother when she achieved a lofty age.

What a terrifying thought.

For her part, Diana was feeling rather cheerful this morning. She'd lain awake far too long last night, reliving Willingham's kiss, and had awoken this morning still focused on the remembered pressure of his mouth on her own. Clearly, she and Willingham should have done this years ago—the attraction that crackled between them wasn't going to vanish on its own, and she was pleased they'd finally decided to take the sensible step toward becoming lovers. They'd have a nice romp or two in bed, and then they'd be ready to move on.

By the time she arrived at the breakfast table, Willingham was already there, but fully ensnared in the clutches of Lady Helen Courtenay. As Diana filled her plate at the sideboard, she caught snatches of their conversation—though "conversation" might have been an overly generous term to describe what sounded more like a lengthy mono-logue on Lady Helen's part, with occasional pauses for Willingham's wordless murmurings of assent.

"... *so* pleased you included me in your invitation," she was saying, as Diana placed a plump piece of spice cake on her plate. "Rothsmere is always so *maddeningly* close-lipped about what you gentlemen get up to, and I, of course, am simply *desperate* to learn all of your scandalous little secrets." The titter that emerged from her mouth at this juncture was a sound that Diana was reasonably certain would haunt her night-mares for years to come.

She made her way to the far end of the table, but Lady Helen's shrill voice carried, so that over the course of the next ten minutes, Diana became intimately familiar with the lady's opinion on fichus—she would not have thought a scrap of lace at the neckline to be worthy of such strong emotion, but according to Lady Helen, they were a last bastion of moral authority before the wastelands of sin—as well as strawberries (delicious), raspberries (disgusting), and musicales (de-lightful, though Diana disagreed).

On the one hand, it was torturous to listen to; on the other, it made for a nice distraction from the uncomfortably fluttery feelings in her abdomen whenever she thought of Willingham's kiss, or recalled the memory of his blue eyes so intent and focused on her own.

Another distraction shortly arose in the form of the dowager mar-chioness, who wasted no time at all in settling herself beside Diana with a cup of tea and a disturbingly innocent smile.

"How did you sleep, my dear Lady Templeton?" asked the dowager marchioness, stirring sugar vigorously into her tea.

"Like a corpse," Diana assured her.

"Good, good," the dowager marchioness muttered, barely seeming to register her reply. "And have you seen my grandson yet this morning?"

"I can hardly see how I might have managed to evade him, given that we are sitting at the same breakfast table." Diana held her breath, waiting; this was pushing it, she knew. The dowager marchioness might be diminutive in stature, but she could be quite terrifying when it suited her. This morning, however, she seemed to have her mind on other things—on one thing in particular, in fact, as Diana was coming to realize with creeping alarm.

"He is looking very well, is he not?" the dowager marchioness asked, giving Diana a beady-eyed stare.

"I suppose," Diana hedged. "If one likes that sort of thing."

The dowager marchioness pounced. "And what sort of thing would that be?"

"Oh, you know," Diana said, affecting breeziness. "Blue eyes. Broad shoulders." She faltered. "Cheekbones."

"Yes, cheekbones," the dowager marchioness agreed sagely, a clearly detectable note of glee in her voice. "I do admire a lady who properly appreciates cheekbones."

Diana liked precisely nothing about where this conversation was going; not only did she have her own fixation on Willingham's kiss to worry about, she apparently had a determined matchmaking grandmother to do battle with as well.

Diana knew herself, and prided herself on being able to honestly assess her own strengths. Willingham, she knew she could beat—no cheekbones or kisses would be powerful enough to defeat her. The dowager marchioness, however, was another matter entirely, and Diana had no desire to be on the receiving end of her scheming.

Diana cast her gaze around the room, as a drowning man might cast about for a raft, and her eyes caught on Willingham and Lady Helen, still cozily tête-à-tête at the other end of the table—and suddenly, Diana realized that the solution to her predicament had already presented itself.

She leaned back in her chair, directing her attention back to the dowager marchioness. "I believe Lady Helen appreciates cheekbones."

The dowager marchioness blinked. "Lady Helen?"

Diana nodded serenely. "Yes, Lady Helen. You know, blond? Slender? Seated approximately ten feet away?"

The dowager marchioness's eyes narrowed. "I am familiar with her, yes."

"Oh, good," Diana said, giving her an angelic smile. "Then surely you must have noticed the particular attention she is paying Willingham this morning. It's really rather sweet."

"I notice quite a bit, my girl," the dowager marchioness said sternly, giving Diana a look that was vaguely reminiscent of the looks Diana's governess had leveled at her more than once.

"Then of course," Diana pressed, "you must realize the spark that I can see so clearly between them?"

The dowager marchioness appeared unmoved, which was, more or less, as Diana had expected; Rome hadn't been built in a day, after all. But if the dowager marchioness was serious about seeing her grandson wed, then Diana was going to use any weapon at hand to ensure that the target of this grandmotherly matchmaking was anyone other than herself.

And, conveniently, Lady Helen's presence at the house party provided just such a weapon.

Not that Willingham would be interested in Lady Helen, of course; she might question the man's judgment at times, but he wasn't completely deranged. But Lady Helen could certainly prove useful, if she kept the dowager marchioness's sights off Diana herself.

In the hands of a lesser intellect, this would not be sufficient to propel a plan into motion, but Diana was decidedly *not* a lesser intellect, and she knew the bones of a perfectly good scheme when she saw them.

Fortunately for Diana's plans, the gentlemen weren't due to begin hunting until the following day; for today, a ride and picnic at Dauntsey Hill had been proposed. While she certainly could have used time apart from Willingham to cozy up to Lady Helen to further plant the seeds of romance, a picnic, too, presented its own sorts of opportunities. All that fresh air. Birds chirping, bees buzzing . . . Lady Helen could hardly fail to capitalize on such a romantic atmosphere.

Or at least, she could hardly fail to do so once Diana had prodded her in that direction.

Of course, it would be easier to focus on the matter at hand—redirecting the dowager marchioness's speculative, matchmaking gaze far, far away from herself—if she weren't still distracted by thoughts of her conversation with Willingham of the night before.

It had been . . . complicated. Complicat*ing*, rather, in that it had thoroughly muddled all the ways she thought about Willingham and herself and the way they worked together. All the neat boxes she had thought she could place the various aspects of their relationship into—intense attraction in this one, overpowering dislike in that one there—had been jumbled up. Now she had gotten a glimpse of a Willingham she didn't just find interesting for purely physical reasons—and, more dangerously, she had also glimpsed a Willingham who saw more of her than she cared to reveal.

There was also the small matter of the thing she had not been able to stop thinking about doing since the moment he left her room last night: kissing him again.

And again. And again.

She felt rather as though she'd lost control of her own body. Despite her best efforts, she could not stop her mind from returning to the feeling of those short hairs at the base of Willingham's neck sliding through her fingers. Or the feeling of his evening stubble scraping against her cheek. Or the roughness of his hand against the smooth skin of her breast.

For heaven's sake, it was *breakfast time*. She hadn't known that thoughts this inappropriate were possible this early in the day. Surely they belonged to candlelit evenings instead. Did everyone feel like this? How did anyone manage to get anything done? Her eyes landed on Violet and Audley with newfound respect—while she had found their antics since their marital reconciliation a bit tiresome, she now felt that they exercised great restraint. Had she a husband she felt this way about, she wasn't certain she'd ever leave their bedchamber again. It was somewhat alarming that these feelings were not directed at a husband at all, but at Willingham, of all people—a man she certainly had no intention of ever wedding.

But she had no time for these dangerous thoughts—she had a scheme to enact, a dowager marchioness to thwart, and a marquess to make miserable. In short, she was *busy*. Busy ladies had no time to dwell on kisses.

Ten

After breakfast, everyone returned to their respective bedchambers to prepare for the day's outing. Diana stood impatiently as Toogood removed her soft blue gown and replaced it with a sturdier riding habit the color of claret. Toogood redressed her hair as well, braiding it into a knot designed to withstand wind and tree branches. Within the hour, the group had reassembled at the stables, where a lengthy debate was undertaken about the merits of various horses. Diana, who was a competent rider but had zero interest in horseflesh, was thoroughly bored by the discussion, and instead wandered around the perimeter of the stable, her eyes scanning the vista before her.

Elderwild was a beautiful estate and she knew, despite his best efforts to convince everyone otherwise, that Willingham was a careful caretaker. The view from the stables behind the house was magnificent, the lawns sloping gently upward, giving way to scenic woodlands; Willingham seemed to think that the natural beauty of Wiltshire was pleasing enough to the eye without attempting to tame every inch of it, and Diana couldn't have agreed more. Her fingers itched to get a brush in her hand—it had been an age since she'd done a proper landscape painting, and the scene before her was practically begging to be painted.

"Here you are," said a voice, and she turned, startled, to see Willingham standing very close to her—she had been so absorbed in her thoughts that she hadn't heard the telltale crunch of boots on gravel signaling his approach. "We've decided on the horses at last. I thought Audley and West were going to come to blows at one point, but it seems to have all been sorted."

"Now that he's given up his own stables, he can't resist offering his opinion on everyone else's horses instead," Diana said, her mouth curling up. She was referring to a recent decision on Audley's part to return ownership of a country house and lucrative stables to his father, a duke, after having spent the past five years managing them. It was of course incumbent on every aristocratic man to have at least a somewhat tortured relationship with his own father, though Audley took this to a greater extreme than most men of Diana's acquaintance.

"Quite," Willingham agreed, his gaze focused on the view beyond her shoulder. She turned as well, soaking it all in, already imagining how to capture the vivid green of the lawn, the darker shade of the leaves on the trees—

"Thinking about painting this?" he asked, interrupting her vision.

She was surprised by his question—she didn't make a habit of discussing her painting with him, and she was a bit unsettled to realize he'd been paying such close attention when she spoke of it. "I was, actually," she admitted, not bothering to turn. "I don't come to the country much anymore, and there are few opportunities for landscape painting in town."

"Didn't Templeton have a country house?"

"He did," she confirmed, "but the new viscount has taken up residence there." When her husband had died, the title had passed to his nephew, who was a few years older than Diana herself. The new viscount was a kind man, and had told her that Templeton House in London was hers as long as she cared to live there. He maintained his own residence in town, but he had young children and spent much of his time at the family seat in the country, which Diana had been only too happy to give up—she could not imagine herself there alone, wandering the drafty halls with only the servants for company.

She had, on occasion, thought of moving elsewhere in London— her husband had left her a hefty portion of his fortune, and she could certainly afford her own home. She wasn't certain what stopped her—pure inertia? She felt *stalled*, somehow, like an insect caught in amber. She watched other lives moving on around her, and yet felt that she hadn't taken a step since her husband's death. She slept in the viscountess's bedchamber, lying in bed each night looking at the connecting door to a room that had lain empty for years now. Why did she do it? Why didn't she move? Or at least invite someone else into that bed with her?

Well, she reminded herself, she was taking steps toward the latter, at least, and the person with whom she was taking those steps was still standing behind her; she could feel him watching her intently. She found this oddly unsettling, and so she said, rather briskly, "Am I holding everyone up? Show me this horse of mine, and let's be off."

She turned to see Willingham gazing at her with a curious expression upon his face—not at all the usual sort of sardonic one he wore when looking at her, but rather one that implied he was actually curious, that he found her painting interesting. It was vastly different from the half-amused, taunting smirk that she usually found herself on the receiving end of. He reached out and grasped her wrist, stopping her when she would have moved past him. "Did you bring your painting supplies with you from London? I'd be happy to send to the village for anything you might need—or even to London, if we're too provincial for whatever supplies you require."

Diana worked hard to keep her surprise from registering on her face, but doubted she was entirely successful—*thoughtful* had never been one of the many adjectives she might have used to describe Willingham.

"I brought my things," she said, walking past him in the direction of the rest of the party before pausing to look back over her shoulder. "But thank you," she added, and then turned before he could make any sort of reply.

It was, she was fairly certain, the first entirely civil interlude they'd shared in years.

And it felt both wrong and right in almost equal measure.

Once Diana and Willingham had rejoined the party and mounted their horses, they were off, taking one of the many paths that wound away from the house and into the forest that surrounded it on all sides. This one led steadily uphill, their ultimate destination being a patch of clear ridgeline that, Willingham claimed, offered one of the finest views for miles. The width of the trail only allowed them to ride two abreast, and Diana found herself next to, of all people, her brother.

"Well," Penvale said after they had ridden in companionable silence for a while, "out with it. What is your plan?"

"My plan?" Diana asked, turning her head to look at him. Her brother, she'd been told often, resembled her quite strongly. They shared the same honey-colored hair and hazel eyes. They even had similar mannerisms, a certain laziness of movement that Diana, at least, found to be useful. It made people relaxed around her, caused them to let their guards down, never dreaming of the sharp, calculating mind behind the pretty face and elegant slouch. She strongly suspected that her brother took similar advantage of the misconception.

At the moment, he was eyeing her speculatively, the reins held loosely in his hands. "For Jeremy and Lady Helen," he clarified, casting a quick glance about to make sure that they couldn't be overheard. There was enough distance between them and the closest riders that they could manage a private conversation.

"Willingham and Lady Helen," she repeated, feigning confusion.

"Don't profess innocence with me, Diana," he said sternly. "I overheard you speaking to the dowager marchioness at breakfast this morning. I know perfectly well that you are up to something nefarious."

"Dear brother of mine," she said with a sunny smile, "I am never *not* up to something nefarious."

Penvale snorted. "You don't need to tell me that, I assure you." He paused for a moment, and they rode a few paces in silence. "Truth be told, despite the farce Violet and Audley have enacted this summer, marriage is more often than not a business arrangement—if you're hoping to pair Jeremy with Lady Helen, you might appeal to his practical side. I understand her dowry is enormous."

"I'm surprised you're not dangling after her, then," Diana said grumpily. "Isn't that your plan, after all? Amass enough of a fortune that Uncle John will consider selling Trethwick Abbey back to you?"

When Penvale and Diana's parents had died when they were children, their ancestral home in Cornwall had been sold to cover death duties—it was the rare seat to a title that was unentailed. There had been a very willing buyer at hand: their father's youngest brother, from whom the late viscount had been long estranged, who had made his fortune with the East India Company. Their father's solicitors had seen little choice but to sell to him, given that there had been no ready money to cover the debts. Diana and Penvale had been bundled off to live with their mother's sister in Hampshire, and Uncle John had been living at Trethwick Abbey ever since.

Even before he had gained his majority, Penvale had been obsessed with buying back the estate that went with his title. Diana knew he was a dab hand at cards, and he had multiplied his initial holdings many times over through the distasteful business of dabbling in the stock market, but it seemed obvious to her that an advantageous marriage would be a clear path to the fortune he needed with the least amount of effort on his part.

Penvale, however, shrugged off her suggestion, as always. "I've other ideas for myself, thank you very much, sister dearest. Meanwhile," he added, ducking under a low-hanging branch, "do tell. What misery have you in store for Willingham? Do you plan to catch him in a compromising position with Lady Helen? Or somehow coach her to be more appealing?"

Some part of her was vaguely nettled to hear her brother so blithely referring to a lady as *unappealing*, even though she happened to agree with him. It seemed unfair—a lady was expected to get herself married off as quickly as possible, without ever giving the appearance of expending any effort toward that aim. It was a delicate balancing act, and an exhausting one at that.

"That is none of your concern," she said. "I've the matter entirely in hand, don't worry."

"Lady Templeton, was that innuendo?" came Willingham's voice from behind them, startling them both.

Diana chanced a glance over her shoulder; Willingham was riding close behind her and Penvale, watching her with a devilish glint in his eye that she liked and disliked in almost equal measure.

"I overheard the words *in hand*, you see," Willingham continued, "and I could not prevent my mind from wandering down a happy mental detour, much as I tried to steer it back on course."

Diana could practically feel her brother's eyes roll, though her gaze remained fixed on the path ahead. "If you are going to flirt with my sister, Willingham, I am going to ride elsewhere," Penvale said. He didn't sound particularly concerned, but he did spur his horse into a faster trot, allowing Willingham to take his spot next to Diana instead.

"Shouldn't you be leading the party?" she asked crabbily. She craned her neck, not seeing anyone behind them. "Are you the last rider? I thought Violet and Audley were back there somewhere."

"Ah, they were," Willingham said in a strangled voice. "Audley and I were having a perfectly pleasant conversation when Violet suddenly invented some calamity—something about her saddle straps needing to be tightened." He grinned at Diana. "They're back there somewhere, but I wouldn't recommend looking for them, lest you see something scarring."

"I appreciate the warning," Diana said, barely suppressing a shudder.

"I frightened off Penvale, I see."

"I should be thanking you for that. There's only so much of my brother's company I can take."

"I'm surprised you weren't cozying up to Lady Helen, enumerating my charms," Willingham said, giving her a dazzling smile. It was one she had seen him use on numerous ladies, with universal success.

She gave him a severe look. His smile widened.

"Are you asking me to do so?" she inquired, deciding that two could play at this game. "I had no idea you were so moved by her great beauty and, er ..." She faltered, searching for another complimentary adjective to describe the lady in question. "Flattery," she finished weakly.

"I'm asking no such thing," he said, seeming unconcerned. "But I saw you and my dear grandmother cozily chatting at the breakfast table, so I thought to warn you now that it would be wasted effort."

"Of course," she said demurely.

He shot her a suspicious look at that.

"You are, as ever, correct," she added innocently.

His look of suspicion became one of alarm. "What are you planning?" he demanded.

"Nothing for you to be concerned about, my dear marquess," she said, smiling at him like the cat that got the cream. "Nothing at all."

Eleven

It was difficult to be terribly concerned about anything, Jeremy reflected, when one was seated upon a soft blanket under a cloudless English summer sky, with good wine and good food at hand.

Difficult, but not impossible. Lady Helen made sure of that.

The lady was seated to his right—he had never seen someone in a corset move as quickly as she had to claim a spot at his elbow—and had spent the past three-quarters of an hour flirting with him in a way that would have been mildly flattering had it not been so terrifying. Rothsmere was seated just one blanket away with Penvale and Langely; surely he would notice the wild improprieties being enacted by his sister. Jeremy tried to catch his friend's eye, with no success whatsoever; Rothsmere appeared entirely occupied with the array of cheeses displayed before him. There would be no help from that quarter, clearly.

Jeremy thought back over his actions of the past twenty-four hours, trying in vain to recall a moment at which he had given Lady Helen any sort of encouragement, and failed—she must just be remarkably determined. It would have been an admirable quality under any other circumstances. Now, however, when that determination resulted in her hand stroking his forearm in a disturbing fashion, it was merely alarming.

"...and that," she concluded, her fingers encircling his wrist, "is how I convinced my brother to purchase me a puppy."

"*Fascinating*, Lady Helen," said Diana, who was sharing their blanket. "It must be so charming to have a puppy about the house."

"Well," Lady Helen said, wrinkling her nose, "the puppy proved to be a bit smellier than I anticipated. It kept having accidents on the rugs. William finally put his foot down and it lives in the stables at the moment. It will be allowed indoors once it's been properly trained."

"Ah, yes, quite understandable," Diana said, blinking solemnly. "Still, you must be very pleased that you were able to so cleverly convince your brother to get you the puppy in the first place."

Lady Helen looked rather taken aback at this unexpected show of approbation, and Jeremy couldn't blame her—wide-eyed simpering did not suit Diana one bit. He gave her a narrow look, which she ignored.

"Willingham," she said, shifting her gaze from Lady Helen to him, "I do believe Lady Helen needs more wine."

"Oh," said Lady Helen, looking down. "Well, Mama always says that only one glass at luncheon is permissible."

"But surely picnics are an exception," Diana pressed. Jeremy leaned closer—good lord, had she just literally batted her eyelashes? "All that fresh air does make one so frightfully thirsty. I'm sure your mama would not object."

"Well," Lady Helen said uncertainly, casting a glance toward her brother.

"I don't think there's any need to ask for Rothsmere's permission. Willingham," Diana added, in an entirely different tone of voice, "refill her glass."

He supposed he should count himself lucky that she hadn't

snapped her fingers at him as she issued the order. He also supposed that he should have his head examined, because the sound of her voice shifting from artificial sugary sweetness to a tone of sharp command was far more appealing than it should have been.

He had clearly been too long absent from a woman's bed—an entire fortnight, he realized, after a bit of mental calculation. It was the longest period of abstinence he had endured since his brother's death. Obviously the state was dangerous for him.

This summer had been a bit of an anomaly for him, in terms of his romantic activities. His affair with Lady Fitzwilliam Bridewell—Sophie—had occupied much of the early half of the summer; he'd quite enjoyed their time together, even if he was fairly certain she was still in love with Audley's brother. He had no proof—and nothing the lady had ever said to him had ever hinted at this—but he'd not been able to escape the niggling suspicion that Sophie was using him to get West's attention. This suspicion had not been at all alleviated when Sophie had—somewhat to his surprise—accepted his invitation to join the house party. They'd parted on amicable terms, to be certain, but he still had expected her to send a note making her excuses once their liaison had ended. And yet, here she was, seated on a blanket with Violet and Audley, chatting merrily and—to his eye, at least—being rather pointed in the way she did *not* cast so much as a single glance over her shoulder at West.

Jeremy supposed he ought to have been offended by the notion of being used as a pawn in someone else's romantic scheming, but he'd been unable to work himself into much of a lather. If women with golden hair and wide brown eyes and surprisingly adventurous tastes in the bedchamber wished to use him to spite or entice former lovers—well, who was he to object?

The affair had run its course, ending amicably, and then nearly immediately afterward he had tumbled into bed with Lady John Marksdale, a very young, very bored lady with a very elderly, very inattentive husband. And *that* particular liaison, as he had already—humiliatingly—been forced to explain to Diana, had ended in a fashion that had been just traumatizing enough to dampen his enthusiasm for the chase.

Or, as it happened, the chase after anyone other than the hazel-eyed harpy smirking at him from the other side of the blanket.

While he had been contemplating this, his hand had been blindly following orders, refilling Lady Helen's glass and then his own. Whatever plan Diana had, he was certain he did not wish to be entirely sober as it played out.

Diana, however, seemed satisfied with the lay of the land at the moment, sipping contentedly from her own wineglass as she surveyed him with amused eyes. The sunlight brought out the green flecks in her eyes, and he wondered idly if the enticing row of freckles upon her nose would be darker by the time they returned to the house.

Lost in an enjoyable, wine-fueled fantasy of tasting every single one of those freckles, he at first failed to notice the hand slowly creeping up his thigh. Eventually, however, reason returned, in time for him to grasp Lady Helen's hand before it compromised his nonexistent virtue entirely.

He smiled at her as best he could, though he rather thought his grin might lack some of the sparkle of his usual smile—he was incapable of performing to his highest standards under such stressful circumstances, after all. He had never known that a girl nearly a decade his junior—and approximately half his size—could be so intimidating. The female sex truly did not receive enough credit.

"Why, Lord Willingham," she said in a breathy tone that Jeremy supposed was meant to be alluring, but which had the perverse effect of making him feel mildly nauseated instead, "did your heart suddenly feel an overpowering desire to beat in rhythm with my own?"

"Er," Jeremy said intelligently. Across the blanket, out of the corner of his eye, he could see Diana trying not to laugh. It appeared to be a losing battle. He gathered as many of his wits about him as he could manage and said, somewhat more coherently, "I don't take your meaning, Lady Helen."

Her limpid blue eyes widened and the blond ringlets framing her face bobbed as she shook her head. "But surely you feel it?" she whispered, and Jeremy realized he was leaning forward slightly to catch her words—which, doubtless, had been her plan all along. "The way, with our palms pressed together, you can feel your own pulse throbbing against my own?"

A few feet away, Diana choked on her wine; Jeremy spared an uncharitable thought to hope that she would spray it all over her bodice, if only so that he might have the pleasure of watching her attempt to mop it up.

At the moment, however, such pleasurable possibilities had to be set aside in the face of the sticky situation in which he now found himself: with Lady Helen Courtenay's hand clutched in his own and the word *throbbing* hanging in the air between them.

It was, all in all, thoroughly disturbing.

With great effort, he extricated his hand from hers.

"It was indeed a soulful moment," he agreed solemnly, "but perhaps best saved for some occasion other than a picnic, you understand."

"Picnics cannot be soulful?" Diana inquired, all innocence.

"Oh, to be sure, Lady Templeton," he said, never breaking eye contact with Lady Helen. "But I prefer my more soulful picnics to be a touch more . . . private."

"Oh, of course!" Diana clapped a dramatic hand to her chest. "Shall I just go . . . over there?" She gestured vaguely in the direction of the blanket currently occupied by West, Belfry, and Emily. "I don't wish to interrupt, you understand."

"That won't be necessary," Jeremy said hastily, looking away from Lady Helen at last, in time to see the flash of laughter in Diana's eyes before she quickly hid it behind her usual mask of lazy indifference. "The mood has been spoiled."

"How tragic," Diana said, the laughter that had been in her eyes a moment ago now evident in her voice.

"Yes, how tragic," Lady Helen echoed in an entirely different tone. Jeremy had nearly forgotten that she was there, despite the fact that, until moments before, he had been staring at her face, holding her hand. The moment he began to speak to Diana—to banter with her, to engage in their constant game of one-upsmanship—everything else around him faded in significance. He had the distinct impression that the woodland they had recently emerged from could have burst into flames and he would not have noticed, had he been occupied with baiting Diana. It was a profoundly unsettling thought.

"Lady Helen, I find myself restless," he said suddenly, springing to his feet, nearly upsetting his own glass of wine. At the moment, it no longer held any appeal for him—he was too alarmed by the potential dangers attached to dulling one's wits in the company of Lady Helen Courtenay. He had not forgotten that hand creeping up his thigh. He felt like a fussy virgin, but really, they were in *public*.

At a *picnic*.

In a *meadow*.

There were things that decent English people simply did not do.

Jeremy had not considered himself to be counted among the ranks of "decent English people," but he was coming to realize that he had more scruples than he realized. Disturbingly sexual advances from eligible virgins appeared to be his limit.

Of course, had the eligible virgin been Diana, he doubted that he would have reacted with such horror. But Diana had not been an eligible virgin in a very long time. That was the reason he was able to anticipate another late-night visit to her bedchamber.

Shaking these thoughts away, he said, "Would you ladies care to accompany me on a walk?"

Lady Helen wrinkled her nose. "Exercise? My dear Lord Willingham, you must be joking."

"For once, Lady Helen and I are in complete agreement," Diana chimed in, helpful as ever. "Unnecessary movement is frightfully bourgeois, Willingham."

In a moment of clarity, however, Jeremy realized that Diana was lying. Or not *lying*, precisely, but putting on the public persona of Diana, Lady Templeton, that he knew was only a small fraction of who she truly was. She had been playing the role for so long that it had become more and more difficult to distinguish between the public Diana and the private Diana, and he counted it as a small victory each time he was able to catch the deception.

He could, of course, say none of this aloud—it would have made him sound like a raving lunatic, or at the very least oddly fixated on his friend's sister.

Which, of course, he was not.

He turned away from Lady Helen to face Diana instead. Offering her his best courtly bow—the one he employed only on very select, important occasions, lest it send all the ladies in his presence into swooning fits—he extended a hand. "Will you walk with me anyway, Lady Templeton?"

Diana, of course, appeared to be in no danger of swooning. Instead, she looked mildly irritated. "Lady Helen does not wish to walk," she said, giving him a mildly terrifying smile. "Why do you not remain here to keep her company?" She cast a look about them. "I had something I wished to speak to Violet about, anyway."

"It can wait, I'm certain," Jeremy insisted.

"But I know you would relish any opportunity to spend even a moment longer in Lady Helen's company," Diana said, her deranged smile widening even further. "I am certain the lady would be amenable to . . . to . . ."

She trailed off, clearly attempting to think of an activity that would meet with Lady Helen's approval. Jeremy waited, amused; with a glance to the side, he saw that Lady Helen was watching Diana curiously as well. There was something shrewd in her gaze, he noticed with a slight pang of alarm; given Diana's and his desire to keep their liaison a secret, he did not think anything that drew unnecessary attention to them was at all a good sign. And Lady Helen, at the moment, was definitely attentive.

His concerns were relegated to the back of his mind a moment later, however, when Diana burst out with: "Poetry!"

"Poetry," Jeremy repeated, drawing the word out into more syllables than naturally inhabited the six letters.

"Lady Helen clearly has a poetic soul," Diana said; it was a testament to how convincing she could be when she put her mind to it that, even now, clearly scrambling, putting in far from her best performance, she did not sound entirely absurd. Largely absurd, yes, but not entirely so.

"A poetic soul," he said. He could not seem to help repeating everything she said, since at the moment he lacked the ability to form any sort of rational response to this claim.

"Of course," she said. "Her appreciation of a soulful picnic clearly indicates the presence of deep . . . er—"

"Poetry?" he suggested.

"*Feeling*," she said firmly. "In her—"

"Soul?" he asked.

"Heart," she said.

"I must confess," Lady Helen said, a startling reminder that they were not, in fact, alone on this blanket, "I have never heard myself described in quite such terms."

"That is why you are fortunate to be in the company of the famously charming Marquess of Willingham, Lady Helen," Diana said. Jeremy felt rather like a slightly bruised apple being shined up and turned just so to attract a willing buyer.

"Of course," Lady Helen said slowly. Jeremy did not think he was imagining the note of doubt in her voice. "Nevertheless, I am perfectly content here on my blanket, and if Lord Willingham is so desperate to accompany you on a walk, Lady Templeton, it would seem churlish of you to deny him." She flashed Diana a venomous smile; Jeremy could practically see Diana's blood boiling—not to mention her contrary instincts flaring to life—but he intervened before she could work herself into too much of a temper.

"There you have it," he said, turning to Diana in triumph. "I have been cruelly rejected by Lady Helen, but when faced with rejection from one quarter, I have turned to a likelier one in hopes of rescue."

"Please explain to me how anything I have said to you in the past quarter hour could possibly cause you to classify me as a 'likelier quarter,'" Diana said peevishly.

"Walk with me, and I will." He gave her his best, cheekiest grin. He knew it was irresistible—no fewer than twelve different ladies had told him so.

Not that he'd been counting, of course.

With bad grace, Diana allowed herself to be pulled to her feet. She made a great show of brushing off her skirts and then shaking them out, then smoothing her hair, shading her eyes from the sunlight, et cetera. You would have thought he had proposed taking her on a jaunt across England rather than a stroll along the hilltop. Finally losing patience with her theatrics, he seized her by the elbow in a grip that was more domineering than gentlemanly and led her away from the cluster of blankets.

Once they were out of earshot, he murmured, "I hope you enjoyed that."

"You manhandling me like I was a recalcitrant sheep?" she said waspishly. "I can't say that I did."

"No," he said with exaggerated patience. "The sight of Lady Helen nearly deflowering me on the blanket for all the world to see."

Diana huffed a laugh. "I believe your defloration is an event so long in the past that schoolboys will be studying it along with the Greeks and the Romans before too long. Although," she added, pausing, mock-thoughtful, "if you think that your virtue was that endangered by a mere hand on your entirely clothed thigh, that implies a lack of understanding of the basic mechanics of the act that might indeed mean you are an innocent."

"I promise you, I'm not that." He gave her a dangerous smile.

She appeared unaffected. "Or," she said, drawing out the word, "perhaps your recently rejected paramour is more justified in her criticism than you'd like to believe. Clothing *does* generally have to be removed, Willingham."

"I cannot tell you how enticing I find that prospect when you discuss it," he said to her in a low, seductive voice. She rolled her eyes but, he could not help noticing, her cheeks were slightly flushed as she did so. From embarrassment? Desire? He wished blushes would be a bit more damned specific. How was a man supposed to interpret them when they went about appearing on ladies' faces under any number of circumstances?

"I suppose there is a reason you dragged me away from my perfectly acceptable lunchtime entertainment to traipse about the woods with you," she said conversationally. Her elbow was still held in his grip, which had loosened with each step. To any outside observers, they might be courting lovers, taking a romantic late-summer stroll through the meadow's tall grasses, surrounded by wildflowers and the gentle buzzing of unseen bees.

Which was not entirely untrue, if one removed all hints of romance or any sort of attempt at proper courtship.

Realizing belatedly that he had not answered her question, he said, "I thought we might discuss this evening."

Diana tripped. He thought it was the clumsiest movement he had ever seen from her, and felt oddly proud to have been the cause of it.

"What about this evening?" she asked, her voice cool even as she allowed him to steady her with one arm about her waist. He dropped his arm as soon as she was on firm footing once more.

"I was hoping you might permit me to pay you another visit."

"Oh," she said faintly. Did she sound nervous? And what did it say about him that his chest swelled—metaphorically—at the prospect?

"We do have an agreement," he reminded her. "I believe a handshake was involved. I thought we might as well get to it."

"Get to it," she repeated, narrowing her eyes at him. "How sentimental, Willingham. It's a miracle you're not yet married. Tell me, do you beat them off with a stick?"

"I should note that Lady Helen seems to find my charms more than satisfactory," he said, smiling smugly at her. "Besides, even if I tried to fend them off, there is not a stick in the world strong enough to counteract the lure of a marquessate."

She smirked at him, the sun hitting her face in just such a way as to light up her hazel eyes. "How true. Indeed, for all you know, you might be the world's worst lover with all the charm of a troll."

He felt as though he'd walked into a cleverly laid trap, except he was fairly certain the trap was of his own—unintentional—devising. "Well, I wouldn't go that far."

"Oh, no, I'd go even further," Diana said, beginning to warm to her subject. "For all you know, you've never left a woman truly satisfied in all your years of . . . raking? Rakedom? Rakehood? Is there a proper word to use to describe this activity?"

"It's not as though we have meetings to discuss it," he said peevishly, even as his mind screamed, *Trap! Trap!*

"But you don't deny that you've no idea whether your legion of conquests have enjoyed their time in your bed."

"No," Jeremy said vehemently. "I certainly *do* deny it."

"So you've asked them, then? You've solicited reviews immediately after the fact?"

"I—" Jeremy paused. He racked his brain. He was trying to think of a good example with which to refute her, but instead found himself wondering: *had* he ever asked a woman if she had enjoyed herself? Surely he had. He couldn't be that much of an ass.

Could he?

He didn't dare ask the question of Diana, of course; he knew precisely what her answer would be. Instead, he took a different tack. "Lady Templeton, are you implying that you have complaints about our interlude last night?"

"Well," she said slowly, affecting the bored tone that he knew she used to disguise the rapid thoughts racing around inside that beautiful head. "I suppose it was not entirely dissatisfying."

He grinned; coming from Diana, directed at him, that was high praise. "Of course," he agreed. "But if you mean to suggest that it was not entirely satisfying, either, then it seems that I've some work to do."

As he spoke, he was leading them into the shadow of the woodland that spread out down one side of the hill, back toward the house. Even a few feet in, they were completely hidden from view; none of the rest of their party could see them, and they were far enough away that they could not be overheard, either. However, the feeling of isolation was false—anyone could stumble across them without much effort, which meant that he had to work fast.

Diana was looking around, confused. "Willingham, I don't wish to go on a nature hike. What do you think you're—" She broke off abruptly as Jeremy pressed her back to a tree and lowered his mouth to hers.

It felt like a homecoming, the feeling of tracing her lips with his tongue, of her mouth opening beneath his and her sighs mingling with his own breaths. He broke the kiss after a moment to place a series of small kisses along the underside of her jaw, slowly moving lower until he reached the high collar of her riding habit.

"Who designed this blasted dress?" he muttered as he pulled it back slightly so that he could place a lingering kiss at the base of her throat where her pulse pounded at what he was certain he was not imagining was a pace much quicker than its usual rate.

Diana gave a breathless laugh. "Someone more concerned with the practicalities of horseback riding than with opportunities for dalliance?" she suggested. Her fingers tangled in his hair, which was already a bit windswept from the ride; God only knew what it would look like later, but Christ that felt good.

"Foolish," he said, his hands sliding up to feel the heavy weight of her breasts beneath the many layers of fabric and corsetry that kept them tantalizingly wrapped up. "Dalliance should always be a consideration."

At some point, her legs had tangled with his, her skirts wrapped all around. They were pressed together from chest to toe, and the feeling of her soft body molded to his own was doing highly inconvenient things to the state of his breeches. The intelligent thing to do would be to break this off before things got out of hand.

Yes. That would be intelligent. Reasonable.

Instead, Jeremy sealed his mouth over hers once more, loving the small, urgent noises she was making in the back of her throat. One of his hands crept downward to get a firm grip on her hip, keeping her pressed as close to him as was physically possible, given the encumbrance of skirts and jacket and all the other damnable fabric that kept her bare skin from touching his own. That hand grew more adventurous, drifting farther down over a tantalizing curve that the fit of ladies' gowns these days did far too much to hide—

"My eyes!"

It was as though they'd been struck by lightning. Diana jerked backward from him so quickly that her head smacked the tree, causing her to howl in pain. Jeremy, meanwhile, had sprung back as though he were a puppet on a string, shaking his head to clear it, then leaning forward to grip her by the shoulder.

"Are you all right?" he asked urgently.

She nodded, her eyes watering a bit. "I may have a knot at the back of my head, but I'll be fine."

"But will *I* be fine?" demanded the voice behind them that had so startled. The voice that, unfortunately, Jeremy recognized all too well.

He turned, very reluctantly.

Standing a few feet away, one of his hands clapped firmly over his eyes, was Penvale.

Twelve

Brothers, Diana fumed. What possible function could they serve? Eating more than their fair share of dessert every evening in the nursery? Chasing their sister up a tree and then refusing to help her down for two whole hours? Getting so blindingly drunk at a sister's seventeenth birthday fete that they were found the next morning in the hayloft?

These were all occasions upon which Diana had had cause to ponder the purpose of elder brothers, and now she had a new one to add to her ever-growing list: interrupting a sister in the middle of a kiss so good that she felt as though she were about to go up in flames?

Useless.

Unfortunately, this was precisely the sort of situation in which one's brother thought himself to be at his most useful. He was entirely mistaken in this regard, of course, but men were mistaken much of the time—so often that they seemed entirely unable to recognize the state. She spared a thought to wonder if medicine would ever progress far enough to allow for the study of the human brain. She had grave doubts that the male brain would compare positively to its female counterpart.

Unfortunately, however, none of that helped in her present situation: her back pressed against a tree, her head throbbing painfully, the taste of Willingham's kiss still upon her tongue, and a visibly traumatized—and, were she to hazard a guess, furious—brother standing before her, covering his eyes, practically vibrating with indignation.

She sighed. Moments like this were when men tended to be their most unreasonable. She would have to act quickly to avert disaster.

"Penvale," she said coolly, using her hands to push herself away from the tree and move around Willingham toward her brother. "You may open your eyes. There is nothing to see that would offend your delicate sensibilities."

Penvale dropped his hand, looking mildly sheepish. The sheepishness vanished, however, when his eyes landed on Willingham, and his gaze took on a decidedly more outraged glint.

"Do stop looking at me like that, Penvale, you're not the dueling type. You'd probably shoot your own foot off by mistake." It was true—her brother was a notoriously awful shot. Willingham, she recalled, was actually a very good shot; it was fortunate that he was not terribly hotheaded, or all of those duels he had fought could very well have ended in a body bleeding out on the grass and Willingham fleeing to the Continent to live out the rest of his life in exile. It was a surprisingly sobering thought.

"I think a man is entitled to look however he wishes when he finds his only sister being mauled by his supposed friend."

"I say," Willingham objected mildly, "I hardly think *mauled* is the appropriate word to use here."

"Particularly not when the activities you witnessed were entirely consensual," Diana added.

Penvale grimaced. "Please don't make me reflect upon it further. I am already terrified that the images will be imprinted upon my mind for the rest of my life."

Diana rolled her eyes. "Penvale, you are making a nuisance of yourself. I'm not an unwed girl whose virtue you need to protect, you know. I can take care of myself."

Even when she *had* been an unwed girl, she had taken care of herself. A childhood spent in a house where she was aware every day that she was a burden, even if it had never been said in so many words, had created a powerful independent streak within her. She had arranged the details of her London Season; she had created her list of acceptable potential husbands; she had planned her own wedding. Penvale was not a bad brother, but even a good brother is no substitute for a mother, and he had been very young at the time—he had kept an eye on her, but the attention of a twenty-three-year-old is easily distracted by a pretty face, or a bottle of brandy, or a high-stakes game of cards.

For this reason, it was incredibly irritating to have him playing the role of her protector now, when she had no need of him.

"You are an unmarried lady," he said.

"A widow," she countered. "An entirely different creature."

"But a lady without the protection of a husband nonetheless," he insisted. "Easy prey for every lecher in the *ton*."

"Should I be offended?" Willingham asked pleasantly. His tone was calm, but Diana could detect an edge of anger beneath it, and thought that Penvale should choose his next words very carefully indeed.

"You know your reputation, Willingham," Penvale said curtly. For Penvale to use Willingham's title was indication that he was very irritated indeed.

"I do," Willingham agreed. "And so I think that we can both agree that, compared to my usual activities, a few kisses in the woods are nothing much to speak of."

Diana felt a surge of irritation at hearing their recent activities described as such—*a few kisses in the woods?* Technically accurate, yes, but a bit dismissive of the kisses in question, which Diana had thought were rather spectacular. Though, considering their audience was her very irate brother, she supposed this might be for the best.

"They are plenty to speak of when it's *my sister,*" Penvale said indignantly. Diana refrained from rolling her eyes with great difficulty. "Besides," Penvale added, trying a new tack, "what are *you* doing, Diana? You were flinging Lady Helen at him at dinner last night—have you changed your mind about that?" He paused. "Are you trying to marry him *yourself?* You two can't get through a conversation without arguing! Has this been some sort of lengthy mating ritual all this time?" He appeared disturbed by the thought, though still less disturbed than she was by this suggestion.

"I have no plans to marry Willingham, thank you very much," she said in as quelling a tone as she could manage. "And none of this has anything to do with the scene you so irritatingly interrupted."

Penvale gave her an assessing look. "As your brother, I really should call him out."

Diana was appalled. "For heaven's sake, Penvale, I am a *widow*. Have you taken leave of your senses? Now kindly go away."

Penvale split a dark look between her and Willingham. "I want the record to show that I approve of this not one whit. And, Jeremy, we will be discussing it later."

"A discussion I will look forward to with great anticipation," Willingham said in a bored tone. Diana simultaneously wished to laugh and to smack him across the face. These were not unusual sentiments where he was concerned, come to think of it.

Fortunately for her temper, her brother departed as quickly as he had arrived, with a parting shot of, "Do try to look less ravished before you rejoin us." Gazing at Willingham's tousled hair and askew collar, Diana wasn't entirely certain whom her brother had been addressing.

A long silence fell in the wake of Penvale's departure. Diana was torn between smoothing down her skirts and departing in the most dignified fashion she could manage and pressing Willingham back against a tree and picking up where they had left off.

Judging by the gleam in his eye as he gave her a thorough once-over, he was having similar thoughts.

Tempting as the prospect was, however, having an interlude disrupted by one's brother did tend to put a bit of a damper on things, so Diana gave an internal sigh and reached up to try to repair some of the damage to her hair. Without a lady's maid, or even a mirror, this was a difficult task, and she shuddered to think what the others would say when she returned in such a state.

"Here," Willingham said, moving quickly to her side, "allow me."

"An expert in women's coiffures, are you?" Diana asked, arching an eyebrow.

"I have some experience with them, yes," he said smugly.

And why, oh *why*, instead of feeling amused, did she suddenly feel ever so slightly . . . jealous?

"I wouldn't look so pleased with myself, Willingham," she said, seeking as ever to regain the upper hand. "You've yet to prove if your hands are similarly adept with other portions of the female anatomy."

He leaned closer, an errant lock of golden hair falling across his brow. "Let's find out this evening then, shall we?"

The rest of the afternoon was a blur, and Diana could not have said with any degree of certainty what she said to a single person. She knew that she and Willingham had rejoined the group, and had been the subject of several looks from their friends—ranging from curious (Emily) to suspicious (Audley)—but had been saved further questioning or ribbing by the general hustle and bustle of loading up their picnic, remounting their horses, and riding back to Elderwild. Diana had taken great care to ride nowhere near Willingham—or near her brother or Violet, either, as she had little doubt that both of them had plenty of things they wished to say to her.

Things that she had no particular interest in hearing.

Thirteen

Diana had as short a respite from her friends as she might have expected. She had retreated to her bedchamber and solicited Toogood's assistance in removing herself from her riding habit and unlacing her corset before dismissing her maid. Clad only in her chemise, Diana wrapped herself in her most luxurious dressing gown—a delicious concoction of embroidered red velvet; she always felt like a courtesan in it, in the best possible sense—and sat down in her room's window seat with a sketch pad.

The view out her window was stunning—a few clouds had appeared in the late-afternoon sky but the sun was doing its best to shine around them upon the rolling green lawns stretching out beyond the house, a corner of the formal gardens that lined the east side of the manor visible from her vantage point. She scarcely noticed said view, however, so occupied were her thoughts with the day's events. She hardly thought mauling Willingham in a forest really suited their respective aims—his to bed a woman and solicit an honest review, hers to gain a bit of experience in the bedroom. When stated that way, the entire agreement sounded rather cold-blooded, and yet it felt anything but. Whenever she was so much as in the same room as Willingham, she found herself seized with an almost unbearable desire to touch him—to run her fingers through that beautiful golden hair of his; to press a kiss to the spot beneath his strong jaw that so tantalized her; to seize his surprisingly rough hand and move it on her own body, learning how she liked to be touched.

It was all thoroughly . . . distracting.

And Diana could not afford to be distracted—she had an affair to conduct and a wager to win. It was an awful lot on one lady's plate. She needed to focus. But how could she focus, when she had become so inconveniently fixated on a certain marquess? She had spent much of her life trying to ensure that no one could have any sort of power over her, so how had she reached this state so quickly?

These unhelpful thoughts were interrupted by a knock on the door; she rose to open it, but Violet and Emily practically tumbled inside before she'd made it halfway across the room.

"I was going to let you in," she said mildly, dropping her untouched sketch pad down on a side table and sinking into an overstuffed arm- chair instead. Violet and Emily, taking this as the invitation that it was, dropped down on the settee that Diana and Willingham had debauched the evening before.

Well, perhaps *debauched* was too strong a word; after all, they had ceased their activities before they'd gotten to any of the truly interest- ing bits. Nevertheless, Diana carefully avoided contemplating this as her happily oblivious friends made themselves comfortable.

"Would you care to offer an explanation for your behavior today?" Violet asked conversationally.

Diana paused, mock-thoughtful. "Not particularly?" she offered.

This, unsurprisingly, was not deemed a satisfactory response.

"Care to try again?" Violet asked.

"Could you be more specific?" Diana asked, stalling desperately.

Emily, seemingly fascinated, was bobbing her head back and forth; Diana wondered what, if anything, Penvale had told them.

"Well," Violet said, drawing out the word into an improbable number of syllables, "let's see." She held up a finger. "You fling Jeremy and Lady Helen together at our picnic today like a puppet master pulling strings."

"I'd no choice!" Diana protested. "His grandmother was making matrimonial eyes at me and I needed to distract her with someone else to focus on. There aren't that many unmarried ladies of the party to choose from, you know."

"Don't you think this might be taking things a bit far?" Violet asked dubiously.

Diana straightened in her seat in indignation. "That is rich, coming from a lady who spent a fortnight this summer *pretending to be dying* rather than just simply telling her husband that she was still in love with him."

Violet colored slightly. "Well, it *worked*."

"Precisely. And if a scheme that unhinged can work out in the end, then I've no doubt my more clever approach will meet with similar success."

"Except that now you've inflicted Lady Helen Courtenay upon poor Jeremy!" Violet wailed dramatically. "We'll be lucky if there's anything left of him in a fortnight."

"I think Willingham can take care of himself," Diana said, unmoved. "Lady Helen already had her eye on him, I've just . . . encouraged her in that direction. All with the aim of getting the dowager marchioness to stop staring at me like I'm a pig on its way to the slaughterhouse."

"You do have such a romantic view of marriage, Diana," Violet said, laughter in her voice.

"Shouldn't you be more concerned about Emily's behavior than mine?" Diana asked, attempting to change the subject. "She needs a chaperone, since Belfry is here." The last was uttered in a dramatic stage whisper; glancing at Emily, she was delighted to see her blushing.

"That's what Jeremy's grandmother is for," Violet said, waving a dismissive hand.

Diana snorted. "She doesn't seem to be overly diligent in that role; I've scarcely seen her today at all. Emily and Belfry could have slipped away to some dark corner and—"

At this point, Emily interrupted Diana, murmuring something under her breath as her cheeks took on a suspiciously rosy glow.

"I'm sorry," Diana said, leaning closer. "Did you just say, '*We might have done*'?"

Emily blushed even harder. "Perhaps," she hedged.

"Emily Turner," Violet said admiringly, "I have clearly underestimated you."

"He asked for a word after breakfast," Emily explained. "He . . . he told me it was nice to see me without my mother or Mr. Cartham lurking nearby, and that he hoped we could use this week to become better acquainted."

"Better acquainted!" Diana said, gleeful. "I'm sure he *does* hope that. Did he try to become, er, *better acquainted* with you right there in that dark corner?"

"Diana, really," Violet objected, close to laughter.

"He was a perfect gentleman," Emily said defensively, straightening. A note of steel ran through her voice as she defended Belfry. Diana rather wished Emily would deploy said note more often where her parents were concerned.

"In any case, we are not discussing me," Emily said sternly. "We were busy discussing your odd behavior."

"Quite right," Violet said, allowing Emily to change the subject without further comment. "Where was I?" She held up another finger. "After flinging Lady Helen at Jeremy at every opportunity, you then vanish with the aforementioned marquess for a suspiciously long period of time, out of sight of everyone in our party, until your *brother* has to go and fetch you."

Diana opened her mouth to speak, but Violet hadn't finished yet. "And your brother then returns looking uncharacteristically disgruntled, I might add." She leaned back on the settee, looking like a cat who had just presented its owner with an impressively large mouse. Diana, at least, felt rather like what she imagined a cat owner would feel in that circumstance.

Emily, helpfully, decided to chime in at this point. "It *was* rather suspicious."

Diana thought it was for the best that this was her first attempt at dalliance, as she clearly was not very good at it—she and Willingham hadn't gotten around to anything more interesting than a few kisses, and already they were the subject of gossip.

Still, she reminded herself, trying to shore up what remained of her morale, her goal *had* been to gain experience. She had certainly learned a few lessons in the past day.

Namely, on how *not* to behave when beginning a liaison with a gentleman.

Emily, seeming to sense her distress, said gently, "Diana, is everything all right?"

Diana gave a helpless shrug. "I had a *plan*," she burst out—seeing as Emily already knew about the arrangement, she supposed it was past time to fill Violet in as well. She could not explain her hesitance to discuss the matter—she, who lived for gossip, who delighted in regaling her friends with the tale of the latest gentleman to flirt with her (or, sometimes, proposition her) of an evening. But despite their agreement that this was anything *but* personal, she found those moments with Willingham, when his body was pressed against hers, when his mouth moved urgently over her own, to be somehow precious, as though something important was being said without any words being uttered.

It made no sense at all, but that knowledge didn't prevent her from feeling it, anyway.

At the moment, however, the desire to unburden herself was more powerful than anything else.

"Willingham approached me with a . . . proposal, of sorts." Seeing the delighted expression on Violet's face, she added hastily, "Not *that* sort of a proposal. Calm down."

Violet sagged.

"He has recently ended his arrangement with his most recent mistress." Emily, of course, was blushing furiously at just the mention of such a relationship; Violet, however, was nodding in a *get on with it* fashion that was not terribly helpful, but *was* terribly Violet.

Diana hesitated, just as she had done when explaining the situation to Emily, unwilling to betray Willingham's confidence; they might not precisely get along, but there was an odd sort of code of honor between them nonetheless.

Much like Emily, however, Violet did not seem to find any explanation necessary.

"Let me guess," Violet said after Diana had remained silent for a moment too long. "He offered the position to you?"

"I don't know that I would phrase it quite like that," Diana said with as much dignity as she could muster. "That makes it sound terribly mercenary. It's not as though I'm a kept woman, or anything so sordid."

"But you are lovers?" Violet pressed, focused as ever on the important bit.

"Well, not quite," Diana said with uncharacteristic primness. "But we are on that path, yes."

Emily, always innocent, frowned. "What does that mean?"

Violet turned to her. "It means they've been engaging in lewd activities in varying states of undress, but have yet to complete the act."

Diana choked. "Violet!" She fully expected Emily, of all people, to blush at this, but instead she looked intrigued.

"Just how many acts are there that involve the removal of clothing that are not *the* act?" she asked. Diana wouldn't have been surprised to see her whip out a pen and begin taking notes.

"Emily, I would be happy to educate you on this further at a later date, but I do think we have more pressing matters to discuss," Violet said.

Emily slumped slightly in her seat. "I suppose you're right."

Diana looked at her with suspicion. "Why are *you* so interested? Did that cozy tête-à-tête with Belfry make these activities sound rather appealing?"

Emily did flush at this. "I am merely seeking to become . . . more well-informed."

"I'd wager Belfry would be more than willing to help you in that endeavor," Diana said sweetly.

"So," Violet said, seeming to think this interlude had gone on quite long enough, "let me be certain I understand this. You and Jeremy are . . ." She waved her hand, searching for the appropriate euphemism. ". . . becoming *intimately acquainted*, shall we say?" She waggled her eyebrows in an exaggeratedly lascivious fashion, and Diana reflected, rather grumpily, that Violet was somewhat insufferable when she was happy. "But you have no desire to marry him, which the dowager marchioness seems to be angling for. So your solution is to—even as you engage in said intimate activities—try to get him married to someone else?"

"I'm not trying to *actually* get him married," Diana said, exasperated. "Or at least not to Lady Helen."

"I would certainly hope not," Violet said. "You're skilled, Diana, but no one's *that* skilled."

"I still have eleven months to see him wed, according to the terms of our wager," Diana said. "There's no need to rush the matter."

But, even as she spoke, the wheels in Diana's mind began to turn. Surely, *surely* Lady Helen could not be as dreadful as she seemed. No one was *that* dreadful. Perhaps she merely needed some assistance in wooing a gentleman as marriage-shy as Willingham.

The fact of the matter was, Diana despised losing—to anyone at all, but particularly to Willingham, with his smirking and his eyebrow-raising and his mere existence. And for that reason, she was determined to see him wed in the next eleven months, no matter what it took. And how much easier it would be to ensure such an outcome if the lady she chose to play this role was the one she had already so conveniently redirected his grandmother's attention to? Willingham was a strong-willed man, but surely even he would crumble beneath the combined will of Diana and the dowager marchioness.

"What are you thinking?" asked Violet, who had been watching Diana's face shrewdly as her mind had raced.

"Well," Diana said slowly, knowing her friends were going to think her mad, "I was just wondering if perhaps we don't give Lady Helen enough credit."

"Credit for being dreadful?" Violet asked. "I assure you, I give her plenty of credit in that regard."

"We've crossed paths a fair number of times, and she is quite awful," Emily agreed.

"Oddly so, in fact," Violet mused. "Her brother is quite alluring." She had a vague, dreamy expression upon her face.

"Violet!" Emily said, shocked. "You are married!"

"And only recently reconciled," Diana chimed in. "Don't ruin your reconciliation by mooning over Rothsmere."

Violet laughed the laugh of happily married women everywhere, secure in their husband's affections. Diana, despite having been married for over two years before Templeton's death, had never laughed that laugh. "I'm married, not dead," Violet said. "Rothsmere is exceedingly handsome. And charming." She gave Emily a speculative look. "In fact . . ."

"Oh, no," Emily said, nipping that line of conversation in the bud before it could even be properly begun. "We are not talking about me anymore. We are discussing Diana."

"So we were," Violet said, but not before giving Emily a glance that said, quite clearly, that she was mentally bookmarking this discussion to be continued later. Diana found it rather disconcerting to realize how much energy Violet had to meddle in her friends' lives now that her own marriage had been so happily, if laboriously, reconciled. The change in her friend, in fact, made Diana feel a bit odd: she realized that Violet had not been quite, well, *Violet* for so many years, and that she, Diana, had not entirely noticed it until Violet was acting like herself again. What kind of friend was Diana? Was she so self-absorbed that she could fail to notice a friend's misery? That thought made her, quite suddenly, think once again about the dark circles beneath Emily's eyes, and she vowed that this was one conversation that she, too, would continue.

At the moment, however, both of her friends were peering at her curiously, rather as though she were a particularly exotic animal. She could not entirely blame them, given the day's events.

"Willingham and I have come to a mutually agreeable arrangement," she said briskly, trying to keep any hint of sentiment out of her voice. Evidently she succeeded, because Emily looked disappointed and Violet rolled her eyes. "This arrangement has no bearing whatsoever on his grandmother's efforts to marry him off, and that is why I've decided to distract her by finding a different matrimonial candidate for him."

"You think he is going to suddenly decide that Lady Helen Courtenay is his ideal wife?" Violet asked, extremely skeptically.

"I'm *saying* that the lady perhaps deserves some further investigation," Diana said carefully. She knew this was a stretch, and yet it seemed too easy an opportunity to pass up entirely. "Her brother is delightful, and seems to like her well enough, so she can't be as dreadful as she seems. It's only a matter of making Willingham realize it."

"Why do you care so much, Diana?" Emily asked curiously.

"Have you *met* his grandmother?" Diana exclaimed. "I've no intention of spending the next fortnight with her trying to trap me in a locked room with her grandson."

"I imagine she won't need to try very hard," Violet said with unholy glee. "I think it likely you'll trap yourself without much prompting."

"That is quite enough commentary from *you*, Violet, thank you very much," Diana said peevishly. "I'm going to seek Lady Helen out and try to get to know her a bit better. She and Willingham might suit perfectly."

And Diana would be one hundred pounds the richer, just like that—and, far more important, she would have the satisfaction of having bested Willingham. She did not wish for much in life—a comfortable house, an extensive wardrobe, and a plentiful supply of paint and canvas were all she really asked for. But the sensation of winning a wager against Willingham? Yes, she would admit to wanting *that* rather badly.

She sat back, feeling rather pleased with herself. It was an entirely sound plan.

Violet and Emily regarded her as though she had recently escaped from Bedlam.

"This is a dreadful plan," Emily said with uncharacteristic bluntness. "I do try to see the good in everyone, but Lady Helen . . . well, she makes it rather difficult."

"This is one of the worst ideas I have ever heard," Violet agreed, and given that this comment was coming from someone who had recently feigned consumption to gain her husband's attention, it had to be said that it stung a bit.

Diana smiled with more confidence than she truly felt. "You say that now. But haven't we learned quite recently that even the most farfetched schemes may ultimately prove successful?"

Emily looked back and forth between the pair of them. "I think that if either of you show the faintest hint of attempting to meddle in *my* romantic affairs, I shall elope."

Diana didn't entirely blame her.

It was just before teatime that Diana enacted the next stage of her plan.

She dawdled in the corridor outside the library, perfectly aware that Lady Helen would have to pass this way en route to the blue drawing room, where tea was being served. Diana spared a longing thought for the treats on offer; Willingham's cook was famous for her raspberry jam, sure to be presented alongside her fluffy, heavenly scones, and postponing such delights in favor of a conversation with Lady Helen Courtenay took reserves of self-discipline that Diana had not been certain she possessed.

Still, it was a desperate time. Scones could wait; arranging her companions like pieces on a chessboard could not.

She turned at the sound of footsteps—she'd been disappointed twice already, once by West and Audley, deep in conversation, and once by Emily and Belfry, suspiciously silent as they passed Diana—but the third time was indeed the charm, for it was Lady Helen now approaching.

Diana straightened and plastered on her best, sunniest smile. "Lady Helen!" she called brightly, waving—*waving*? O, the depths to which she had fallen in her quest to avoid emotional entanglement. But still, needs must—so energetically that Lady Helen stopped in her tracks, glancing over her shoulder as if to assure herself that these attentions were, in fact, directed at her.

"Lady Templeton," she said, a note of suspicion in her voice confirming that however irritating she might be, stupid she was not. "I was just on my way to tea."

"As am I," Diana agreed. "But I thought you and I might have a word first?" She phrased it as a question, even as she took Lady Helen's elbow in a firm grip and began to steer her toward the library.

"There," she said cheerfully, closing the door behind her. Lady Helen stood behind her, looking distinctly ruffled, clearly about to object, so Diana barreled on before she could do so.

"I could not help noticing that some degree of feeling seemed to be emerging between yourself and Lord Willingham," Diana said, strolling idly to a wall to examine a map of Elderwild and the surrounding countryside.

"Of course you could not," Lady Helen said stiffly. "The deep emotion already present between us indicates two souls so wholly in communion, so perfectly in tune with one another, that it is as the relation between a great composer and his prized violin."

"Mmmm," Diana murmured as she contemplated gagging into the decorative urn on a nearby end table. "I could hardly have said it better myself."

"It is as you said this afternoon, Lady Templeton: I have a poetic soul," Lady Helen said smugly. Diana, with great effort, resisted rolling her eyes.

"I could not agree more," she said, then tried a different tack. "Still, the Marquess of Willingham is notoriously marriage-shy, as I'm certain you are aware. His reputation—well, it is perhaps best not spoken of."

"Yet do not they always say that reformed rakes make the best husbands?" Lady Helen asked brightly. "I am certain that he will be suitably tame once the noose is around his neck."

Diana paused at this; given Lady Helen's apparent eagerness to be wed, it was somewhat surprising that she seemed to view herself as the hangman and her future husband as her victim.

"My concern was more in regard to your ability to catch him," she said after a moment, determinedly maintaining her light tone. "Men like Willingham . . . well, they're not easy to snare. They have an eye out for all of the normal sorts of tricks. I was thinking perhaps you might like some advice, from someone who is a bit more intimately acquainted with him?"

Lady Helen's gaze sharpened on Diana at last; she had been idly glancing around the room, her arms crossed over her chest, as though this conversation were not of terribly great interest to her, but it seemed that Diana finally had her attention.

"Yes," she said slowly, drawing the word out. "I have been wondering just how *intimately* it is that you are acquainted with Lord Willingham."

Diana considered pretending not to take her meaning but wasn't sure she could manage it convincingly—after all, a doe-eyed innocent she was not. Instead, she decided to laugh it off.

"Willingham and *I*?" she asked, injecting just the right note of incredulity into her voice. "You must be joking, Lady Helen. The man and I can barely exchange three sentences without quarreling."

"I've noticed that," Lady Helen agreed. "But it does nothing to dissuade me from my suspicions."

"Why on earth would I be *here*, offering to help you woo him, if I had designs on him for myself?" Diana asked airily, posing a question that some small internal part of her would also very much have liked the answer to, but which she had no notion of indulging.

"I don't know," Lady Helen admitted, frustrated. "It's all very odd."

"I'm offering to give you advice in pursuit of the gentleman you wish to wed, and you're too busy asking *me* questions to let me assist you."

Lady Helen laughed haughtily. "Lady Templeton, you cannot possibly imagine that I need help snaring Lord Willingham? I am the daughter and sister of an earl; I'm pleasing to look upon; I play the pianoforte exceedingly well. I am exactly the sort of lady a marquess should choose for a wife, once he decided to take one."

"It's the 'deciding to take one' bit that I think will be likely to give you trouble," Diana replied. "Willingham seems entirely disinterested in the matrimony—not one month ago, in fact, he was willing to wager a substantial sum that he will not be married in the next twelvemonth."

Lady Helen took two steps toward Diana. "I like a challenge," she said, her eyes locking onto Diana's own. "And even if I didn't—even if I did need help—I can assure you I'd not beg the assistance of a widow with a reputation of her own." Diana felt as though she'd been slapped; she nearly took a step backward.

"After all," Lady Helen continued, "I hardly see gentlemen flooding you with offers—at least, not of the matrimonial variety."

Diana took two steps forward of her own; there were now scarcely six inches of space between them. "I've already played that game and won," she said softly. "I've found my freedom; I merely thought to offer you help in finding yours. Clearly, I was mistaken." For a brief moment, some unidentifiable emotion flickered across Lady Helen's face, but it was gone before Diana could put a name to it.

Without another word, Diana turned and left the room, uncomfortably aware that, whatever her earlier hopes, Lady Helen seemed to be just as odious as she appeared. Which, in turn, begged the question: how was Diana possibly going to convince Willingham to marry the lady?

Fourteen

Jeremy had planned to visit Diana's bedchamber again as soon as everyone had settled in for the night, but the evening's entertainments had stretched into the wee hours of the morning. Dinner had been a long, chatty affair that had endured well past the traditional hour as they lingered at the table, and the trend had continued for the rest of the evening. The gentlemen dawdled over their port and then upon rejoining the ladies had been drawn into a highly competitive game of charades.

The dowager marchioness, as it turned out, was a surprisingly adept actress. He'd had no idea that one could so clearly convey the idea of a sheep without emitting a single *baa*.

His grandmother was, incidentally, the reason he was so late in visiting Diana. Just as the party finally dispersed for the evening, the dowager marchioness had crossed the room to join him where he stood, placing a hand on his arm with a surprisingly firm grip for a woman in her seventies.

"A word, Jeremy," she said tremulously, and he was instantly on alert—many adjectives could be used to describe the dowager marchioness, but *frail* was not one of them. If she wished to project that appearance, she was clearly up to no good. He had learned long ago that where the dowager marchioness was concerned, one could not let one's guard down for a single second.

He, of course, said none of this, but instead gave her his best and most charming smile, as well as a smooth, "But of course, dearest Grandmama."

She gave him a dark look in response, but was forestalled from further conversation until the rest of his guests had bade them good night. Diana, he saw, cast a look at him, standing there with his arm still in his grandmother's grasp, and offered him a small but decidedly smug smile. Jeremy was beginning to wonder if monks weren't on to something—women were nice, but he questioned whether they were quite worth all the bother.

As soon as the last guest had left the library—which was where they had assembled, as it offered the largest expanse of open floor, an important consideration when playing charades—the dowager marchioness crossed to the sideboard and unstoppered his decanter of brandy, pouring sizable splashes into two tumblers, one of which she handed to him. He had imbibed less than usual that evening, wanting to keep his wits about him—and all body parts appropriately functioning—for his rendezvous with Diana later on. But he had no doubt at all that he was not going to enjoy whatever his grandmother had to say.

"I must confess, Jeremy, that I recently heard some unflattering gossip about you back in London," she said, diving straight to the heart of the matter, as was her wont. "The Countess of Cliffdale is one of my dearest friends, you know, and her granddaughter is married to—"

"Lord John Marksdale, yes," Jeremy said, in as bored a tone as he could manage. He could already tell where this conversation was going, and he did not like it one bit. He would not have liked to be having it with *anyone*, but having it with his grandmother, of all people, was particularly mortifying.

"I will spare you the specifics of Lady John's complaints, which I am certain are already known to you, but needless to say, the lady in question is less than pleased with your behavior of late."

"I am aware," Jeremy said quietly, casting wildly about in his mind, wondering if he'd ever heard any rumor of a sinkhole beneath Elderwild. It would be a highly convenient time for one to develop.

"I have to say, Jeremy, I tend to turn a blind eye to your behavior—you are young, and heaven knows your father sowed his fair share of wild oats when he was your age. It seems unfair to hold you to an unrealistic standard, when I know that most gentlemen your age act similarly." She paused. "Furthermore, I am not unsympathetic to the difficult path you have traveled these past few years, after your brother's death."

Jeremy felt his chest tighten at the mention of David. He managed to avoid discussing him as much as possible—he avoided even *thinking* of him. West's presence at this house party made that difficult, of course—West had been the other participant in the curricle race that had killed David. Not that Jeremy blamed West, not even initially—both men had been caught up in the heat of the moment, young and, on that occasion, uncharacteristically reckless. And West himself had been terribly injured in the ensuing crash, walking with a limp to this day.

But still, the sight of West's face tended to bring back memories of that day, and the days that had followed—what little Jeremy could remember of them, that was. He had drowned his sorrows so thoroughly in spirits that it was a miracle he could even remember a single detail from that—how long had it been? A week? More? Even now, he was unsure.

But it had been his grandmother who had pulled him out of that hole, who had presented herself at his door day after day, who had drawn him out of his dark well of grief, and for that he was eternally grateful—which was why he now stood quietly, drink in hand, allowing her to say her piece.

"However, there is a limit to what even my affection for you will allow." Her voice had become steely. "This is behavior that is unfitting of the man I know you to be."

He forced out a light laugh, but it sounded strained even to his own ears. "I think this is behavior exactly fitting the man I am." Or the man he had become, ever since his brother's death. Jeremy had always been rather rakish—certainly more irresponsible than his elder brother, who had borne the burden of the title he was to inherit. But it was only after David died that Jeremy had gotten up to the worst of his exploits, almost as though he were thumbing his nose at the brother who had left him with this title and responsibility he had never wanted.

Who had left him here, alone.

His grandmother was having none of it. "That is where you are wrong, my boy." He had the distinct impression that, had his grandmother had a fan in her hand at that precise moment, she would have rapped his knuckles with it. "*This* is not who you are—sneaking out of ladies' bedchambers at all hours of the evening, fighting duels at dawn, showing up in my drawing room at four in the afternoon, still foxed from the night before. Ending a liaison in such a ham-handed fashion that the lady has cause to complain to her *mother*, of all people." Who had then, presumably, complained to *her* mother, who had then relayed the entire sordid tale to Jeremy's grandmother. Christ, what a mess. He made a mental note to check the family tree of all future bed partners to ensure that their grandmothers shared no more than a nodding acquaintance with his own.

Though, knowing the dowager marchioness's ability to sniff out scandal, even that might be too dangerous. Perhaps he should turn his attentions beyond London for his entertainments. Was Scotland removed enough from his grandmother's all-seeing eye?

Or Peru? It was still the dry season in Peru.

"This is why it has become even more evident that it is high time you were married," the dowager marchioness said decisively, drawing Jeremy rather abruptly out of his ruminations.

"Yes, you've made your thoughts on this abundantly clear," he said, affecting a bored tone that he vehemently hoped would discourage this line of conversation.

Unsurprisingly, his grandmother was not so easily deterred. "How convenient, then, that Lady Helen Courtenay is here, so eagerly putting herself forward as a prime matrimonial candidate."

Jeremy had to laugh at that. "You cannot be serious."

"I am deadly serious, Jeremy," his grandmother said, her tone unusually stern. "If marriage is what it takes to stop you from sending respectable society wives weeping into their mothers' arms with tales of bedroom misbehavior, then I would be perfectly happy to see you settle down with the butcher's daughter. So please understand me when I say that an earl's sister seems like a very appealing option to me at the moment."

"You won't be able to enjoy your victory for long if I fling myself out a window a fortnight into the marriage," Jeremy said darkly.

The dowager marchioness tutted. "You young people. So certain that you're *different*, that you'll evade the parson's mousetrap, or that you'll find a love match."

"Who said anything about a love match?" Jeremy objected indignantly. "I'm not averse to marrying Lady Helen because I'm holding out for love; I'm averse to the idea because I'd like to not be legshackled to someone who would lead me to stab myself with a toasting fork."

His grandmother rolled her eyes. "So dramatic, Jeremy, it's most unseemly." She paused, a crafty expression crossing her face. "*Unless,*" she said slowly, "you object to the idea because your affections are otherwise engaged?" She paused expectantly, giving him a shrewd look that implied she saw right through him. It was unsettling.

Like everything else about this conversation, in fact. "No," he said firmly, determinedly *not* thinking of Diana, awaiting him in her bedchamber at that very moment. Because whatever sentiments their arrangement involved, affection was not one of them.

"Good," his grandmother said, not seeming the slightest bit deterred by this reply. "Then I look forward to seeing many more happy, intimate moments between yourself and Lady Helen." Before Jeremy could offer a rejoinder—really, this conversation would go on all night at this rate—she gave an enormous, patently false yawn, and rose to her feet.

"Now, if you'll excuse me, my dear boy, I must find my way to bed." She produced a faint tremble of the lips, and raised a slightly shaking hand to pat his cheek affectionately. Jeremy stared at her, unmoved. "It would be such a comfort, in my twilight years, to see you properly settled," she offered by way of a parting shot as she made her way feebly from the room at half her normal speed.

Jeremy sighed and downed the rest of his brandy. He really should go back to his bedroom and allow his valet to undress him, splash his face, and just take a moment to be alone. To think.

However, he didn't want to do any of those things. He just wanted to see Diana, and perhaps it was his exhaustion, but he wasted no time fighting the impulse. He strode purposefully toward her room, where he softly knocked on her door.

She was slower answering tonight than she had been the night before, and he wondered for an instant if perhaps she was not expecting him. Perhaps she had already gone to bed—it was quite late, after all, and rather presumptuous of him to be here. Before he had a chance to talk himself out of it, however, the door opened and Diana was there, stepping back to allow him to enter the room.

She had already made herself ready for bed—she was wearing a high-necked nightgown that looked incongruously innocent, and her glorious hair was braided over one shoulder. It was the least seductive bedtime ensemble imaginable—barring ones that involved flannel, he supposed—and yet he felt a bolt of lust shoot through him at the sight of her. She had left one button undone at her neck, and it was enough to allow him the sight of her pulse fluttering at the base of her throat. The sight of that faint beat reminded him of the feeling of sealing his lips over that very spot, and from there it was a mere hop, skip, and jump, mentally speaking, to envisioning her spread out on the bed before him, the nightgown lying in tatters around her.

Knowing Diana, however, she would then rise up on her elbows and give him a thorough scolding for destroying a perfectly good nightgown, which rather spoiled the fantasy. She was the oddest combination of seductive and practical that he had ever encountered, and yet he didn't think he wanted her in spite of her practicality, but rather, in some way, because of it. It was part and parcel of her and, at the moment, every part of him wanted every single part of her.

"I'm sorry it's so late," he said, feeling uncharacteristically ill at ease.

He never felt awkward around anyone except her—what was it that she did to him? Was it merely lust? Did so much of his blood flee south at the mere sight of her that there was none left in his brain to allow him to produce any sort of intelligent conversation?

That was the simple explanation but not, he thought, the wholly accurate one. What happened to him in her presence—the conflicting need to press her up against the closest piece of furniture *and* to rile her until she threw claret in his face—was something that he, at least, did not understand well enough to put into words.

"I was beginning to wonder if you were coming," she said. "It's been a long day." She reached out and placed a hand on his arm, and there was something so casually intimate about the gesture that he froze, like an adolescent boy who had never been touched by a girl before. Sensing his stiffening, she started to take her hand away, and Jeremy seized it, not wanting her to mistake his reaction for distaste. Instead, he held her warm hand in his as he spoke, lacing her fingers through his own.

"My grandmother wanted a word. Several words, actually." He paused, drew a breath. Diana's hand squeezed his, the movement somehow silently encouraging him to continue. "She was full of complaints about my recent behavior."

Diana arched an eyebrow. Of course. If he had any artistic talent whatsoever, and someone asked him to paint her, the painting he produced would feature her staring directly at the viewer with that frank, unsettling hazel gaze of hers, one eyebrow ironically arched.

"Only your recent behavior?" she asked. "I don't see what you've done recently that is any more meriting of complaint than usual."

She was entirely right, of course, and yet somehow he didn't like to hear himself described this way, or at least not by her. It was nothing more than the reputation he had deliberately cultivated, and yet he wanted her to see beyond it, past it. And sometimes, he thought that she did. And yet other times, she spoke like this. They had built a wall of animosity, of teasing and bantering and needling, between them, and it was remarkably difficult to break down. They had created cracks in it recently, but it was still there.

"My grandmother is friends with the Countess of Cliffdale, whose granddaughter is Lady John Marksdale." He paused, waiting.

Diana looked at him, not comprehending. "What does that have to do with—" She broke off with a gasp, her eyes widening as her hands came up to cover her mouth. "Oh, no." Her voice sounded suspiciously close to laughter. "Don't tell me that Lady John is who you recently wronged so grievously?"

Jeremy rubbed the bridge of his nose, sighing. "I'm glad this is so amusing to you."

"Willingham, you utter idiot," Diana said, but it was an affectionate sort of insult, and it had the rather perverse effect of making him feel warm all over. Being called an idiot by Diana was better than any of Lady Helen's flattery—or, indeed, any other compliment he'd ever received.

Perhaps he truly was losing his mind.

"Well," she said, leading him further into the room with the hand she still held, "I hope this has been a valuable lesson for you. I'm sure you've a copy of *Debrett's* floating around somewhere—perhaps you should consider using it the next time you set your sights on a lady, to ensure none of her relations are friends of your grandmother's."

He narrowed his eyes at her as she drew him down onto the same settee they had sat on before. He felt the tension that he had held within him all day beginning to unspool, even as her mere proximity sent a new sort of awareness coursing through him.

He made as if he were going to stand. "Shall I go consult it now? Do you have some relative who is going to come haring after me once all of this is over?" He spoke lightly, trying to mask the distaste he felt for that notion—the idea of *this*, whatever it was between them, having run its course. He couldn't imagine it—but perhaps only because he had not yet bedded her. That was the explanation, of course.

Diana tugged him back down, rolling her eyes. "Only Penvale." She snorted. "And I wouldn't worry too much about how you'd fare against him, if it came to a duel."

"He can run faster than I can, though," Jeremy said. "Shouldn't like it if he decided to give chase and just . . . tackle me."

"I would pay money to see it," Diana said cheerfully. Jeremy cast her a baleful look, which only seemed to heighten her amusement.

"In any case, my grandmother was not pleased to catch wind of this, and informed me it's time I settle down. Stop bringing shame on the family. Et cetera." Even as the words came out, he wondered why he was sharing this with her—theirs had never been a friendship of intimate confidences.

"She does seem rather determined to see you wed," Diana agreed. "All the better for me, if it helps me win our wager."

"I wouldn't start counting your winnings just yet," he warned her. "I've evaded the parson's mousetrap this long, so I don't see why I should stumble into it now."

"You've never found yourself up against the combined will of me *and* the dowager marchioness," Diana said, smiling in a self-satisfied manner. "You don't stand a chance." She hesitated a moment, and then added, "You *will* have to marry someday, you know. You've worked so hard to make your estate solvent again—you wouldn't just throw that all away by never fathering an heir, would you?"

Jeremy stiffened, though he knew Diana was unaware that she'd trodden onto dangerous ground. "I'm so glad that the sole aim of my existence is now to find a woman I can tolerate, get her with child, and then pass this pressure and responsibility onto my son someday. What a bloody lovely prospect."

Diana frowned. "Welcome to the aristocracy—which I believe you've inhabited all your life? I shouldn't think this would come as a surprise to you."

"I'll remind you, I spent most of that life assuming that it wouldn't matter much to anyone else what I did, because I wasn't the one with the title."

"You're hardly the only second son to ever inherit a title unexpectedly, Willingham." She paused, her expression softening. "It was terrible, what happened to your brother. And it was terrible that you couldn't simply mourn him in peace, but that you had to instantly figure out how to keep the estate afloat. But you did that, and it's not so absurd that your grandmother should expect you to marry someone and have a son to pass it on to.

"Now," she added, her eyes flashing, "if you'd like to discuss the absurdity of the fact that it has to be your *son* who inherits it—that if you had an entire manor house full of daughters, none of them could be the next Marchioness of Willingham—then *that* I'd be more than happy to talk about."

"Why am I not surprised?" he asked, giving her a ghost of a smile. "But the fact remains, I don't feel any pressing obligation to marry some woman I can barely stand and saddle my son with all the responsibility I feel, just because I'm unlucky enough to have an elder brother who couldn't say no to a stupid challenge."

He broke off, surprised at the raw note he detected in his voice—

one that Diana evidently heard as well, judging by the wrinkling of her brow.

"Willingham," she said, "if you've things about your brother that you wish to get off your chest—"

"Nothing of the sort," he said, forcing a laugh that he didn't think was terribly convincing. "I'm not certain what's gotten into me this evening, but I don't think I'm terribly good company. Could we perhaps postpone this until tomorrow?"

"Of course," she said, still looking at him with something close to concern. "We've plenty of time left, after all, for me to tell you that you're brilliant in bed and send you back off into the world with your confidence newly restored."

While this was, technically, precisely what they had agreed upon— or, rather, what he'd hoped the outcome of their agreement would be—it all sounded rather unsavory when stated like that. All he said in response, however, was, "Too right."

"Good night, Willingham," she said as he rose to his feet. He debated with himself with every step he took to the door, then turned just before opening it and said, "You know, Diana, my friends call me Jeremy."

The word hung in the air between them: *friends*.

"And is that what we are?"

"I do not think a word has yet been invented to describe what we are," he called over his shoulder, and was maddeningly pleased with himself as he shut the door on the sound of her laugh.

Fifteen

Diana lay in bed for as long as could possibly be deemed polite the next morning. Toogood delivered her a tray of toast and chocolate at some point, muttering under her breath all the while.

"It's all right for some, I suppose, when others have been awake for hours . . ." And then, after a pause, "Last I checked ladies have two good feet just like the rest of us, but walking downstairs for breakfast is still somehow too much of a burden—"

"And two perfectly good ears as well, Toogood!" Diana called sweetly after her maid's retreating back. She knew that any lady in her right mind would have shown Toogood the door years before, and yet Diana had become oddly fond of the woman over time. It was refreshing to know exactly what one's help thought of one, rather than having to guess.

She lay back in bed, sipping her chocolate slowly, contemplating the view out her window. It looked unfortunately . . . gray.

Dark gray.

Since the world tended to look gray when there was water falling from the sky in a torrential downpour.

Which there currently was.

Every curse word Diana's brother had ever taught her—along

with a few she had picked up on her own—flashed through her mind. Weather like this meant there would be no hunting today. Which meant the gentlemen would be scattered about the house, generally making a nuisance of themselves, poking their heads into every conversation, offering a never-ending litany of unsolicited opinions, et cetera. Male things.

However, in the interest of total honesty, Diana was forced to admit to herself that this prospect was not what truly concerned her—after all, if a lady found the specter of unwanted male opinions so daunting as to force her to remain abed, she would never leave her bedchamber again. No, it was the possibility of encountering one gentleman in particular that she found so alarming.

Diana wasn't quite sure what had occurred between herself and Willingham the night before, but it made her deeply uneasy. Their discussion of his brother's death was unquestionably the most serious conversation they'd ever had—and it was, she thought, the most vulnerable she'd ever seen Willingham.

She had been perfectly comfortable with their arrangement when it had seemed that she would be able to continue to keep Willingham tidily in the mental box she had assigned to him: charming, flirtatious, utterly maddening. She was far less comfortable now that she had seen this other, even more appealing side to his character. Did anyone else see this, or was it only her? Even thinking that made her feel laughably presumptuous, and yet she knew that he must keep his more serious side buried deeply away, for the sake of his reputation if nothing else.

She sighed, allowing her head to flop back upon the mountain of pillows behind her. She and Willingham were too much alike—that was the problem here.

Not Willingham, she mentally corrected herself. *Jeremy.* The name sounded strange even in her mind, despite the fact that she had heard Penvale, Audley, Violet, and most of his other friends address him as such for years. But she supposed it was past time she started using it—after all, *he* used *her* Christian name.

Not, of course, that she had given him leave to do so. She wasn't sure when she'd grown accustomed to hearing him call her Diana rather than Lady Templeton, but she found she rather liked it—he had always said her title with just a touch of laughter in his voice, too faint for her to object aloud but present nonetheless.

It was one of the countless things about him that made him easily the most frustrating man of her acquaintance. Or, she was quite sure, of *anyone's* acquaintance.

She raised her cup to her lips only to find that it was empty—she had finished her chocolate without realizing it. Blinking down at the tray on her lap, she realized that she had eaten all of her toast, too. This was truly a worrisome sign—no matter how perturbed her mental state, Diana prided herself on being able to enjoy her meals. She sighed again and rang for Toogood. There was no avoiding it: she would have to go downstairs for breakfast.

By the time she arrived downstairs, it was late enough that much of the party had already breakfasted, leaving only a few stragglers behind. Jeremy, mercifully, was not one of them; Emily, however, was—and, more interestingly, so was Lord Julian Belfry. They were sitting next to each other at one end of the table, several chairs removed from their closest breakfast companion, and though both were silent and appeared rather dedicated to the food before them, Diana had the distinct impression that the air around them was vibrating with some sort of tension, indicating words either recently or soon to be spoken. For the sake of her own nosiness, she hoped it was the latter.

Being the shameless creature that she was, Diana loaded up her plate at the sideboard and dropped into the seat directly next to Emily. Smiling at both of them—it was difficult to say who looked less comfortable—she lifted the teapot and said brightly, "Tea?"

Belfry shook his head jerkily and gave a sort of grunt that Diana supposed she was meant to interpret in the negative; it was a far cry from his normally urbane conversation. Emily, however, gave a half-hearted smile and a nod.

"And how are *you* this morning, Lord Julian?" Diana asked as she refilled Emily's cup.

"Quite well, thank you," came the stiff reply.

"Sleep well?" she asked innocently. His appearance indicated quite the opposite—the circles under his eyes rivaled Emily's, and she had the distinct impression that, were he not bound by the manners of good society that constrained them all, he would have taken great pleasure in telling her to bugger off.

Which was another insult she had picked up from her brother, incidentally. He had proved distressingly unforthcoming when pressed to actually define the word *bugger*; that, however, was what books were for.

"I feel that I should be asking you that question, Lady Templeton," Belfry replied mildly, and Diana arched a brow, one worthy opponent acknowledging another.

"You are too kind, sir," she said, her tone indicating that she felt just the opposite. "I myself passed quite a restful evening."

"Indeed? How . . . unexpected."

"And why should it be?" She smiled sweetly at him, daring him to state outright what he was implying. Any other man of the *ton* would have backed down at this point, unless he were an utter blackguard— she was a lady, after all, and it was beyond the pale to accuse her of loose behavior to her face. Behind her back, of course, was an entirely different matter, as more than one unfortunate lady had cause to know. But to make such an accusation directly . . . no. It would be entirely unseemly.

She had forgotten, of course, that the usual rules of the *ton* did not apply when one was conversing with a man who had been disinherited by his father and operated a scandalous theater in Piccadilly.

"I just thought you might have had . . . company." His eyes were dancing with laughter, and while coming from any other man, the intimation would have offended Diana, she somehow found it entertaining rather than off-putting coming from Belfry. Possibly because she knew that, in truth, he had little regard for the rules of polite society—he was just trying to get a rise out of her.

Unfortunately for him, while he was skilled, he had not yet reached Jeremy's level of mastery, and she was unfazed.

"My maid is not terribly attentive," she said, deliberately misunderstanding him.

"Ah," he murmured, "what a shame. You must have dearly missed . . . her company."

"Oh, for heaven's sake," Emily muttered, setting down her teacup with a clatter. "My lord, surely even you cannot think this is acceptable breakfast-table conversation."

The instant Emily spoke, Belfry's gaze sharpened on her with such intense focus that Diana marveled that Emily's skin was not burning. Instantly, she understood that his entire conversation with her had been designed to nettle not *her*, but Emily. Now that he had achieved his aim, his attention was so entirely devoted to Emily that Diana was certain she herself could have plunged through a hole in the floor and he would scarcely have noticed.

It was all extremely interesting.

"I apologize," Belfry said to Emily in tones of such exaggerated courtesy that Diana was instantly suspicious. "Did you wish to resume our previous discussion, then?"

Emily flushed. "I didn't think we had anything left to discuss."

Belfry leaned back in his chair. "Interesting. I'd thought we were in the middle of a conversation—one I was rather eager to finish." His gaze on Emily was unwavering, his blue eyes sharp. He was an exceptionally handsome man, Diana thought—not for the first time or, if he continued to make himself a constant presence in Emily's life, the last.

"I don't think you understand what you're suggesting," Emily said, so quietly that Diana was forced to abandon all dignity whatsoever and lean sideways in her chair to better hear her friend.

"I rather believe I do," Belfry said in an undertone. His gaze flicked to Diana, who did not even attempt to feign disinterest. "I've told you more than once, I know things about Cartham that could prove most inconvenient if they were brought to light, and—"

Whatever else he had to say was drowned out by the sound of Jeremy's voice—he had entered the room without Diana noticing and, at the moment, given the conversation he'd just interrupted, she could have cheerfully murdered him.

"Ah, there you are," he said, although, since he was addressing the table at large, she couldn't be entirely certain that his gaze had lingered on her for a second longer than was necessary. "We are gathering in the drawing room to begin a game of hide-and-seek—would you care to join in?"

"Really, Jeremy," drawled Lord Monmouth, one of Jeremy's university friends seated at the opposite end of the table, "have we reverted to childhood? I don't think I've played hide-and-seek since I was in leading strings."

"Audley suggested it," Jeremy said, unbothered. "Though if you ask me, it was more an excuse to hole up with his wife in some cozy corner than anything else. . . ."

The prospect of finding a lady in a similar private hiding spot was apparently enticing enough to forestall any further complaint, as everyone finished their breakfast in short order and reconvened in the blue drawing room. Belfry had fallen silent upon Jeremy's interruption, and Emily took the opportunity to engage Diana in a spirited discussion on the virtues of poached eggs, a topic Diana had never heard her friend—or anyone else—discuss with such fervor. Belfry watched her with an amused gleam in his eye that Diana thought did not bode well for Emily's attempts to forestall their aborted conversation for very long.

Diana herself pondered escaping back to her room for her sketchbook and sequestering herself somewhere for a morning of drawing instead—Jeremy had a lovely gallery with several impressive sculptures in it, she recalled, and it had been quite awhile since she'd last done any drawings of the human form. Emily, however, cast an expectant look at her—was she afraid of being left alone in Belfry's company? With a mental sigh, Diana followed her along the winding hallways of Elderwild until she reached the drawing room—or, rather, one of them. If she recalled correctly, the house had five.

Audley was standing in the center of the room, looking as excited about the prospect of hiding himself in a linen cupboard as any small boy; his cheeks were flushed, and his usually vaguely distant manner was entirely absent as he explained the rules.

" . . . gentlemen have drawn straws and Rothsmere is the lucky—or unlucky—man who shall begin the search. He will close his eyes and count to one hundred before beginning, and each person he finds will join him in the quest to hunt down all the others. The last person to be discovered is, of course, the victor."

He rubbed his hands in anticipation; for a moment, he looked no older than he had done the first time Diana had met him, on some school holiday or another, when he was seventeen or so. It was strangely endearing; she had spent the past several years viewing Audley with vague suspicion, since he and Violet had been estranged and she'd had no knowledge of the nature of the argument that had caused their split. Now that he and Violet were reconciled, it was rather nice to be able to look at him and see only the school friend of her brother, overly interested in mathematics and with no notion of how handsome he was.

Not that tall and dark had ever been her preference. It seemed, unfortunately, that she had a weakness for blond hair instead.

"Shall we begin?" asked the golden-haired source of all her present problems. Jeremy looked no worse the wear for the late evening; no trace of the concern that had marked his features the night before was visible, and he was his usual carefree self. Diana had never previously thought of his typical demeanor as a mask, and yet now she wondered—he could not be as blithe as he seemed. The man who had visited her room the night before had certainly not been. It made her wonder what else she had overlooked about him over the years.

For so long, bickering with Jeremy had been something of a habit—comforting, almost, in its familiarity. She had always found him to be rather . . . unserious. This was not a complaint she tended to level against gentlemen as a rule, but something about Jeremy's manner had always irked her. He was too handsome, too charming, too flirtatious—she didn't trust him, not one bit. But it had taken only a couple of days for her to begin revising that opinion of him, and the idea that there might be more to him than she had thought was more intriguing than she cared to admit. She didn't like the newfound fascination he held for her, and she felt certain nothing good could come of it—it made her feel powerless, and that was something she refused to be. Ever.

She would simply have to remain focused on the task at hand: seeing Willingham married off, posthaste.

The guests scattered as Rothsmere began to count, his hand held theatrically before his eyes. Diana contemplated remaining in the room for a moment, thinking that Rothsmere might rush out so quickly once he finished counting that he wouldn't search it thoroughly, but she saw Langely eyeing one of the shadowy corners of the room and realized that her idea had already been taken. Instead, she went out into the corridor, turning in the opposite direction of the majority of the crowd at each corner until, after a few minutes, she was entirely alone. She knew that Rothsmere must have finished counting by now, but also found it unlikely that he was moving terribly quickly, so she took her time, wandering into and out of several rooms before finally finding a place that suited her needs.

She had never stumbled across this room on her previous visits to Elderwild. This didn't surprise her—she'd taken quite a meandering path to discover it this time, and was not at all certain that she'd be able to find her way back to the drawing room without getting lost along the way. She had discovered a small sitting room, tucked away in a corner of the manor—the windows lining two walls instead of one informed her of this much, at least. Rich blue wallpaper covered the walls, cheerful against the gray day visible outside the windows, and she imagined it would look equally welcoming on a sunny or snowy day. It was full of second-best furniture, which was, of course, the very best sort—not so new or fancy as to be uncomfortable, the perfect amount of worn in. A window seat was set into one of the bay windows, and low bookshelves lined the walls underneath the windows on either side of the seat.

She knew in an instant that someone had loved this room very much—everything about it, from the wallpaper to the eclectic collection of artwork on the walls to the cracked spines on nearly every book on the shelves, told her that this had been someone's retreat. Someone's hideaway. Someone's safe place.

However, it also had a disused feeling about it—Jeremy's servants were quite diligent, so every surface was dusted and the furniture hadn't been covered in sheets, as it so often was in unused rooms in country houses. But the air felt still and stuffy, as though the sound of laughter and conversation had not echoed within these walls for a very long time. She could not explain how she knew this, but her awareness gave her an odd pang of melancholy.

However, the room made a perfect hiding place. She scanned her surroundings, hands on hips, trying to decide where someone would be least likely to look. Her eyes landed on the drapes at the window seat. At the moment they were open, but they could be drawn to hide the seat from view, and the gloomy weather outside would ensure that her silhouette would not be visible. It was perfect.

She crossed the room and sat on the window seat, tucking her feet up beneath her, and pulled the drapes closed. She stared out the window at the rain beating against the glass, and at the smudged landscape behind it, the rain making the rolling green hills and woods look blurry and indistinct. She was just wishing that she had gone back to her room to fetch her sketchbook when she stiffened at the distinct sound of footsteps.

How was it possible? There was no way Rothsmere could have found her so quickly, and she was certain that no one in the group had followed her. The footsteps did not proceed with the halting progress indicating that their maker was searching for people in hiding. Instead, they were purposeful, growing louder every second. There was, she realized in a flash, only one person who would move through such a remote corner of the house with such deliberate intent; equally unfortunately, she knew, there was nothing she could do to escape him.

The footsteps halted for a moment, as the person to whom they belonged no doubt took in the drapes closed across the window seat. They resumed a moment later, now muffled by the rug, and Diana closed her eyes and sighed as they came to a halt directly before her.

A moment later, the drapes were twitched back, and she opened her eyes to find Jeremy staring at her, his expression a cross between amused and disgruntled.

"I suppose," he said after a moment's silence, "it would be too much to ask that you not poach the best hiding spot in the entire house."

Diana scoffed. "I find that hard to believe. There must be some cupboard in the kitchen or eerie attic corner that would serve much better."

"I stand corrected," he said, sweeping a gallant bow. "The best hiding spot in the house for those of us who are somewhat lazy."

Diana's mouth quirked. "I suppose I should take offense at that, but I find I haven't the energy." She made no move to remove herself from her present position. "Did you need help finding somewhere else to hide?"

"This is *my* house," Jeremy pointed out. "I think according to any notion of private property, I have the right to select where I wish to hide within it."

"It's this sort of attitude," Diana said primly, "that is going to lead to revolution, you know."

"Why, Diana Templeton," he said, placing a hand to his heart, "I never would have taken you for a revolutionary. Will you be handing out pamphlets next?"

"I wouldn't be surprised if you drove me to it," she said sweetly. "The thought of a guillotine on your lawn does hold a certain appeal."

He laughed at that, and Diana could not help but join in. The joke was undoubtedly in poor taste, given how recently English soldiers had spilled their blood to defeat Napoleon, and yet it was a relief to laugh with someone who shared her inappropriate sense of humor. Who did not chide her when she made an off-color joke, or expect her to be better and more ladylike than she actually was.

His laughter died after a moment, and he nudged her with his knee. "Move over," he ordered, without a hint of the solicitousness any other gentleman would have employed with a lady whose bed he was hoping to visit. "If you won't yield this hiding spot to its rightful owner, I shall have to join you."

Diana knew, to the core of her being, that sharing a cozy, cushioned window seat on a rainy day with the Marquess of Willingham and his charming smile could only lead to trouble—and yet, she was already moving, scooting to the side so that he could fold himself up on the cushion next to her, twitching the drapes closed once again.

He looked considerably less comfortable than she did, which was unsurprising given that he had an advantage of approximately six inches of height on her—rather than tucking his legs underneath his body, as she had done, he folded his knees up to his chest, wrapping his arms around them.

"How cozy," she said dryly. He cast her a withering look. "If you are uncomfortable, my lord, I'm certain this old pile has a number of other corners in which you might hide." She batted her eyelashes.

He scowled. "I'll have you know, this window seat is perfectly comfortable when only occupied by one person."

She smiled flirtatiously, because she seemed unable to help herself when she was in his presence. "I'd imagine there's a way for it to be perfectly comfortable for two as well."

He arched a brow. "Was that an invitation?"

"I think not."

They lapsed into silence for a moment; for her part, Diana felt the weight of the previous evening upon her, and could not help wondering if he was thinking of it, too.

"What is this room?" she asked, partly to break the silence and partly out of genuine curiosity. She leaned her head back against the cool glass of the window.

"A sitting room," Jeremy said at once, and she rolled her eyes, waving a hand in wordless indication that he should elaborate. He was silent for long enough that she cut a curious sideways glance at him. He was frowning slightly, staring with unusual intensity at the heavy fabric of the drapes that shielded them from view, creating their own private corner, hidden away from the rest of the world. His handsome face held none of its usual bored amusement, and there was a faint line between his brows. It smoothed after a moment, but she noticed a crease that remained even after the frown had vanished, indicating that such an expression was not uncommon on his face. And yet, Diana had rarely ever seen him frown. Was this another of his private faces, then?

"It was my mother's favorite sitting room," he said at last, and Diana, without thinking, reached out to place a hand on his knee. He glanced down as she did so, and she nearly snatched her hand back again, but some vein of—courage? Stubbornness?—within her prevented her from doing so. After another moment, he continued speaking. "She designed everything about this room—chose the wallpaper and which artwork should be displayed. Which furniture would be in here—much of it from her own childhood home. Every single book on these shelves was one that she had read and enjoyed, often many times before. She was a great reader, apparently," he added softly.

"She died when you were quite young?" Diana asked—she knew the marchioness had caught a chill and fever one winter and never recovered, but she'd never heard Willingham discuss his mother before.

"When I was six," he confirmed. "I can't remember her very well—I don't think she and my father were terribly happy in their marriage, but my memories of her with David and me always involve laughter." Diana thought that that was a lovely way to be remembered—she'd been so young when her own parents died that she barely remembered them at all, though she did have one vague memory of crying over a skinned knee and being pressed in a warm embrace.

"Does anyone use the room now?" she asked, seeking to distract herself from her melancholy thoughts. "It's perfectly maintained, but it feels . . . abandoned," she said, for lack of a better word, still unable to explain the feeling the room gave her.

"No," he said, still in that soft, serious voice so unlike his usual laughter-filled tone. "My father had everything covered in sheets after my mother died—said there was no point in paying servants to clean a room no one used." His tone was mild, but Diana could hear the bitterness underneath. "My brother had it opened back up again, after my father's death," he continued. "He never used it, I don't think, but he had servants come in and clean, made sure everything was in immaculate condition, should it ever be wanted. I've often wondered if he was preserving it for his wife."

Diana held her breath, scarcely daring to breathe, lest she break this spell. After their conversation the previous night, she didn't want to push him too much on the subject of his brother, but she found herself curious.

"Did your brother have an . . . attachment, then?" she asked hesitantly. She had never heard the previous Marquess of Willingham's name mentioned in connection with any lady in particular, unlike that of West, whose aborted courtship of Sophie she assumed to be another casualty of that blasted curricle accident.

"Not that I'm aware of, no," Jeremy said with a shrug. "He had a mistress at the time of his death—I know, because I paid her off rather handsomely once he died. He hadn't thought to make any provision for her himself, of course—he was only twenty-four. Why would he think about dying?" There was a faint note of bitterness to the words.

Diana decided to press her luck. "When you speak of your brother, you seem . . . angry," she said hesitantly, after trying and failing to come up with a better adjective.

Jeremy recoiled as if he'd been physically struck. "I'm not angry," he said, an unmistakable note of defensiveness in his voice. "It's hardly his fault that he died."

"No one forced him to get in that curricle that day," Diana said, and nearly wished the words unsaid a moment later, when something raw and dark flashed through his eyes. "I don't mean to say that you *blame* him, just—"

"In any case," Jeremy said loudly, drowning her out entirely, "I think it was more of a hypothetical future wife who might use the room." Diana opened her mouth, then closed it again; if he didn't wish to discuss this subject, who was she to press him on the matter? After a moment, seeing that she was going to allow him to return to the original subject of conversation, he gave her a crooked sideways grin that almost, *almost* fooled her into forgetting the pained expression on his face moments before. "Gentlemen aren't opposed to the idea of wives in *theory*, you see. Just so long as the theoretical wife never seems any closer than a decade in the future."

"Does that mean, *theoretically*, that had I extended the time frame of my wager with you, you might not have been so quick to take it?"

"My dear Lady Templeton," he said, "since spiting you is one of my life's great pleasures, you could have bet me that I'd be married within the next *twenty* years and I'd still have remained a bachelor, just for the satisfaction of thwarting you."

She narrowed her eyes at him. "You're a marquess, you know," she said. "You *will* need to sire heirs at some point."

He widened his eyes in mock horror. "Are you implying that, at the ripe old age of eight-and-forty, I will be unable to, shall we say, rise to the occasion? I might as well kill myself now, if that's the fate that awaits me."

"You are quite insufferable—you are aware of that?" she said conversationally.

"So I've been told, many times," he said, unruffled. "Most of them by you, though, so perhaps I should seek a wider sample of opinions."

"You do that," she said placidly. "I'll just wait right here."

"On second thought," he said, shifting with a slight wince—his current seating position could not be terribly comfortable—"I'm not sure I trust my knees to hold my weight at the moment, so perhaps I won't."

Diana didn't know what it was that possessed her in that moment—some madness inspired, no doubt, by the slight dimple in his right cheek, or the way, in his current position, his jacket stretched very appealingly over his broad shoulders. Or perhaps, most likely of all, it had been that faint crease between his eyebrows that she had never noticed before, and the ragged note in his voice when he spoke of his brother. Regardless of what caused it, the fact was that Diana took momentary leave of her senses and said, "You can make yourself more comfortable, you know."

He quirked a brow at her yet again, all seductive innuendo. "Is that so?"

She rolled her eyes. "Not like *that*. But if you should like to use my lap so that you might stretch out more comfortably, you are welcome to." When she issued this invitation, she had a mental image of him toeing off his boots and resting his feet in her lap, which, while certainly inappropriate, was rather lacking in romantic charm.

He, however, had other ideas. "Better yet," he said, and there was a light gleaming in his eyes that she didn't like one bit, "why don't we use *my* lap?"

Diana opened her mouth—to issue some cutting set-down, she assured herself—but before she could speak, in a sudden flurry of movement, Jeremy dropped his knees, seized her waist, and lifted her bodily onto his lap.

There were a few moments of adjustment as Jeremy got all of his limbs comfortably situated—he turned his back to rest against the curve of the window and stretched his legs out fully on the seat before him—as, all the while, Diana trembled with indignation atop him.

Only with indignation, she reminded herself firmly, though she was not certain she had been entirely convincing.

"That was not precisely what I had in mind," she said stiffly, alarmed to discover that the most comfortable posture in this new seating arrangement involved her reclining against his chest. She fought the temptation, keeping her spine uncomfortably straight, even as something deep within her urged her to sink back against him.

"And yet look how nicely it serves us," he said, his voice lazy and seductive and amused. An arm snaked around her waist, and she stiffened further. "Relax," he murmured in her ear. "You're supposed to *enjoy* my touch, remember?"

"I believe that *that* is entirely up to you," she replied, but she abandoned her resistance and sank back against him. The solid warmth of his chest against her back was surprisingly comforting, and she racked her brain for a moment, trying to think if a man had ever held her so. She thought not.

"How right you are," he said, his mouth still perilously close to her ear, and a moment later she felt the warmth of his lips against the side of her neck, tracing a path from the underside of her jaw down to her collarbone. Her traitorous body responded immediately, of course; her breath quickened as her heart began to pound more rapidly in her chest, and she hoped that he was too occupied with the task at hand—which currently involved placing a lingering kiss at the spot where her neck met her shoulder—to notice. His hands were tucked snugly around her waist, keeping her pressed tight against him, and his hair tickled under her chin where his head was bent. She used her last passing moment of lucidity to wonder if he was going to get a crick in his neck from keeping it at such an angle for so long. At that moment, however, one of his hands slid upward to cup the heavy weight of her breast, and all intelligent thought abandoned her.

She reached her hand up to cradle the back of his head, twisting her head and drawing his mouth up to meet hers in a hot, open-mouthed kiss. His tongue twined with hers, and suddenly her body was awash in sensation from the base of her stomach, where a fire was slowly building, to the delicate place between her legs, where her pulse was pounding. She broke away with a gasp, attempting to turn so that she could kiss him properly, but he pressed her back against him more firmly, preventing her from moving.

"Willingham—" she said breathlessly.

"What did we discuss about your use of my name?" There was a teasing note in his voice, as ever, but she was pleased to hear the ragged edge of his breathing.

"Jeremy," she said from between gritted teeth, but he silenced her with another kiss. She was so consumed by the heat of his mouth and the warmth of his hand at her breast that at first she didn't notice the downward progress his free hand was making as it inched south, working its way between the layers of skirt and petticoat that shielded her skin from view. She closed her eyes again with a moan at the first kiss of cool air upon her ankle, then moaned again as his warm hand slid up, up along her thigh, growing closer to where she needed him so desperately.

She drew his tongue into her mouth and sucked just as his hand slid between her thighs—

And then, suddenly, everything ceased to be quite so lovely.

It wasn't that Jeremy was doing anything precisely *wrong*, of course—he had his hand in the right general area, and even seemed to know which specific portion of her anatomy was most desirous of his attention. Diana had limited experience in this regard, but she understood from other ladies that even this was something of an achievement. His technique, unfortunately, left something to be desired. He was simultaneously moving too fast with one finger and too slowly with another, leaving nothing in his wake so much as a general feeling of frustration.

And while some frustration, of course, heightened the anticipation in these circumstances, Diana thought she had had quite enough anticipation. She was ready for—well, for something she had never experienced with a man before, given that her late husband had been a rather unenthusiastic lover.

Men were confused creatures, and they undoubtedly lacked the capacity to think clearly in these circumstances. Perhaps Jeremy simply needed a bit of silent encouragement.

She tilted her hips upward, trying to force him into a rhythm that was more comfortable for her. He, however, seemed to take her motion as endorsement of his efforts, with the effect being his redoubling of them, to her continued dissatisfaction.

Drat. She was starting to lose some of the lovely, lust-induced fuzziness in her mind. Even his kisses—distracting as they were— were losing their power, as her attention focused on a more southern part of her anatomy.

At last, deciding that the time had really come for action, she broke the kiss, raising her hand to forestall another. She panted for a moment, and felt him breathing heavily behind her. His hand below had, mercifully, stilled, and she decided that this was a perfect opportunity for an instructive moment. Because while Diana might not have had as much practical experience as she might have wished by this point in her life, she had done her best to make up for it with avid—perhaps excessive—reading.

About this topic alone, of course. Heaven forbid anyone ever accuse her of being a bluestocking.

"Something wrong?" Jeremy asked as she pondered how precisely to begin. The lazy, seductive note in his voice was a clear indication that he expected a reply in the negative.

He therefore immediately stiffened when she said, "Since you mention it, yes."

His hand was absent from beneath her skirts so quickly that she might have thought she'd imagined its presence there in the first place, and he made no move to stop her this time as she shifted forward slightly on the window seat so that she could turn to face him.

"That was . . . pleasant," she said, searching for an inoffensive word. Judging by the appalled look on his face, she hadn't quite hit the mark.

"*Pleasant?*" he sputtered.

"Now, Jeremy, don't react like this," she began, belatedly realizing as she spoke that employing the tones of a nanny scolding her young charge might not be the wisest tactic. "I've no complaints with the kissing, you see," she added, stumbling over her words in an attempt to mollify him. "But . . . well . . . we might need to work on the other bits."

"Other bits?" He leaned back against the window, crossing his arms over his chest. His cheeks were slightly flushed, though she couldn't tell if that was a result of their kisses or this conversation.

"The bits that came after," she hedged.

"And which bits would those be, precisely?" He fixed her with a look of polite inquiry. Damn the man, he was going to make her say it.

"The part with your hand under my skirts," she said, brazening it out. She willed herself not to blush—she was not prone to blushing as a rule, but even ladies with unusual amounts of sangfroid had their limits.

"And what, precisely, was your complaint?"

Diana realized, perilously close to hysterical laughter, that she had possibly never heard him speak so formally to her, which was amusing, given the subject matter at hand.

"You didn't have quite the right . . . rhythm," she said, having searched for and located the most appropriate word.

His brow furrowed. "How so?"

"It was . . . well, too slow in one bit and too fast in another."

"You're not making any sense at all!"

Diana threw her hands up. "I don't know how else to explain it, barring producing a medical text and beginning to throw all sorts of Latin words about!" She sighed. "You have to . . . well, you have to pay attention."

Jeremy's look of confusion would have been maddening had it not been so obviously sincere. Or perhaps its sincerity made it all the more enraging? "I don't understand how I could possibly be paying you any more attention than I was at that moment, with my tongue in your mouth and my hand between your legs."

Diana didn't break eye contact with him, knowing that he was deliberately trying to embarrass her. And, damn it, she was a widow, albeit a distressingly uninformed one, not to mention one of the most notorious flirts in the *ton*. She would not be cowed by this . . . this . . .

"Strumpet."

She didn't realize she'd said the word aloud until both of Jeremy's eyebrows shot so high toward his hairline that they were in danger of vanishing entirely.

"Did you just call me a strumpet?"

"I didn't mean to say it aloud," Diana said with as much dignity as she could muster, "but yes. Only a strumpet speaks the way you just did."

Jeremy's shoulders were shaking with barely suppressed mirth.

"I've been called worse, I suppose," he said, laughter evident in his voice as well.

"I don't doubt that," she said acerbically.

"You do realize some people enjoy a bit of lewd banter in the bedroom, don't you?" he asked conversationally.

"I'm sure they do," she said, lifting her chin. "But you won't have the opportunity to engage in any if we don't sort out our current issue."

"Ah, yes," Jeremy said, his mouth flattening into a line. "My . . . *rhythm.*" Something about the way he said the word instantly raised Diana's hackles; it wasn't precisely sarcastic, but his tone implied that she was the one being unreasonable, and that he, the man nobly suffering her whims, was exchanging weary winks with an unseen audience.

"Need I remind you that this was *your* idea in the first place?" she asked coldly, keeping as tight a leash on her anger as possible. "*You* are the one who received a complaint from a lady, and so *you* came to *me* to ask for my help in the matter. I don't know why I'm surprised, though—if a gentleman's response to hearing his bedroom performance critiqued is to instantly take up with someone new in the hopes of receiving a more favorable review, I shouldn't have expected him to respond well to honest criticism."

"I feel like I'm back at school again, about to be sent down for poor marks." There was no heat in his voice, however, a fact Diana noted with relief.

"You're the one who came to me as if you were proposing a business partnership," she shot back. "You can't complain about the tone when you set it."

"Touché," was all he said before waving a hand expansively to indicate that she should continue.

Diana, never one to waste a perfectly good opportunity to opine at length before a captive audience, continued. "The trouble with gentlemen," she began, ignoring what she was fairly certain was a barely stifled groan from Jeremy, "is that they are too used to getting their own way." She crossed her legs underneath her like a child, the last lingering hints of desire from their unfulfilling interlude driven away. Who could worry about kisses when there was a man to educate?

"You don't pay attention to ladies, because you've never had to." Jeremy opened his mouth, and she forestalled his objection. "And before you tell me that not all men behave this way, I am of course not speaking about you in particular, so you don't need to go getting yourself worked into knots about it. But the fact remains that gentlemen—and particularly wealthy, titled gentlemen—hold a disproportionate amount of power within our society, and as such are unused to having to consider the needs or wishes of anyone but themselves.

"Now, I've no doubt that you've had women falling all over themselves to tell you what a brilliant lover you are, ever since you were an inexperienced boy—and come now, Jeremy. Doesn't that tell you enough?" She was really beginning to warm to her subject now—the longer Jeremy went without interrupting her, the more confident she grew. "What are the odds that a sixteen-year-old boy can possibly be that skilled a lover? Practically nonexistent. But I've no doubt she was a milkmaid or a tavern wench or involved in some such similarly rustic profession, and she was leaping at the chance to involve herself with the son of a marquess."

Jeremy cleared his throat. "Seventeen."

Diana paused, her next thought forgotten. "I beg your pardon?"

"I was seventeen, not sixteen, the first time I went to bed with someone."

Diana raised an eyebrow. "Well, I must give you credit, Jeremy. That displays a degree of restraint I did not think you capable of."

"My father set a rather appalling example when it came to womanizing," Jeremy said, his voice uncharacteristically even, his eyes never leaving hers. "And whilst I have certainly had my share of conquests, as you are well aware, I did strive to keep myself at a level of conduct at least somewhat elevated above his. The number of maids dismissed from our house when I was a boy because they were with child—with *his* child, you understand—numbers at eleven, and I thought that, at the very least, I could behave in a slightly more admirable fashion. So I did indeed refrain until I was the lofty age of seventeen, and the lady I selected was a widow in town. She was, as you correctly surmised, not of an equal social station to my own, but she was not a virgin milkmaid, and she was very . . . kind."

She had the distinct impression that he had been searching for another word entirely—he looked faintly surprised, as though that had not been what he intended to say at all. Diana, however, was stuck on something else he had said.

"How do you know it was eleven?"

His brow furrowed as he failed for a moment to take her meaning.

"Eleven housemaids," she clarified. "How can you possibly know the number with such certainty? Surely this began when you were a very small child—or even before you were born. How can you know the number so precisely?"

Jeremy shrugged, displaying a nonchalance that did not fool Diana for one instant, despite the strange feeling she had that it might have fooled just about anyone else. "It was a guess."

"No, it wasn't," Diana said firmly. "It was not at all a guess." She eyed him for a moment—he was avoiding her gaze in that clever way that made it look like he wasn't; he was looking in her general direction without quite meeting her eyes. A sneaking suspicion began to snake through her, growing stronger with each passing second.

"You found them all." She didn't phrase it as a question, because the moment she spoke, she somehow knew that that was precisely what he had done. Something within her clenched at the thought.

"I might have done," he said softly, still not quite meeting her eyes. The weak gray light from outdoors made his eyes appear a lighter shade of blue than normal as he gazed at some point just past her ear, his jaw tight. "It was after David died that I learned of their existence. I was going through my father's papers—David had started doing it, but he wasn't marquess for very long, and he hadn't finished the job. I found letters from a couple of the women, begging for assistance— letters I assume my father ignored," he added, and Diana noted that he made no effort to keep the bitterness from his voice. Not that she could blame him, of course, but it still surprised her. Even now, even as she had come to realize that the charming, shallow Marquess of Willing- ham was only the very surface of Jeremy, she still had moments where she was surprised by her glimpses of the man underneath—one with a history of pain and anger that he could never allow to creep across the surface of his always-amused facade.

"I offered my financial support to both the women and the chil- dren," he added, still looking rather uncomfortable with this entire line of discussion. "Not much at first, given what dire financial straits the estate was in, but I've been able to increase it in the years since."

"Jeremy," she said, and waited until he had made eye contact with her—*proper* eye contact. There was something embarrassed and self-effacing in his expression, and she knew that she needed to choose her next words carefully. They were not used to being gentle with each other, after all. "Why are you acting as though you did something to be ashamed of? It was the height of honor."

"No," he said, just as quietly but with a core of steel underlying the word. "I did what any responsible man would have done in my shoes. I did what my father should have done years ago—but he didn't do it, of course, so I did. My brother didn't do it, either—he was only marquess for a year, but—"

He cut himself off abruptly and looked away from her again, making an awkward sort of shifting gesture from his shoulders all the way down to his hips that was striking for its unfamiliarity—he was many things, but never awkward. "Weren't we supposed to be discussing my lovemaking technique? I can't imagine how we strayed so far from the topic at hand."

Diana gave him a long, considering look. "This must be a remarkably uncomfortable subject for you if you'd rather discuss your shortcomings in the boudoir."

"I beg your pardon, madam, but when I attended you in your boudoir, I do not recall hearing any complaints."

Diana rolled her eyes. "Yes, well, we did not make it very far in the proceedings on that occasion."

He arched an eyebrow. "As opposed to today? I daresay I had not quite achieved my aim before being rather forcefully interrupted."

"Because I had—notes!" she burst out. "I had notes!"

"This is rather like a conversation with my secretary," Jeremy murmured. "Though, mercifully, he has never offered me any notes on this particular matter."

"Willingham," Diana said between clenched teeth, "if you continue to speak, I am going to stab you with a hairpin." She found it frankly astonishing that she had felt uncharacteristically tender toward the man only a moment before. "Now, as I was saying several minutes ago before we were sidetracked, you are not accustomed to considering the needs of the women you go to bed with. As a marquess, you likely hear nothing but panting and exaggerated moans and then heaps of lavish praise regarding your shoulder muscles."

"You've noticed my shoulder muscles, then?" Jeremy asked, preening a bit.

Diana saw no point in denying this when, after all, some things were simple fact. "They are . . . admirable," she said grudgingly.

Jeremy grinned. "I can feel my head swelling already. Although," he added, his grin slanting into something slightly more wicked, "the resentful tone *did* prove effective at preventing certain other portions of the anatomy from swelling."

Diana decided that, under the circumstances, her only option was to ignore that particular bit of commentary. "In any case, I think that you need a lesson in *paying attention*. There is a world of difference between a lady who is in the throes of passion and one who is merely pretending, and it's past time you learned to spot it. Ladies also often offer subtle cues—you missed me raising my hips to attempt to direct you earlier, and that was a fatal mistake. Next time I'll expect you to pay closer attention."

"Ah, so I am to be granted another chance?" Diana was irritated to note that his voice still held a trace of amusement.

"You are," she said briskly, lowering her knees and stretching her feet out so that they peeked beneath the underside of the curtains that hid them. "But if you don't learn to take your time and notice when I am clearly not enjoying myself, I don't think it will end any better than this interlude." She could feel herself growing agitated again as she spoke, and inhaled deeply. "In any case, now is hardly the moment to continue. We've been tucked away here for quite a while—surely we must be on the verge of being discovered."

As though her words had summoned them, the sounds of voices in animated discussion suddenly became audible—Diana wondered if she and Jeremy had simply been so wrapped up in their conversation that neither of them had noticed. She detected Rothsmere's voice, of course, but also distinctly heard those of her brother, Emily, and Belfry as well.

She hastily shuffled as far to the right as space would allow, hugging herself into the curve of the window and pulling the curtains around her, leaving Jeremy exposed just a moment before the group rounded a corner and entered the room.

"Not much of a hiding spot if you're in plain sight, Jeremy," Penvale said amiably, to the sound of collective laughter.

"And yet I still remained hidden longer than you did," Jeremy replied. Diana heard him stand and join the group. Exchanging barbs with his friends, he left the room without revealing Diana's hiding spot, which she thought quite decent of him—she might be a widow and therefore granted more leniency by the rigid rules of society, but being found tucked cozily in a window seat with a gentleman would still be taking things a bit far.

She waited for the sounds of their voices to fade a bit before getting up—she would follow them down the hallway and then hail them, pretending that they had overlooked her in some alcove or another, professing her boredom with the game. Which was true enough, she supposed—she found parlor games a trifle tiresome at times. But nothing about the past half hour had been tiresome. It had been maddening and passionate and, unexpectedly, enlightening—she felt as though she had learned something about Jeremy that he would rather she hadn't, and she felt a bit giddy with the power. But beyond that she also felt sad—for this man who was torn between his fear of becoming his father and his own expectations that he would never manage to do much else. For his determination to live down to those expectations, in the wake of his brother's death. For the complicated mixture of emotions he still held for his brother, and the circumstances of his death—grief, yes, and yet also something sharper-edged, angry and raw.

Something within Diana told her that Jeremy would need to come to terms with this on his own. And yet, equally strong was another feeling within her—one that made her want to turn toward him, take his hand, and walk with him down that path. And it was this feeling that gave her the first signal that she might be in trouble.

Sixteen

Diana retired to her bedroom soon after dinner, pleading exhaus-
tion, but sleep did not come easily to her that evening. Jeremy had
given her an inquisitive look as she'd taken her leave of the group,
but she'd merely shaken her head at him and given him a smile that
did nothing to erase the worried crease between his eyebrows. She'd
passed a solitary evening in her room, reading and sketching by the
fire, but found herself unable to focus much on either book or sketch
pad, so occupied was her mind with its worries.

Or, rather, a single worry: the undeniable fact that she was growing
dangerously attached to the Marquess of Willingham.

Later, as she lay in bed, she could not stop her mind returning to
him—she had known the man for a decade, and yet somehow he had
become endlessly novel and fascinating in the past few days. It was not
just that she found herself drawn to him physically—that had been
the case for years, loath though she'd always been to admit it. It was
something much more alarming: the fact that each time they had a
lengthy, serious conversation about themselves, she was left eager for
more. He had become fascinating to her, and that was the undeniable
signal that this had gone too far.

Not that she intended to give up their affair, of course; it hadn't even properly gotten started, and she was still eager to gain some practical experience that might serve her well in the future. But her decision to encourage his grandmother's matchmaking, which she'd initially done in the interest of winning her wager with Willingham and nothing more, had suddenly become of the utmost importance. If Willingham was courting someone else, then Diana never need worry that things between them would progress beyond the physical. Which was, of course, the only sort of relationship she wanted.

But therein lay her dilemma: her conversation with Lady Helen the day before had confirmed that the lady was, unfortunately, just as odious as she appeared upon initial conversation. Jeremy was a trifle foolish, but he wasn't a complete imbecile, and Diana knew he could never be persuaded to marry someone so dreadful. But then, who remained? This house party was hardly overflowing with eligible ladies, and it was deeply unfortunate that the one currently flinging herself at Willingham was more likely to send him fleeing into someone else's arms than into her own.

But wait.

That was it, she realized all of a sudden. That was the solution. Lady Helen must behave so dreadfully that any other eligible lady looked appealing by comparison. But who? Not Diana, obviously— that was rather the entire point. Not Emily, either—she seemed to be more than occupied with Belfry at the moment. Not Sophie, of course—she'd only recently finished her liaison with Jeremy, and hardly seemed to be collapsing in despair at this outcome.

But then, why *not* Sophie? The affair had clearly ended amicably, if her presence at this house party was any indication. She was beautiful, intelligent, and all-around good company; Diana had little doubt that the affair had ended more because Willingham was allergic to any sort of commitment lasting much longer than a fortnight than for any other reason. And clever, lovely Sophie would seem extra appealing by comparison to Lady Helen Courtenay, of course.

There *was* the matter of Sophie's long-standing attachment to Audley's brother, but Diana had seen no indication from either Sophie or West that they intended to rekindle any flames between them. Well, unless one counted the occasional longing look from each party.

No, Sophie would be the perfect bride for Jeremy—and, of course, there were advantages for Sophie as well. She clearly found Jeremy attractive, and it would undoubtedly be more pleasant for her to share Jeremy's spacious London town house than to live all alone in the home she'd once shared with her late husband.

You *live alone, in* your *late husband's house*, the irritating little voice at the back of her mind that she usually did her best to ignore reminded her.

But that was different. *She* was different. She had no wish to remarry—not Jeremy, not anyone. She valued her freedom too greatly. Other ladies likely did not feel the same; surely Sophie would be different. Surely she would be receptive to Jeremy's renewing his affections.

The trick now was just making him realize he wanted to do so.

The following day dawned rainy once more, again scuttling plans for the hunt. While yesterday's parlor games had proved amusing enough, the general mood of the party seemed to be listlessness at the prospect of another day trapped indoors. Everyone rose rather late, appearing at the breakfast table in a slow trickle and then disappearing once more for largely solitary pursuits. They reconvened for a simple luncheon of cold meats and cheeses in the early afternoon, looking hopefully out the windows at the sky, which seemed to be a lighter shade of gray, even as the rain continued to fall. After the meal, several of the gentlemen retreated to the library with plans for a game of vingt-et-un and, most likely, several bottles of brandy. Sophie and West professed an intention to admire Jeremy's portrait gallery and set off arm in arm, watched with avid interest by Violet and Audley, and with an odd, frustrated expression by Diana. Violet, Diana, and Lady Emily retreated to a corner of the drawing room, their chairs drawn close together, heads bent in consultation.

"I wouldn't try to interrupt them," Audley advised from just behind Jeremy's shoulder. Jeremy turned; Audley's gaze was on his wife, an expression on his face that was a strange mixture of fondness and exasperation. It softened his sometimes stern features, and his mouth curved up slightly at one corner in a smile that Jeremy didn't understand, and was sure he wasn't meant to. Across the room, Violet looked up and met her husband's gaze; she quirked her mouth slightly and raised her eyebrows inquisitively. Something she read in Audley's expression caused her smile to broaden, and she turned her attention back to her friends with a faint smile still playing about her lips.

"I wasn't planning to," Jeremy said, in response to Audley's original warning. "Do I need to advise *you* to stop mooning?"

Audley, unruffled, gave his wife one last lingering look before turning his gaze fully on Jeremy. "If you think I'm mooning, then I'd be interested to hear what you consider what *you're* doing to be."

Jeremy narrowed his eyes. "I haven't the faintest idea what you mean."

"Of course you don't," Audley said amiably, lifting a glass of claret in a mocking salute. "You know, for someone who has blunt on the line, you don't seem to be doing a very good job of avoiding the parson's mousetrap."

"You must be joking," Jeremy said, crossing his arms over his chest, feeling vaguely like a petulant child. "In case you haven't noticed, I've been keeping a healthy distance between Rothsmere's sister and myself all day."

"Indeed," Audley agreed. "But she wasn't the lady I was referring to."

Unable to help himself, Jeremy let his eyes drift to Diana. She was speaking animatedly to Violet and Lady Emily, gesturing with one hand. Like all of her movements, the motion seemed calculated to be neither too fast and frenetic nor too lethargic. It was just lazy enough to put one in mind of other slow, languorous activities.

"You continue to prove my point," Audley murmured. With great difficulty, Jeremy tore his eyes from Diana to glare at his friend.

"You must be mad."

"You only say that because you can't see the look on your own face," Audley said with a grin. "It's practically indecent."

"That is my normal facial expression," Jeremy said.

"No," Audley said firmly. "If it were, you'd never be invited out in polite society. It's positively lecherous."

Jeremy, sensing an unproductive line of debate, redirected the conversation. "Never mind all that. I've no intention of marrying Lady Templeton—or anyone else," he added hastily.

"If you say so," Audley agreed—except that he agreed in a fashion that somehow made it sound as though he was doing just the opposite, but Jeremy couldn't work out how to call him out on this without sounding like a madman.

"I do say so," was the response he settled on, which even to his own ears sounded a bit feeble. "Even were I the marrying type—perish the thought—Lady Templeton is hardly the lady I'd set my sights upon. In case you haven't noticed, she and I don't get on. Never have."

Audley's mouth flattened into a line as he gave Jeremy a long, surveying sort of look that Jeremy didn't like one bit. "I don't know if that's exactly how I'd describe it," he said after a moment. "You two have been at each other's throats for years—since she made her debut, at least—but I've always gotten the impression that you rather enjoyed it."

Jeremy opened his mouth to reply, then shut it again. He thought back on the long years of his acquaintance with Diana, which dated back to his days at Eton; back then, the five years' difference in their ages had stretched between them like an uncrossable void. For years, he hadn't given her much thought—she was Penvale's annoying little sister, who laughed a bit too loudly and spoke a bit too boldly for her own good. However, as they'd grown older, their interactions had taken on an edge. She had begun to mock him mercilessly, and he, a young buck with a hot head, had given as good as he received.

It was in her debut Season, however, watching the calculating light in her eyes as she surveyed the gentlemen at a ball or during an outing to the theater, that the first hints of something . . . different had begun to make themselves known in his feelings for her. And how had he handled this? He, who took nothing seriously, who tried his damnedest to treat everything in his life as a joke? He'd proposed to her, half in jest—and she had shot him down, as he'd surely deserved.

And they'd barely been able to hold a polite conversation since. And yet . . . wasn't Audley right, much as it pained him to admit it? Wasn't needling Diana all part of the fun?

He realized that, as he'd been occupied by his own thoughts,

Audley had stood there in silence, awaiting his reply, a maddeningly superior expression upon his face.

"I don't know that I'd go that far," Jeremy hedged.

"I would," Audley said smugly. "You bicker with each other because you're too much alike. You see too much of yourselves in each other, which is why you can't carry on a conversation for more than ten seconds without trying to get a rise out of one another."

Jeremy sputtered. "That's ridiculous."

"Of course," Audley agreed solemnly.

"I grant you, there are some passing similarities, but I can hardly help it if she's the best-looking woman of my acquaintance, and I myself am obviously a fine specimen of masculine glory"—at this, Audley rolled his eyes so hard that Jeremy was surprised they didn't roll out of his head entirely—"and so it is only natural that you find us superficially similar."

Audley shrugged, clearly regretting having begun this conversation, and made to move past him toward the ladies. "Whatever you say, Jeremy. Do try to keep your hands off of her when Penvale's about, though—I'm not sure he'll react so benignly if he catches you in flagrante again."

Before Jeremy could object—to multiple parts of this accusation, in fact—Audley was striding toward his wife, leaning over her to murmur in her ear. Whatever he said made her color slightly, and she cast a flirtatious look up at him through her lashes. She mouthed something at him and he planted a completely inappropriate kiss upon her neck before retreating. Violet, Jeremy noticed, watched him go, and there was something about this entire exchange that caused a pang within him that was as foreign as it was unexpected. It was clearly a sign that he needed a good romp in bed—something he had been tantalizingly close to achieving the day before, until he was so rudely interrupted.

Truth be told, when he had asked Diana to . . . well, to reassure him, he'd envisioned one evening of passion, after which she'd fall into raptures at his feet, declaring him to be God's gift to womankind. The fact that this scenario was not remotely consistent with anything of the real flesh-and-blood Diana was immaterial. A man had to have his dreams.

However, after his discussion with her yesterday, he was beginning to have his doubts. Because, in truth, the assessment of him she had offered was not entirely off the mark. He *was* a marquess, after all, and before he'd become that, he'd been a marquess's son. While he made a point of not taking advantage of desperate women—nor ones who relied on him for employment—the fact still remained that there was not a woman of his acquaintance that he did not enjoy an advantage over. Even a duchess only held her title by virtue of her marriage—it was nothing she possessed in her own right.

And, without making any pretense at false modesty, Jeremy knew that he was something of a catch. It had, at some point, become a challenge to himself over the years—what had started as youthful lust and exuberance had become something more. No sooner had he finished with a woman than he'd set his eyes on the next conquest—whom could he tempt next? A duchess? A Russian princess? The latest star of the stage?

Yes, yes, and yes, for the record.

And while he made certain that the ladies fully understood their arrangement before he so much as laid a finger on them—while he compensated them handsomely for their company (even the ones who had no need for his funds were the recipients of lavish gifts)—

the fact still remained that he was one of the most powerful men in England. And they, regardless of their status, wealth, or beauty, were women.

And it was possible—just oh so slightly possible—that Diana might have a point. That he might not have been the recipient of any sort of honest opinion from the women he'd been with in the past. And while that stung his pride rather more than he wanted to admit, he would have been a fool twice over to ignore this chance to correct course.

With this thought in mind, he was half a second away from luring Diana out of the room on some invented pretext when she glanced up and, in a display of surprise that was so wide-eyed Jeremy was certain it had to be false, said in a simper, "Lady Helen! There you are!"

With a sinking feeling in the pit of his stomach that told him nothing good could come of this development, Jeremy turned. Lady Helen was indeed standing in the doorway of the drawing room, accompanied by—God preserve him—his grandmother. The dowager marchioness, unsurprisingly, had a vaguely pained expression on her face that Jeremy would have found amusing had he not been so certain that his life was going to decrease in quality quite drastically over the next thirty seconds.

"Lord Willingham!" Lady Helen said in the sort of tone that, in Jeremy's opinion, should only have been directed at puppies and children below the age of intelligent speech. "How positively delightful to see you. Your grandmother mentioned that we might order some tea and have a cozy chat in the drawing room, and I'd no notion that you'd be here as well! I thought you would have joined the other gentlemen in more ... *manly* pursuits."

"But *my* presence here is no doubt unsurprising," Audley said solemnly, with only the slightest twitch at the corner of his mouth betraying his amusement. "Manly pursuits don't really seem like something I'd be involved in, eh?"

Lady Helen produced a fan from some hidden fold of her skirts—Jeremy wasn't quite certain how she managed the trick—and fluttered it before her face as she let out a shrill giggle. "Oh, Lord James, how you do tease me! I of course knew that you would not be able to tear yourself away from the presence of your beautiful wife, as you have seemed so devoted to her of late. No one could expect you to be more than a few feet from her side, ready to spring into action should she take a chill or experience a moment of faintness."

Violet, who seemed to be trying very hard not to laugh, said, "It's true that I *have* been feeling somewhat unwell of late, James. Your presence is much appreciated." She coughed delicately into a handkerchief. Her husband seemed torn between the desire to roll his eyes and the desire to burst out laughing.

Lady Helen cast one last misty-eyed look at Violet and James, who were locked in some sort of silent conversation, and redirected her focus, alarmingly, to Jeremy.

"Lord Willingham, will you be joining us for tea?"

"Do say you will, Jeremy," his grandmother said briskly, seizing his arm in an iron grip and giving him a look that, coming from another woman, he would have characterized as . . . desperate.

Lady Helen Courtenay apparently had unanticipated skills, if she was able to provoke that reaction in the Dowager Marchioness of Willingham.

Jeremy wondered if he had underestimated Lady Helen—and if, in fact, he should be concerned.

At the moment, however, he had been left no polite option other than to say, "I would be delighted to join you ladies for tea. And Audley, too, I hope?"

"Only a fool would turn down the opportunity for a scone."

"Excellent," the dowager marchioness said, "since I requested enough food to feed a small army, assuming at least a couple of gentlemen would be present."

In short order the group had arranged themselves in the chairs before the fireplace, and before long, a pair of maids carried into the room an enormous tea service, piled high with sandwiches, scones, and enticing-looking pastries. Lady Helen extended an arm, seemingly reaching for the teapot to assume the duty of pouring, but Diana beat her to it. Jeremy wasn't certain how she managed it, since nothing about the movement seemed rushed, and yet there she was, teapot in hand, calmly pouring the first cup, while Lady Helen had to awkwardly attempt to cover her motion by reaching for a scone instead.

"Lady Helen," Diana said as she handed a cup of tea to the dowager marchioness and lifted the teapot again to pour a second cup, "have you enjoyed your stay at Elderwild thus far?"

"But of course, Lady Templeton," Lady Helen said, giving Jeremy a smile that could only accurately be classified as terrifying. "It would be impossible to not enjoy oneself when staying with a host as charming, as courteous, as entirely perfect as Lord Willingham."

Violet broke into a fit of coughing at that; Jeremy, who had become rather familiar with the sound of her cough over the course of the summer, was nearly certain that this one was designed to hide a laugh. He looked at Diana, fully expecting her to pounce upon on this opportunity to deliver him a glorious set-down, but found her with a strange expression on her face.

"How right you are, Lady Helen," Diana agreed, and Jeremy belatedly realized that the expression was supposed to be a smile. "And how fortunate for Lord Willingham that he has such charming company to entertain him."

"Lady Templeton, are you feeling at all well?" his grandmother asked; she had lifted her teacup halfway to her mouth, where it was suspended in her grasp as she looked at Diana with some degree of concern.

"Never better," Diana assured her. She turned back to Lady Helen. "Lady Helen, you must find it trying to be one of the only unmarried ladies present. How fortunate you are that our oh-so-gracious host has been so attentive to you."

Lady Helen simpered. Jeremy glowered at Diana, who merely finished pouring the final cup of tea, then lifted her own cup to him in a mock salute.

"I believe I strive to be attentive to all of my guests, Lady Templeton," Jeremy said, undoubtedly without his usual degree of charm—but then, truly, a man had his limits.

"Oh, to be sure," Diana agreed, wide-eyed. "You are all that is welcoming charity. And yet, I could not help but detect a certain extra effort on your part to ensure that Lady Helen felt comfortable." There was a barely detectable pause before the final word, but Jeremy was certain everyone in the room had noted it just as he had.

"Indeed, Jeremy, it has been most touching," his grandmother chimed in; Jeremy leveled a look of wounded betrayal upon her. It was one thing to be conspired against by the likes of Diana—she did not seem to be able to help herself in this regard, at least where he was concerned. But to be betrayed by his own flesh and blood?

"I'm not certain," his own flesh and blood continued, "that I've ever seen you pay such particular attention to a lady." She gave a merry sort of chortle as she lifted her teacup to her lips; Jeremy was quite certain that such a sound had never come out of her mouth prior to this moment.

"I was *just* thinking the same thing," Diana exclaimed, by all appearances delighted. "It was particularly striking considering it was just yesterday that Lord Willingham confessed to me his intention to take a bride!"

Mercifully, Jeremy had not yet raised his teacup to his mouth. It did clatter rather loudly in the saucer, though, as he set it down quite firmly on the side table next to his armchair. "Is that what I said, Lady Templeton?"

Diana tapped a finger against her lips contemplatively—an unfair tactic, Jeremy thought, since it brought his attention to the lips in question, which made it very difficult for him to focus on anything else at all.

"I believe, Lord Willingham, that you mentioned something about the fact that you weren't growing any younger."

Jeremy narrowed his eyes. "Of course," he said. "I recall it perfectly now. And I mentioned how of course I would need a wife who was young enough still to have plenty of breeding years ahead of her. No older than eighteen, I believe I said."

It was Diana's turn for narrowed eyes. "I seem to recall the conversation a bit differently, my lord. The bit that really stuck with me was when you mentioned your desire for a wife with a good aristocratic pedigree. An impressive lineage, you understand."

Lady Helen stiffened and gazed at them so avidly that Jeremy felt it was only a matter of time before she leaned so far forward that she toppled out of her chair entirely.

"I think I said that the most desirable trait would be that the lady be in her first Season," he said determinedly. "In fact, I cannot imagine that I ever would have said anything else."

"But don't you feel that a few Seasons give a girl a certain . . . polish? I often think that twenty is the perfect age for marriage."

"Not for this man," Jeremy said firmly. "I should like either an exceedingly young wife or a somewhat older one."

Diana's eyes were instantly wary. "Older?"

"Yes," Jeremy said slowly, thoughtfully. "Not *elderly*, of course—no offense, Grandmama," he added as an aside to the dowager marchioness.

"I would have to consider myself as belonging to that category of people in order to take offense," the dowager marchioness said placidly.

"But," Jeremy continued, as though this interruption had never happened, "just a *bit* older. A bit long in the tooth, if you will."

"Please define 'long in the tooth,' sir," Diana said.

"Oh, I don't know." Jeremy heaved a dramatic sigh, gazing off into the middle distance as though deep in thought. "Perhaps . . . three-and-twenty?"

"Surely that is a bit absurd, Jeremy," Violet said, with a worried glance at Emily, who, Jeremy belatedly realized, was the same age as Diana, and still unmarried. Lady Emily, however, seemed to be thoroughly amused by the entire conversation, much to his relief. He shot her a look that he hoped translated as apologetic, and she lifted her teacup to him merrily in return. She seemed in remarkably good spirits, and he wondered to what extent the whispered conversations he had noticed between her and Belfry were the cause of this.

"I mean no offense, Violet," Jeremy said, all innocence. "I just find older women so terribly . . . enticing. If she were previously unwed, of course. An unwed lady of a certain age has had time to gain a full understanding of herself and her preferences, and should make an admirable wife, I think, despite her advanced years. A widow, of course, would be an entirely different matter." He wasn't even certain what he was saying anymore, just that he was driven, as ever, by his relentless desire to needle Diana.

"Oh?" Jeremy nearly laughed aloud at the strangled note in Diana's voice; she seemed to be at war with herself, torn between the desire to quarrel with him on this point, and the desire to project an air of blithe unconcern.

"Indeed," he said mournfully. "Widows are so . . . headstrong. So stubborn. So stuck in their ways. I just do not think I could ever marry one."

His grandmother was watching him with an expression that he realized, too late, was one to be wary of. "I have not heard anyone suggest that you should, Jeremy," she said in a deceptively innocent tone. "Unless it is you who have been considering the possibility?"

"Not at all," Jeremy replied swiftly, sensing danger. "I just want to be certain we were all in agreement on what a disagreeable sort of species the English widow is."

Lady Helen leaned forward in her chair, even going so far as to set down her teacup so as to be able to more easily cup her mouth with both hands. "Lord Willingham," she said in a dramatic stage whisper, "have you forgotten that Lady Templeton is a widow?"

"Yes, Willingham," Diana said lazily, "how foolish of you to have forgotten that particularly salient detail. Perhaps it is your advanced years?" She paused thoughtfully. "That is, of course, why it is so imperative that you marry soon—if you wait much longer, you'll be unable to recognize your wife from one morning to the next."

"Depending on who the lady was, that might not be such a bad thing," Jeremy said, giving her his best, most deadly smile.

"Jeremy, do cease this line of conversation at once," his grandmother said sharply. "This is entirely inappropriate talk for the drawing room—or for anywhere else," she added severely. Ordinarily, one look from her would have been enough to cow him, but, as was always the case when Diana was near, he was feeling reckless.

"But surely, your ladyship, you see that an obvious solution to your grandson's marital woes has presented itself." Diana cast a significant look in Lady Helen's direction, as though everyone present were not already perfectly aware what she was alluding to.

"I see a great deal, Lady Templeton," the dowager marchioness said thoughtfully.

"I'm so glad," Diana said, sounding pleased, though Jeremy could have warned her that the shrewd look his grandmother was giving her spelled trouble. He, however, was not feeling terribly charitable, particularly not when Diana turned to him and added, "I take it you recollect our conversation better now, Willingham?"

"Perhaps not in quite the same amount of detail that you seem to recall, Lady Templeton," he said with a thin smile.

"I suppose I was just so touched by the sound of you confessing your desire for love and companionship that I committed every detail to memory," she said, laying a theatrical hand upon her chest.

"I thought we were discussing matrimony," he replied. "I'm not certain that the state necessarily goes hand in hand with the others."

"A cynic!" she cried dramatically. "Clearly, you have yet to have your heart pierced by Cupid's arrow."

"I should certainly hope not. It sounds like a rather painful, bloody business."

"All the better to allow you to properly empathize with your wife during childbirth, then," Diana said solemnly.

"Lady Templeton!"

This, apparently, was a bridge too far. His grandmother's tone was sufficiently arctic to quell even the boldest among them, and Diana fell silent, looking abashed as she sipped her tea. Jeremy was certain her expression was entirely feigned. He'd never seen Diana look abashed in the more than ten years of their acquaintance.

"Er," Lady Emily said, clearly attempting to rescue what had become a near-unsalvageable situation. "It seems as though the rain might be letting up outdoors. Perhaps we could take a stroll about the gardens after tea?"

"A capital idea," agreed Violet, who seemed to share Emily's desire to escape their awkward teatime. "Fresh air, particularly fresh *damp* air, is so good for . . . for—" She broke off, clearly grasping wildly at straws. "The heart?" she offered weakly.

Audley cast an amused glance at his wife.

"I don't think I've ever heard of such a thing, Lady James," Lady Helen said with a sniff. "And besides, my slippers are certain to be ruined if I go traipsing about in all that mud."

"Well, I did think a change in footwear might be needed first," Violet said with as much patience as she seemed capable of mustering.

"I don't know," Lady Helen fretted. "I don't know that I care to risk muddying any of my shoes—and what if I should slip and turn my ankle, and then I should be forced to remain here . . . well, *indefinitely*, really." She cast a crafty look at Jeremy, who felt the blood drain from his face.

"Lady Helen, I should be happy to loan you a pair of my shoes," Diana said sweetly. "We would all—Willingham in particular, I expect—be positively devastated by your absence from the party. It would be even more catastrophic than the sight of mud upon your lovely slippers."

There was a scattered round of—rather halfhearted, it must be said—murmurs of assent from the group and thus it was settled: for now, tea; then, a walk. Jeremy eyed Diana suspiciously as she spread jam upon a scone in what seemed to him an unnecessarily self-satisfied manner. He had never in his life felt such a definite feeling of doom while watching someone prepare a scone.

She had a plan, he was certain.

And he was equally certain that he was not going to like it one bit.

Seventeen

Diana thought that it was a great shame she had been born female,
for she would have made an admirable general. All the people around
her were players on a chessboard, moving about the board according
to her plans. She felt a nearly uncontrollable desire to cackle but
refrained—not only would it alert her companions to her scheming, it
would likely make her appear a madwoman.

Which, in all honesty, was how she was beginning to feel.

It was entirely Jeremy's fault, of course—as always. He just made
her so irritated that she was unable to resist poking at him in the hopes
of provoking a reaction. She had to admit that the teatime battle of
words had gotten a bit away from her—had she really discussed *childbirth* before the Dowager Marchioness of Willingham?—but all was
back on course now, and Lady Helen was nothing more than a puppet
dancing on Diana's carefully hidden strings.

At the moment, her puppet was walking arm in arm with Jeremy,
and Diana was already congratulating herself for this early success. Say
what one might about the rules-obsessed world of the English upper
class—and she had, on occasion, said quite a bit on this subject—but
the rigid code of honor came in handy sometimes.

Such as, for example, when a lady tripped in walking boots that were at least two sizes too large for her, leaving a certain marquess no option but to lunge to her rescue before she toppled over into a nearby hydrangea bush.

And Lady Helen, being no fool, was certainly not going to let go of the arm of a marquess once she'd seized it. Diana wondered idly if Jeremy would have finger-shaped bruises all along his arm the next day.

Everything was, in other words, going just according to plan. Although *plan* might be an overgenerous term to employ for what was, she had to admit, a rather hastily cobbled together scheme. Hardly her finest work.

However, it would do in a pinch, and it was time to make her next move.

"Lord Willingham," she called from where she walked behind the pair with Sophie, Violet and Emily just behind them. "Lady Helen appears to be limping."

As a matter of fact, Lady Helen *was* walking strangely, but Diana was fairly certain that it was merely owing to the fact that her tiny feet were slipping around in the boots she'd borrowed from Diana. However, she was not about to let the truth get in the way of her matchmaking, the importance of which had been reinforced to Diana by a few unsettlingly perceptive looks from the dowager marchioness at teatime.

"I think perhaps she might appreciate a chance to rest," Diana added, all solicitous concern.

Jeremy gave the lady on his arm a cursory glance before directing a sharp look at Diana. "Perhaps we should all pause for a moment to admire the natural beauty that surrounds us, then," he offered blandly. Had Diana not been searching for it, she might have missed the challenging look in his eye.

It was a look that seemed to ask if she had forgotten with whom she was dealing—if she really thought he could be so easily trapped. She met his gaze with an entirely self-assured look of her own, refusing to break eye contact. She was not about to concede an inch to this man.

"Diana, you can go an impressively long time without blinking," Violet interjected, breaking up their silent battle.

"I do not feel in need of a rest," Diana announced loudly, ignoring Violet completely and focusing the entirety of her attention on Jeremy and Lady Helen. "I think the rest of us should continue onward and allow you to wait with Lady Helen until she feels sufficiently able to resume walking."

"I hardly think that would be appropriate," Jeremy said hastily, and Diana was pleased to note a definite hint of unease in his voice. That would teach him to underestimate her, she thought smugly.

"Very well," she said thoughtfully. She paused, allowing him to think he had avoided danger—indeed, the other members of their party, thinking the discussion at an end, made as if to move onward—and then into the silence she offered: "Then perhaps you should carry Lady Helen instead?"

"Oh!" Lady Helen said dramatically, clutching at her bosom. While the bosom in question did not rival Diana's own, the human male is physically incapable of looking away when attention is drawn to such a spot on the body, and Jeremy proved himself no different from any other man in this regard.

"I think that might be a bit of an overreac—" Jeremy began, but was distracted from his objection by a sort of wailing swoon on the part of Lady Helen, which of course required him to leap into action to break her fall. The lady seemed remarkably unstable. Perhaps medical attention truly was necessary.

And so, there they were: Jeremy with an armful of delicate, vaporish virgin, Diana attempting to rearrange her features into an expression of mild alarm rather than smug glee, and the rest of their party regarding this little tableau as though it were a Drury Lane production. And really, who could blame them?

"May I escort you back to the house, Lady Helen?" Jeremy asked politely and—to his credit—without the slightest hint of shortness of breath. Despite herself, Diana was impressed—Lady Helen was slender, it was true, but she was on the tallish side and must have weighed at least nine stone.

"Oh," was the lady's feeble reply. "I could never think to trouble you so much, my lord. If you would merely find a convenient bench or rock to perch me atop, I am certain I shall be right as rain in but a moment."

Jeremy's facial expression said that he thought this unlikely in the extreme, as did the lady's tone itself. He cast his gaze about, clearly looking for a spot where he could relieve himself of his burden without appearing ungentlemanly, and his eyes landed on a delicate wrought-iron bench some twenty feet away. It was set in a curve in the gravel path that led through the neatly manicured gardens, and was bordered on either side by bushes that gave the illusion of privacy.

It was perfect for Diana's purposes.

"There!" she called gaily, waving an arm toward the bench in question. She found herself on the receiving end of more than one curious look from their companions, but persevered. "I am certain that with a few minutes' rest, Lady Helen will be recovered and you will be able to rejoin us on our walk."

Jeremy, however, did not budge. "Only if you accompany us, Lady Templeton," he said with a show of great courtesy. His tone was that of the utmost politeness, and his expression held nothing but bland invitation.

This was where the next portion of Diana's plan came in, and it would require careful maneuvering on her part. "I thought perhaps Lady Fitzwilliam might join you instead."

Next to her, Sophie stiffened and turned to look at her questioningly. "Oh?" she asked simply, her lovely face as smooth and untroubled as a still pond, only the slightest spark in her eye indicating some combination of irritation and amusement warring for dominance within her.

"I have noticed you slowing, Sophie," Diana said earnestly. "I know that your stride is not as long as mine and thought that you might appreciate a respite from the punishing pace I set us." And, more important, sharing a bench with both Lady Helen *and* Sophie—especially when matrimony had so recently been discussed!—should make Jeremy quickly realize that an easy escape from one lady's maneuverings lay in his other bench companion.

This would be an easier scheme to execute, of course, if Sophie were willing to go along with it.

Unfortunately, however, West, who had been walking ahead with Audley but who had turned back to rejoin the party upon noticing the holdup, chose this moment to intervene.

"If Lady Fitzwilliam is finding the pace too quick, I would be pleased to walk with her myself."

Diana snuck a sideways glance at Sophie at this; as though unable to control their motion, Sophie had allowed her eyes to flicker to West's at his words, and held them there. After a moment's charged silence, she spoke. "I am not certain why everyone is quite so concerned with my ability to walk about a garden, but nonetheless I should be happy for your escort, my lord."

Barely had the words escaped from Sophie's mouth than West was moving toward her as quickly as his bad leg allowed, offering her his arm. There was the briefest moment of hesitation, then she reached out and took it. He began leading her along one of the paths that intersected the main one upon which they walked; Diana's gaze happened to land on Audley, who was watching his brother with intensity.

"This still leaves me with the question of who is to chaperone myself and Lady Helen," Jeremy said a few seconds later, breaking into the silence that had momentarily overtaken the group. He turned his most innocent, questioning smile upon Diana. "Lady Templeton?"

Resisting the temptation to throw her hands in the air in frustration, Diana mentally conceded that her oh-so-brilliant plan for their walk was not going to end well. "Of course," she said through gritted teeth. "I should be delighted."

"We'll just carry on without you, shall we?" Violet called behind them.

"Do you need any assistance, Willingham?" Audley asked, casting a concerned look at Lady Helen. "I should be happy to fetch the lady's brother . . . or a physician—"

"Capital idea!" Jeremy said, as a drowning man might lunge for a raft.

"I don't think that will be necessary," Diana said loudly. She made a shooing motion with her hands, as though Audley were a disobedient sheepdog—not at all an inaccurate comparison for most men, she thought, though it might be a trifle unfair to sheepdogs. "A moment of rest and we'll rejoin you." She smiled brightly at him, which Audley looked mildly disturbed by. She cast a speaking glance at Violet, who seized her husband's elbow and steered him rather firmly down the path behind Emily, who was now conversing animatedly with Penvale.

Diana saw, with a sideways glance at Jeremy, that he was watching them as a man marooned on a desert island would watch a ship pass by.

Clearly resigning himself to his current predicament, however, he quickly settled Lady Helen on the bench and then made a great show of offering Diana a hand and seating her carefully next to that lady.

The bench, naturally, was only large enough for two.

Diana could not help scowling; with a sideways glance, she saw a similar expression mirrored upon the face of Lady Helen, who was no doubt fuming that her plans to secret herself away with a certain marquess had been foiled. By the marquess himself, Diana felt like pointing out, since she had a sneaking suspicion that a fair bit of Lady Helen's anger was radiating toward her own person.

"Well," Diana said brightly, smoothing her skirts, "here we are."

Jeremy's reply was the sort of inarticulate grunt that men seemed to believe substituted adequately for actual words. Lady Helen's was an eye roll.

"It is a lovely day," Diana tried again, her companions' less-than-satisfying reaction serving to only provoke her own contrary nature.

"And how nice it is that we are able to appreciate it in such solitude," Jeremy said dryly.

"I quite agree," Diana said. Turning to Lady Helen, she offered, "How does your ankle fare?"

"Tolerably well," was the lady's cool response. "I expect I only twisted it a bit in these boats of yours."

Ignoring the jab at her shoe size, Diana persevered. "And how kind of Lord Willingham to spring into action to come to your rescue."

"Yes," agreed Lady Helen. "It was indeed the stuff all romances are made of."

It was then that Diana noticed it. The oh-so-slight *something* that was strange about Lady Helen's tone. For while the words were entirely correct, there was a certain wryness to the delivery that was not at all fitting with the Lady Helen that Diana knew.

Or that she thought she knew.

She cast a quick glance upward at Jeremy, only to see that he had vanished.

Not entirely, of course, but he had moved several feet away, as if desperate to put as much distance as courtesy allowed between himself and an eligible young lady. He was currently giving a great deal of attention to a rosebush.

Suppressing a sigh with great difficulty—and conceding that her plan to leave Jeremy and Lady Helen in cozy seclusion among the flowering shrubs had been destined for failure—Diana cleared her throat.

Jeremy straightened at once, and Diana could not help admiring with a sort of artistic appreciation the graceful, fluid motion of his tall form as he moved toward them. His steps were smooth, almost languid, and the sunlight glinted off his golden head as it would off a new coin. She was all at once full with an almost irrepressible desire to paint him. Portraits were not her line of expertise, as a rule—she enjoyed landscapes and still lifes because of their absence of people, in fact, the way that she could entirely immerse herself in rolling green hills and forget that everything about her bright, glittering, artificial world existed—but her fingers practically itched to seize hold of a paintbrush. She clenched her hands in her skirts instead.

"How might I be of service, fair lady?" Jeremy asked with a wry twist to his mouth as he halted before them, and Diana flattened her lips, refusing to allow herself an answering smile.

"I think Lady Helen is feeling sufficiently recovered to rejoin the party," she said briskly, pushing herself off the bench and ignoring entirely his proffered hand.

"Actually," Lady Helen said, rising as well, "I think I should like to retire to my room for a spell. My ankle feels fine, but I don't relish the thought of walking much farther in these shoes."

"May I escort you back to the house?" Jeremy asked politely.

"No, thank you, my lord," Lady Helen said, to Diana's surprise. She was already beginning to walk in the direction of the house. Diana would have expected her to jump at the opportunity to be escorted by Jeremy—particularly since it would have allowed her to rid herself of Diana's company.

"You and Lady Templeton must rejoin the party," Lady Helen continued, "and not allow me to spoil the rest of your walk." She spoke absently, as though her mind were on something else, and as soon as she had finished speaking she was gone, moving with decisive steps back toward Elderwild and not betraying the slightest sign of a limp.

Jeremy, staring after her, began to laugh.

"What, precisely, is so amusing?" Diana asked, narrowing her eyes at him.

Jeremy turned slightly to face her head-on, still laughing. His face was alight with humor, his blue eyes dancing, and Diana averted her gaze slightly, much as one would when faced with the direct glare of the sun. Oh, this was dangerous, dangerous, dangerous.

"Well," he said, "you rather twisted yourself into knots trying to ensure that I would be left alone with the lady in a compromising situation, and yet I find myself alone with you instead."

"How do you know that wasn't my true aim all along?" Diana asked without thinking, and could she have willed those words back into her mouth a moment later, she would have done so. Flirting came so naturally to her that it was like breathing sometimes—a way to continue the conversation without really saying anything at all.

Except, of course, she had forgotten to whom she was speaking, and the fact that he would not hesitate to take this as an invitation. In an instant, his eyes darkened and he took a step toward her. Diana resisted the instinctive urge to take a step back, as one would from a predator, and instead raised her chin. She had said the thing, so she might as well brazen it out.

She made a mental note to have that motto engraved upon her tombstone, but that was her last coherent thought before Jeremy's hands slid into her hair, pulling her face toward his own. Her eyes fluttered shut, but he did not kiss her at once. Instead, he rested his forehead upon hers, and she allowed her eyes to open once again, staring into his own from such close proximity that she could see nothing else.

"Diana," he murmured, his breath warm against her skin. Something deep within her heated at the sound of her name uttered in his deep voice, slightly ragged at the edges in a way that was not all in keeping with his usual smooth demeanor. She had the fleeting thought that she wanted to hear him say her name like that every day for the rest of her life.

She tilted her chin up and captured his lips with her own, and immediately she was drowning in sensation: in the heat of his mouth and the taste of him—the black tea he had been drinking earlier, mixed with something else entirely his own. One of his hands cupped the nape of her neck, then slid upward to cradle her cheek. He made no further move to claim her, did not attempt to draw them closer together, and yet she felt warmth course through her body at his touch. His tongue teased her lips apart and explored her mouth in a leisurely fashion, and she reached up to grip him by the shoulders to ensure that she kept her balance, given the sudden weakening of her knees.

He took a step forward then, and then another, and she backed up until her knees hit the edge of the bench. Without relinquishing her grip on him, she sank down onto it, drawing him down with her. And while he had seemed content a moment before to kiss her in a slow, unhurried fashion, something changed the instant they were seated, and his mouth began to move with greater force, creating a slowly intensifying heat between them that she was helpless to resist flinging herself into. He drew her closer toward him, as close as the frustrating volume of her skirts would allow, and he wrapped his free arm around her waist, pressing their chests together and letting her feel the rapid, staccato beat of his heart, racing in time with her own.

Time seemed to slow, and she lost all sense of the world around them—the warmth of the August sunlight peeking out from behind the clouds, the lazy buzzing of bees at a nearby flower. . . . She felt slow and languid and as though her entire body had been weighted down. She moved her arms from his shoulders to twine around his neck and pressed herself even closer—close enough that she could feel him stiffening against her hip, and a primal, feminine part of her thrilled at this power, even as the sensation brought her reluctantly back to earth.

She pulled away from him. "We can't do this here," she said breathlessly, though her arms remained in place around his neck, and his face was still so close to hers that she could see the faint laugh lines at the corners of his eyes. They would deepen with time, she thought, and he would be all the more handsome for it. She had never given a moment's thought to Jeremy as an older man—in her mind, he was so much the youthful rake that she almost had difficulty imagining it—and yet in that instant she could see it all too clearly. He would settle down and marry a beautiful woman and—this she knew with a sudden, clenching certainty—be a devoted father. *He* could not see this future, she knew, but she could. And the thought made her feel oddly lonely all of a sudden.

"You're right," he admitted, his tone reluctant, and then his brow furrowed at whatever he saw in her expression. "Are you all right?"

"Fine, fine," she said in as breezy a tone as she could manage, drawing back farther to put some much-needed space between them. "Just distracted."

"Just what every chap wants to hear from the lady he's been kissing," Jeremy muttered.

Without thinking—*why* did she never think?—she replied, "Your kisses are not your problem, my lord. Indeed, if you were any more proficient at them, I should find it a bit dangerous."

He preened. "Dangerous?" She could practically see his chest expanding with pride, like a balloon, and she quickly summoned a verbal needle.

"Yes, well, as we have discussed, there are other parts of your repertoire that leave room for improvement." He deflated. "But I am willing to work on those with you."

He arched a brow. "Are you, then?" he murmured.

Diana resisted the urge to blush, of all things. "I feel that it's the least I could do."

"Ah," he said, leaning forward again so that their foreheads touched once more. "All out of a spirit of charity, then?" He angled his head so that his lips brushed, whisper-soft, against her temple, and gooseflesh rose along the back of her neck immediately in response. "No personal gain whatsoever?" He ducked his head and pressed another feather-light kiss to the underside of her jaw, and she felt the hair along her arms rise. "How positively saintly of you, Lady Templeton," he murmured, one of his hands moving on a steadily upward course toward her breasts.

"I just . . ." she began, with no clear idea of what she was going to say, and he slid away from her, all traces of seduction gone, and raised an inquiring brow.

"Yes?" he asked politely.

"I . . ." Her mind felt as though it could not hold two thoughts in it at once, so distracted was she by his proximity, the heat of his body, the scent of his skin. It was maddening—it made her feel positively itchy.

And was causing other, entirely unmentionable sensations.

"I would like you to let me paint you," she blurted out. She was momentarily pleased with herself for accomplishing the Herculean task of stringing together a grammatically correct sentence in a reasonably calm tone, until she realized what the actual *content* of the sentence had been. She could not think what had possessed her to admit such a thing—it felt entirely too intimate, as though confessing her wish to paint him also laid bare the manner in which he had come to consume her thoughts.

Hastily, she added, "That is to say, you have a—a pleasing form." She sounded like her great-aunt Mildred, who had lived to the ripe old age of eighty-eight, never wed, was always clothed in a prim gown of an indeterminate shade of dark blue, and had pursed her lips at anything even slightly suggesting carnal relations or physical attraction. To draw such a comparison, even in the privacy of her own mind, was somewhat lowering.

"A pleasing form," Jeremy repeated.

"Yes." She nodded briskly. "I think it would look rather well on canvas."

He gave her a sort of scrutinizing look she didn't like one bit, but she raised her chin and met his gaze steadily.

"I thought you didn't paint portraits."

"I don't terribly often," she admitted, "which is all the more reason for me to practice. I don't like having such an obvious weakness."

"You wouldn't," he muttered, but before she could respond to that, he barreled on. "And you'd like to use me as your . . . test subject?"

"Isn't it rather in keeping with the theme of our current relationship?" she asked. As soon as she said it, though, she knew it wasn't true. She didn't want to paint him to practice her portraiture, though she certainly needed practice; rather, she wanted to paint him because he was beautiful, and far more complicated than she had ever given him credit for in all their years of acquaintance, and the thought of trying to capture even a fragment of that complexity was an almost irresistible challenge to her.

And neither was it accurate to reduce their entire relationship to one of physical experimentation with a willing partner; to do so felt entirely inadequate, a complete failure to encompass whatever this complicated, undefinable feeling was that seemed to grow between them whenever they were together.

However, she would rather have died than admit any of this to him at the moment. A week ago, she would have assumed he'd laugh in her face; now she knew him a bit better, but she thought that whatever his reaction would be—most likely born of pity—would still be more than she could bear.

"I suppose so," he said in response to her question, and it took her a moment to recollect what she'd said. His tone was surprisingly hesitant, and *hesitant* wasn't an adjective she normally associated with Willingham. Before she could respond, however, an expression of alarm crossed his face. "Wait a moment. The two things wouldn't be … *related*, would they?"

Diana frowned. "What do you mean?"

Did her eyes deceive her, or did the Marquess of Willingham actually *blush*? He appeared to be struggling for words. This just kept getting better and better, really. "I mean—that is to say, I don't wish to assume anything—I'm not trying to imply that you'd be in the habit of doing this—"

"Out with it, Jeremy," she said calmly.

"You wouldn't expect to be painting me, er, au naturel, would you?" He could barely meet her eyes; Diana wished she kept a diary, merely for the purpose of recording this entire conversation.

"Willingham," she said in a voice of deadly calm, "are you asking if I intend to paint you in the nude?"

"Yes, damn it!"

She burst out laughing. It was not the laugh she usually employed at a social event—light and carefree—or the one she used when flirting with a gentleman—coy and throaty—but the honest, open laughter she tended to share with Violet, Emily, and her brother, and no one else. After a moment, she realized he was looking at her oddly, as though he had never properly seen her before, and it made her feel as naked as he'd been imagining himself in this hypothetical portrait sitting.

"No," she managed to get out, bringing herself back under control with some difficulty, though in some sense she felt it was already too late—he had caught a glimpse of a side to her that he'd never seen, one that she took care to never show anyone, and she could not remove that knowledge now that he possessed it. "I imagined you would be entirely clothed, my lord. I know I have a bit of a scandalous reputation, but I do draw the line at erotic paintings."

"I just wanted to be certain I understood where we stood," he muttered, still having difficulty meeting her eyes, like a shy virgin. His discomfort was utterly charming, unfortunately.

"And now you do. Everything aboveboard, so to speak. All clothes in their proper places. No one's virtue shall be compromised—not that I think you've much of that to concern yourself with."

"Well, one still likes to leave something to the imagination." He waggled his eyebrows in an exaggeratedly lascivious fashion. She rolled her eyes.

"Do we have an agreement then?" she asked, all business.

"You shall paint my angelic visage, and in exchange you will inform me—in unfortunately blunt detail, I have no doubt—exactly what my failings are in the boudoir?" To his great credit, he was able to say this in apparent good humor, and for a moment she thought about how rare and precious this was. How many men in a hundred, or a thousand, would take a woman's criticism seriously, without taking offense? Without resorting to bluster, or worse? She marveled at this, and at the vast gulf she was coming to understand existed between the man she had thought she'd known, and the man he actually was.

"Shall we say midnight, then?"

"My room or yours?"

"Mine," she said in brisk tones. "I think your reputation can endure your being caught wandering the halls at an illicit hour better than mine can."

"Of course," he said, sounding a bit rueful. "Foolish question." He looked at her dead-on then, and humor flashed across his face, making him look very much like the boy she had first met a dozen years ago. "I feel as though we should shake on it."

"As gentlemen?" she asked wryly, extending her hand nonetheless.

"Believe me, Diana," he said, even as he shook her hand firmly, "I am not in any danger of mistaking you for a gentleman."

Eighteen

"Jeremy," called his grandmother feebly as he reentered the house, and he was immediately on his guard. The dowager marchioness might have been rather elderly, but she was astonishingly hale and healthy. "Come here." She beckoned him imperiously from where she stood on the second-floor landing; he was careful to keep a bland smile upon his face as he ascended the stairs, even as a selection of choice curses ran through his mind.

"Wipe that addlepated expression off your face at once," his grandmother added sternly, and Jeremy was happy to comply; he was an intelligent enough man to know when his efforts were wasted. Moreover, he was suddenly not at all in the mood to wear the Willingham mask that normally came so easily to him.

"How can I be of assistance, dearest Grandmama?" he asked. She scowled at him; he could distinctly recall being struck dumb with terror upon being on the receiving end of that expression as a boy.

"I would like for you to explain to me what exactly is going on," she said, taking his proffered arm and leading him back down the hallway in the direction of the bedchamber that she occupied; for as long as Jeremy could recall, she had taken up residence in the grandest of all the guest bedrooms on the second floor during her visits to Elderwild, to the point that he never offered the room to anyone else, so linked in his mind was the room to the dowager marchioness. It was strange to think that she had once ruled over this entire house during his grandfather's years as the marquess; she spent the whole year in London now, and it was odd to imagine her rusticating in the country for months on end.

His musings were interrupted by a sharp poke in his side as the dowager marchioness led him into the small sitting room that opened onto her bedroom. "Have you been listening to a word I've just said?" she asked sharply.

"Not really," he answered honestly, settling her in an armchair before seating himself in the one next to it. "I apologize."

"I was asking what on earth happened on that garden walk you young fools went on," his grandmother said waspishly. "First I see young Weston and Lady Fitzwilliam walking back to the house—*very cozily*, I might add. I'd wager a hefty sum there are wedding bells in their future at last—"

"I wouldn't bet on it," Jeremy said warningly, with the wisdom of a man who had recently found himself enmeshed in a matrimonial gamble. "I'm coming to think one should never wager on marriage."

"Worried you've set yourself up to lose some blunt, my boy?" the dowager marchioness asked shrewdly.

"Nothing of the sort. I just think it's bad form."

"Pot, kettle, and all that. But back to my point: I then see Lady Helen Courtenay stomping back up to the house in quite a hurry— she tried to throw me off with some story of a twisted ankle, but she was moving mighty quickly for someone with an injury, I don't mind telling you. And then you and that widow of yours return separately from the rest of the group—"

"Don't you have other things to do than keep tabs on the comings and goings of everyone in this house?" Jeremy asked peevishly.

"Not particularly," his grandmother said serenely.

"And Lady Templeton is not *my* widow," he added belatedly, though this conversation was beginning to make him wish he were deceased.

"If you say so."

"Was there anything else you wished to discuss, Grandmama?" He tugged at his neckcloth; was it warm in here? He was beginning to think it was just as well that he'd never joined the army—he didn't think he'd hold up well under interrogation.

"I would like you to go apologize to Lady Helen for whatever it is you've done to offend her," his grandmother said simply. This, he suspected, was the real reason he'd been dragged up here in the first place.

"*I* have done nothing to offend the lady," he said with an air of wounded outrage that he didn't feel was entirely unearned. He, after all, had been nothing but unfailingly polite to Lady Helen for the duration of the house party thus far; he was certainly not to blame if Diana was practically flinging the lady at him. To be fair, Lady Helen hardly seemed to need any encouragement in that vein.

"I won't deny that she's a bold little thing," his grandmother admitted before pinning him in place with a sharp look. "But, tiresome as Lady Rothsmere is, she wields a great deal of power in the *ton* and I won't have her complaining to all and sundry about my rake of a grandson leaving her daughter heartbroken. She entrusted her daughter to my care for the duration of this house party, and if the lady returns to London giving even the slightest impression of a woebegone calf, I'm certain Lady Rothsmere will be more than happy to lay the blame at your feet. And mine."

"If the lady is heartbroken, I'm hardly to blame," Jeremy objected. "I've certainly done nothing to encourage her."

"I'm not saying that you have, but the fact is, Willingham, you have something of a reputation—one that you've very intentionally created for yourself, I've no doubt. As I told you just the other night, the act is wearing thin with me, but if you're going to insist on behaving like a man without a scrap of conscience, then the very least you can do is not embarrass me publicly by creating a scandal with the daughter of an earl. It is apparently too much to ask that you sincerely consider the idea of courting her—"

He could not allow this to pass without comment. "You cannot be serious."

"I'm entirely serious, my boy," the dowager marchioness said, surveying him in a way that made him wonder what, exactly, she saw within him. "It's high time you were wed, as I've made abundantly clear, and one could hardly ask for a more willing candidate for a wife. You'd barely have to expend any energy at all—it seems the perfect solution."

"Barring the minor detail that I would be utterly miserable for the rest of my days!" Jeremy said, nettled.

His grandmother waved a hand dismissively. "I never took you for a romantic, Jeremy." Before he could offer a vehement protest to that particular bit of commentary, she rose, rubbing her hands together in businesslike fashion. "Now, go soothe the lady's wounded sensibilities. I don't want to hear another word about it."

Somehow, in short order, Jeremy found himself out in the hallway, rather like a subject whose audience with the king had been declared at an end; he had no doubt that his grandmother would not object to this characterization of their relationship. Deciding that there was no point in putting off an unpleasant task—and shuddering to think what the dowager marchioness's reaction would be if he did not follow her instructions—he walked a few doors farther down the hall, stopping before the bedchamber that had been given to Lady Helen.

He had a vague thought of knocking on the door and asking her if she would like to accompany him downstairs for another cup of tea, but he paused in the act of raising his fist when he realized that the door before him was slightly ajar. Elderwild was an old house, and many of the heavy doors, if not shut sufficiently firmly, would fail to latch and swing back slightly, which was what appeared to have happened here. He was about to go ahead and knock anyway when a sound from within made him freeze.

A moan.

Jeremy was a man of simple pleasures: a fine glass of brandy, a hard ride on a horse, a good round of boxing at Gentleman Jackson's, a tumble with a willing woman. None of these occupations provided him with expertise that he generally had much cause to call upon, but in that moment, he knew one thing with the utmost certainty: that moan had not been one of pain, but of pleasure.

He lowered his fist, the rest of him frozen in shock. Lady Helen with a lover? He would never have thought her capable of it; in truth, he was a bit impressed. Her reputation was impeccable—never so much as a whiff of scandal. Who could the gentleman possibly be?

He knew that the honorable thing to do now would be to attempt to shut the door without the parties within noticing, and walk away, but he found himself leaning forward slightly, pressing his face to the crack in the door.

And then he blinked. And blinked again.

For Lady Helen was indeed within, pressed up against a wall, her skirts rucked up and a lover's hand working beneath them. But the lover in question was not one of the gentlemen of the house party.

It was one of the servants.

Specifically, it was Sutton—her lady's maid.

Later, Jeremy thought, he would look back on this evening and laugh. At the moment, he felt rather too shocked to do anything of the sort, even as the events around him devolved into farce.

Dinner had been a lengthy affair, as usual, the table groaning under the weight of numerous dishes making up each course. Jeremy—who was beginning to seriously wonder at the wisdom of allowing his housekeeper to be in charge of the seating arrangements—had found himself seated between Lady Helen and Diana, with Audley, Violet, and Penvale directly opposite. This arrangement seemed entirely to the latter three's satisfaction, as they watched the ensuing conversation between Jeremy and his seatmates rather like spectators at a boxing match.

"Lady Helen," Diana said sweetly as the soup course was cleared away, "are you finding your ankle much recovered?" This was, of course, a ludicrous breach of etiquette—Diana was meant to be talking to Jeremy, who was seated directly to her left; on his other side, Lady Helen was regaling Belfry with some sort of lengthy monologue. Jeremy noticed that Belfry was drinking rather deeply from his wineglass.

At Diana's interruption, however, Lady Helen broke off her discussion with Belfry and slowly turned. She gave a sort of trembling sigh clearly meant to indicate long, noble suffering. "I am, Lady Templeton," she said mournfully. She had to lean forward slightly to speak across Jeremy to Diana, and she placed a hand on his sleeve as she did so. Several hours earlier, this breach of propriety would have had him crawling under the table to escape; now, however, he merely watched her, wondering what, precisely, her plan was.

She turned to him, batting her eyelashes so heavily that he was tempted to ask her if she had something in her eye. "Lord Willingham, the strength of your arm undoubtedly played a role in my speedy recovery."

Across the table, Jeremy saw Penvale choke on his Madeira.

"Oh, yes," Diana agreed solemnly, leaning a bit forward as well. This movement, given the cut of her bodice, made it extremely difficult for Jeremy to keep his gaze fixed on the lady's eyes, which were at the moment round and innocent. Given that her brother was seated directly opposite them, however, he did his best in this regard.

"Willingham can be quite solicitous when the fancy strikes him," Diana continued; a more halfhearted endorsement of one's chivalry Jeremy wasn't sure he'd ever heard, but he had too many other concerns at the moment to take offense. "And of course . . ." She trailed off, pausing dramatically. Jeremy once again glanced at Penvale, Audley, and Violet, all of whom were watching Diana expectantly, appearing to be enjoying themselves thoroughly.

". . . when Cupid's arrow has struck, you cannot but expect him to spring into action to spare his delicate flower any discomfort." Diana blinked rapidly, as though suppressing tears.

"Are you quite all right?" Jeremy asked politely, watching as she dabbed at her eyes with her napkin. It seemed a shame not to pay her the courtesy of playing along, now that she'd really gotten into the spirit of this performance.

"Merely touched," she assured him with a watery smile.

"In the head?" he asked.

On his other side, Lady Helen gave a shrill sort of giggle, once more placing her hand on his sleeve, drawing his attention back to her. Was it his imagination, or had her nails dug into his arm? "Oh, Lord Willingham!" she said with slightly manic glee. "So droll! So frightfully droll!"

"Yes, frightful," Jeremy agreed, nodding fervently. He picked up his fork, attempting to refocus on the food before him. It was difficult to concentrate on much of anything with Diana's theatrics on one side and Lady Helen's on the other.

Because he was now almost certain that Lady Helen's behavior was indeed just that: an act. He had beaten a hasty retreat away from her door once he had realized just who she was tangled up with—and had tripped rather spectacularly, and sworn even more colorfully at an elevated volume, once he was a bit farther down the hallway. He hoped he'd been sufficiently noisy to interrupt the ladies and at least make them realize that the door was not shut before anyone else discovered them.

He felt oddly protective of Lady Helen's secret; he had stumbled upon her by accident, she'd no notion that he knew, and it didn't feel sporting to gossip about her like a mean-spirited dowager, even with his closest friends.

However, he could not stop thinking about what he'd seen. He was not shocked at the existence of sapphists, of course, but rather amazed that Lady Helen counted herself among them. What the devil was she doing, then, dangling after him? Was she trying to catch a rich husband and be done with it, so that she might continue liaising with her maid whenever she wished? He could not fault her for this, in truth; the world of the *ton* was a difficult place for any woman, much less one who wished for something beyond the bounds of a traditional family and home. But why did she behave so dreadfully? It had to be an act; he couldn't countenance the idea of a servant carrying on with an aristocrat as insufferable as Lady Helen seemed, unless she was being compelled. And Sutton had looked exceptionally enthusiastic that afternoon.

Perhaps she planned to find herself in a compromising situation with an eligible man, but to have made herself so undesirable a companion that he would have little to do with her once they were wed? That would certainly give her plenty of time to make love to her maid instead. If that was her plan, he had better watch his step: just because he felt sympathy for her situation and somewhat admired her cunning didn't mean he had any wish to make her the Marchioness of Willingham.

He spent the rest of the evening fending off a double set of advances: Lady Helen's, and Diana's further attempts to force Lady Helen upon him. The remainder of the dinner passed in a series of mishaps: the remains of a glass of wine spilled onto Jeremy's thigh, resulting in some highly inappropriate dabbing at the area with a napkin wielded by Lady Helen; Diana repeatedly asking him to move his chair farther to the left, claiming she had nowhere near enough room, so that by the meal's end Jeremy was nearly sitting in Lady Helen's lap; Lady Helen offering him a taste of her asparagus, waving a fork in his face with such enthusiasm that he had obediently opened his mouth to ensure she did not poke out one of his eyes.

"Mmmm," he said weakly, giving Lady Helen a smile that he could only imagine made him look entirely deranged. "Delicious."

"Jeremy," Violet said from across the table; he was fairly certain she had interrupted her husband mid-sentence to speak to him, but

Audley merely appeared amused. "I had no idea you were so fond of asparagus. You already have a generous portion of it on your plate, and yet you still could not resist?" She blinked at him with an expression of innocent inquiry that Jeremy was not fooled by for a second.

"It is a . . . newfound passion."

"Ah, yes," she agreed, nodding. "You seem to have discovered more than one of those this week."

It would be too much to hope, of course, that Lady Helen had not noticed that comment. "Oh?" she asked. "What else has caught your fancy this week, my lord?"

"Riding?" Diana asked innocently; it was Audley who choked on his wine this time. Penvale gave his sister a look that was uncannily reminiscent of a maiden aunt chaperone regarding her unruly charge.

"I think Jeremy already enjoyed riding," Violet said thoughtfully, ignoring Penvale entirely and giving Diana an encouraging smile.

"Fair enough, Violet, fair enough," Diana agreed, nodding at her friend across the table. "Was it . . . planting? I know you've become very invested in the fates of your tenant farmers, Willingham."

"Scattering all those seeds about," Violet said, straight-faced.

Jeremy contemplated the sweet release of death. "I believe it was shooting," he said firmly. "I never quite appreciated the satisfaction in blood sport before."

"Ah, yes," Diana agreed. "Hunting. The pursuit. The chase. It's most . . . invigorating." She smiled at him sweetly. On his other side, Lady Helen's hand crept to his thigh.

Belfry chose this moment to chime in, leaning around Lady Helen to peer at Jeremy's face. "Willingham, are you feeling well? You don't look quite the thing at all."

"Merely contemplating the virtues of a lengthy stay in the Outer

Hebrides," Jeremy assured him. Next to him, Lady Helen tittered. Across from him, Violet—and her husband, damn him—grinned. And, most alarmingly of all, Diana smirked like the cat that got the cream.

It was much later, as the parlor games were breaking up and the party was beginning to scatter for the evening, that Penvale cornered him. Jeremy had just finished bowing over Lady Emily's hand in an excessive display of gallantry engineered mainly to irk Belfry, who had seemed suspiciously attuned to every move Emily had made all evening. No sooner had Jeremy raised his eyebrows at the dark look Belfry leveled in his direction than Penvale was upon him, a firm hand on his shoulder making escape all but impossible.

"Jeremy," he said in a tone of false heartiness that had Jeremy on his guard at once. "Fancy a nightcap?"

"I don't imagine I've much say in the matter," Jeremy said; Penvale barely seemed to hear him, turning to hail Audley, who was hand in hand with Violet, his head bent slightly to listen to whatever impropriety she was whispering in his ear. "Audley!" he called. "A nightcap?"

"I don't think—" Audley began, but was immediately interrupted by Penvale again.

"Good, good! Violet, I'll send him along shortly."

Violet raised her eyebrows at her husband and departed before he could object further, leaving a visibly disgruntled Audley standing alone by the doorway. He moved back toward Penvale and Jeremy, muttering under his breath all the while.

". . . late the hour is, and a man just wants to be tucked up with his wife in bed—"

"I'll return you to Violet's clutches in just a moment, never fear," Penvale said blithely, pressing a glass of brandy into Audley's hand before turning to Jeremy and offering him one as well. Jeremy supposed he should rather object to being treated like a guest in his own home, but he had too many other pressing concerns at the moment.

So, too, apparently, did Penvale. "How, precisely, do matters currently stand between you and my sister?"

Jeremy sighed, lifting his free hand to rub at the bridge of his nose. "I don't know what you mean," he said, taking a few steps to sink into one of the armchairs that bracketed the fireplace. Audley joined him, sipping at his brandy in a considering manner, but Penvale remained standing.

"Please don't waste my time," Penvale said pleasantly. "I did, after all, see the two of you mauling each other in the woods."

"What a mental image," Audley murmured, taking another sip.

"Is this the part where you threaten me if I so much as touch your sister?" Jeremy asked, taking a leisurely sip of his own. "Because in the interest of honesty, I feel the need to confess it's a bit late for that."

"Hardly," Penvale said, shaking his head. "I'm more concerned about you than her."

"Me?" Jeremy attempted a devil-may-care sort of laugh, but the effect was somewhat spoiled when he choked on his brandy and collapsed in a fit of wheezing.

"This is precisely what I was worried about," Penvale said, watching him with what Jeremy was very much afraid was pity. "You're already a shadow of your former self."

"I beg to differ," Jeremy objected. "Or were you not at the same dinner table I was? I am apparently a prime specimen on the marriage mart, judging by Lady Helen's behavior."

Penvale ignored this. "I just want you to be . . . careful." He seemed to be selecting his words with caution, and there was not the slightest trace of humor on his face. His gaze on Jeremy was razor-sharp, and Jeremy found himself fighting the uncomfortable urge to shift in his seat like a naughty schoolboy. "My sister is . . . calculating. I don't want you to fall in love with her and get your heart broken."

"In *love?*" Jeremy asked, his voice cracking on the word. "I can assure you, I'm in no danger of that."

"Mmm," Penvale said skeptically, but before he could elaborate further, Audley chimed in.

"I have always thought you might be a bit besotted with her, Jeremy."

"*Besotted?*" This conversation kept growing worse and worse; Jeremy gathered the remaining fragments of his dignity about himself and stood, chin up, projecting every bit of aristocratic froideur he could manage. "I have never been besotted with anyone in my entire life, and I certainly don't intend to start with a lady I can barely exchange three civil sentences in a row with."

"I myself have found recently that the more one denies the existence of deeper feelings, the more likely they are to exist," Audley commented, studying his tumbler with more interest than Jeremy felt was warranted.

"I don't wish to quarrel about this, Jeremy," Penvale said, reaching out to grip his shoulder once more. "Nor, in perfect honesty, do I really wish to spend much time contemplating the idea of you and Diana being romantically involved." He paused. "But she can take care of herself. And I know you can, too. Just . . . don't fall in love with her. I've heard her rail against marriage more times than I can count. And of the two of you, I think you're the one more likely to be disappointed with how this ends."

Jeremy scarcely knew how to respond. He was indignant at the idea that he would be left brokenhearted by anyone, much less a certain sharp-tongued widow; he thought that Penvale did not perhaps do his sister enough credit—the Diana that Jeremy had grown to know was capable of far deeper feeling than her brother seemed to believe. Underneath it all, though, he was grateful for a friend who he knew had his best interests at heart.

"I do not anticipate Diana breaking my heart," he said evenly at last, draining his glass in one burning gulp and setting it down on an end table with a heavy thunk. "And I think your sister is a more complicated person than you perhaps understand her to be. I'm *not* in love with her," he added firmly, "but I've come to realize that there's far more to her than meets the eye, and I pity anyone who can't see that—and appreciate it." Relishing the sight of Penvale and Audley both rendered momentarily speechless, Jeremy nodded to them amiably.

"Good night, chaps," he said, feeling unaccountably cheerful all of a sudden as he strode from the room.

Nineteen

The clock had barely ceased tolling the midnight hour when Jeremy rapped upon Diana's door.

For a moment, he experienced a fleeting, entirely uncharacteristic feeling of uncertainty—was he too punctual? Would she think him overeager? They had not been keeping terribly late hours thus far in the house party, but the late stragglers had only broken up downstairs half an hour earlier—was that enough time for her? Despite the number of women he'd bedded, the intricacies of ladies' toilettes remained something of a mystery to him. Was thirty minutes enough time to undress and do whatever mysterious things they did in preparation for an evening of rest—or of no rest, as the case might be?

Fortunately, she saved him from himself by opening her door only a few seconds after he knocked, clad in a nightgown and wrapper and looking entirely unsurprised to see him. He must not be too early, then.

As she cast a leisurely glance up and down his person, however, new causes for anxiety reared their ugly heads. Was he attired appropriately? He'd dismissed his valet and undressed without assistance, but then had hesitated. She had assured him—in what surely had to be one of the more humiliating moments of his life—that she did not expect to paint him naked, but what *did* she expect him to wear? He, of course, had failed to ask, and had hovered in his dressing room for a solid ten minutes, casting uncertain glances around at his many, all somehow inappropriate, articles of clothing.

Eventually, he had settled on a pair of fawn-colored breeches and a white shirt, cravat-less under a forest green banyan. He'd no idea if it was what she'd envisioned, but he also refused to spend a moment more contemplating the matter. A man had his dignity to consider, after all.

Except, of course, that in this moment he was certain that he'd chosen all wrong, that she wouldn't wish to paint him at all, that she'd cast him out of her bedchamber—

"Come in," she said, stepping back to allow him entrance, neatly nipping his anxiety in the bud. As he walked into the room, he gave himself a bit of a mental shake; he'd bedded some of the most beautiful women of the *ton*, for Christ's sake. Why should one sharp-tongued widow reduce him to his current state of incoherence?

As she closed and bolted the door behind him, he paused to survey the room. A fire crackled in the fireplace, casting a romantic glow upon their surroundings; she also had the heavy drapes at the window flung wide, allowing moonlight to flood the room. She had set up an easel and canvas before the window, and had moved one of the armchairs a bit back from the fireplace so that it faced her instead.

"I take it I'm to sit there?" he asked, gesturing toward the chair as she moved past him deeper into the room.

"I think so." She stood with her hands on her hips, surveying the scene before them. The moonlight gilded her skin, making her complexion even more luminous than usual; he clenched his hands at his sides to resist the urge to reach out and touch her, to claim all of that soft, glowing skin with his own flesh.

"I don't want you in direct moonlight because I think firelight will suit you better," she explained, turning to him. "But I didn't want you to sit too close to the fireplace, since that corner of the room is full of shadows. But I think that if you sit in that chair"—she gestured at it casually, and he was somehow fascinated by the lazy grace of that single hand movement—"then we'll strike the right balance." She bit her lip. "Does that suit you?"

It took him a moment to register her question, so distracted was he by the way her curves were silhouetted by the moonlight behind her. "Er," he said belatedly, dragging his eyes upward to her face with some difficulty, "whatever you think is best."

She batted her eyelashes. "Oh, how I have waited these many years to hear you say those words." She motioned to the chair. "Sit."

"Yes, madam." He brushed past her to take a seat in the chair indicated, unashamed to admit that he walked significantly closer to her than was strictly necessary in the process. He did not think he had imagined her sharp intake of breath as he did so. He paused in the act of lowering himself into his seat. "Shall I remove the banyan, or . . . ?"

She scrutinized him for a moment, her brow slightly furrowed. Perversely, he rather enjoyed this look—there was nothing remotely amorous in it, and he knew that, in that moment, she was examining him in a purely objective, aesthetic sense. But he liked watching her do it—he liked the faint line between her eyebrows and the way she tapped her chin gently with an index finger, her elbow cushioned in one palm. When she was in company, everything about her seemed oh-so-slightly calculated—her posture just so, the arching of an eyebrow in invitation. It was refreshing to see her like this instead, entirely unaware of her appearance, completely focused on something else.

Some*one* else, in this case: him.

"Leave it on for now," she said after a few moments of thought. "I think it brings out the warmth of your skin." She shrugged with a bit of a laugh. "Not that it matters terribly much at the moment—I'll just be sketching you first." She retreated to her easel and, ignoring the canvas, picked up a worn leather-bound notebook that he hadn't noticed. She seated herself on a stool that he thought she might have purloined from her dressing table, picked up a worn stub of pencil, and opened the notebook. She lifted her knees so that her bare feet rested on an ottoman she'd placed before her and the notebook could perch on her knees; then she looked up and met his gaze. Her mouth twitched.

"You can relax a bit," she said. "You look like a young lady at finishing school, about to be asked to walk about the room with a book on her head."

He allowed his posture to slacken, sinking back deeper into the armchair. He was surprised at how uncomfortable he felt, fully clothed, sitting here before her. He couldn't remember the last time he'd been this nervous to be alone with a woman. "Do they really do that? At finishing schools, I mean?"

Her mouth quirked up on one side even as she lifted her pencil and began to make a series of rapid strokes. "Never having been to school myself, I can't say for sure, but I've heard the anecdote from more than one lady of my acquaintance."

"All private governesses for you, if I recall?" he asked—he found that filling the space between them with conversation made him feel less like he was a fish in a fishbowl.

"For a while," she agreed, her eyes on the paper before her. "My uncle and aunt allowed me to be tutored with Penvale, until he went away to Eton—I think they didn't want the expense of hiring a separate governess for me until it was necessary, but I had no complaint, since it ensured I received a far more useful education than I might have otherwise. Until he left, of course." The movement of her hand paused for a moment and her eyes flicked upward to study him again. In the candlelight, they appeared more brown than hazel.

"Once Penvale left for school, they hired a governess for me for a spell—I was the daughter of a viscount, after all, and they didn't want anyone to claim they weren't giving me a proper education. I was taught watercolors. We continued with my study of French, and I dabbled a bit on the pianoforte. I was dreadful at it," she added.

"Too impatient to practice?" he guessed.

She grinned at him, a lopsided grin that he'd never seen from her before. "Indeed. I caused my governess no end of despair—she couldn't understand how I could hide myself away in the gardens for hours sketching the same flower over and over but couldn't bear to seat myself before a musical instrument for more than ten minutes at a time." She shrugged a bit, her attention once more on the sketch taking form before her. "I couldn't explain it, either—when I have a pencil or charcoal or a paintbrush in my hand, everything around me goes still. It's as though time slows to a trickle, and someone could be standing beside me speaking directly into my ear for some minutes before I realize they are there. Sitting at a pianoforte, by contrast, makes me feel like I'm about to climb out of my skin.

"They dismissed the governess after a while—I think they considered it a waste of money, and they felt that they'd already invested enough in Penvale and myself, considering that we weren't exactly able to provide much in the way of funds."

"Was there no money left over after the sale of Trethwick Abbey?"

Jeremy asked. He had a vague notion of the situation from years of friendship with Penvale, for whom reclaiming ownership of the estate was something perilously close to an obsession, but he wasn't sure he'd realized quite how desperate their situation must have been.

"Enough to pay for Penvale's Eton fees, and to set aside for a pathetic dowry for myself, but nothing else," she said. "My aunt and uncle paid for the entirety of the cost of clothing and feeding us, for launching me into society. Penvale borrowed blunt from my uncle for his Oxford fees, and paid him back as quickly as he was able—he said it was smart investing, but I suspect the gaming tables were the real source of that particular windfall."

Jeremy held his tongue, not wishing to betray any confidences by telling her that her guess was entirely correct.

Instead, he asked: "Was it so dreadful, with your aunt and uncle?"

She did not reply for a long moment, her eyes fixed upon the page before her, her hand moving rapidly. He did not prompt her further, merely waited her out.

"No, and yes." More silence, even as the hand continued in motion. After several seconds had elapsed, however, her hand stilled and she looked up once again.

"They were never unkind to us, you understand. This isn't some tragic tale out of a penny novel. They always provided for us, as far as their means allowed. We had new clothes each season, and plenty to eat, and essentially free rein of the house and grounds. We had a tutor, and of course we had each other."

"But?" he asked, after a lengthy pause. She had not resumed her drawing and was staring past him, at some point in the middle distance, and he was certain she was not seeing anything physically in the room at all. Her gaze was distant, and there was a look in her eyes—not pained, exactly, but somehow forlorn nonetheless—that he had never seen there before.

"They never said anything explicitly, but Penvale and I were somehow always made to understand that we were a burden," she said at last. "We were never allowed to forget that our parents had left us with very little in the way of inheritance, and that most of what was left to us would have to be spent on Penvale's schooling. Anytime he did poorly on an exam, he returned home to be reminded that he was wasting the bulk of our inheritance if he was not excelling at school. And I was always on the receiving end of . . . comments."

"What sorts of comments?" Jeremy asked with more calm than he felt at the moment. Indeed, he felt a peculiar sensation growing within him, rather as though something were slowly coming to a boil.

"Just remarks in passing, now and then. Comments that it was a mercy I'd such a pretty face, since I'd likely need it. Gratitude that my looks would make an advantageous marriage likely, so I wouldn't have to remain at home beyond my first Season. Nothing that was overtly cruel, you understand, just a steady litany that made me understand that my face was my only asset, and I was to use it as soon as possible to cease making myself an inconvenience to them."

"The bloody buggering nerve," he said, not bothering to apologize for his language. He realized, with a strange sort of removed tranquility, that he was really quite angry. "You were their family—your aunt's own flesh and blood—and you were orphaned, left in circumstances that were no fault of your own."

"And I'm sure if anyone had ever made such a comment to them, they would have agreed wholeheartedly," she said, looking at him steadily. "I don't even know that they were truly aware they were doing it. Which might be even worse, I think—if they were making us feel unwelcome, a burden, without even trying to do so at all. Careless cruelty is the worst sort, I sometimes think."

"This explains why you were so determined to marry well your first Season," he said slowly. At the time, he had understood that she had a small dowry, that she was going to have to rely on her face and figure and charm to land a husband of means. But he hadn't understood quite why she was so desperate—her aunt and uncle seemed to lead a comfortable enough life as middling members of the *ton*; surely she did not need to be quite so mercenary?

But now it made perfect sense. Of course she did not wish to remain in a home with these people a moment longer than necessary. Of course she wanted to find a husband wealthy and staid enough to ensure security, stability, a permanent place.

Of course she had no desire to marry a profligate, debt-ridden marquess.

"It felt as though I could never breathe deeply," she said softly, her hazel eyes locked with his blue ones. "As though my entire life, I'd been wearing the tightest corset imaginable, taking shallow little breaths, never able to get quite enough air. And that first night of my marriage to Templeton—even having married someone so much older, someone I knew wanted me for my appearance alone, as some sort of prize—it felt like I was at last able to inhale properly. It was dizzying." She took a deep breath, as if to illustrate her point.

"It was not a terrible marriage, you know. It was somewhat comforting, in fact, that it wasn't a love match—it felt like we didn't have unrealistic expectations of each other. The bit in the bedroom was uninspiring, I'll confess, but he was never terribly interested in me— physically, I mean. I sometimes wonder if he was interested in ladies at all, for that matter. He had his nephew next in line, and he was fond enough of him, so I don't think he was terribly bothered about producing an heir. He had his pursuits, and I had mine. He was generous with my pin money, and I was able to paint as much as I wanted. I could go about in society and do all the things I loved—dance and socialize and, yes, flirt—without being under constant pressure to find someone to marry, now, and it was all rather pleasant.

"And then Templeton died, and I was sorry about it, because he had been kind enough to me. But even mourning was not so dreadful, because it was an excuse to stay home and paint and be no one but myself, and that was another new sort of freedom for me. And when my mourning period was over, and I was able to be back out among society, and the first flood of invitations came in and I realized I could do whatever I chose, with no one to answer to, with money that was mine, forever . . ."

She trailed off.

"You got to experience what it is like to live as a man," he finished for her.

"A very privileged sort of man," she amended with a quirk to her mouth. "Yes." She paused, took another breath. "Penvale grew up in that house, too, and I think he felt what I did to a certain extent, but, well . . . he was able to leave. I had to stay until I was married. And each day that I stayed, I was conscious of what I was costing them."

She looked down at the pencil in her hands, turning it over between her fingers. "I've offered to help Penvale, you know," she said quietly. "With the cost of buying back Trethwick Abbey. I don't even know if our uncle would sell it to him, but I told Penvale that if he were willing, I could put up half of the cost." She looked up again, meeting Jeremy's eyes, an expression of fond exasperation upon her face. "He refused, of course. Just as he refuses to marry a wealthy heiress to solve his problems. He's determined to do it himself—to not rely on anyone else."

She sighed, the quiet exhalation of breath so soft that Jeremy would not have heard it if he hadn't been listening so carefully to every word she spoke. "It's the Bourne curse, apparently—or at least for our particular branch of the family tree. We don't wish to be a burden on anyone else. We just want our independence—the independence we never had as children."

She fell silent at last, and Jeremy sat as though frozen in his seat, unable to break her gaze and equally unable to stem the flow of shame he was feeling. He remembered, during her first Season, at some ball or other, mocking her for the list of potential suitors she was keeping. He had dismissed her as cold and mercenary. But he had never truly understood. He'd had his fair share of financial difficulties, particularly after the death of David, but at the end of the day he'd been a marquess—and, prior to inheriting, the second son of a marquess, with an allowance befitting his position. He'd never felt this helpless sense of dependence that she had experienced. How could he fault her for using the one weapon she had in her arsenal?

"Have you finished sketching me?" he asked, his voice rough at the edges.

She blinked, then looked down, appearing surprised to see the sketch pad before her and the pencil still clutched in her hand. "I suppose I have. This is certainly a good enough start for this evening."

"Good." He rose in one fluid motion and walked toward her. He reached down and plucked the sketch pad and pencil from her hand, laying them down carefully on a nearby table. He then took her hands in his and drew her to her feet. The firelight flickered across her face, creating shadows against her cheekbones, dancing across the smattering of freckles on her nose. He drew her forward until they were pressed together and he could feel the steady beat of her heart pounding against his chest.

"I'm sorry for judging you. In the past, I mean," he added, seeing her slight frown. "I didn't understand. I couldn't possibly have understood. But I understand a bit better now, and I apologize for how I behaved then. It's years too late, but—"

"Better late than never," she said softly, but there was a warmth to her gaze that let him know he was forgiven—a warmth that he was not certain he'd ever seen directed at him, from her.

A warmth that made other parts of him begin to heat in response.

"It feels rather presumptuous to ask for anything, when I've just had to apologize to you," he said, leaning forward slowly, bringing his face oh so close to her own.

"But . . . ?" she breathed against his mouth.

"I'm ready for my next lesson," he said, and claimed her mouth with his.

He had a wild, fleeting thought that he would never grow tired of kissing her. And that was madness, of course—it *had* to be madness, because there was not a woman of his acquaintance that he'd not eventually grown tired of kissing. He saw no reason that this trend should change now. And yet, somehow, it seemed impossible to him that he should ever grow weary of the warmth of her mouth, of the soft little sigh she made at the back of her throat as she settled more deeply into the kiss, of the taste of her, of the feeling of her tongue tangling with his own.

One of his hands sank into her thick, glorious hair while the other reached for her waist, undoing the laces there and a moment later shoving her wrapper from her shoulders and down her arms to pool at her feet on the floor. His own banyan followed a moment later, and he pressed himself more firmly against her, the heat of their skin separated now only by the fine material of his shirt and her nightgown. He felt her hand scrabbling at his waist, and in the next instant it had worked its way beneath his shirt, resting flat against his abdomen and making it very hard for him to concentrate on anything happening above that particular region of his body. A moment later, she was tugging at the hem of the shirt, and he stepped back to pull it over his head in one fluid motion and toss it aside.

And now, he did allow himself a moment of male smugness, because the way she was staring at his naked chest was nothing if not flattering. Had it been any of his previous bed partners, he would have offered a seductive "Like what you see?" accompanied by the requisite arching of one devilish brow, but he rather thought that any so blatant attempt at seduction with *this* particular lady would result in nothing more than laughter on her part—and laughter did, at key moments, have a rather deflating effect upon the proceedings.

So instead, he merely closed the distance between them once more, seized her about the waist, and resumed where they had left off a moment before.

Some indeterminate amount of time later, Diana asked breathlessly, "Should we move to the bed?" After a moment of lazy incomprehension—his mind never did seem able to move terribly swiftly in these sorts of situations—he nodded in agreement, and shortly thereafter found himself braced on one elbow as he slowly drew her nightgown over her head. Each inch of skin that he revealed was more enticing than the last: her long legs; the nip of her waist; the full breasts that had occupied no inconsiderable amount of his attention over the years. At last she was naked before him, and with a bit of hasty maneuvering—and an awkward sort of high leg kick that would not perhaps go down in his seduction archives as one of his finer moments—he, too, was in a similar state of undress.

Normally, at this juncture in the proceedings, he would have plunged forward boldly—a hand between her legs, or perhaps his mouth, depending on how things were going; the quick application of a French letter; and then, bliss—but tonight, he hesitated. He met her eyes for a moment, feeling more uncertain than he had at any point since he'd been an actual virgin, and she smiled.

"Good," she said lightly, "you're already learning." His confusion must have been evident upon his face, because she added, "It's not a race. We've made it this far in relatively little time; there's no harm in pausing the proceedings for a bit."

"I find it a trifle difficult to be patient at the moment," he said through gritted teeth, and her eyes flicked downward. She met his gaze again a moment later and her mouth curved into a very feline sort of smile.

"Shall I take pity on you?" she murmured, and a moment later her small hand curved around him, making him jerk involuntarily in her grip. "Is that better?" she asked innocently, blinking at him. He resisted the urge to moan with great difficulty, and instead thrust into her palm again, the heat and friction of her hand so maddening that it was all he could do to keep his eyes from rolling back in his head. She tightened her hold on him and stroked him slowly; he reached down and seized her hand, adjusting her grip, showing her the pace he liked. Her brow furrowed in concentration, and before long his arm gave out beneath him and he collapsed onto his side even as she rolled onto hers, allowing herself better access to the portion of his anatomy she was presently interested in.

At one point, she allowed her eyes to flick up to his face for a moment, gauging his reaction, before casting them back down once more, evidently satisfied with whatever she saw in his expression.

"I thought," he managed to get out, after some indeterminate period of bliss.

"Mmm?" She gave an inquisitive hum, never removing her attention from the task at hand. Literally.

"I thought . . . Jesus Christ." This time he *did* moan. "I thought you were supposed to be teaching *me* how to please *you*."

"But doing this *does* please me," she said, and there was a note of wonder to her voice—the pleased surprise at learning something new about herself. He would have enjoyed watching her make this realization, had he not been focusing all of his attention on not spilling in her hand.

He pulled himself away from her a moment later, his chest heaving. "Enough," he said on a gasp, lacing her fingers through his own to ensure that they could enact no further mischief. He kissed her, effectively silencing any protest she would have made, and his own hands began their steady journey south. They were delayed for some time at her breasts, it was true—and who could blame them, really?—but eventually made their way as far as her navel, and then lower still, until one hand slid into the slick warmth between her legs and began to move.

At this point in the proceedings, she stiffened. He, being a wiser man than he'd been the day before, stilled his hand immediately. He looked into her eyes and said simply, "Show me."

"The trick," she said, as one of her hands slid around his wrist and moved his fingers slightly upward, "is to listen to the lady's breathing." Her own breaths came more quickly a moment later as he resumed his movements in this slightly adjusted location. "You have to pay attention to these cues, because most ladies won't feel comfortable telling you if you're doing something they dislike. We've been taught all our lives that what happens in the bedchamber is something to be tolerated at best, so there's no expectation among many ladies that they should receive any pleasure from the act."

His hand stilled for a moment as he processed this information. "But surely the sorts of women I—" He broke off with an embarrassed cough; somehow, he did not think that discussing previous conquests while naked with his hand between a lady's legs was terribly good form.

Diana, however, in her typical fashion, was undeterred. "Yes, even some of those sorts of women," she said. "Ones who've indulged in their fair share of liaisons—many of them expect to enjoy the proceedings, I'm sure, but some doubtless do it for the power, or the material advantages their lover can grant them; they don't necessarily count on enjoying the physical aspect of the relationship."

"Have you been interviewing widows and actresses, then?" he asked, quirking a brow at her.

She rolled her eyes. "Don't be absurd." There was a flash of impatience across her face, and a slow roll of her hips that he thought might have been unintentional. "Weren't you in the middle of a task? I do apologize for interrupting you."

He leaned forward, even as his hand resumed its previous activities.

"What are you doing?" she breathed against his lips, her voice a bit ragged.

"Listening to your breathing, of course," he said, capturing her mouth in a long, slow kiss—one that she eventually broke with a moan as he brought his previously underutilized thumb into the proceedings.

"Harder," she said into his ear, locking her arms around his neck.

He obliged. "*Harder*," she said again, moving her hips restlessly against his hand.

"Truly?" he asked, a bit surprised.

"Do I seem likely to *lie* to you at this particular moment?" she asked breathlessly, a note of frustration in her voice.

Acknowledging the soundness of her logic, he redoubled his efforts, and after some indeterminate period of time—seconds? Minutes? He'd utterly lost the ability to judge anything with any degree of accuracy—she broke against him with a last, long moan. Her arms were still locked around his neck in a grip that was rapidly becoming uncomfortable; he was still painfully stiff against her hip; and yet the look of contented bliss upon her face was such a revelation that his bodily concerns faded into nothing.

After a moment, she opened her eyes and quirked her mouth in a lopsided smile. "Full marks."

He grinned back at her helplessly like a lovestruck boy. "I must confess that while I refuse to believe that all of my previous paramours were as dissatisfied as the most recent lady, I don't know that I've ever inspired quite such an enthusiastic reaction before."

She unwound her arms from his neck and patted him fondly on the shoulder. "You just weren't paying close enough attention. Now you'll know."

That remark had the effect of cold water dumped atop his head.

Now you'll know. For future lovers, at some future date when he and Diana were no longer anything to one another other than verbal sparring partners at dull balls. The prospect should not have been so unsettling—it was nothing more than what they had agreed to—and yet so distracted was he by it, and so disturbed was he by his reaction to it, that he must have given some outward sign of his thoughts.

"What is it?" Diana asked, drawing back from him slightly. He rolled over onto his back, tucking one arm behind his head while the other lay at his side. Diana—still gloriously, distractingly naked—wormed her way into the cushion of space between that arm and his body like a particularly determined mole, and rested her head on his shoulder. His arm came around her to toy with the loose strands of her shining hair, slightly sweat-dampened from her—*his*, really—exertions.

"I was just thinking about what you told me before, about your marriage," he said, which was not entirely true, but he did not at all fancy the idea of confessing his maudlin thoughts to her, when he had no doubt she would laugh them off—or, worse, treat him with *pity* of all things, as she gently reminded him that he was nothing more than a convenient warm body. However, he was sure that his thoughts *would* have returned to this subject before too long, so it was not so much of a lie as to make it difficult to pass off as truth.

"What about it?" she asked, a definite note of caution in her voice. He wondered if she regretted telling him already, and the thought that she might was unexpectedly painful.

"What you said about Templeton's death giving you freedom," he said, speaking more carefully than he was accustomed to doing. It turned out speaking as oneself, rather than while wearing a hollow mask of revelry, required a bit more thought. "Do you never intend to remarry, then?"

It occurred to him a moment too late, in the silence that followed, that asking a lady about marriage while lying next to her, in bed, in a state of undress, her skin still glistening from the pleasure he'd recently given her, might be an example of poor timing.

"Willingham," she said after a moment, bracing herself on one elbow with a hand to his chest, "if you are about to propose to me, I might advise you that this is hardly the time or place." She quirked her mouth at him. "Don't come over missish on me now—do I need to explain to you the benefits of a discreet, mutually enjoyable affair?"

"*Missish?*" he asked, ignoring the rest of her sentence entirely.

She nodded solemnly, her hazel eyes wide. "Not everyone can be wise to the ways of the world, you see, and I feel that I perhaps need to keep a wary eye on you. You might fall prey to some unscrupulous seductress—"

Silent as a cat, he sprang into action, drawing her onto his lap to straddle his hips and leaning back against the headboard before she seemed to quite realize what had happened. Certain portions of his anatomy woke up again at this unexpected, enticing dose of female proximity. She adjusted to their situation with her typical speed, however, and reached a hand down to wrap around him once more. He bit back a groan as she leaned forward and placed a series of kisses along the underside of his jaw, and flung his head back so sharply that it hit the headboard a few moments later when she sank down atop him.

She didn't move for a moment, staring at him in concern. "Are you all right?"

He opened his eyes, ignoring the faint throbbing in his head, far more focused on other sensations. "I have, quite literally, never been better."

She grinned as she rose to her knees and sank back down onto him, and his heart stuttered at the sight of her, naked and beautiful and smiling. "It seems I fell prey to an unscrupulous seductress after all," he said on a gasp, anchoring her hips with his hands to slow their rhythm slightly.

"Indeed it does," she said solemnly. "Fortunately, I shall take pity on you"—she gasped at a particularly well-timed thrust on his part—"and ensure that you know what you're doing."

Jeremy forbore to remark that, based on her breathing and the urgent sounds coming from the back of her throat, he thought he had a fairly good idea already. She leaned forward to brace her hands on his shoulders, and he stole a lingering kiss from her, their tongues twining and mimicking the movements of their bodies.

He felt heat building at the base of his spine and knew he could not hold off much longer. Previously, he would have plunged onward without further thought—he had, after all, satisfied the lady in the not-at-all-distant past—but now, listening to the sound of her breathing, he instead redoubled his efforts, sliding a hand between them and applying the same vigorous effort that had yielded such pleasant results some minutes before. He was rewarded, several minutes later, by the sensation of her tightening around him in helpless pleasure, and he dropped his hand, wrapped both arms around her waist, and—with a display of will that he thought worthy of some sort of medal—withdrew, just before joining her in the plummet to mindless release.

It was several minutes before either of them mustered much in the way of words. She was slumped atop him, her head resting on his chest, his cheek against her hair, his hand stroking up and down the smooth skin of her back. At last she mumbled something, the words indecipherable against his skin.

"I beg your pardon?" he asked—slurred? He felt as though he'd been drugged.

"I *said*," she said, tilting her head up slightly so that her mouth was no longer pressed against his shoulder, "you're a remarkably quick study."

He quirked a smile at her. "I do have some experience, you know. It was more a matter of . . . polishing my skills."

She rolled her eyes. "I don't know why I expected you to exhibit some humble gratitude at this particular moment."

"Neither do I. I am feeling rather nauseatingly self-satisfied at present, if you must know. You should count yourself lucky that I'm not preening."

"Aren't you?" she asked, giving him a skeptical look.

He shrugged. "I'm not perfect."

"Of that, I promise you I am perfectly aware," she said, sitting up straight, then glancing down and wrinkling her nose at the mess they had left behind.

"I'll fetch a cloth," he said, lifting her by the waist and depositing her next to him before rising to his feet and crossing to the washbasin in the corner. He dampened a cloth and gave it to her to use before he attended to the mess on the bed.

"This bit isn't terribly romantic, is it?" she asked with characteristic candor, watching as he discarded the cloth and returned to sit beside her. He stretched out his legs and leaned back against the headboard, wrapping an arm around her shoulders. He half expected her to stiffen and pull away, now that the evening's physical activities were at an end, but she rested the back of her head on his arm and looked up at the ceiling.

"It's not the portion of the proceedings I'd choose to write poetry about," he agreed. "But it's either withdraw or use a French letter, and I didn't have one to hand, so this charming scene is the result." She snorted, the noise indelicate and unladylike, a sound that he could not imagine any of his previous paramours making at any point, much less when they were naked in bed with him. A fortnight ago, he would have said that Diana was as full of artifice as any woman of his acquaintance—because even then he had known the face she showed to the public, the face she allowed him to see, was not the *real* Diana. But now, he also knew that no other woman he had ever met—and certainly none that he had bedded—had been as honest with him as she had been these past few days.

She stifled a yawn against the back of her hand, and Jeremy cast a glance at the clock hanging above the mantel. It was nearly two, and his body was beginning to recognize that fact, growing slow and languorous from the combined effects of a long day and an active evening. "I should go back to my room," he said reluctantly, easing his arm out from behind her and rising to his feet. "I can't risk falling asleep here and being discovered by one of the housemaids."

"I think they'll know I had a visitor," she said with a significant glance at the bedsheets. "But you're right—it's likely best if they don't know it's you. A loose widow is far less interesting than a loose widow engaged in licentious acts with the master of the house himself."

Jeremy was moving about the room as she spoke, gathering his discarded articles of clothing. He hastily began to dress. "Shall I come again tomorrow evening?" he asked over his shoulder as he did up the buttons on his breeches. He caught her eyes fixed on him in rapt attention, and she smiled, entirely unashamed to be caught gawking.

"Yes—hopefully in both senses of the word," she said; he paused for a second, then burst out laughing, almost in unison with her, and as he laughed helplessly, the thought rose to his mind unbidden: he loved her.

That, at least, was sufficient to bring his laughter to an abrupt end, and he was able to finish dressing in a hurry by the time her own giggles had trailed off. He tried not to look too carefully at her—naked and tousled, giggling helplessly at her own bawdy joke—for the sake of his dignity; if a thought like that could pop into his mind out of nowhere, it seemed only a matter of time before it popped out of his mouth, and he shuddered to think what her reaction to *that* would be, given her earlier response to the merest mention of marriage. And marriage, after all, was a far sight less serious than *love*.

Mastering herself at last, she added, "I want to start painting tomorrow."

"I'm at your disposal, madam," he said, offering her a courtly bow—a barefoot courtly bow, it was true, but he still thought he made a rather good show of it.

"I know," she said cheerfully, dimpling at him. "I'm still feeling a bit wobbly as a result of that fact."

He gave her a knowing smirk as he backed out of the room to the sound of her renewed laughter, and it was only once he was in the hall, having shut the door quietly behind him, that he allowed his smile to fade. He braced his forearms on the wall next to her door and allowed his forehead to fall forward to rest upon them with a muffled sort of thud.

"Bloody buggering fuck," he said with feeling.

MARTHA WATERS

Twenty

Diana slept even later than usual the next morning, and when she awoke she was gloriously, blissfully sore in certain muscles that hadn't received any exercise in quite a few years—and which had *never* been worked so thoroughly, at that. She stretched her arms above her head and pointed her toes, staring up at the canopy over her bed, which was dappled with enough sunlight to tell her it was late morning. She contemplated ringing for Toogood and dressing in a hurry, but instead, when her maid responded to her summons, requested a breakfast tray.

"It would be too much effort to actually leave the bed to eat, I suppose," Toogood said with her typical utter lack of grace. "Some of us have been awake for hours, whilst others lie abed until noon, a day slipping by outdoors whilst they slumber off the evening's excesses."

"Some toast and chocolate, Toogood," Diana said serenely, too pleased with the success of the previous evening to even work herself up about her maid's typical rudeness.

Toogood, unsurprisingly, ignored her. "Whilst you're not as bad as Lady Helen, I'll confess, I still think it a sign of a lack of moral fiber to spend quite this much time in bed."

Diana's ears perked up at the sound of Lady Helen's name. "What do you mean?" she asked.

"You see, if you weren't so lazy . . ." Toogood began, with the closest thing to joy Diana had ever seen in her manner. Evidently, the opportunity to expand upon her mistress's character failings was akin to Christmas come early.

"No, I meant about Lady Helen," Diana interrupted, waving her hand impatiently. "She's usually at the breakfast table before I am in the morning."

Toogood muttered something that *might* have been, "That's not saying much," but followed it up with the information Diana desired before any reprimand could be directed at her. "She's awake early enough in the morning, but she takes to her room in the afternoon almost every day—some nonsense about becoming overtired, and from *what*, I ask you?—and she insists her maid remain with her the entire time. Can't even nap alone! What sort of person can't nap alone?"

Toogood, having discovered a new target for her irritation, expanded upon this subject with great fervor, and at considerable length, but Diana stopped listening, distracted by what Toogood had just told her.

How odd. Diana wasn't surprised that Lady Helen rested in the afternoon—it was just the sort of insipid thing society ladies did with great frequency, as though the effort of eating a meal and exchanging conversation over tea was so taxing that an afternoon nap was necessary to recoup one's strength—but her insistence on her maid remaining present seemed peculiar in the extreme. She supposed the lady wouldn't hesitate to inconvenience one of her servants, but it still seemed strange to be so desirous of her maid's company while sleeping.

An idea was slowly beginning to take shape in Diana's mind—a wild, improbable, utterly scandalous idea—and she was desperate to know if she had the right of it. And, if she did have the right of it, she was similarly desperate to know who the gentleman was. Langely? Monmouth? Neither of them seemed particularly likely candidates, and yet . . .

The idea of Lady Helen taking a lover—for would this not perfectly explain why she needed her maid to remain with her during her "naps," to act as lookout?—was so preposterous that Diana was tempted to reject it as quickly as it had occurred to her. And yet, if there was one thing she loved more than gossip—and make no mistake, she was *exceptionally* fond of gossip, so long as it wasn't about her—it was secrets so delicious and well-kept that no one even whispered of them. It wasn't often one was privy to such a confidence, and she was positively *desperate*, all of a sudden, to know if she had been so lucky.

But how to find out? She and Lady Helen were hardly bosom companions—a less likely confidant Diana could scarcely imagine. But if she were correct in her wild supposition, then it was possible that she had badly misjudged Lady Helen, in which case . . .

Well, she didn't know quite what.

"My breakfast, please, Toogood," she said briskly, interrupting her maid's diatribe, which seemed to have turned to the subject of naps in general, and the loose, reckless nature of those who took them. With a few last muttered grievances—and a very dark look—Toogood departed, leaving Diana alone with her suddenly quite fascinating thoughts. How best to approach this situation? She had nothing but a vague theory—and a wildly improbable one at that.

Although, if it were true, Diana was not at all certain where it left her plans to see Jeremy married. If Lady Helen was liaising with someone else, was her interest in Jeremy entirely feigned—a front to disguise her actual activities? Not that anything Jeremy had said to her had given her the slightest indication that he now considered matrimony—to Lady Helen, or anyone else—to be an appealing prospect, in any case.

But then, there *had* been that moment last night, in bed . . .

Diana lost track of her own thoughts for a moment, remembering. It should have been nothing more than an idle, curious comment, but there had been something in his expression—an intensity, an interest in her response—when he asked her if she intended to wed again that had made her take notice. Which was sufficiently alarming, for reasons she didn't care to delve into very deeply, that she had wasted no time in shutting down that line of inquiry with one of her typical breezy jokes.

The fact was, her own intimacy with Jeremy did not seem to have given her any great insight into his mind. Did she understand him better than she had a week ago? Undoubtedly—and she liked him a dangerous amount, as a result. Did she know what he was looking for in a wife? Absolutely not—and the idea of such a person existing was suddenly more distasteful to her than she would have liked it to be. Some primal, traitorous part of her whispered, *Mine*, when she thought of him, and it simply would not do.

She knew it must be a simple result of their physical relationship— she had never taken a lover before, after all, and she had certainly never found so much satisfaction in the bedchamber, despite his early fumbling. She was, in fact, remarkably pleased on that front; she admitted that her own limited experience offered little by way of comparison, but she was certain that the previous night's activities had been exceptional by anyone's measure. He had needed a bit of guidance, of course—but Diana suspected this weakness was common to men in the bedroom, just as it was in so many situations outside of the bedroom, too. He had accepted her instructions with remarkably good grace, and it in fact did something strange and squirmy to her insides to think of him touching her, listening to her words, working his hardest to bring her release.

He had certainly succeeded spectacularly on that front, she reflected; had she known the marital act could be like this, she would have taken a lover before Templeton was cold in the ground. She, fool that she was, hadn't even been able to maintain an aura of cool reserve after the fact; she had no idea what the size of Jeremy's head would be today, but she'd no doubt that the man would be insufferably smug about the entire experience, and the worst bit was that he probably deserved to be.

The long and short of it was, Lady John Marksdale had clearly been exaggerating her complaints. There had been a bit of fumbling at the beginning, it was true, but things had improved considerably from that point. Diana liked to think that she was doing a sort of community service to all the future actresses and opera dancers and merry widows who would make their way into Jeremy's bed; he knew how to pay a bit closer attention now, and she'd no doubt that women would be reaping the benefits of this lesson for years to come.

This thought was unexpectedly depressing, and she refocused her attention on the matter at hand: namely, that she still had no idea how she was going to get the man married, and the more she felt herself growing attached, the more necessary this goal became. If Jeremy was married to someone else, he was safe; she might be many things, but she was not the sort of hopeless creature to fall in love with another woman's husband. Her scheme had taken advantage of Lady Helen's blatant attempts to fling herself at Jeremy to make some other eligible lady look attractive by comparison—but Diana now, all of a sudden, was uncertain as to *why*, exactly, Lady Helen was behaving this way toward Jeremy. If she was liaising with another gentleman, shouldn't she be attempting to marry him instead?

The entire situation was enough to give her a headache. And while the last thing she needed at the moment was yet another complication to her scheme, she also couldn't stand being in the dark—and nothing about Lady Helen's behavior at the moment made sense, if Diana's suspicion was correct. She was determined to speak to the lady before the day was out—the only question that remained was, how?

As it turned out, fortune conspired in Diana's favor that afternoon. The gentlemen of the party were absent by the time she had breakfasted, dressed, and made her way downstairs; the fine weather was too appealing for them to remain indoors a moment past breakfast, and a hunting party had departed on horseback in apparently high spirits. The ladies of the party, being forsaken by their gentlemen companions, had gone on a walk after breakfast, declaring that if the gentlemen were going to take advantage of the sunshine, so, too, should they.

Diana, however, made her excuses and absented herself from the party. She gathered her sketchbook and a packet of pastels and took herself to the gardens, settling on the same bench she had sat upon with Jeremy and Lady Helen the day before and beginning a detailed rendition of the roses growing nearby. So absorbed was she in her work that she did not hear the footsteps that signaled the approach of another person, and it was only when a shadow was cast upon the page before her that she glanced up in surprise.

Lady Helen stood above her, peering down at her sketchbook with an expression of surprised interest on her face. "That's remarkably good," she said, a tone of mild astonishment in her voice. "I'd never heard you were an artist."

"Oh," Diana said, feeling uncommonly flustered. Having others look at her artwork always made her feel rather as though she were naked and on display, and having Lady Helen of all people being the one staring down at her did nothing to lessen this sensation. "I'm not. I just dabble a bit."

Lady Helen frowned. "I'm no expert, but this looks like more than dabbling to me. When you compare it to the bland watercolors that most ladies of our class produce . . . well, it's astonishing."

"That's because it's a pastel, not a watercolor," Diana said with what she felt was admirable patience. "They look entirely different—pastels allow you much bolder colors, and to compare them is . . . well, it doesn't make any sense at all. They're two entirely different mediums."

"You don't sound like a casual hobbyist," Lady Helen said, giving her a speculative glance. It was a glance that made Diana distinctly uncomfortable, in part because it was such a far cry from the idea of Lady Helen Courtenay that she had built over the course of her entire acquaintance with the lady. Diana disliked having to revise her assumptions about people—it was so tiresome to have to admit that she'd been wrong. But, she supposed, in this particular case that ship had already sailed.

"Can I help you with something?" Diana asked, shading her eyes against the sun as she gazed up at Lady Helen. Would she never re-member a hat? This was why she had those accursed freckles across her nose that never seemed to fade, even in the dead of winter.

Freckles that, she suddenly recalled with a rush of heat, Jeremy had trailed his lips over the evening before.

Giving herself a stern mental shake, she leveled an even stare up at Lady Helen, who was looking down at her in an assessing fashion. Seeming to come to some sort of internal conclusion, Lady Helen seated herself on the bench next to Diana and said, "I heard that you were asking your maid about me."

Diana's jaw did not literally drop, but it was a very close thing. "How could you *possibly* have heard that so quickly? It couldn't have been more than two hours ago."

"I have my ways," Lady Helen said primly, then added, "I believe your maid ran into mine on the stairs. She was evidently in the midst of a fit of pique, and nearly talked Sutton's ear off before she was able to make her escape."

Diana heaved a sigh that, heavy as it was, still did not feel out of proportion to the situation. "I really must find a new lady's maid," she muttered.

"I would if I were you," Lady Helen agreed.

"I've grown rather accustomed to her, after all this time," Diana confessed. "And I somehow find her complaining more comforting than any simpering prattle I could receive from another maid."

"It is possible to employ a maid who lands somewhere in between those two options," Lady Helen pointed out, and there was something in her tone as she said it that made Diana—metaphorically—sit up and take notice.

"I suppose you're correct," Diana conceded. "But yes, to return to the topic at hand—Toogood mentioned something about you that I found rather interesting, and I inquired a bit more of her. I didn't think it enough to warrant gossip, but I suppose I should never underestimate the ire of a grudging maid."

"What was it that had you curious, my lady? My maid was not very specific regarding the details." Lady Helen's voice was as cool as ever, but there was something in her tone that made Diana think she might be the slightest bit nervous. She was certainly watching Diana with rapt attention, as though whatever her answer would be was of the utmost importance to her.

"Well," Diana said, drawing the word out for no other reason than to be difficult, "Toogood mentioned that you were in the habit of napping every afternoon."

Lady Helen's lips pursed. "Yes. I find the rigors of a country house party rather more than my delicate constitution can handle. I can't expect you to understand, of course—you are just so much more . . ." She paused, as though searching for the right word, though Diana had no doubt that she already knew exactly what she was going to say. ". . . robust."

Well played, Diana thought. Never had she felt quite so much like a horse. She pasted a sweet smile upon her face. "I am not unsympathetic to your weariness, my lady. Who, after all, can be expected to breakfast, take a turn about the gardens, and perhaps play a game of whist without retiring to one's bed? It is entirely understandable."

Lady Helen's eyes narrowed, but Diana continued speaking. "However, the piece of Toogood's report that I found so interesting was the fact that your maid apparently remains with you for the entire duration of your rest."

"Yes," Lady Helen said calmly, "it is helpful to have her at hand should I need anything."

"Mmm, yes," Diana murmured sweetly, trailing off as though contemplating Lady Helen's reply. "It is fortunate that you have found a maid so . . . *devoted* to you." She placed just the right amount of emphasis on the word—enough to make Lady Helen notice, but not enough to rob Diana of the ability to deny that she had done any such thing.

"I don't know what you mean," Lady Helen said calmly—and that was her critical mistake. She should have agreed with Diana, of course—murmured some nonsense about the pleasures of finding a truly loyal servant, complained about the difficulty of finding reliable help, anything, really. But to claim ignorance entirely—no. It was completely the wrong answer—and it made Diana feel even more convinced that her wild theory might just be true.

She decided there was nothing for it but to pretend to more knowledge than she actually possessed. Fortunately, feigning confidence had never been difficult for her.

"I think you do," she said sweetly. "I think you insist your maid remains with you because you are not actually resting at all." Here, she paused. How to phrase it, exactly? How did one imply an affair—imply that one's maid had been bribed to serve as lookout to ensure that no one interrupted unexpectedly while one cavorted with a gentleman?

"I believe that you are having an affair," Diana said at last, deciding to abandon subtlety entirely and instead brazen the thing out with a bit more confidence than she actually felt.

This bet paid off immediately, as Lady Helen looked around them frantically, her eyes wild.

"Keep your voice down! Do you want the entire household to hear?"

"Of course n—" Diana began to say, but Lady Helen continued speaking, growing increasingly fervent the longer she spoke.

"I would be ruined—utterly, truly ruined. And whilst I've obviously no desire to marry, I shouldn't wish to cause my mother pain, or to blacken my brother's name."

Diana opened her mouth to reply, then paused. No desire to

marry? But surely Lady Helen wished to marry whoever the gentleman was that she was carrying on with—why else would she be willing to sacrifice her virtue, if not in pursuit of some plump matrimonial prize?

"If my mother were to find out, she would cast Sutton out without a reference, and she'd never be able to find another post again. The thought of her suffering, all because I could not help myself . . ." Her bottom lip trembled, and Diana was momentarily struck dumb. She would never have guessed that Lady Helen possessed the compassion necessary to feel so deeply for a member of the hired help, to feel so personally responsible for the woman's fate. It spoke well of her character, and Diana opened her mouth to magnanimously tell her so, when she was once again forestalled.

"And of course, I am the one who led Sutton down this path in the first place—she might have continued on, ignorant of her own preferences, had I not met her." Diana frowned, confused—*preferences?* "But I took one look at her, and I just could not resist"—Diana began to receive the impression that she had badly misunderstood the situation at hand—"and of course, it was even worse once I came to truly *know* her, and our attachment was no longer merely physical. Once I realized what a remarkable woman she is . . . well, there was simply no way I could give her up."

"I beg your pardon," Diana said at last as Lady Helen paused for breath, gazing at her with imploring eyes. Diana felt considerably at sea, and more naive than she had felt in years. It would have been galling, had it not been so entirely shocking. "Are you implying that your lover is . . . your *maid?*"

Lady Helen blinked. "Are *you* implying that you didn't already know?" She blinked again. "Did I just confess for no reason at all? Oh, this is utterly maddening—I should have just behaved like a villain in a novel and murdered you and hidden the body beneath the church flagstones."

Diana interrupted this bit of criminal fantasy before Lady Helen could get too carried away. "I supposed that some sort of bedroom activities were underway," she assured—*assured?!*—Lady Helen. "I, however, must have too conventional a mind. I assumed that you had a gentleman lover, and that your maid—Sutton, is it?—was standing guard to ensure that you were not interrupted at a delicate moment."

Lady Helen snorted, the sound the least delicate Diana had yet heard from her. "I should be offended, truly I should. As if I would be so foolhardy as to sacrifice my virtue to one of the—doubtless incompetent—gentlemen at this house party."

"But sacrificing your virtue to a *lady* is acceptable?" Diana asked incredulously; she had no objection to this practice, but would have thought that Lady Helen—or at least the Lady Helen she thought she had known—would.

Lady Helen smirked slightly; the smirk had a rather saucy edge to it, one that Diana would never have thought to see on the face of Lady Helen Courtenay. "In the interest of strict accuracy, I would like to note that my virtue is entirely intact. It is an advantage of being a sapphist, you see."

Choosing not to follow the conversational direction her curious mind so desperately wished to pursue—surely one of Violet's beloved poets had something to say on the matter; Diana would inquire later—Diana instead said, "What are you about, then, flinging yourself after Jer—Willingham, if you have no interest in marrying?"

Lady Helen's smile widened. "It's all part of my plan, you see.

Merely the latest chapter in what has been a lengthy, yearslong strategy."

Diana was beginning to get the sense that she was in the presence of a mind far more devious than her own, and the feeling was simultaneously alarming and intriguing. "Explain."

Lady Helen settled herself back upon the bench. "If a lady does not wish to wed," she explained, "and she is fair of face and from a respectable, moneyed background, she is confronted with a bit of a challenge. However, she has several options open to her. The most obvious option is to ruin herself. This itself is a bit risky—there is every chance her parents will force her into matrimony with the man she selects for her ruination, so if a lady chooses this path, she must only do so if she knows her parents sufficiently well to feel confident that they won't force her hand.

"For many ladies, however, this option is too risky. Another possibility is to transform oneself into a bluestocking—spectacles, ink-stained fingers, dull pedantries at every social event she attends. This often does the trick, but this, too, has its attendant risk—what if her parents decide to find her a dull sort of younger son? A vicar, or a scholar, someone who finds her academic nature appealing? One could find oneself shipped off to a vicarage in Shropshire before one even realizes what is happening. Again, risky.

"Naturally, I considered both of these choices as I was approaching my own come-out," Lady Helen added. "I had known for some years that I was not attracted to men, but for a while I assumed I would merely make a go of it, marry some aristocratic gentleman I did not love, and hope that he took up with a mistress in short order. My mother hired Sutton for me when I was sixteen, however, and . . . well, once we came to an understanding, I knew that there was no possibility of my marrying. Even if we could manage to conceal our feelings from my husband, even if we could carry on under his nose with him none the wiser, the thought of living such a lie for the rest of my life was too appalling to be bearable. It was then that I began to plot how to evade this trap."

"And what did you land on, then?" Diana asked, fascinated despite herself. Lady Helen's plight rather cast her own woes in her debut Season in the shade.

"A more cunning line of deception," Lady Helen said with some degree of self-satisfaction—probably entirely earned, Diana thought. "I would play society's game, give them every appearance of a lady desperate for marriage. I am an observant person, Lady Templeton—I have watched ladies and gentlemen perform the courting ritual and I've noticed the ladies who are *too* desperate, who make themselves unattractive in the wanting." Her voice took on a slightly bitter edge. "Because of course, they have been told their entire lives that matrimony to the most eligible gentleman possible is their raison d'être, and yet if they want it too badly—if they get the slightest bit desperate to achieve this thing that they have been told is the only thing they should ever desire—well . . . how *pathetic*."

Diana's mouth actually *was* agape by this point. This entire conversation gave her the feeling of being in the company of a creature one had assumed was a rather unintelligent lapdog who turned out, in fact, to be a wolf.

"It wasn't too difficult to turn myself into the sort of lady that no gentleman actually wants to marry. One who laughs too shrilly, who clutches a gentleman's arm too tightly, who praises too lavishly—and, for the record, you've *no idea* how excessive one's praise of a titled gentleman must be before he finally thinks you've taken it too far." She allowed herself an eye roll. "It was a delicate endeavor—I couldn't be too obvious about it, or my mother and brother would have realized what I was doing. I had to give the impression of a lady being slowly worn down by the marriage mart, of becoming a lady so desperate to wed that she no longer even resembled her former self."

She paused for a moment, her gaze fixed on her lap. "I am fond of my brother, and my only regret regarding this deception is that I am certain it has altered his opinion of me. If I could but trust him to never force me to wed, I would let him in on my secret, but I fear my mother's influence would wear him down eventually, even if he were sympathetic to my plight."

"So Willingham was all part of this scheme?" Diana asked, feeling a guilty twinge at the role she had played in this entire saga.

"It was too good an opportunity to pass up," Lady Helen explained. "I thought if I flung myself at a *marquess*, of all people, and were rebuffed, gossip might start to spread. I'm getting older, but I'm not on the shelf yet, and I thought that whispers about my conduct here might hurry me down that path. It was all the easier when you began conspiring to trap me alone with him—for reasons I'm still not entirely certain I understand."

"Willingham and I made a wager about him being married within a year," Diana said, feeling a bit sheepish.

Lady Helen frowned. "But surely you couldn't have thought Lord Willingham would want to marry a lady like me? Or rather, the Lady Helen Courtenay he thinks he knows?"

"No," Diana admitted, "but I was hopeful that if I flung him together with you enough, it would make him reconsider some of the other ladies of his acquaintance—might make them appear more appealing prospects by comparison."

"So you were essentially using me to *scare* him into matrimony?" Lady Helen asked, arching a brow.

Diana was beginning to feel rather ashamed of herself. "Well . . . yes, I suppose that is the most succinct way to put it."

Lady Helen burst out laughing, her real laugh, happy and unguarded, a far cry from the shrill giggles Diana had previously heard her emit. It had a transformative effect—her entire face softened, the cool, haughty look that she usually wore having completely vanished. "I really should thank you," she said after a moment, still giggling. "If ever I needed confirmation that my efforts are working, you have just given it to me. Not only have I made myself an unappealing matrimonial prospect, I have in fact become so dreadful that the mere specter of marriage to me can be used to scare gentlemen into marrying others."

"When you put it like that, I feel rather ashamed of myself," Diana confessed. "I should offer you an apology."

Lady Helen waved a hand dismissively. "Don't bother with all that. What I'd like to know, however, is why it is that you are trying to get Lord Willingham married to someone else when it is obvious that you're in love with him."

Diana felt the blood drain from her face. "I'm certain I don't know what you mean," she said stiffly—and, she feared, entirely unconvincingly.

"Oh, come now, I thought we were being honest with each other," Lady Helen said, fixing her with a beady-eyed stare. "It might not be obvious to everyone, but to me, at least—well, it's quite the experience to have another lady conspiring to get you alone with a certain gentleman at every possible opportunity, and yet also glaring every time she succeeded."

Diana sighed. "Willingham and I have a bit of an . . . arrangement, at the moment," she said carefully. "However, it is entirely temporary, and I've no wish for another loveless marriage of convenience."

"Love can exist without marriage, just as much as the opposite is true. I promise you, I'm quite certainly in love with Sutton, and we'll never be married," Lady Helen said. "It seems to me that there is a fair amount of feeling between you and Lord Willingham, even if you never marry."

"I didn't . . ." Diana hesitated, floundering. "Willingham and I have a casual arrangement."

Lady Helen snorted, the sound yet another reminder—if Diana needed one—that the lady before her bore little resemblance to the one Diana had thought she'd known. "It doesn't seem all that casual to me, judging by the way you look at each other."

Diana opened her mouth to object—her natural response to any insinuation of deeper sentiment on her part, about anyone at all, but most particularly Jeremy—but then closed it again. And, for perhaps the first time, paused to ask herself: *did* she love Jeremy?

She had spent so much time insisting—to Jeremy, to Violet and Emily, to herself—that their arrangement was based on nothing more than mutual attraction and convenience, and brutally suppressing every hint of true feeling the moment it attempted to emerge, that she had not taken even a moment to ask herself this simple question.

She thought of Jeremy—of the man she'd thought she'd known so well, and of the one he was revealing himself to be bit by bit, conversation by conversation. She thought of the laugh lines at the corners of his blue eyes, and of the particular quirk to one side of his mouth when he was bickering with her, waiting to see if she'd rise to the bait. She thought of the intensity of his gaze on her when they were naked in bed, her hand moving with his to find the rhythm she wanted.

Most of all, she thought of the thrill she felt every time he walked into a room, every time she scored a point in one of their never-ending arguments, every time his face lit up with amusement at whatever setdown she'd just delivered him.

And she realized that of course she loved him.

Now what on earth was she to do about it?

Lady Helen, of course, had been privy to none of these thoughts, but she'd been watching Diana carefully and seemed to guess at some of what had crossed her mind.

"Not so casual, then?" she asked. "I thought not," she added, not even waiting for a reply.

"You needn't sound so smug," Diana grumbled.

"I rather think I'm entitled to it," Lady Helen said airily, which, Diana reflected, was true. Lady Helen had successfully enacted an elaborate, yearslong ruse that had fooled the entire *ton*, while Diana couldn't even carry on a discreet affair without falling in love in painfully obvious fashion.

"I'd appreciate your keeping this to yourself," she said briskly. "I've no intention of risking looking ridiculous by declaring myself to Willingham, so this need go no further than the two of us."

"Whatever you wish," Lady Helen said, waving an idle hand. "You might consider that some things are worth the risk, though."

"And what are you risking all of this for, then?" Diana asked curiously. "What is your plan, precisely?"

"I only need another year or two before I am so firmly on the shelf that I hope to convince my brother to purchase me a cottage in the countryside where I can rusticate in peace with a single servant," Lady Helen confided. "It has been a great deal of trouble, making it this far, but the end is in sight."

All at once, Diana felt more than a little ashamed. Lady Helen had risked everything for Sutton, for the chance of some semblance of a happy life together, even if that life would undoubtedly be far less comfortable than the luxury to which she had been born. Was Diana not willing to risk far less than that for the chance of keeping Jeremy—the private Jeremy, the *real* Jeremy?

She had no ready answer, and it was deeply unsettling.

"I think I shall leave you to your thoughts," Lady Helen said, standing and brushing off her skirts in rather ostentatious fashion. "Please do not allow this discussion to change anything in your manner toward me—I have worked quite hard to craft this particular image of myself, as I have just explained, and I shall be most vexed if you undo all of my labor with a sympathetic glance."

"You have my solemn vow that I shall continue to speak to you with thinly veiled distaste," Diana said. "Shall I continue to fling Willingham in your direction, then?"

"That, my lady, is entirely up to you," was Lady Helen's reply. "I certainly do not intend to change anything in my manner to him. Whether you continue to enable my attempts to seduce him, however, is of no matter to me—and should the gentleman suddenly find himself otherwise engaged, I shall of course retreat hastily, albeit with very bad grace."

"Duly noted," Diana said, not entirely certain what other response she could offer to this.

"Hire a new maid," was Lady Helen's parting shot over her shoulder as she floated away through the gardens in the direction of the house, leaving Diana alone with her very complicated, very inconvenient thoughts.

Twenty-One

The gentlemen were not yet returned from their day of shooting helpless creatures in a rustic woodland setting when Diana returned to the house to seek out Violet and Emily. She found them in the library, tucked into a window seat together, a book spread across their knees. As Diana drew closer, she could see that it had illustrations, which Violet pointed to as she spoke in a low voice to Emily. Emily, it should be noted, sported cheeks even rosier than usual, and was emitting a rather shocked giggle at the moment Diana came within earshot.

". . . have found that friction in this particular area produces extremely positive results," Violet was saying. "But I think it's likely different for everyone, so it's particularly useful to discover for yourself what you might enjoy before finding yourself called upon to instruct a gentleman in this regard."

Diana stopped in her tracks. "Are you looking at *lewd* illustrations?" she asked. "Not that I'm surprised Willingham would leave such a book lying around the library—it seems entirely in keeping with his character—but you might have found somewhere more discreet to look at it, for heaven's sake."

Violet looked up, startled, evidently having been so involved in her instructive lecture to Emily that she hadn't heard Diana's approaching footsteps. "For your information," she said, with great dignity, "this is an anatomy text."

Diana blinked, and looked closer. Violet was entirely correct. The book was full of text set in very small type, which seemed dreadfully dull, but also—as Violet illustrated by flipping through a few pages—littered with extremely interesting, and accurate, anatomical illustrations.

"I am merely trying to offer Emily the assistance that no one gave me before my own marriage," she explained.

Diana arched an eyebrow. "Please, Emily, tell me Cartham hasn't proposed. I don't know how I shall bear it."

"Fortunately, he has not," Emily said with a barely suppressed shudder at the thought—which was as close as she'd ever gotten to complaining about the situation. Had Diana been in her shoes, she would have been hollering to the rooftops—not to mention plotting how to ruin herself at the earliest possible opportunity, to ensure that Cartham no longer found her company so elevating—but Emily had precious little to say of the years (years!) she had spent in the man's company, her father rejecting all other suitors who looked twice at the beautiful daughter of an impoverished marquess.

"It's always best to be prepared, however," Violet said. "One can't necessarily rely on a gentleman to know all of these things, though I must confess that I've never had any complaints in that regard." Her lips curved upward in an expression that Diana—who was not, perhaps, feeling her most charitable at the moment—could only describe as smug.

"Yes, Violet, we are both very pleased for your newfound matrimonial bliss," Diana said acerbically. Violet's smile slipped, and Diana cursed herself—she did this sometimes, spoke without thinking of how her words would sound.

"We truly are pleased," she said more softly. "You know that. I'm sorry, I'm all at sixes and sevens at the moment and I hardly know what I'm saying."

"What's wrong?" Emily asked, scooting to one side so that Diana could squeeze between them on the window seat. Violet—after casting an approving glance at an incredibly detailed illustration of the male reproductive organ—closed the book in her lap and set it on the floor. Diana leaned back, feeling the cool glass of the window at her back and, toeing off her shoes, drew her knees up to her chest.

Diana hesitated—Lady Helen had entrusted her with an extremely important secret, and Diana didn't feel quite right about betraying her confidence so quickly. However, she knew Violet and Emily were entirely trustworthy—and, furthermore, if she didn't tell someone all that was on her mind, she thought she might burst.

"I made a rather interesting discovery about Lady Helen this morning," she said after a moment during which both Emily and Violet watched her expectantly.

Emily's brow wrinkled slightly. Clearly, this was not the salvo with which she'd expected Diana to open.

"What I'm about to tell you cannot move beyond the three of us—not even to Audley, Violet, because he's friends with Rothsmere, and whilst I know he can keep a secret, I worry he would give it away by some accidental tell, without even meaning to." Seeing Violet's nod of assent, Diana continued, lowering her voice even further. "Lady Helen prefers the company of other women, and has been carrying on an affair with her lady's maid for some years now."

"*What?*" Violet asked; had she been drinking anything at the moment, Diana was certain she would have spit it out. Emily sat quietly, frowning.

"But she's been flinging herself at Jeremy for the better part of a week!" Violet protested.

"All part of a rather cunning plan to make herself seem so desperate and grasping that no man could possibly wish to marry her, so that eventually she can retire to a cottage in the country with her maid."

"Well," Violet said, crossing her arms over her chest and tapping her chin with one finger, "I must admit I'm rather impressed in spite of myself."

"That was entirely my reaction as well," Diana assured her. "One doesn't know quite what to say in the face of such craftiness."

"'Congratulations,' perhaps?" Violet suggested.

"You're right," Diana said slowly. "That would have been the correct response. I bungled it horribly, I think."

Beside them, Emily was still silently frowning. Violet looked at her. "What is it, Emily? Did you not know such inclinations existed?"

"No," Emily said slowly, clearly still deep in thought. "I've read enough of those scandalous poems you've forced on me over the years to understand that some ladies prefer ladies, and some men prefer men." She paused for a moment, staring into the middle distance, still deep in thought. "However," she continued at last, "I'm not sure how to put this in the context of what you just told me today." She turned to Violet. "How, exactly, do two ladies achieve the matrimonial act, when they are lacking a necessary piece of . . . er . . ."

"Equipment?" Diana suggested innocently.

"Yes, quite," Emily agreed eagerly, even as Violet shot a reproving look at Diana.

"Yes, Violet, do instruct us," Diana agreed, turning to Violet and attempting to mirror Emily's look of eager inquisitiveness as closely as she could.

"Why don't *you* inform us, Diana?" Violet shot back. "I assume you've been gaining a fair share of firsthand experience of your own this week, have you not?"

It was now Diana's turn to smile smugly. "I might have done," she admitted. "But I think it only fair that, since you commenced this lesson with Emily, you be the one to complete it."

"Very well," Violet said through gritted teeth. She looked at Emily once more. "There are—other ways to achieve completion, without the presence of a . . . um . . ." She floundered.

"Instrument of love," Diana said, straight-faced.

"Phallus," Violet said firmly, clearly deciding that safety lay in Latin. "When Diana walked in, we were discussing how some friction in a certain area can be very pleasant—you recall the region in particular I was describing?" Emily nodded eagerly; Diana had the distinct impression that, had she a pen and piece of paper at hand, she would be taking diligent notes. "Well, in the absence of a male partner, I believe ladies devote even more attention to that particular region."

"With fingers alone?" Emily inquired.

"Um," Violet said. Was she blushing? Diana thought her color looked high. "And their tongues," she added in a rush.

"Tongues!" Emily repeated in amazement. "Down there?"

"The sensation is remarkably pleasant," Violet said, blushing in earnest now, an expression upon her face that implied fond reminiscence of an enjoyable interlude.

"I believe there are also certain substitutes for the male organ in question, which one can purchase," Diana chimed in—if they were going to corrupt a virgin, they might as well do a thorough job of it.

"I've yet to see one of these for myself, sadly, but I've heard whispers of them. I'd be unsurprised to learn that ladies of Lady Helen's inclinations make use of these as well."

"It's really rather clever," Emily said slowly. "If the female body is so designed that pleasure can be achieved from—or is, as you said Violet, rather dependent on—an area not necessary to the reproductive act . . ." She trailed off for a moment, deep in thought once more. ". . . and if there are even *imitations* of the male organ that can be acquired, for ladies who happen to enjoy its sensation . . ." Another moment of thoughtful silence. "Why, it's almost as though men aren't necessary at all!" She beamed at the pair of them, like a pupil who had just worked out a particularly thorny mathematical equation.

"A comforting thought, is it not?" Diana asked her.

"It's much more *pleasant* with a man," Violet said, seeming to think that her instruction session had veered a bit off course. "If one's inclinations lie in that direction, I mean."

"Still, this is useful knowledge," Emily mused. She blinked and redirected her attention to Diana. "But what does all of this have to do with whatever is bothering you?"

"Oh," Diana said, her smile fading; for a moment, she had forgotten what she'd come here to discuss in the first place. "Well . . ." She paused. Her insides squirmed. The thought of being candid about how she felt—about how she *truly* felt, and about Jeremy, of all people—made the idea of flinging herself off the roof sound more appealing than it probably should . . . and yet wasn't that the root of her problem? If she could not voice her feelings to her two closest friends, to Violet and Emily, whom she'd known for half her life, how could she ever muster the courage to tell Jeremy himself?

"It made me think, for a moment, about how much more difficult life is for people like Lady Helen. And for men who prefer men. About what they're willing to risk, just to be with the person they love." She paused, her mind still working, snagging on one thing in particular. "And about how marriage probably doesn't seem like a trap to them at all, but a glorious, impossible dream." Marriage had never felt like that to her—but it had, once upon a time, been a means of escape, and she had reached for it eagerly with both hands. If marriage to Templeton, a man she had barely known and had not loved, could have been an escape, how much more could it be with a man she cared for—and desired—a great deal?

"Marriage has never felt like a trap to me," Violet said carefully, clearly recognizing how difficult it had been for Diana to speak even this much. "Even when James and I were in our worst moments, when we were sitting silently across the dinner table from one another, not saying a word, it never felt like a trap. It felt like something precious and wonderful that we had broken."

"Marriage to someone of my own choosing is more than I have ever truly hoped for," Emily said quietly. "It still seems out of my reach. But I am starting to think that if there is someone who makes that risk worthwhile, it might be worth taking." She paused, a distant expression on her face; Diana and Violet watched her eagerly, and when she did not continue speaking after a moment, Violet broke the silence.

"Emily," she said slowly, "has Belfry proposed to you?"

Emily shook her head. "Not in so many words. But he's implied . . . well, he's told me that he has more than enough money to pay off my father's gambling debts—and that he knows something about Mr. Cartham, something about his past, that he could use to end Mr. Cartham's blackmail of my father. I could be free," she added, her voice faltering on the word, one she clearly barely even dared voice for fear it would vanish in a puff of smoke. "It would not be a love match, of course—but I like the fact that he spoke honestly to me. He . . . respects me." Her tone was slightly wondering, as if this was something she had not thought possible, and Diana felt painfully sad for Emily, in a way she'd not felt in a while.

"In any case, he hasn't even properly asked," Emily said, her manner more businesslike all of a sudden. "But I'm starting to think that it might be worth the risk."

For the second time that day, Diana was struck by her own cowardice. Lady Helen was willing to risk her reputation, her very future to be with the woman she loved; Emily was willing to risk marriage to a man she barely knew, to have some taste of freedom. But she, Diana, could not even risk uttering three small words, and seeing if Jeremy returned them?

"You're making me feel rather ashamed of myself, all of a sudden," she confessed. "My own romantic problems seem rather pitiful by comparison."

"Is this about Jeremy?" Violet asked.

Diana sighed, nodding. "We came to our current arrangement under the understanding that it was to be temporary, mutually beneficial, and that we would go our separate ways when it ceased to please us both. But . . ."

She trailed off, at a loss to explain the complex whirlwind of emotions that had taken up residence within her without her consent. That was the trouble with feelings—they so rarely appeared when it was convenient, and even more rarely did they appear in a desirable configuration. It was one of the many reasons she had done her best to protect herself against them, but a certain maddening marquess had apparently fought his way through her defenses.

"Speaking to Lady Helen today gave me much to think on, appalling as that is to admit," she said at last. "And it occurred to me that if she is willing to risk her name, her entire future, all to have some semblance of a life with the person she loves . . . well, it strikes me as being rather cowardly that I refuse to speak a fraction of my feelings." And, indeed, she did not feel at all brave as she spoke these words aloud—so accustomed was she to keeping her deepest feelings tucked close against her heart that even this hedging sort of admission, which did not *really* admit anything at all, made her feel naked and exposed in a way that was utterly terrifying.

And yet, she knew that the words she had just spoken were true— and if there was one thing she could not stand the thought of being, it was a coward. She took a deep breath.

"I think I love Jeremy," she said quietly, forcing herself to state the words simply, without hesitation. "I've no idea *why*," she added, unable to help herself, "considering he's vain and maddening and I can barely converse with him without wanting to stab him with a fork, but apparently that is what love looks like for me. And," she added, her mind lingering on the look in his eye when he gazed at her sometimes, as though marveling at her very existence, "I think he might love me, too—though, being a man, I expect he's too dense to realize it." As she spoke, identical grins spread across Violet and Emily's faces; at the same time, she could not help noting—rather grumpily—that neither of them looked remotely surprised.

"I can't say this comes as a shock," Violet said, confirming this impression; next to her, Emily had clasped her hands together, an expression of rapturous joy upon her face.

"Don't get too excited," Diana warned. "I'm hardly about to start spouting off sonnets."

"So what will you do?" Violet asked. There was a gleam in her eye that Diana recognized all too well, and she knew that she would be spending the next fortnight feigning a wasting disease for Jeremy's benefit if she did not head Violet off.

"I think I will . . . well, I think I will speak to Willingham." It sounded rather pathetic, put like that—it didn't sound like much action at all, no matter what it felt like deep within her. "I shall speak honestly to him at last."

"And agree to marry!" Emily cried joyfully.

"Certainly not," Diana said, alarmed. "I was thinking more that I should indicate that we should continue our liaison for a longer duration than we originally envisioned. I don't wish to spook him, after all—men and horses really are remarkably similar, you know."

"O, Diana of the romantic soul," Violet intoned dramatically, clutching at her own chest. "The bards will sing of this most heart-rending of gestures."

"That is quite enough of that," Diana said acerbically. She cast Emily, who appeared to be stifling laughter, a withering look. "From both of you," she added. "I think I shall start small and see how things progress. I'm not . . ." She trailed off for a moment, hesitating. "I'm not averse to the idea of marrying Jeremy, if I absolutely had to marry again"—even admitting this much made her feel as though she were stripping naked and parading down the street, so vulnerable did she feel—"but I shall begin by simply telling him how I feel. This is all rather new to me, you know. Emotions," she clarified, seeing their confused looks. "Communication."

Violet heaved a long-suffering sigh. "It is a shame you were born a woman, Diana, truly it is. You have the emotional range of the most repressed English gentleman at your very core."

Diana arched a brow. "Coming from the lady who recently spent a fortnight coughing into handkerchiefs whilst refusing to have a single honest conversation with her husband? I think I might be excused for not being overly wounded by your critique."

To this, Violet—satisfyingly—had no reply.

Twenty-Two

Jeremy, meanwhile, had similarly busy thoughts that day. It was unfortunate timing, really, that the weather had been so fine that morning—the sky a deep, sharp blue, fluffy white clouds floating above on the faint breeze that had whispered against their cheeks all day. There had been no excuse at all not to join the hunting party, not when conditions were so ideal and it was, in fact, *his* hunting party. But still, Jeremy had never felt less able to be trusted with a firearm in his hands, so distracted was he by his tumultuous thoughts. His aim was abysmal—he was as likely to shoot a member of his own party as a deer—and after a few wild misfires, he limited his participation to unhelpful commentary on his friends' efforts.

Even this, however, fell far short of his usual standards. When Penvale took a particularly wild shot that hit the trunk of a tree several feet away, Jeremy's mockery was so halfhearted that he caught sight of Audley giving him a concerned look out of the corner of his eye. The fact was, he couldn't concentrate on anything, because his mind was so bloody full of the events of the night before—and the way he had almost ruined it all with his foolish question about marriage and his sudden realization of his own feelings.

There was undoubtedly some irony to the fact that he, positively *in-*

famous for his reputation as a bachelor, so unlikely to wed that even the gleam of his title was insufficient to entice most matchmaking mamas—that *he* should nearly destroy an affair before it had properly begun by coming perilously close to uttering a particular four-letter word.

Not his favorite four-letter word, mind you, but one which started with *l* and which he'd spent years ensuring that no one could ever expect to hear him speak.

For that was true, was it not? Hadn't he done everything he possibly could since David's death to make certain that no one would ever expect anything much of him? He certainly hadn't expected much of himself beyond securing the estate—because, as undeserving as he still felt of the title that never should have been his, he knew that he owed it to his tenants to get Elderwild back on solid ground, and at this, at least—miraculously—he had succeeded.

But in all other regards, the past six years had been one long exercise in irresponsibility, ensuring that no one ever took him too seriously. And he was reaping his reward. He'd taken up with a woman even more averse to emotion than he was, and he was mooning over her like a lovesick calf.

A very strapping, charming sort of lovesick calf, he mentally amended, because a man had to have *some* self-respect, after all.

But a lovesick calf nonetheless.

In any case, something had to be done. If he carried on like this much longer, he'd find himself spouting poetry at her feet—and *why?* What was it about her that had him behaving this way? Was it because she'd shown him how to touch her in the bedroom? Surely not—though, admittedly, that had been a most instructive experience.

Was it because she never, for one second, seemed remotely impressed by anything about him—not his title, not his looks, not the particularly charming smile he had perfected for the sole purpose of dalliance?

Again, almost assuredly not. Though he could not prevent himself from preening a bit mentally when he recalled her obvious appreciation for his unclad form.

No, it was something more complicated, more difficult to comprehend—it was the way he felt when he was around her, as though he could lay aside his title and his reputation and be no one but Jeremy Overington. Who was a person he hadn't felt much like in a very long time.

Which of course meant that he needed to end this . . . this . . . this *thing* between them, whatever it was, as quickly as possible. Because if he didn't, she certainly would, once she realized what a fool he had become over her.

The thought of ending their liaison was not a pleasant one, in truth—the night before had been something of a revelation, even for a man who numbered his conquests in the dozens, and he was quite eager for a repeat session. But not if he could not get control of himself. Not if he could not trust himself to keep all of these inconvenient, embarrassing emotions bottled up—because he knew that if he didn't, he would scare her off without question.

If only there were some way to keep himself in check, to ensure that he didn't do anything foolhardy or rash . . .

If Diana feared being trapped, he needed to prove to her that he had no interest in trapping her. If he could not trust himself not to utter his feelings aloud, he needed to prove to her that he was making no demands upon her. That he could be content with however much of herself she wished to give him, and nothing more.

That he was in no position to offer her too much of himself, either. If, for example, he were involved with someone else . . . or even *engaged* . . .

His eyes alighted upon Rothsmere, who was pointing his gun, eyes narrowed in concentration.

Oh.

Of course there was a way. It had been staring him in the face— and clutching him by the arm and batting its eyelashes at him at every opportune moment—for the better part of a week. There was a very obvious prospect for matrimony—one who suddenly did not seem nearly as dreadful as she had previously appeared.

All that this course of action required was a willingness to forfeit a certain wager. . . .

It seemed the evening would never end.

Diana, clad in her favorite gown of forest green, put on a good show—she laughed at jokes; she flirted with every gentleman within reach; she batted her eyelashes. She won a game of vingt-et-un and then another, having rather scandalously insisted that rather than separating after dinner, both sexes reconvene for cards and drinks— tea, brandy, port—in the library. She was in the highest of spirits, her cheeks flushed, her smile dazzling.

She was utterly terrified.

"Are you quite all right?" her brother asked her at one point in the evening's proceedings. They were both at the sideboard—he to refill his tumbler with brandy; she to splash a furtive dose of the same into her teacup—and their backs were to the room, giving them the illusion of privacy.

"What do you mean?" she asked, raising her teacup to her lips. The warmth of the brandy began to spread through her from the very first sip, soothing her frazzled nerves somewhat.

"You're in rather a state," Penvale said, giving her a sideways look, a reminder that her oh-so-obtuse brother was really nothing of the sort. He was dressed, as always, with great care, his attire entirely correct. His hair was neatly cut, his jaw smoothly shaven. She saw more than one lady present giving him an admiring glance.

Her brother, typically, noticed none of it. He had just won a handy sum off Rothsmere in a game of cards, and she could practically see the wheels inside his mind turning, calculating the return on these winnings he could gain from one of his various investments. His single-minded focus on regaining their ancestral home was something she simultaneously admired and felt alarmed by.

To Diana, who had spent her adult life doing nothing much of importance—she was a viscountess, after all, and what truly was expected of her beyond throwing lavish entertainments and smiling over tea?—his focus on this one aim seemed almost something to be envied, a purpose that she often felt she lacked.

In truth, she often felt similarly driven regarding her painting, but she didn't feel comfortable admitting that to anyone, even Violet and Emily. Even her brother.

Except Jeremy, a voice whispered in her head. She ignored it.

Her painting, she sometimes felt, was what kept her sane. It gave her an outlet for her thoughts, her feelings, for everything about her that had no place in polite society. Everything rough and raw about her she poured onto canvas in bold strokes of pigment—and perhaps this was why she had always felt so uncharacteristically shy about her artwork. It was entirely acceptable—desirable, even—for ladies to dabble in art. A lovely watercolor or a particularly fine portrait was something to be unveiled in the drawing room to admiring oohs and ahhs.

Diana, though, had never felt particularly like showing her paintings to a drawing room full of people. She had no ability to look at her own work objectively—though she believed her brother and friends when they told her she was very good—but she somehow thought that there was no chance that the feelings she kept bottled up within her did not spill onto the canvas somehow. And those feelings were certainly not the stuff of polite drawing room chatter. They were nothing that anyone else had any desire to see.

"I'm not in any state at all," Diana said, realizing she'd allowed the silence between herself and Penvale to drag out slightly too long. "Unless you mean a state of smugness over my superior card skills. Perhaps it runs in the family," she added, lifting her teacup in a toast.

Penvale clinked his tumbler gently against the delicate china of her cup. "Is this about Jeremy?"

Diana, who had just taken another sip of brandy-infused tea, choked. Penvale, like the loving, sensitive creature that he was, thumped her on the back so hard he nearly knocked her into the sideboard.

"Why would it be about Willingham?" Diana asked once she had recovered her composure and her balance.

Penvale gave her a withering look, and she sagged. "Did he say something?" she asked in an undertone, hating that she had become a person who would ask such a question—and of her *brother*, of all people. It was undoubtedly a low point.

"Not in so many words," Penvale said, looking pained. "He seemed a bit distracted whilst we were out hunting today is all."

"Perhaps he found pointing a gun at some fast-moving thing with antlers to offer insufficient intellectual stimulation," Diana suggested sweetly.

Penvale gave her a speaking look. "Diana. This is *Jeremy* we're discussing. He requires approximately as much intellectual stimulation as a field mouse."

All at once, Diana was angry. She was not routinely angry with her infuriating brother, as was usual, but instead felt a surge of protective rage on the part of someone else that she'd never experienced before. Logically, some part of her knew that Penvale was Jeremy's friend—one of his two dearest friends, and someone who had been close to Jeremy for far longer than she had, in fact—but that knowledge did not do much to suppress the entirely illogical, out-of-proportion feeling of fury coursing through her.

"Has it ever occurred to you, Penvale, that Jeremy might have intellectual depths that he has chosen not to share with you?" she asked icily. "Perhaps because he might expect just such a reaction, in fact? Or," she added, really getting into the spirit of the thing now, "perhaps because he knows that your pea-size brain couldn't possibly hope to keep up?"

Rather than looking offended, Penvale grinned at her. "It's 'Jeremy' now, is it?"

Diana mentally cursed. She had stubbornly continued to address Jeremy by his title long after she might reasonably have ceased to do so; her use of his given name now gave her brother far more information about the status of her relationship with Jeremy than she was comfortable with Penvale having. Nevertheless, she resisted the urge to rise to his bait, as she learned to do the hard way, and many times over, throughout the course of their childhood.

"What it is or isn't is none of your concern," she said in the haughtiest tones that she reserved solely for her brother. She was naturally not about to inform him that she planned that very evening to lay her heart at Jeremy's feet—possibly after enjoying a satisfying bout of amorous congress. She had no desire to have Penvale either warn her off *or* make the sort of threatening mutterings about his sister's paramour that men seemed to believe was required of them in such situations.

"Just . . . be careful with him, Diana," Penvale said quietly, and his tone was entirely serious.

"I can take care of myself," Diana informed him.

"I know you can," he said in that same low, grave voice. "I meant . . . take care with him. I've always been under the impression that he was rather carrying a torch for you all these years—I can't think why else he would spend so much time provoking you."

Diana simultaneously wanted to tell him that this was ridiculous and to admit that he was entirely right—for she knew, deep down, that she had always understood that there was something more to her relationship with Jeremy than mere antagonism. She had never allowed it, even to herself, of course. But she couldn't say this. The words she held within her were for Jeremy, and no one else.

If this blasted evening would ever end and let her speak them, that is.

Jeremy, in some sense, hoped that the evening would never end—the longer it dragged on, the longer before he had to tell Diana of his plans to propose to Lady Helen.

He had spent a fair amount of time the past few hours in close proximity to the lady, and now that he knew her act for what it was—

for an act it surely had to be—he was able to regard her performance appreciatively, like a theater-goer, rather than with the abject horror previously provoked by her fawning (and by her occasionally bold hands).

However, despite his newfound understanding that the lady was something more than the marriage-obsessed miss that she appeared, he did not look forward to the thought of informing Diana of his plan with any great enthusiasm. For the one, he hated being bested—particularly by her. And he was not eager to admit that he was surrendering in their wager. No, a smug Diana was not a prospect to be relished, even if a bet was worth losing if doing so earned him more nights in her bed.

Furthermore, however, he dreaded the possibility of other emotions he would see on her face. He wasn't terribly certain he could tolerate seeing relief in her eyes—she would try to hide it, he was certain, but he'd become quite skilled at reading her expressions.

At last, however, the party broke up amid much grumbling at the vowels Penvale was collecting, though anyone who sat down at a card table with Penvale knew that he risked being fleeced out of a sizable share of blunt. The minutes seemed to trickle by as Jeremy dismissed his valet and paced his bedroom, waiting for the hallway to have been silent for long enough for him to risk venturing out. The moment arrived at last, and he scarcely had to scratch at Diana's door before she flung it open and pulled him inside.

He had given a great deal of thought to how he would tell her—he'd let her work on her portrait of him for a bit, since he wasn't entirely certain how this conversation would go, and he didn't wish to distract her from her art. The look of peace mingled with concentration that spread across her face while she was painting or sketching was one that he could happily look at every day for the rest of his life—and it was dangerous thoughts like *that* that had convinced him of the necessity of this action in the first place.

However, he thought it unwise to allow matters to proceed too far before telling her, so he planned to interrupt her painting after a while to share the news of his impending engagement. He wasn't entirely certain what to expect when he told her, but rather hoped she'd appreciate this sacrifice on his part—she'd see that once he was engaged, they could continue their affair without any pressure of marriage or commitment. He hoped that she'd be so pleased that they could then immediately continue about their—considerably less clothed— evening's business.

All of these thoughts, however, were wiped from his mind, because the second the door closed behind him, he found himself pressed up against it, Diana's mouth on his own. And while plans were very well and good, he'd always liked to consider himself a man capable of flexibility—quite literally, on one memorable occasion— and he decided that he could allow this amendment to his agenda for the evening.

That was, naturally, the last intelligent thought to cross his mind for some time, so consumed did he become by the softness of her body pressed against his, the feeling of her mouth sucking on his neck. His hands ran over her curves greedily, the weight of a breast filling one hand, the roundness of her bottom occupying the other. He leaned his head back to rest against the door as she continued to move her mouth down the column of his throat, resisting only with great effort the temptation to roll his hips against hers. He felt as though there were flames licking at his skin wherever her body was touching his, and was so stiff in his trousers that he feared embarrassing himself like a schoolboy—which was, honestly, how he felt whenever his bare skin was in close proximity to hers.

Her hands slid to the waistband of his trousers, undoing the buttons and dipping inside to wrap around him. He thrust into her grip without meaning to, but before he could achieve any sort of rhythm, she undid the placket of the breeches and sank to her knees before him, licking her lips as she did so. His mouth went dry at the sight of her, hair unbound around her face, full lips slightly parted, tantalizingly close to a portion of his anatomy that would desperately like her attention. And all of a sudden, he knew he had to put a stop to it.

"Wait," he said, his voice hoarse. He cleared his throat and said again, "Wait." His body screamed at him in protest as he leaned forward to cup her elbows and draw her to her feet. It felt wrong, somehow, to have her perform this act for him when he intended to tell her that he was going to propose to someone else. If the situation with Lady John Marksdale had taught him anything, it was that ladies preferred to receive news of this nature before any articles of clothing had been removed.

"What's wrong?" she asked, wrinkling her brow in confusion. "I've been wanting to try that. Violet made me read a *very* naughty poem about it once."

He stared at her, resisting the urge to laugh, because *of course* Diana would read some sort of pornographic poetry about fellatio and, rather than being horrified, would think to herself, *I can be good at that, too.* Rather than laughing, however, he said, "I'm going to propose to Lady Helen."

In his mind, when he'd attempted to plan out this moment, he'd imagined himself prefacing this information with some sort of thoughtful, intelligent introduction—he'd imagined his tone as cool, dispassionate. He'd imagined himself calmly taking a pinch of snuff afterward, as though the information was of no importance whatsoever—not that he actually took snuff, of course, but it did make for a nice mental picture. Perhaps he should take up the habit.

In actuality, however, there was nothing calm or cool about him. He blurted out the words too quickly, so they escaped his mouth in a rush and Diana cocked her head to the side as she processed them. He saw the moment the words registered, however—shock, then an icy coolness.

Well, he told himself, at least it wasn't relief, as he'd feared.

No, the look on her face wasn't one of relief. But it wasn't much better, either.

"Shall I wish you happy, then?" she asked, sounding bored. Whatever response he'd been expecting, it hadn't been this. "And shall I collect my earnings now, or must I wait until the church bells are ringing? I suppose there's always the chance something could go horribly wrong." She paused for a moment, as something occurred to her. "Wait. You said you're *going* to propose?" She looked almost as though she hated herself for asking, as though she despised herself for showing any interest at all in the matter, but Jeremy, for once, was fervently grateful for her penetrating line of questioning. Curiosity was far more comfortable to deal with than cool boredom.

"Yes," he said, feeling slightly uncomfortable as he realized they were still standing pressed together against the door—he with his breeches still undone, for that matter. He quickly remedied the situation. "Er," he said, gesturing vaguely in the direction of the armchairs arranged before the fireplace. "Shall we—"

"What? Oh, yes, if you wish." Her tone was distracted, her mind clearly still occupied. She took a seat in the armchair closest to the fireplace, tucking her knees up beneath her chin and wrapping her arms around her legs to hold them close. She looked younger than usual. "So I take it you've yet to actually extend your offer?"

"Yes," Jeremy confirmed, taking the chair nearest hers and dragging it closer to her for good measure. Her eyes narrowed slightly, but she made no comment. "I thought it the gentlemanly thing to do. To tell you first."

"Yes," she said, her tone as dry as toast. "You're a paragon of chivalry, Jeremy."

"I just thought that announcing the engagement as a fait accompli at the breakfast table one morning would be unfair to you," he protested, feeling that he was somehow digging himself into a deeper and deeper hole but unsure of how to free himself from it.

She raised one eyebrow slowly. "You're certain of being accepted, then?"

Jeremy puffed out his chest a bit. He didn't even *mean* to—it was some sort of deeply ingrained masculine instinct that he hadn't realized he possessed until that very moment. No wonder women were so disgusted with the entire male sex, he thought in a moment of clarity. "Not certain, no," he said. "I should never presume to understand the female mind well enough to be assured of my success." She narrowed her eyes at him, but he continued speaking as though she hadn't. "However, I am a reasonably good catch, I've been led to understand, and the lady's behavior toward me of late has led me to believe that my suit would not be rebuffed."

She snorted. "I wouldn't be so certain."

He opened his mouth to object, then paused. Why would she say that? Unless *she* knew what *he* knew? Surely not. Surely such knowledge would shock any gently reared lady down to her very core. For all her worldliness, even Diana could not know about *that*.

"She doesn't like men," his innocent flower said in businesslike fashion.

"I beg your *pardon?*" Jeremy asked, sounding more like his grandmother than he had ever done in his entire life.

"She. Prefers. Women," Diana said slowly, enunciating each word very clearly, as though speaking to a small child, or a deaf octogenarian. "And this is something that was shared with me in confidence, so please take care not to go blabbing about it to Audley and Penvale and ruin everything. I just felt that this was something you might wish to know, before you go making an ass of yourself strewing rose petals at her feet or whatever other ideas you have within that thick skull of yours."

"As it happens," Jeremy said, with what little sangfroid he could muster, "I was already aware of this. It is, in fact, the knowledge that led me to this plan of action in the first place."

It was, he noted smugly, Diana's turn to look shocked. "How could *you* possibly know?" she asked, incredulity tinging her voice. "Surely you couldn't have puzzled it out." The definitive tone with which she said this did not speak highly of her opinion of his intellectual capabilities, but for once he decided to ignore this. A man could only fight a battle on so many fronts at once, after all.

"I happened to catch her in a rather delicate situation with her maid," Jeremy said casually. "The experience was fairly educational, truth be told."

Diana's mouth quirked up at one side. "I imagine it was. To think I could have saved us all this time and merely drilled a peephole in her door instead." He didn't wish to be oversensitive, but he couldn't help but think that he detected a note of relief in her voice upon learning that he had not, in fact, deduced this about Lady Helen in the absence of hard evidence, as though her world had been set to rights by confirming that he was not quite *that* clever.

Before he had a chance to reply, however, she continued. "Could you please explain to me how your knowledge of the lady's complete disinterest in the male sex makes you convinced that marriage between the two of you would be a beneficial arrangement?"

"She needs security," he explained. "If she were to marry me, with the full understanding that our marriage should never be anything other than an arrangement of convenience, she could remain in London and carry on as she wishes, with a much larger purse than Rothsmere is likely to grant her."

"You need an heir," Diana pointed out, ever practical.

"We'd grit our teeth and do the necessary until she was with child, and then we'd never need to have much to do with each other ever again," Jeremy said, feeling pleased to have a ready response for her. "Then we could each carry on as we wished. She and that maid could do—er—whatever it is that ladies do together, and I could take any lover I desired." He was aware of his heart rate increasing as he said this last bit, worrying that she would see right through his casual tone and understand that "any lover he desired" really meant her. But if he framed it all as an affair, no commitment required, surely she would not be so easily frightened. Because the truth was, he wanted her—in his bed, painting his portrait, making him laugh and making him fume with equal frequency—and he would take her however he could get her.

She had made it abundantly clear that she had no interest in marriage—or in anything that implied permanence, sentiment, attachment. Surely if *he* were married, she'd never suspect that he'd actually fallen in love with her. And if she didn't suspect *that*, she wouldn't be frightened away.

He watched her with a fair amount of trepidation—he was a bit afraid she'd shy at this hint of his desire to continue their affair—but he was still unprepared for the flash of rage that crossed her face, just as quickly suppressed and replaced by her usual cool mask.

"That's a lovely plan, Willingham," she said, her use of his title akin to a slap across the face; he was surprised he didn't physically recoil. "I suppose now that you've experienced one evening in the bedroom in which you were absolutely certain the lady was genuinely enjoying herself, you thought, *Well, I've learned it all. Better find my next mistress posthaste.*"

"That's not—"

"But of course," Diana continued, "you wouldn't want your next lover to get any ideas about where she stood with you, and how better to achieve that than by racing to the altar first? Just to ensure that the lady understood how she ranked, of course."

"I didn't mean—"

"And, of course, who better to marry than a woman who is guaranteed never to expect much of anything at all from you? Isn't that what you want, after all? For no one to expect much from you?"

"Yes, it bloody is," Jeremy said heatedly, his mouth racing ahead of his mind by several measures, and he unable to give much of a damn about it. "Because I don't have anything to offer! It's best that everyone knows where we stand when we begin." He sprang to his feet, unable to remain seated for one moment longer. "I'm not fit to be any sort of husband to anyone, so why not marry someone who doesn't want a husband at all?"

Diana did not join him on his feet, instead remaining almost eerily still, her gaze on him unblinking. "And those future mistresses?"

"I wasn't thinking about any goddamned future mistresses!" he burst out, frustrated. "I was only thinking about you!"

His words fell heavily into the silence between them, like rocks dropped into a still pond. He didn't even wish them unspoken—it was an enormous relief to have them out in the open rather than at the tip of his tongue, threatening to spill out each time he spoke to her.

"Am I supposed to be flattered?" she asked quietly after the silence had dragged out to a length that could only be classified as excruciating. Her face was pale, and her eyes glittered. "Am I supposed to swoon at your feet with the knowledge that you wish only to bed *me* for the immediate future, even as you plan to woo and wed another woman?"

"Only so that I could still be with you!" he said heatedly, his mouth now apparently operating entirely independently of the rest of his body—a novel occurrence, to say the least. "You're the one who has made such a point of the fact that you never wish to remarry, that you value your *independence* above all else—and all I am doing is coming up with a solution that allows us to be together without asking you to sacrifice that!"

"Is that supposed to be *romantic?*" she asked incredulously, unfolding her legs and rising to her feet at last. "Do you think you're making some sort of grand gesture by not asking anything of me, ever?"

"I'm trying to give you what you want!" He raked a hand through his hair, frustrated. She was standing very close to him, and even through his anger he was unable to help noticing the becoming flush that had replaced the paleness of her cheeks a few moments before. It was probably inappropriate to react to a woman's anger with desire. He assumed. He didn't think asking Diana's opinion on the matter would yield positive results at the moment—which was, in and of itself, perhaps an answer to his question.

"But what do *you* want?" she asked, pressing closer to him, and he was instantly distracted by the heat emanating from her skin, the subtle scent of her, the smattering of freckles across her nose with which he feared he was becoming perversely obsessed.

"That doesn't matter," he managed to say, tearing his eyes from those accursed freckles with great effort. Logically, he understood they were mere dark spots on her nose; illogically, he wondered if they possessed some sort of peculiar, trance-creating witchcraft.

"It should," she said, her face suddenly erased of all expression, as if by magic—and if it was magic, then it was a sort of magic he absolutely despised. "I had a plan for this evening, you know. I planned to be honest with you—to tell you that I have . . ." She trailed off; he held his breath. "I have feelings for you. No, I think I love you—or at least I *hope* I do, because if anything less than love is causing me this degree of emotional turmoil, then I assure you I have no interest in the real thing."

He was vaguely aware that she was still speaking, but his mind was stuck on a single word: *love*. She *loved* him. At least, he was fairly certain that was what she was saying.

"You love me?" he croaked. He'd like to have imagined some more dashing, romantic way of describing the sound of his voice at that precise moment, but strict honesty compelled him to admit that *croak* was really the most accurate word.

"That isn't the point," she snapped. Her assertion seemed a trifle unfair to him—it was a very rare situation in which someone declared their love for another person and it wasn't at least *somewhat* the point. "I don't know what I was thinking! I can't imagine why I possibly thought this was a good idea!"

"*Love?*" he asked again incredulously, feeling as though he were scrambling after her as fast as he could but was always, *always* at least twenty feet behind. "But I—but you—" He had the vague impression that this response was not going to gain him any admiration from her; his suspicion was confirmed a moment later.

"Don't be too flattered," she snapped. "I assure you, if I had any control over the matter, this would not have happened!" She sighed heavily, as though this was all a frightful burden. "In light of this . . . unexpected development, I wanted to discuss your own sentiments, and the prospect of prolonging things between us, and then seeing where that led . . ." She shook her head in disgust. "Don't worry," she added with haughty froideur. "I see now that I must have taken temporary leave of my senses, and I shall no doubt be back in my right mind again almost immediately. I find there is nothing quite like the object of one's affections discussing marriage to another woman to make one reconsider one's preferences."

"But you said you never wanted to remarry!" he protested weakly.

"I'm not saying I wish to now!" she said. "But I've experienced something of a deepening of my feelings, and I—foolishly, apparently—thought that you might be feeling the same way. I thought that you might have changed your mind and seen a different path forward for us." She was so close to him that when she huffed an indignant breath, he could feel it on his cheek. "Clearly, I was wrong—and I can assure you, I won't make this mistake again."

He inhaled a deep breath, feeling rather as though he'd been punched in the stomach repeatedly. If this was what came of feeling genuine concern for a woman, then he had clearly been wise to avoid any such emotional entanglements in the past. He suspected, however, that it would be rather more restful to fall in love with—well, with just about *anyone* other than Diana.

Unfortunately for his sanity, however, restfulness didn't seem to be what he was after.

"Diana," he said in what he felt was an admirably calm tone of voice, "we had an arrangement, which I have done my best to adhere to. I have found myself, of late, devoting rather more mental energy to you than I am accustomed to giving other people, and it occurred to me that I was unwilling to allow our liaison to end anytime soon. Considering the parameters you set out at the beginning of our arrangement, I was given to understand that you had a strong aversion to marriage—an aversion that, until quite recently, I entirely shared.

"When I discovered that my emotions had become inconveniently engaged, I set out to determine a way to extend our arrangement without causing you undue distress. I thought I had landed upon just such a method. Clearly, I was wrong. I apologize for any offense I may have given, and will take this opportunity to humbly withdraw." He finished speaking at last, vaguely aware that he sounded like he had a stick shoved up his arse but unable to care overly much. He hadn't known any other way to speak in the moment—the situation was too dangerous, his emotions riding too close to the surface. He had spent the past six years doing his utmost to ensure that his emotions—toward the brother who had died, leaving him with a whole heap of unwanted responsibility; toward himself, and the disgust he felt at his inability to live up to his brother's memory; and certainly toward anyone else—were kept tightly reined, never allowed to govern his actions. He wasn't going to falter now.

"That's not what I'm asking you to do!" she burst out in frustration. "I'm just asking you not to be a *complete* ass, for once in your life, by perhaps not proposing to one woman whilst you claim to have feelings for another?"

"I'm trying to give you what you want!" he burst out, resisting the temptation to clutch at his own hair with some difficulty. He felt as though they were talking in circles, and yet each time he opened his mouth, he thought that this time, somehow, he would make her see reason.

"I want *you*," she snapped back. "The *real* you. I don't want to be your damned lover whilst you're married to another lady—I don't want to be someone who has no expectations of you."

"If it's expectations you have, I'd recommend revising them," he said with a hollow laugh. "What haven't you seen over the past week? I'm a degenerate marquess who's trying his best to fill the shoes of the man who was meant for the role. I don't have anything to offer anyone. I've grown far too attached to you for my own good *or* yours, and I'm trying to arrange things so that we can continue seeing each other without it ending in disappointment."

She stepped forward, lifted a hand, and laid it gently on his cheek—truth be told, he would have been less shocked if she'd slapped him, given the way the conversation had gone thus far. "No, you're not," she said, her voice suddenly quiet. "You're a man who's still in pain, and grieving, and who thinks too little of himself. You're a man who is angry at his brother but doesn't want to admit it."

"I'm not—"

"You are," she said simply. "I've been trying to tell you every time we've discussed him all week."

"I suppose we got too sidetracked discussing my shortcomings in the bedroom to focus on this other, larger defect in my personality," he said bitterly.

"Jeremy, it's not a shortcoming!" she said, her tone sliding from tenderness to exasperation in a split second. "You're allowed to be angry at your brother—it doesn't mean you love him any less. It doesn't make you any less worthy of a man. But if you can't see yourself as you truly are, then I don't want to waste my time trying to convince you otherwise."

"Perhaps I'd better go, then," he snapped angrily, "and you can summon me back to your bed once you've worked out what, precisely, it is that you want from me."

"I thought I'd spent the past five minutes explaining just that," she said coldly, her voice gone deadly quiet. He would have been less alarmed had she been shouting. "You just don't seem to be listening." Out of the corner of his eye, he saw her flexing her hand at her side, as though she were positively itching to slap him. He couldn't say he blamed her—he *had* just announced his intent to propose to someone else—and yet he could not control the anger that coursed through him at the moment. He was following the rules, and she had changed them.

"You should be thanking me," he said, gripped by that relentless desire to have the last word in every argument they'd ever shared. "If I marry Lady Helen, you'll win our bloody wager." He sketched an ironic bow. "Isn't that what you wanted? I'm always happy to assist."

"You think you're fooling everyone when you use that tone," she said, crossing her arms—regrettably—over her chest. "But just so you know, you're not fooling me. You're more than a charming rake, Jeremy, and you'll realize soon enough that you're not fooling yourself, either. But don't expect me to wait around for that moment to arrive.

"Now," she added quietly, her eyes never leaving his, "get out."

He clenched his jaw, let himself out of the room, and just barely resisted the urge to slam the door behind him.

Twenty-Three

The weather the next morning suited Jeremy's mood perfectly. He awoke after tossing and turning for much of the night to find the sky full of heavy gray clouds, a halfhearted drizzle spitting against the windows already, with no end in sight to the gloomy weather. He was torn between the desire to remain in bed indefinitely, burying his head beneath the pillows and blocking out everything and everyone in the world around him, and jumping on his horse and riding like hell until he collapsed from exhaustion.

Unfortunately, the presence of a number of houseguests and the inclement weather made both of these fantasies unworkable and, as little as he wished to speak to anyone at the moment, he more or less had no choice in the matter. He should, he knew, ring for his valet and dress and make his way downstairs—a glance at the clock on the wall confirmed that there were likely already guests at the breakfast table—but he delayed, hoping to put off the moment he'd have to see Diana for as long as possible.

Instead, he rose from bed, ignoring the slight chill in the room that bit into his naked skin. He stood at the window, watching the clouds roll in, his thoughts full of the angry words he and Diana had exchanged the night before.

309

You're not fooling yourself, either.

It was that parting shot that dug deeper than all of her other verbal barbs combined. Because wasn't that precisely what he had been attempting to do—not just for the past fortnight, but for the past six years? He had been trying to fool everyone around him, yes—convince them that the Marquess of Willingham was no one to be listened to, no one to take seriously, nothing but a pale imitation of the brother who had rightfully held the title before him. No one to pin any hopes or expectations on. But, more important, he'd been trying to fool himself, too—to convince himself that the fact that David was dead didn't matter, that he was standing here in his brother's house, wearing his brother's title, was fine, when of course it wasn't. It would never be fine. Restoring the family fortunes hadn't made it fine—sleeping with half of the women of the *ton*, drinking his body weight in brandy every night for years hadn't made it fine, either. And it hadn't made the barely suppressed anger—that anger which he'd never dared admit to, and yet which Diana had spotted so easily, from the first moment he'd discussed David with her—vanish, either.

Leave it to Diana to make him excruciatingly, clearly aware of these facts.

And now he'd cocked things up so royally that he was unlikely to ever hear anything from her ever again, other than his name paired with a curse—and then only if he was lucky.

On the bright side, he would not be losing one hundred pounds to Diana today—or, likely, any day. Because not only was he *not* going to propose to Lady Helen—what was the point, if he'd lost Diana anyway?—he found it difficult to imagine himself proposing to anyone. Ever. He would continue with his string of conquests with no strings attached, and he would never again risk feeling as he did right now: like he had been punched repeatedly in the chest.

He should have known, of course. He should have known that he could not be trusted around her, that any sort of arrangement with Diana would become complicated entirely too quickly. He'd been fascinated by her for years—their verbal sparring matches had been his favorite part of every social event he'd ever attended—and he should have known that an affair with her would only lead to trouble.

He'd made a mistake, and he was suffering for it now. But he would not make such a mistake again.

With a determined nod, he turned from the window to ring for his valet and begin the day.

Diana had slept like a baby.

Well, that might not have been strictly accurate. Because while she had, on occasion, observed a baby in a heavy slumber, she doubted that this effect was achieved by the application of a dose of brandy, administered rather liberally. Rather, she hoped not, for the baby's sake.

Because no baby deserved to be feeling how she was feeling at the moment: like she had been run down by a carriage. Or as though a flock of sheep milled about on her head.

"Ouch!" she said, clapping a hand to the aching head in question after a particularly sharp tug of the hairbrush as Toogood dressed her hair.

"Apologies, my lady," Toogood said, not sounding sorry at all. She gave her mistress an assessing look in the mirror, and Diana straightened her shoulders, attempting to appear bright-eyed and refreshed. Like a heroine from a romantic novel.

Or a rabbit.

"I don't think you need to apply quite so much force, Toogood," she said mildly, examining her nails in a casual fashion.

"I don't think you need to apply quite so many spirits, my lady," was her maid's reply.

"I beg your pardon, Toogood?" she asked sweetly. "Surely mine ears did not detect the sound of my *maid*, of all people, offering commentary on my behavior?"

"No indeed, my lady," Toogood agreed, securing a hairpin with a jab that Diana could only describe as vicious. "You must have misheard. Perhaps a poor night's sleep has your ears struggling to work properly this morning?" Another hairpin, another sharp jab.

"I'll have you know that I slept extremely well last night," Diana said pleasantly. "Like the dead, some might say."

"Some might," Toogood concurred. "Or like the inebriated, some others might say." She jabbed yet another hairpin into the knot at the nape of Diana's neck.

"How many pins does this coiffure require, Toogood?"

"About as many tots of brandy as widows require, I expect." *Jab. Jab. Jab.*

"Toogood, do you have something you wish to say to me?" Diana asked severely.

"Not at all." *Jab.* "Just offering some conversation to pass the time." *Jab.* "Thought it might brighten your spirits." *Jab.*

This torture session was mercifully interrupted by a sharp knock at the door. Diana stiffened, wondering who it might be—it was late morning, and she had neglected to put in an appearance at the breakfast table, instead taking a tray in her room. Surely it wasn't Jeremy? Surely he could not possibly think she wished to speak to him after the fiasco of the previous evening?

Surely nothing, she thought darkly. Making assumptions based on the presumed common sense of the male sex was a recipe for disaster. A moment later, however, her worries were dissipated by the sound of Violet's voice.

"I know you're in there! I will burst into this room even if I need to fetch a battering ram to do it—*what*, Emily?" The response was indecipherable through the thick wood of the door; a moment later, Violet exclaimed, "What do you mean, you can pick locks?"

"Let them in, Toogood," Diana said, somehow suppressing a sigh and a smile at the same time. A moment later she had been descended upon by her two dearest friends in the world, whom she loved as much as she loved anyone—and whom she very much did not wish to see at this particular moment.

They, however, decidedly *did* wish to see her; with a nod at Toogood, who speedily departed, Diana turned on her stool to face the inquisition.

"Good morning," she said calmly, folding her hands in her lap. She was wearing one of her favorite morning gowns of periwinkle blue, having decided that even if she felt, physically and emotionally, as though she had been dragged behind a cart down a bumpy country lane for ten miles, there was no reason for her outward appearance to reflect that.

"You weren't at breakfast," Violet said, stating the obvious.

"*You* weren't at breakfast," Emily said to Violet, a note of mild objection in her voice. "You only know Diana wasn't there because I told you."

Violet's cheeks flushed. "I was . . . otherwise occupied. That's not the point!"

"How do you know *I* wasn't 'otherwise occupied'?" Diana asked, attempting to forestall the moment of explanation for as long as possible.

"Because Jeremy was there," Emily said quietly. "Looking as though he hadn't slept a wink. And *not* in a good way," she added hastily. "He looked, in fact, about as miserable as you do at the moment."

This was, in some sense, gratifying to hear—Diana should have hated to have worked herself into such a state over a man who was indifferent to her, after all. But in large part, this merely served to stoke her ire even further, considering that the unhappiness on both their parts was entirely of his own making.

"I assure you he deserves every bit of misery he has experienced," she said viciously, rising to her feet and commencing to pace back and forth across the length of her bedchamber.

"I take it your conversation last night did not go well?" Violet asked, perching atop the arm of one of the chairs clustered before the fireplace.

"You might say that."

"Does he not share your feelings?" Emily asked hesitantly, drawing her hands into a knot before her, her eyes tracking Diana's movements across the room.

"Oh, no, he shares them," Diana said with complete confidence. "But he informed me last night that he intends to propose to Lady Helen today."

"He *what?*" Violet screeched.

"But didn't you just tell us that Lady Helen . . ." Emily trailed off, blushing.

"Oh, he is perfectly well aware of that," Diana assured her. "In fact, it is why he thought a marriage between them made so much sense, apparently. You see, if they married, she could continue to carry on with her maid and he could continue to carry on with me and I'd never get any sort of wild ideas in my mind about *love* or *marriage* or anything that requires the least bit of commitment on his part."

Violet held up a hand, effectively halting Diana's rant just as she was getting into the spirit of the thing. "Let me be certain I understand. He was prepared to *marry someone else* just so that he might continue to be with you?"

"Yes!" Diana said indignantly. "Isn't that the most ridiculous, insulting—"

"And," Violet said, in a slightly raised voice, speaking over Diana, "didn't you assure him at the outset of this little liaison—and, I'm assuming, many times since—that you had no interest in remarrying, or in any sort of emotional entanglement?"

"I did!" Diana agreed heatedly. "And then, when I tell him I've changed my mind—"

"And," Violet interrupted, "had you given him any prior indication that your sentiments on this matter had changed?"

"Well, no," Diana was forced to admit.

"And, when he told you that he intended to propose to Lady Helen, was it before or after you had told him that your sentiments had changed?"

Diana paused. "Before."

"Meaning he had no way of knowing that what he was proposing would not seem like a perfect solution to the situation as he understood it?"

Diana was silent. It was true, blast it all. Jeremy had taken a set of facts as he understood them, and had come up with a solution he thought would suit them both. She'd been entirely unreasonable to hope for anything else—to hope for anything *more*.

And yet . . .

And yet.

She had been willing to make a fool of herself. She thought his feelings had changed, it was true, but she hadn't been assured of that fact. And yet she had been willing to risk outright rejection and bare her heart to him regardless. Was it so unreasonable that she hoped for a similar amount of courage from him?

"I just . . ." she started, then trailed off. Confessions of this sort did not come naturally to her—nor would they ever, she suspected. But she was trying. "I was willing to be honest with him. Is it so wrong for me to have hoped that he would risk honesty in return?"

Violet's face softened. "Of course not."

"Very well." She sniffed, which made no sense, because sniffing was generally what one did in response to crying, and of the many, many things that Diana did, crying was most assuredly not one of them. She reached a hand up to her cheek and felt a suspicious dampness there.

"Oh, Diana," Emily said in her quiet, soothing fashion, which did nothing other than make the tears—because yes, they were tears—fall faster. She reached out a gentle hand and took Diana's own hand in hers.

"This is really too far!" Diana said furiously, reaching into her bodice for a handkerchief. She usually kept one handy, though generally for the purpose of drawing attention to that portion of her anatomy rather than out of actual practical concern. "I refuse to turn into a watering pot for the sake of a man who thinks that discussing marriage to another woman is an intelligent way to woo someone!"

"I feel that I must observe that, based on the behavior of the two of you this summer, love does not appear to be a terribly restful state," Emily said to the room at large in a conversational tone.

"It isn't!" Diana informed her. "And don't listen to anything Violet will tell you about how it is worth all the tears and sleepless nights, because I can assure you that I have never been so miserable in my life. And over a man. The very idea!" She felt somehow offended by herself—as though the rational, cool, cunning mind that had always been so reliable a companion had suddenly let her down.

"So what are you going to do?" Emily asked bluntly.

Diana slumped down into a chair, the righteous indignation that had fueled her pacing leaving her all in a rush.

"Nothing," she said.

"Are you feeling quite all right?" Emily asked, reaching out a concerned hand to feel Diana's brow. Diana swatted her away.

"He knows how I feel," she explained, the echo of the words they'd exchanged the previous night still ringing in her ears. "And it's his turn to be brave."

"And what will you do if he doesn't declare himself?" Emily asked hesitantly.

Diana gave her as dangerous a smile as she could manage at the moment. It was a touch wobbly, it was true, but the spirit was there. "Find another lover, and rub it in Jeremy's face for every second it lasts."

In a weaker moment some days earlier, Jeremy had agreed with Lady Helen's insistence that an "evening of light musical entertainment," as she put it, would be an enjoyable occasion. This was what came of allowing too many women at a house party, he thought as he watched some unfortunate spinster from the village pluck away enthusiastically at her violin. He had prided himself, in previous years, on only allowing a select cohort of ladies to attend his shooting parties—women like Violet, whom one could trust to behave in a generally reasonable fashion.

Jeremy was unlike many men of his acquaintance in that he suffered under no misapprehensions regarding the relative intellect of men and women. It was obvious that, in general, ladies were the vastly more intelligent sex, but they did have a few blind spots in their otherwise sound minds, and their preference for watching a group of people saw away at instruments for an hour was undoubtedly one of them. He thought longingly of the evening he could have been having instead, had he been a bit stronger-willed in the face of female determination: it would have involved brandy and cards and hopefully Diana at as far a remove as was possible.

Instead, she was seated one row ahead of him. They were assembled in the music room, of course, a row of chairs having been rather hastily erected for the occasion. Jeremy had seated himself in the back of the room, so as to place as much distance as possible between himself and the instruments that were about to be wielded. He'd been under no illusions about the quality of the entertainment he'd arranged: he'd known that there were several ladies in the village who had been taking music lessons for some time—he'd heard enthusiastic reports to this effect from their mothers on his most recent jaunts down to the local shops—and he'd thought it would likely thrill them to have the opportunity to perform at Elderwild.

His charity extended only so far, however, and he was unwilling to place himself directly in the line of fire. He was just eyeballing the candles burning in sconces on the wall and wondering if it would be too noticeable if he were to use some of the melted wax to fashion earplugs when Diana swept into the room, imperious as a queen, and took the seat directly in front of him.

Meaning that now, while his ears were being assaulted with something that might have, in a former life, been Bach, he was being tormented by the sight of a single curl that had come loose from her coiffure, curling against the smooth expanse of her neck.

It was, logically, a lock of hair. Everyone had them.

It was, illogically, the single most enticing thing he had ever seen in his life.

How long had he been staring at that single curl? Too long, undoubtedly—and yet he couldn't tear his gaze away. He thought that he might be content to sit here, in this uncomfortable chair, listening to this mildly painful violin solo, staring at this curl, for the rest of his life.

It was in the midst of that undeniably disturbing thought that the violin solo in question mercifully came to an end, and a scattered round of rather unenthusiastic applause interrupted his reverie before he could lose his head entirely.

But, of course, the reprieve was only temporary—the violinist was replaced by sisters at the piano, who he was forced to admit were quite tolerable, though had he been their music teacher he might have steered them away from Italian songs until they could better pronounce even a fraction of the words contained therein.

During this bit of creative linguistic interpretation, it was the delicate curve of Diana's ear that caught his attention. And, truly, had it come to this? A few kisses and suddenly he was contemplating ears?

And hands, as he learned over the course of a rather lugubrious cello performance, an ensemble piece that he *thought* was supposed to be Mozart, and some remarkably energetic fluting. And shoulders. And—most pathetic of all—elbows.

He'd never known the female body had quite so many hidden places, all designed to torment him. He was familiar with the more popular haunts, of course, but it turned out that the female form—or perhaps just Diana's form in particular—had been designed with a seemingly limitless supply of tempting hollows and angles.

All of this was to say that Jeremy heard precious little of the music on offer—which, in truth, might have been a blessing—but became exceedingly familiar with the back of Diana's head.

For amid all of his emotional, mental, and physical turmoil, not once did she so much as glance back over her shoulder. He was reasonably certain that she was aware of his presence behind her—if she wasn't, he was a trifle concerned for her eyesight—but she had given no outward sign that there was anyone in her immediate proximity with whom she had recently enjoyed a night of passion and a singularly awful row.

Eventually, the musical portion of the evening's events ended, and they retreated to the drawing room for tea, brandy, and a fine selection of his cook's blueberry tarts. Jeremy ignored the brandy entirely as he beat an eager path toward the tarts; while he usually did not hesitate to fill his tumbler at the earliest possible opportunity—and was, in truth, feeling rather badly in need of a drink at the moment—he was helpless to resist the allure of a good blueberry tart, and Mrs. Lucas's blueberry tarts were the very best. He was just about to lift one eagerly to his mouth when the sound of his grandmother's voice froze his hand in the air.

"What have you done now?"

He turned, blueberry tart still suspended in midair, to find the dowager marchioness eyeing him through a lorgnette—a ridiculous affectation if he had ever seen one, considering her eyesight was likely better than his own, despite her being fifty years his senior. He considered her comment, decided that he should likely take offense, and then realized that he hadn't the energy.

"Dear Grandmama," he said, stooping down to kiss her cheek before taking an enormous bite out of his tart. "How delightful to see you."

"Do not play stupid with me, young man," she said, lowering her lorgnette and fixing him with a beady-eyed stare. Braver men than he had quailed before such a look, but he stood his ground, shoving the other half of his tart into his mouth, which had the advantage of momentarily preventing him from answering.

As he'd expected, she did not hesitate to fill the silence. "You and Lady Templeton could barely keep your eyes off of each other a few days ago—made me deucedly uncomfortable, if you must know. It felt as though we were interrupting something, merely by being in the same room with you. It was positively indecent." Jeremy noted absently that he distinctly did *not* enjoy hearing Diana being called by her late husband's title, despite the fact that it was, of course, her name, and the only one by which she could reasonably expect to be called. "Now she won't even look at you. So I repeat"—and here the dowager marchioness reached out a bony but deceptively strong hand, extended her index finger, and jabbed him in the chest with each word—"what. Have. You. Done?"

"A difference of opinion on a trifling matter, no more," Jeremy said dismissively, plastering his face with his best devil-may-care smile. "I expect we will be right as rain in no time." He expected nothing of the sort, of course, and in fact considered it a minor miracle that Diana hadn't yet seized one of the serving knives and used it to pin him to the wall for target practice.

"You think that addlepated smile works to fool everyone around you, and perhaps it does, but please understand that it has no effect on me whatsoever," his grandmother said crisply. "If you think that drinking and smiling and whoring your way through society will make me forget that you are the most intelligent man in your family, or possibly of my acquaintance, then you are very wrong indeed."

"David was the most intelligent man in the family," Jeremy said automatically. He felt as though he had some sort of mental registry of comments about his brother on which he could rely at any necessary moment. All of them true, all of them accurate representations of his feelings for and memories of David, but all of them by now so rote that he could utter them without having to actually *think* about David, about the fact that he was no longer alive and that he, Jeremy, was standing here in his shoes instead.

"What utter nonsense," his grandmother said, drawing him out of his thoughts rather effectively. His eyes flicked to her face and held there, startled by the fervent gleam he saw in her gaze. "Is that what you've been telling yourself?"

"I . . . well . . ." He wasn't at all sure how to respond to such an inquiry, and settled on a feeble "Yes?"

"The man got himself killed in a curricle accident," she said, clearly enunciating each word. "He was hardly a staggering intellectual giant."

"West was in the same accident, and I think he's quite intelligent," Jeremy said, nodding across the room to where Audley's brother stood deep in conversation with Lady Emily. His cane was in one hand, as always, though Jeremy thought he didn't seem to be leaning upon it very heavily. As Jeremy watched, West's eyes flicked to the side and landed on Sophie, who was chatting animatedly with Violet and Audley. A look of great tenderness mixed with great pain flickered across West's face in an instant, vanishing before Jeremy could even properly register what he was seeing.

"And young Weston is still alive, is he not?" the dowager marchioness said, effectively bringing Jeremy's attention back to the conversation at hand. He recoiled—he actually physically recoiled—at this verbal blow, and his grandmother's face softened. "It was a terrible accident, Jeremy, there's no way around it. I've no doubt Weston regrets it every day of his life, and I'm certain that had your brother survived it, he would feel the same way. It was a mistake, and he should have known better, but he was *human*. He miscalculated, and he paid with his life. He was reckless, and he left a younger brother in possession of a title he never wanted, and a whole host of financial burdens that should never have been his."

This was, Jeremy reflected, uncannily similar to something Diana had said when he'd discussed his brother with her; at the time, he hadn't thought much of it, and yet now he realized, all at once, how well she knew him. The fact that he had spoken to her of his brother, of his complicated grief and guilt and other, darker emotions—this meant something. He'd already realized he loved her—but now, thinking back on that conversation, on the dark, vulnerable side of himself he'd allowed her to see, he reflected on the fact that she loved him, too.

She'd seen the real Jeremy, the man behind the flirtation and good cheer and reckless charm, and she loved him anyway. She hadn't spoken the words lightly—it must have taken her enormous courage, in fact. But she had spoken them with full knowledge of the real Jeremy Overington, and of the complicated well of grief and guilt and anger that he held within him. She knew of that, and she loved him still.

And he'd thrown it all away.

Even as the thought flitted across his mind, he saw Diana herself murmur something in Violet's ear and begin to make her way to the corner of the room. His eyes followed her movements without any conscious thought on his part; after a moment, his grandmother noticed his attention was fixed elsewhere and glanced over her shoulder.

"Ah," she said, in a tone of great smugness.

"What is that supposed to mean?" Jeremy asked grumpily, tearing his eyes from Diana with great difficulty to focus once more on the dowager marchioness, who was regarding him with a mixture of exasperation, amusement, and what he very much feared was pity.

"Why don't you go after her?" she asked.

"I'm fairly certain my company wouldn't be welcome at present," Jeremy said, his mind once again returning to the evening before. God, how he'd bungled things.

"Well, you can't hope to remedy things without speaking to her, can you?" his grandmother asked practically. "And you *do* wish to do so, I take it?"

Jeremy opened his mouth to deny this—to offer some carefree, blatantly untrue remark about it not much mattering to him one way or the other. To insist that Diana was simply a woman he enjoyed bantering with, flirting with, and nothing more—but all at once, he didn't have the energy. What was the point in lying any longer? He wanted her quite desperately, and just yesterday had been prepared to go to somewhat alarming lengths to keep her. Why bother denying that fact?

"I do," he acknowledged, and his grandmother's face lit up with glee. He frowned at her, something niggling at his mind. "I thought you wanted me to marry Lady Helen, though." His frown deepened. "You mentioned her as a marriage prospect more than once." He didn't know why he ever bothered to attempt to keep pace with the motivations of women; doing so seemed to be a nearly impossible task.

His grandmother snorted. "Of course I didn't. What sort of a fool do you take me for? But if that horrid creature's attempts to seduce you made you realize Lady Templeton was right there under your nose, well, who was I to resist suggesting the idea to you? Though," she added, her gaze flicking across the room to where Lady Helen was in conversation with Rothsmere, "I must say, she's barely looked your way all night. I'm beginning to wonder if she won't be at all heartbroken if she finds out your affections are otherwise engaged."

"I believe you are entirely correct," Jeremy said, deciding it wisest to leave it at that. He glanced over his grandmother's shoulder and saw that Diana had vanished. He had to make things more right between them, even if she wouldn't forgive him for the night before. He had to at least try.

"I must ask you to excuse me," he said shortly, and his grandmother waved him off cheerfully, not displaying the slightest hint of surprise at his unusual behavior. He gave a short bow and crossed the room to slip out the door. He looked left and right down the hallway; seeing the train of Diana's dress vanishing around a corner to the left, he set off in pursuit. Rounding the corner, he saw Diana pause as she walked past an open doorway, then duck inside.

Jeremy paused in the doorway, watching her. Of course she'd stop in this room. It was the portrait gallery.

She moved slowly from painting to painting, standing very close to each one, only a few inches separating the tip of her nose from the brushstrokes on the canvas. After scrutinizing a work at close proximity, she stepped back, taking in the whole scene, then moved back farther still, as if to see what impression it made from a distance.

He stood there watching her for a couple of minutes before the sudden stiffening of her shoulders indicated her awareness of his presence. She did not turn to look at him, but he pushed himself upright from where he'd been leaning with one shoulder propped in the doorway and walked slowly toward her. She kept her gaze firmly fixed on the painting before her—a Rubens, if he wasn't mistaken—and remained silent even as he drew up alongside her.

"I want my paintings to make people feel the way this makes me feel," she said at last, her gaze still fixed on the canvas, which depicted a hunt scene, bold strokes of white and gray creating an overcast sky through which an eerie light filtered down on the scene below. Though Diana spoke quietly, the room was silent around them and every word was crisp and clear.

"And how does it make you feel?"

"Alive," she said without hesitation. "The way he's made the sky balance out the landscape below—the use of light—it feels so vivid and real. I want everything I paint to feel like this." She inhaled sharply and turned to him. She opened her mouth to speak, but her gaze caught and fixed on something behind him and she moved past him, drawing up before a small painting on the opposite wall. Most of the paintings in this room were either works by masters—like the Rubens she'd been admiring—that spoke to the Overingtons' power and wealth in possessing them, or stiff, formal portraits of family members of various generations.

The painting Diana was examining with great interest was a portrait, but there was nothing stiff or formal about it. It depicted two young boys sitting side by side atop a blanket in the grass. Sunshine beat down upon them, making their identical mops of golden hair gleam in the light. One boy appeared to be about seven or eight, the other a couple of years younger; the elder boy had his arm slung casually around the younger boy's shoulders, and they wore the bright, happy smiles of childhood.

"You and David," Diana said softly; it wasn't a question.

"Painted by my mother," he said, moving to stand next to her. "The summer before she died."

"I'd forgotten how much the two of you resembled each other," she said, her eyes still fixed on the artwork before her.

"Yes. I—" He hesitated, then nodded at the portrait next to it, which was significantly larger and in a gilt frame. "It was traditional for the heir to be painted on his eighteenth birthday—that's David's portrait just there." He looked at both versions of his brother—the child David, with his arm around Jeremy, and David at eighteen, handsome and proud. The sight of his brother caused a pang of sorrow, but it was made more tolerable by Diana's presence at his side. "I've never been painted since I inherited the title. The idea of the two portraits hanging there, side by side, with us looking so much alike, I just didn't think—" He broke off, because he had the most curious feeling that if he continued speaking he would begin to weep. He took a deep breath. "I didn't think I could bear it. A constant reminder that I was here, with the title that should be his, doing the job that should be his, all because he was a bloody idiot who couldn't say no to a challenge." His voice darkened with anger, but he didn't try to suppress it—not here, not with her. For so long, he had been berating himself—not good enough, not deserving enough, to hold his brother's title. Because if he was angry at himself, then he couldn't be angry at David.

It was she who had made him realize this—that he could be angry with his brother and not love him any less. She who had given him this gift. He loved her—for this, and for so much else. And now, he knew, she loved him, too. Was he really going to throw that all away?

Diana turned to face him slowly, her eyes wide. He stared back at her, not understanding the cause of her expression, until she said, "You've not been painted since David's death?"

"No," he said, "not until . . ." *Not until you.* He didn't finish the sentence, but the words hung there in the air, understood by them both.

"Jeremy," she said, her gaze on him intent, "why did you follow me?"

It was a typically Diana sort of question. Nothing coy or timid about it—simple and straightforward and to the point, as though she valued her own time too much to waste it on niceties.

"Because . . ." He trailed off. Because he missed her. Because he wanted her. Because he'd ruined everything.

"Because I love you," he said, the words coming out of him in a rush. "Because you were brave yesterday, and I was an ass, and you deserve better. Because I was afraid to tell you how I felt, I was afraid I couldn't be the person you think you see in me—but you deserve someone who isn't afraid. Because I've spent the past six years trying not to think about David, about all the ways that I'm not measuring up to him, about all the ways I'm still angry with him—and you've made me realize it's all right. I feel like . . . like *Jeremy* again when I'm around you. And it feels like that's enough."

He didn't know quite how it happened, but a moment later, Diana was in his arms—or he was in hers—and his cheek was pressed against her hair and her arms were tight around his waist and one of them was trembling and he had an awful feeling that it wasn't her.

"I'm sorry," he said against her hair, his words coming out muffled and indistinct. "I don't mean to—"

"Don't apologize," came her equally muffled reply from where her face was pressed against his chest. "This is long overdue, I think."

So he didn't apologize, not for his trembling, not for the overly tight grip with which he held her, not for the occasional kiss he pressed to the top of her head. Not for the tears she was too diplomatic to mention, though she must have felt them, wet and hot against his skin and hers.

When at last he had himself sufficiently under control—though whether a minute or an hour had passed, he couldn't have said—he drew back slightly, keeping his arms loosely wrapped around her but creating enough space between them for him to peer down into her face.

"I'm sorry for . . . for last night," he said again, the words feeling woefully inadequate.

"I'd imagine you are," she said, sniffing. She raised her nose in the air as she did so, giving the impression of a very haughty rabbit.

A very haughty, very attractive rabbit.

He was beginning to think there was something seriously wrong with him.

"I concede now that announcing one's plans to propose to another woman isn't the best way to earn a lady's trust and affection," he added, and was rewarded with that oh-so-Diana eye roll that he loved so much.

"You don't say," she said.

"It's just—you caught me off guard, and I'd worked out this entire *plan*—oh God, I can't believe I was actually planning to *propose* to Lady Helen Courtenay." He was suddenly wide-eyed with horror. He seized her elbows. "Have I lost my mind? Is this what love does to a person?"

"I've been wondering the same thing the past twenty-four hours," she assured him grimly. "It's all very alarming."

"Do you," he started, then halted, floundering. "That is—I know I bollocksed things up last night, but I've never been in love, and I think I just . . . panicked," he finished lamely.

"I know," she interrupted serenely. "That was part of the reason I was angry with you, you see."

"You knew I was in love with you?"

She huffed in irritation. "Of course."

"I see," he said slowly, which was as far from the truth as any two words he'd ever uttered in his life. He saw nothing. Women were entirely perplexing creatures.

"Of course you don't," she said matter-of-factly.

"No," he agreed.

"I knew you loved me," she explained slowly, as one might to a child. "I knew I loved you. You, however, seemed to know neither of these things, and, moreover, seemed to think that *proposing to another woman* was somehow a satisfactory resolution to our situation." He could see her getting worked up again just speaking of it, and he hastily headed her off before she could get into a proper fury, because Diana in a proper fury was a dangerous thing.

He took a deep breath. "I'm not good at things like this," he confessed. Diana let out a laugh that was an extremely close relation to a snort. "All right," he amended, "I'm utterly rubbish at this. I made a mistake. But I've never had to—well, this is going to make me sound like a prize ass—"

"Too late."

"Thank you," he said, giving her a withering look. She smirked back at him. "I've never had to try terribly hard with women, you see."

She lifted an eyebrow with such expressive skepticism that he was surprised barbed insults didn't spring into midair between them, fully formed. "You're right, that does make you sound like a prize ass."

It should not have been alluring to hear her insult him, and yet somehow it was. He was beginning to think himself curiously perverse where she was concerned—first the freckles, and now this?

"But—well—you know. The title. The money. The . . . well, my appearance. I'm told it's tolerable." He gave her his best rakish smile. Naturally, it seemed to have no effect on her whatsoever, which was of course all part of the appeal she held for him. "I wouldn't go so far as to say they were lining up, but . . . it was never terribly difficult. And I never promised them anything, and they knew not to expect anything. We didn't go so far as to shake on it, like you and I did, but it was the same general understanding. And there were never any issues, because we both knew the rules.

"But, with you . . . the rules changed. I found myself feeling things that I've never felt for anyone before, that I've never *let* myself feel for anyone. Caring for people is dangerous, you see. I learned that one the hard way."

"With your brother," she said quietly.

He nodded, unable to speak for a moment. "I was . . . in a bad way after he died. I was grieving him, and it wasn't so long after my father had died, either. My father was a bit of a bastard, but it's still something to find yourself all alone in the world at the age of two-and-twenty, with an indebted estate and a whole host of people who are depending on you for their very livelihood. I acted out a bit, I suppose. And I realized that it was easier that way, to play the character rather than to be myself. If everyone believed the idea of who the Marquess of Willingham was, I didn't have to worry about any of them knowing who I really was instead."

"I understand that," she said under her breath, and he believed her—he believed her as he would have believed no one else in that moment, because of course she did. She had been doing much the same thing he had, for years and years.

"So when I found myself caring too much for you, I knew I had to be careful—I couldn't scare you away. So I thought I was coming up with the next best option—a way to have you without really *having* you. Without insulting you by asking for your hand."

"I might have overreacted last night," she said, surprising him. "I think I owe you an apology, too. You were trying to find a way to make things work within the boundaries we'd set. You were only doing what I'd asked you to do—you weren't demanding anything I wasn't ready to give."

"I am," he said. He reached out to take her hands. "Demanding things, that is. If you—" He hesitated, his heart pounding. "That is, if you've truly changed your mind."

"Jeremy," she said, her eyes flicking back and forth between their entwined hands and his face.

"If you still don't wish to marry, tell me now," he said, plunging on recklessly, while he still had the courage. "If you want me to be your lover for the next forty years, I'll gladly do that instead—I'll do whatever it takes, Diana, to keep you with me." His gaze was locked on hers, and her eyes, as she gazed steadily back at him, were suspiciously bright.

A small dimple started to form in one cheek as she stared at him, a precursor to that lopsided smile that he loved so much. "You know, there are plenty of more eligible misses on the market. There's no need to settle for a widow with a sharp tongue," she said, and that was all he needed in the way of encouragement.

"I love sharp tongues. I should find married life insufferably dull if it didn't begin with at least three verbal lashings before breakfast."

"Only verbal ones?" she asked innocently, batting her eyelashes.

"We can negotiate on that," he said in a strangled sort of voice.

"I thought I never wished to marry again," she said slowly. "I didn't think anything was worth risking my independence for, and I didn't like the idea of relying on someone else—expecting things from them—ever again."

"I want you to expect things of me," he said hoarsely, never once moving his gaze from hers. "I want you to demand them. I want to be the person you know you can demand everything of, because you deserve everything. You deserve someone . . ." He trailed off as an idea formed in his mind. He squeezed her hands tightly and leaned in close to give her a fierce kiss.

"I've changed my mind," he said once they broke apart for air.

Her mouth dropped open in an expression of genuine shock. "You've *what?*"

"Changed my mind," he said casually, grinning at her. She dropped his hands, but he merely reached an arm out to seize her about the waist and haul her close. "I'm not proposing tonight," he said, dropping a kiss on her nose, her eyes looking daggers at him mere inches away. "I fully *intend* to propose, don't make any mistake on that front, but I'm retracting my offer temporarily."

"Would you care to share *why*, by any chance?" she asked through gritted teeth.

"You'll see," he said, and kissed her again.

"I've only recently changed my mind on the institution," she said darkly. "Is your intent to make me reconsider that change of heart already?"

"No," he said cheerfully.

"Jeremy, if this is about that ridiculous wager, and you plan to hold off for another eleven months until—"

He cut her off with another kiss. "It's not the wager. Besides," he added with a grin, "once we are wed, all of your money will legally belong to me anyway, so I really think I'll be getting the better end of the deal."

"If you think teasing me about our society's horrifying laws about women is supposed to make me want to marry you," she began heatedly, before he stopped her words with his mouth yet again. He supposed that putting his mouth anywhere near her teeth at the moment was a slightly risky endeavor, but when he found his tongue tangling with hers a moment later, he decided that it had been worth it.

Twenty-Four

*Diana spent the next day and a half in a state of giddy joy, irrita-*tion, and sexual frustration. It was a confusing bit of emotional tur-moil, to say the least, and all the more so for the fact that it was, in her opinion, entirely unnecessary.

"He won't tell you *when* he's intending to propose?" Violet asked the morning of the second day since Diana and Jeremy's emotional interlude in the gallery. Violet, Diana, and Emily were gathered in Violet's bedroom, Audley having made himself scarce—or, as he put it, "seeking more masculine breakfast company." Strictly speaking, as an unmarried lady, Emily should have been breakfasting downstairs; this, however, was the advantage to having the Dowager Marchioness of Willingham, rather than her mother, serving as her chaperone: a certain convenient tendency on the part of that lady to turn a blind eye.

"No," Diana said, taking an irritated sip of tea. She hadn't known it was even possible to sip tea irritatedly, but leave it to Jeremy to lead her to this revelation.

"Doesn't it rather take the romance out of it, knowing it's coming?" Emily asked curiously. She had a plate of toast in front of her and was working her way through it at an impressively steady pace, pausing only to liberally apply butter and jam to each fresh slice.

Diana sighed. "That's what's so maddening. It *should*. And yet . . . somehow . . . knowing that he's preparing whatever it is that he's planning, it's . . . it rather . . ." She closed her eyes, mortified. "It makes me *swoon*."

Emily dropped her toast. Violet dropped her teaspoon.

"*Diana*," Violet said in a hushed voice.

"Are you dying?" Emily asked.

"I *know*," Diana said, burying her face in her hands. "It's horrid! I don't know what's happened to me."

"I do," Violet said smugly. Diana raised her head to see that the expression on Violet's face rather resembled that of the cat that got the cream. "You're *in love*."

"I know that," Diana snapped. "I didn't know it meant I had to act like I haven't the sense God gave a field mouse, however."

"Careful observation of Violet and Lord James should have made you understand that already," Emily said primly. A moment later, she was forced to duck a bit of crust Violet tossed at her head. The thought of what either Violet's or Emily's mothers would say, could they see them at this precise moment, was enough to send Diana into a fit of hysterical laughter.

A moment later, she realized that Violet and Emily were staring at her, and her laughter died down. "What?"

"I haven't seen you laugh like that in . . ." Violet began, and then trailed off, clearly at a loss.

"Ever," Emily finished for her, smiling softly at Diana.

"Don't come over sentimental on me," Diana warned, shaking a teaspoon at them severely.

"It's just nice to see you happy," Violet said mistily.

"I'm not happy," Diana said, frowning into her teacup. "I'm living in fear that a marquess with a distractingly good jawline and hands that, with careful instruction, proved to be rather talented, is going to jump out from behind a piece of statuary and propose at any moment."

Violet held up a hand. "I want no details about jawlines or talented hands, thank you very much. It's all very well to hear Jeremy discussing his mistresses in the abstract, but I'd like to refrain from ever thinking of the two of you together in the carnal sense."

"*I* should like all of the carnal details," Emily said, and Diana nearly fell off her chair.

"Do you have something you wish to tell us?" she demanded. "You spoke to Belfry for quite a while after dinner last night."

"Not yet," Emily said vaguely, calmly sipping her tea. "And don't try to change the subject. Let's focus on the situation at hand: Diana's in love. Lord Willingham may or may not be about to propose at any moment. Wedding bells will soon be ringing out from the parish church . . ." She trailed off, misty-eyed.

"What do you need from us?" Violet asked Diana, more pragmatic. "Emotional support? Crumpets? Brandy?"

"I need—" Diana had no idea what would have come out of her mouth had she been allowed to complete that sentence—what *did* she need? Possibly to have her head examined—but she was interrupted by a tap at the door. Violet called an invitation, and Toogood's surly face peered around the door a moment later.

"Yes, Toogood?" Diana asked wearily, already exhausted at the thought of what her maid was here to harangue her about—sleeping too late? Bodice cut too low? Toogood had been the one to dress her, so the latter would have been positively galling.

"Your presence has been requested in the gallery, my lady," Toogood said stiffly, offering a curtsey so elaborate that it was impossible not to find it a trifle mocking.

"Whatever for?" Diana asked blankly.

"You'll see when you get there, won't you?" Toogood asked, her tone carefully calibrated to remain just on the acceptable side of sarcastic; then she vanished.

"Diana, you really must do something about her," Violet said, rising to her feet, Emily alongside her.

"I'm afraid I've grown too accustomed to her at this point," Diana said with a shrug. "If I had a maid who was actually polite, I would die of shock." She sighed, rising to her feet as well. "Let's see what this is about, shall we?"

As it turned out, Diana's fear that Jeremy would jump out from behind a piece of statuary was not far off the mark. She arrived at the portrait gallery to find Penvale and Audley there, grinning madly at her in a way that made her instantly suspicious.

"What are you doing here?" she asked her brother with a frown.

"Providing emotional support," he replied with an infuriating smirk.

"To whom?" she asked, but a throat cleared behind her before Penvale could reply. She turned, knowing exactly who it would be, and found Jeremy standing there, a smile of such maddening self-confidence on his face that she thought it should probably be illegal.

He looked, of course, entirely distracting. It was early enough yet that she wouldn't have been surprised to find him still abed, or at least clad somewhat casually, but he was dressed to perfection, neckcloth tied just so, hair mussed to such a perfect degree that she wondered if he'd directed his valet to do it on purpose. His blue eyes were trained steadily on her face in such a way that made her suddenly conscious of her hair, which was coming undone slightly around her face, and her gown—the simplest yellow morning gown she'd brought with her for her stay. She hardly presented the picture of the perfectly coiffed flirt that she'd worked so hard to perfect—and, judging by his gaze, he didn't mind in the slightest.

"Diana," he said, and despite the fact that she knew Penvale and Audley were hovering somewhere behind her, despite the fact that she could see Violet and Emily grinning in the space behind Jeremy, and—oh Lord, was that the dowager marchioness smirking over in the corner?—something about the low pitch of his voice made a shiver run through her as though they were entirely alone.

"Yes?" she said. She meant it to come out cool and bored, but even she could hear the breathless, questioning note to her voice.

He smiled slowly, letting her know in no uncertain terms that he had heard it, too. "Turn around," he said.

"I—what?"

His smile widened, causing faint laugh lines to appear at the corners of his blue eyes. It was a smile that made her feel unsteady, off-kilter in the best possible way. "Turn. Around," he said slowly, enunciating both words very clearly.

It was a sign of how truly flustered she was at the moment that, rather than arguing with him for daring to give her any sort of an order, as would have been her usual habit, she merely followed his instructions and turned.

At first she didn't know what she was supposed to be looking at. There were her brother and Audley, grinning at her like the two fools that they were—nothing out of the ordinary there. Her eyes scanned the room, confused, then flicked back again, catching on a piece of art on the wall.

It was a sketch of Jeremy, so unlike every other stuffy painting in the room as to be almost laughable. He was sketched in rough strokes, at closer range than any of the other Overingtons of years past depicted in the paintings on the walls around him. His collar was loose, showing the long, seductive column of his throat; his hair was tousled; but it was his face that caught the eye and held it.

It was her sketch, of course, but seeing it sitting there on the wall, in a gilt frame, surrounded by portraits of Jeremy's forebearers, she was able to view it more objectively. And, she had to confess, it was good. No, it was better than good—it was a mere sketch, a preliminary to the portrait she intended to begin work on shortly, and yet its bold strokes and the raw honesty of Jeremy's gaze were arresting.

She was not used to standing in awe of her own artwork. She knew that she enjoyed creating it; she knew that others (the few others who had seen her art, at least) told her that she was talented; but that was an entirely different thing from seeing something she had created with her own hands and knowing beyond a shadow of a doubt that it was good. That this simple sketch was able to hold its own among the formal portraits that surrounded it.

Jeremy's face as she had drawn it was entirely stripped of the mask of cool sophistication that would have been so familiar to so many of his acquaintances; instead, he stared directly at the viewer, his gaze open. There was so much in that gaze: a bit of vulnerability; a touch of desire, yes—enough that Diana felt her cheeks warm, knowing the others were seeing this, too; a look of confidence, of a man who knew—or was learning—his place in the world; and a look of love, directed straight at the viewer.

Or, as Diana knew to really be the case, the artist.

It was Jeremy as she saw him. And he had hung it here, in this gallery, surrounded by paintings of his father and grandfather and all the marquesses before them. As she glanced around, she noticed empty frames scattered about the walls. Beautiful, ornate, undoubtedly expensive frames. Frames containing nothing.

"They're for you to fill," came Jeremy's voice, low in her ear. She felt his breath against her neck, goose bumps rising in its wake. She turned, and there he was—tall, golden, insufferably handsome, and looking at her as though she was the only thing he saw. The only thing that mattered.

Some dim part of her realized that she had been waiting her entire life for someone to look at her like that, without ever admitting it— because to admit it would have been to confess weakness. Admitting it would have meant she wanted it. Admitting it would have meant that she needed someone else, for more than social advantage or a healthy bank balance. Admitting it would have made her vulnerable, and that was the one thing she had refused to be.

Until now.

"Please, fill them," he said, his voice still low, rough with emotion. "Marry me. Live here with me. Paint me—or the furniture—or the blasted sheep, I don't care. Just stay here with me." His brow furrowed, and he hastily added, "Unless you'd rather live in London year-round. That's fine, too. I don't give a damn, so long as you're there with me." He reached out a hand that a dim, clinical part of Diana's brain noted was trembling, and cupped her cheek in his palm.

"I love you, Diana. I love your mind and your art and your freckles and every single other inch of your body, and I want to marry you." He reached his free hand into his coat, and before Diana could ask him what he was doing, he extended a closed hand to her. Startled, she held out her hand and felt the press of a fat wad of paper in her palm. She looked down, her brow furrowed, not understanding—

And then, of course, it clicked.

"One hundred pounds, I presume?" she asked, looking up and arching a brow at him.

"You have my solemn vow, down to the very last penny," he said, placing a dramatic hand to his heart.

"I assure you I shall be counting it later," she informed him; then she was in his arms, his mouth warm and urgent on hers, every other thought she had ever had fleeing her mind.

"I love you," she murmured against his smile, her own mouth stretching into an answering grin.

Dimly, she heard the sound of appreciative applause and—if she was not mistaken—the dowager marchioness's smug voice saying, "This has all turned out *exactly* as I predicted."

She wrapped her arms around his neck, barely noticing as the notes in her hand fluttered loose.

Winning a wager had never been so sweet.

Acknowledgments

I have been distressed to learn that writing a second book is not, in fact, any easier than writing a first book—you're simply expected to do it more quickly. Writing can be lonely sometimes, but publishing is not, and I'm grateful to so many people, including:

My editor, Kaitlin Olson, and my agent, Taylor Haggerty, both of whom helped make this book infinitely better with their questions and feedback. I adore both of you.

The stellar, hardworking team at Atria, including Isabel DaSilva and Megan Rudloff, who make sure my books are read by all the right people; Polly Watson, for her keen (and hilarious) copyedits; and Sherry Wasserman. Thanks also to Kate Byrne and the team at Headline Eternal for giving my books such a warm welcome to the United Kingdom.

The many, many people who helped make launching a debut novel in the middle of a global pandemic somehow still feel special. At Root Literary, Melanie Castillo, Taylor Haggerty, and Alyssa Moore were clutch with their social media savvy and willingness to try new things

ACKNOWLEDGMENTS

in unusual times, and Holly Root's words of wisdom for authors in an unprecedented year were much appreciated. I'm incredibly grateful to my fellow Root Lit authors who so kindly stepped up for debut authors in a time of need, including Becky Albertalli, Gretchen Anthony, Lauren Billings, Kate Clayborn, Jen DeLuca, Jasmine Guillory, Rachel Hawkins, Emily Henry, Christina Hobbs, Ashley Poston, Sally Thorne, and Sara Bennett Wealer. To my debut day twins and co-conspirators, Marisa Kanter and Cameron Lund, an extra big (metaphorical) hug. Thanks also to Sarah Hogle and Margo Lipschultz for the world's most hilariously chaotic Twitter event.

Kate Clayborn, Jen DeLuca, and Lauren Willig, for being so generous with their time and kind words for a debut author.

The booksellers, librarians, book bloggers, and bookstagrammers who spread the word about my books, and make the online book community such a joyful, vibrant place.

And, as always, my family, friends, and coworkers, who are unfailing in their enthusiasm and support for my writing. Thanks especially this time to Kristyn Saroff, who came up with the title for this book.

Don't miss *To Have and to Hoax,*
Martha Waters' first laugh-out-loud, charming and
swoonworthy Regency rom-com …

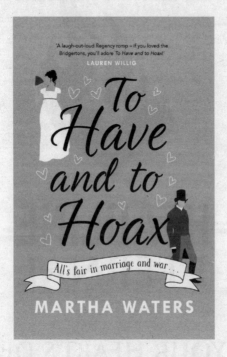

'If you loved the Bridgertons, you'll adore
To Have and to Hoax!'
Lauren Willig, *New York Times* bestselling author

Available now from

HEADLINE
ETERNAL

FIND YOUR HEART'S DESIRE...